Defiance

by

Klaire de Lys

CHAPTERS

Map Of Ammasteinn ....

Detailed Map ....

Astrid & Jarl's Journey ....

GLOSSARY 1

AWE AND TERROR..4

POINTS OF VIEW..28

BITTER..44

PILLARS PASS..58

HUNT 82

QUIET MOMENTS 92

ARRIVAL..106

A LITTLE HELP 118

LITTLE FOX..128

THE OAK TREE 136

HOLMVÉ..154

TREACHERY 160

LOBA..170

LITTLE KINGS 188

UNWELCOME GUESTS 196

OLD TRADITIONS 214

ACCEPTANCE 222

SACRIFICE 240

HÆTTA 250

HATE 268

DANGEROUS PREDICTIONS........................... 282

LIMITATIONS 296

BAD OMENS 306

COME BACK SOON 316

A TRICK OF THE LIGHT 328

GHOST... 334

KELICS 346

BROKEN FALLS.. 358

BAD LUCK 370

REDEMPTION 382

THE IRON KING 394

WAIDU 406

SKY STABLES.. 418

OUT OF TURN 432

SICK.. 444

EGGS 456

THE WOLF OF WAIDU 468

A LITTLE FAITH... 482

RAGANA.. 498

READING THE WREATH.................................... 508

LOGBERG.. 522

THE WOLF IS COMING 536

THREE HOURS 546

JUDGEMENT... 556

FAMILY.. 568

LET'S GO HOME 576

BOOK DEDICATION 587

WEB LINKS 588

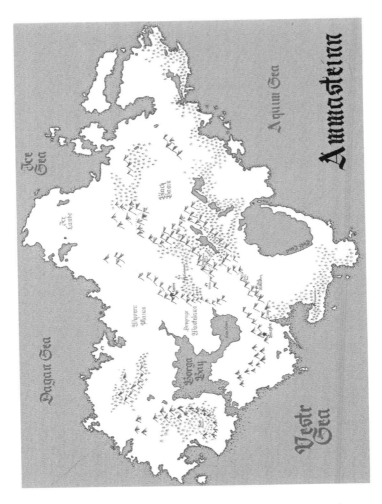

Map Of Ammasteinn

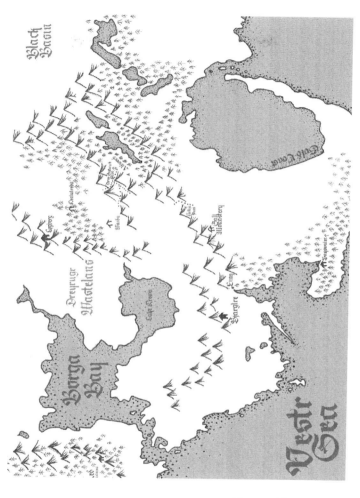

Detailed Map

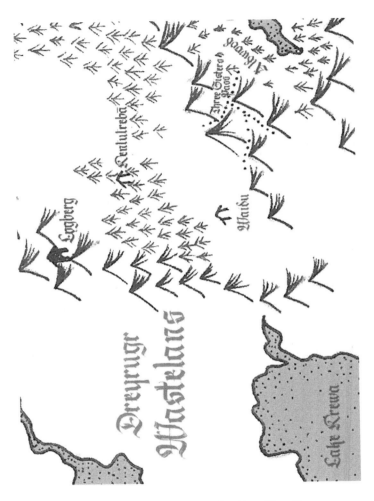

Astrid & Jarl's Journey

GLOSSARY

Mál (Dwarf Language)

Blanda blóð - Mixed blood
Brojóta burðr - Rape Child
Goðgá - Blasphemy
Ósómi - Dishonoured
Hlaupa - Social climber
Sótthringr - Scars left from surviving the Red Plague
Heit - Rare Dwarf money. Can be used by humans to pass through the Kaito Passage and trade with Lǫgberg. Extremely valuable to traders.
Fé - Dwarf Money
Bjartr Dagr - An annual dwarf feast celebrate the end of the Rojóða wars.
Miðsumar - Midsummer
Frǫðleikr - Magic people
Sváss - Beloved
The Gróf - A dwarf prison run by Ope (Demons)
Ríkr Gluggr - Great Window

Nida - Heaven
Úti - Homeless, an outsider.
Faðir - Father

Hætta - A yearly cull on the goblins

Axtī (Elvish)

Jaxī - High (formal) Elvish
Korro - Stunted or short. An insult.

Keiwo - Human
Mewa -Dirty
Jakkito - The ability to heal with life energy
Atibiw - An elvish healing dagger used to transfer energy to heal, used by elves who do not have Jakkito healing powers.
Merkā - Daughter
Mātīr - Mother
Kāsni Kroukā - The ruins of an old middle ground between Kentutrebā and Lǫgberg.
Moi Kridjo - An expression of love meaning 'My heart".

OTHER WORDS

Oddr attacks - An attack tactic used by the goblins.
Knāto - The metamorphosis of a Sylph from air to a physical body.
Agrokū - Meaning battle hound. A goblin leader which had conquered and assimilated several tribes or more.
Maadii - A Vârcolac word for Mother.

EXPRESSIONS

A witches Fé: A coin taken from a witch which will provide good luck and safety for a short time before it causes the death of the owner.

(Due to restrictions in the Kindle software certain names originally containing macron's will differ from the paperback version)

2

DEFIANCE

AWE AND TERROR

It was cold outside the tent; the air crisp and clear. Last night's thunderstorm had finally washed away the thick, heavy atmosphere that had plagued the area around Lake Krewa for weeks now. The air was so clean it almost hurt to inhale it. Each ice-cold breath Ulf exhaled billowed from his mouth in a stream of smoke, like a dragon's.

With his arms folded tightly across his chest and his cold blue eyes pressed together in a tight line, Ulf gazed out over the camp and past the trees that stood in their thousands like a wall of green giants. The sun had only just risen over the Riddari Hǫfuð and he squinted slightly to shield his eyes from the light. The magnificent mountains were so far away he could hold his spear up to the level of his eyes and block them

4

out; they were nothing but a distant row of dark blue peaks on the horizon. It was strange how the plains, which stretched from the Dreyrugr Wastelands and curled around Lake Krewa for hundreds of miles, were stopped so abruptly by the mountains.

Ulf didn't think he would ever get used to seeing them. He was used to the plains. He was born on and had grown up on the plains, where miles upon miles of harsh winds swept over barren grassland and where rodents, rabid Dip wolves, wild horses, and bison were the only plentiful thing upon them. Even the Wyvern plains with their jagged pinnacle of rock, which clawed its way up into the sky for hundreds of feet, did not induce such a feeling of awe. Terror, yes. The Wyvern plains were more that capable of that. But awe...awe was such a different emotion.

Mountains, real mountains, have a way of impressing anyone, Ulf thought. Human, elf, goblin, it made no difference. It was just a shame the mountains were infested with dwarves. His upper lip curled a little with disgust at the thought of it. It was so like the dwarves to inhabit mountains to try and project a grand view of themselves. In a way, though, it made sense. They were strong but they were short, the average dwarf's head standing no taller than Ulf's lowest rib bone. Short and slow, that's what they were. In the mountains the dwarves could hide and dig themselves in, but now *they* were here, so could the goblins. He was determined to live and die among mountain peaks, away from the hardship and humiliation the plains carried with them.

Another early morning breeze brushed past and the large yurt tent behind him shook in the wind. The layers of thickly-stitched hides, which stretched over the lattice frame of the yurt, shuddered and billowed, slapping against the wood and bones.

"Ulf! Ulf!" a female called from inside the yurt, her voice strong enough to be heard through the thick tent walls.

Turning around, Ulf nodded at the goblin who pushed out through the layers of bison skin hanging over the tent entrance. Her large belly was the first thing to appear, before her face - with firm, intelligent green eyes - followed soon after. She shivered slightly, her long pointed goblin ears flitting like a fox's, and she pulled her wrap closer around her shoulders.

"Dreaming again?" Her two, sharp, front teeth glistened like newly polished steel as she smiled through the split in the middle of her upper lip. "Dreaming of our new home?"

Ulf said nothing for a moment but there was a small twitch of a smirk at the corner of his lips as he knelt down in front of her and leant his head against her belly. A small foot, barely half the size of his little finger, kicked his ear the minute it was pressed against his wife's stomach.

"She's getting stronger!" Ulf said, gazing up at her.

"She? You will have a son, Ulf!"

Ulf got to his feet. "No. She's a girl, large and strong. And she is impatient, just like my wife." The she-goblin slapped her husband's head fondly and growled at him from the back of her throat. "I say it will be a boy! I'm carrying him; *he* has no choice." She pulled her shawl tighter around her, the wind a little too cold for her, and tried to walk past him and out into the camp. Ulf blocked her way instantly, his arm around her shoulder.

"You should stay inside, Melrakki. Just for the morning."

"Why?" Meeting his gaze, the pupils of her eyes stretched upwards into sharp slits and her ears pricked up. He never called her by her full name, except when he was angry or worried. It was always *Rakki* to him, never Melrakki, unless they were in the presence of the tribe or his generals. Something was wrong.

"Áki. It's Áki, isn't it?"

Ulf nodded. She had always had a gift for knowing exactly what was on his mind, and on more than one occasion this gift had proven to be extremely useful.

"Stay inside."

Rakki groaned. "He'll be kicking all day now! I need to walk!"

Her walk was more of a waddle, each step forward achieved by a slow rock from side to side. Her baby kicked even more as she turned back into the tent as if it wanted to voice its protest. She groaned again, her hands pressed against her stomach, trying to stroke the child to sleep through the skin of her belly. "Shhh! Stop moving!"

For her first child the pregnancy was going remarkably well. Or rather, that was what every woman in the camp who had ever carried a child had told Ulf repeatedly, to the point of annoyance. She had not suffered from sickness in the mornings and she had only recently started to feel uncomfortable. The baby was so large that each time it moved she could feel it press on all her lower organs.

Her craving for bison stew had become voracious. Ulf had lost count over the past few months how many times he had turned onto his side and reached out across the bed for his wife, only to find cold furs and an empty space beside him, with the crackle of the fire and the smell of boiled stew wafting through the yurt. She would never wake him though. It was not in Rakki's nature to ask for help if she could do something herself. Ulf doubted she would even want the doula in the tent when the time to deliver the baby came. In all likelihood, his mother would be the only woman present. Gríð was just as stubborn as Rakki. There was not a single goblin in the entire camp who would dare to stop her entering Ulf's yurt when Rakki's time came.

"Shhh!" she whispered again, her voice so deep it was more of a rumble, which vibrated through her body. The child's movements grew more and more sluggish, each kick and push less forceful until, finally, the movements stopped and it was lulled back to sleep.

Boy or girl, it will be strong either way, Rakki thought, as she sank down onto one of the multiple cushions strewn around the middle of the yurt. They were all a dark, muddy brown or green colour, patterns of bison, horses and fire the most prominent themes among them. Flashes of fiery red, yellow and orange embroidery shimmered against their dull counterparts.

In front of her, and placed firmly in the middle of the tent so as to take advantage of the light that came through the tono, a large map made of grass paper and drawn with a mixture of fine ash and bison blood was spread across the low table. Picking up the bone quill, Rakki dipped the nib into the small pot of liquid - *niyk,* as they called it – and with her right hand steady and her left hand pressed reassuringly over her belly she scratched the pen nib against the rough, ridged paper.

The paper was so corrugated it made the pen shudder slightly, despite Rakki holding it as firmly as she could, and tiny flecks of niyk flew through the air with each of her meticulous strokes.

For a moment Ulf watched her, his eyes soft, a look he reserved for his wife only. In contrast to the beiges and dark browns of her surroundings, Rakki looked quite striking in her off-white gown with its thick, double-folded hems covered in a heavy but simple brocade. Vivid blue thread was woven together with the white and there were no images or characters depicted in the patterns - no fire, no horses or bison - just uninterrupted filigrene patterns that swirled in and out, with no other purpose than to look pretty.

It had taken over five weeks to make the one robe and three more had been made shortly after the first had been finished. The cloth had been bleached repeatedly with lye - a mixture of animal fat and ash water - before it had been laid out in the sun for several days. Eventually, the naturally beige-coloured cloth had faded and the only trace of its original colour was in the warmth of the almond-white hue left behind. The material was then beaten and pressed by hand until it was paper thin - the texture smoother, its coarseness polished away - before it was cut, folded and embroidered over a period of almost three weeks. Three tailors had worked on it from dawn till dusk in rotation until, finally, they were able to present the finished gown to Rakki. Every goblin in the camp had gathered for the occasion, the women pushing past each other impatiently to try and get a glimpse of it and gasping with envy when Rakki took it from the tailors' hands and held it up to admire it. They had never seen anything so beautiful. Their own clothes were dull and plain; nothing but grubby shades of brown.

In his mind, as she had help it up, Ulf couldn't help but think that by dwarf standards the gown would appear plain, simple and crude, a laughable attempt by a brutish race to cultivate some form of culture. Even the few dwarf soldiers and merchants they had killed in the last few months had worn finer clothes. But any dwarf who understood the goblin culture would have realised the significance it held. Clothes, especially clothes that took so long to make, were only made by powerful tribes. It was not just a dress to the goblins of his tribe, it was a symbol that they had reached a certain level of power and, with that, a certain amount of peace could be expected.

Barely two years ago the many goblins who now formed his army would have been at each other's throats, as petty quarrels and infighting was the standard. It was commonplace for entire families and tribes to be wiped from the face of Ammasteinn overnight by a warring tribe, if not by the dwarves. Death was a way of life. Now, the same goblins who would have happily murdered one another slept with their yurts barely a few feet apart.

Ulf felt an immense measure of pride each time he thought of what he had managed to accomplish. He had given his people a unity that had never been achieved before and now anyone, be they elf, dwarf or goblin, who stood between him and his vision would be destroyed. He would unite the goblins; he had to. Unless they were united he knew they would never be able to stand against, let alone defeat any of the dwarves. They could potentially defeat Bjargtre now, but the retaliation from Lǫgberg would be swift and brutal. Vígdís would not be so easily defeated. He would need more than numbers; he would need cunning. And there was nobody more cunning than his wife.

A small gust of wind blew past Ulf and rattled the lattice walls. The domed roof, weighed down by the multiple packed bags that hung from the ceiling around the circular tono, sunk further into the yurt. The bags, although balanced out so that no single roof pole was overburdened, creaked a little as they swung back and forth. A little of the early morning light hit Rakki's face through the tono above her, making the distinct, green undertone of her skin slightly golden in appearance. The small decorative blades tied into the ends of her long, braided hair glinted in the sunlight. Taking a deep breath, Ulf turned away.

Rakki looked up for a moment and smiled. Áki was a coward; Ulf was not. There was no need to worry.

As he stepped away from the yurt, Ulf ran his hand along the back of his head. Each of his fingers touched the multiple cuffs that were wound together with the braids of his long black hair, which held soft tints of red only visible in direct sunlight. Each bracelet looped over an adjoining one to form a tiered chain from the front of his head all the way down to the middle of his back. The older cuffs at the top of his head had faded to a dull coppery colour, while the newer ones glistened in the sunlight: some silver, some iron and some bronze. Each had a distinct design forged into it, the open ends unique to the tribe to which it belonged. Some had simple rounded ends with a plain, twisted band around the base. Others were meticulously decorated: A Dip wolf's head snarling; eagles, bison, snakes, and a clenched goblin fist. On each cuff the metalwork was different, some of it faultless, the rest crude, the metal far from pure. One cuff, the third that had been added to his braided collection, had started to bend and crack and several hairline fractures curled around it. Another few months and it would probably break in two but, even if it did, Ulf would not remove it permanently. It would be re-wrought and woven back into his hair again, even if the whole process would only have to be repeated a few short months later. Apart from each cuff being a symbol of a conquest, it would be a grave insult to the tribe to whom it belonged if he were to remove it. An Agrokū, especially one as young as he was, could not afford to make enemies. He already had natural enemies. Warring among the goblins was just a way of life - a way of life he was trying to eradicate, but with strong opposition. It would be unwise to remove any cuffs permanently, no matter how damaged and pathetic they looked. The cuffs were a reminder of his power and of the loyalties owed to him. He would never remove them.

The camp was still and quiet. Apart from the wind and the occasional mutter of a guard, almost every living soul was asleep. Soon, Ulf would hear the first wails of waking goblin babes before their mothers would try to lull them back to slumber in order to steal a few more moments of precious rest.

Unlike in other goblin camps where tents were often pitched sporadically, Ulf did not allow the yurts to be speckled about. It left them too vulnerable. His camp was set up in an almost perfect circle with his own yurt erected at the centre and the yurts of his generals forming an inner circle around it. The remainder of the tribe formed an outer circle, with the bison penned around the perimeter. The goblins stationed in the outer circle had no need to worry though, the alarm was always raised long before the camp could be attacked. Guards and their Dip wolves patrolled the camp all night, some of them at fixed points while others circled the boundaries. Although they had been attacked many times over the past few months by other tribes, they had never been caught by surprise.

Ulf reached the pens outside the camp and strode towards a large yurt that had been erected inside one of them. It was covered in a plain cloth instead of animal skins, but built so that it was much taller than any other yurt in the camp. Numerous hoof prints were ground into the earth, the tough grass trampled to a pulp. Ulf thrust his spear into the ground and slipped inside.

A huge black horse made his way from the far side of the yurt towards Ulf, his thick scales glistening like steel as he passed through the pillar of light plunging from the open tono in the ceiling. It was almost as if he knew the light made his hide appear all the more magnificent. His hooves, situated at the back of his feet and each the width of a man's head, had three, sharp, lizard-like claws curled over it. They ploughed at the ground as he approached.

Ulf reached for the animal's face as he stood proudly before him. His eyes, a bright red and green and slit like a lizards, were still for a moment before a silver translucent membrane slid vertically across them and opened again.

"Bál!" Ulf smiled. The horse shook his head at the sound of Ulf's voice, his whinny more like a deep rumble that started in his mouth and ended in his stomach, like he had swallowed a thunderstorm.

Along the lattice walls, several grass fibre brushes hung from small wooden pegs. Ulf took the largest one and began to brush firmly at Bál's hard scales. He had been in the mud again and dust flew into the air as Ulf brushed the coat, the flecks quite beautiful as they floated in the beam of light in the centre of the yurt. Some of the mud was so firmly embedded between the scales that Ulf had to pick it away with his nails.

"A vain animal that likes dirt, eh?" he chuckled. Bál turned to look at him, his dragon horse's eyes glowing in the dim light, and he snorted, the distinct smell of meat on his hot breath. "Hungry?" Bál shook his wiry mane and snorted again, then turned his head towards the doorway and pawed at the ground, the claws of his feet extending slowly.

Out of the corner of his eye Ulf saw a glimpse of a figure at the yurt's entrance, but he did not turn to look. A second figure appeared beside the first.

"Ulf."

Still Ulf ignored them. The grass brush in his hand swept over Bál's scales with fierce repetition and small waves of dust swirled in the air with each brush stroke. He didn't have to look to know that the doorway was now completely blocked by several figures and that their hands were already at their hilts; he could hear the sound of the thick tribal cuffs they each wore around their wrists clinking against them.

Lifting his great weight onto the front of his feet, Bál's claws flexed and his thick wiry mane flicked up and down like a cat's tail. Ulf fixed his eyes on it; it would tell him all he needed to know about what was happening in the doorway.

He had managed to clean enough of Bál's scales to move further down the animal, a vertical stripe now polished perfectly. As the coarse grass fibers scraped down over his skin, a horrible high pitched *shuuushk* sound repeated again and again.

Unlike a horse's, Bál's tail was not made of multiple soft hairs. It was more like that of a lizard - thin - and the tip razor sharp with a small cluster of black spike-like hairs that made it look more like a mace. Ulf watched as it swayed to and fro, alert and wary. The minute a goblin moved towards him, he knew Bál would rattle the end of it. Until then he would keep his back towards them.

Shuuushk! Shuuushk! The noise came over and again as Ulf swept the coarse grass hairs over stony black scales.

"Ulf! Come out!" Áki couldn't stop the stammer in his voice as he spoke; everything about Ulf's manner made him nervous. The dragon horse was enough to frighten any goblin, but Ulf's silent indifference was terrifying. It was as if he didn't even fear them, that they did not even deserve to be acknowledged. They were insignificant to him.

Shuuushk! Shuuushk!

Beside Áki, a larger goblin grunted, angry that Áki would not enter the yurt. "Coward!" he hissed, and Áki whimpered and tried to shuffle away. The goblin opposite him blocked his path.

Shuuushk! Shuuushk!

"Ulf! Come out!" the large goblin bellowed. Ulf still ignored them.

The large goblin stepped into the yurt.

Bál's tail-tip rattled.

From the doorway, Áki wasn't able to see what Ulf had struck the large goblin with but they all saw his arm swinging down onto the goblin's head. A sound similar to that of fresh meat being struck with a large cleaver resonated through the air. The goblin stood still, swayed for a moment, and then crashed onto his back like a felled oak, the side of his face dented by the edge of the hair brush, the force of the blow so violent that his eyeball loosened and protruded from his head.

All of the goblins yelped and jumped back from the entrance.

Ulf strode towards them, tossing the bloodied brush onto the ground next to the dead goblin. Bál followed behind him.

Hearing the commotion, a small crowd had gathered around the pen and Ulf faced them, calm and emotionless. But his wild eyes were ablaze and Áki, terrified, tried to run. The others held him back, their swords drawn.

Ulf stood silently in front of them and Bál rested his massive head on his shoulder. Ulf reached up to stroke the side of his face, his eyes still fixed on the goblins.

"Our tribes leave! Today!" one of the goblins behind Áki barked, before he quickly hid behind the group, too frightened to let Ulf see his face.

Ulf shook his head. "You swore fealty to me."

The goblins growled and held onto their weapons with a little more determination, but were still not confident enough to approach him, not with the dragon horse behind him, his head burrowed into Ulf's shoulder like a cat that wanted nothing more than to be petted.

"I swore to you I would protect any goblin who followed me," Ulf said. "Leave now and I will forget this ever happened." Bál clawed at the ground, his scales and tail starting to bristle and shake.

Two of the goblins at the back of the group turned and scampered away before the others could stop them. A third tried to follow but was roughly pulled back.

"Traitors!" Ulf hissed, narrowing his eyes. His lips curled in disgust, exposing both of his sharp, front teeth.

"Goblins have no king!" Áki whimpered, the tone of his voice a high pitched drone. Ulf wondered how many times Áki had repeated the sentence to himself before he'd finally had the courage to blurt it out. The goblins nodded in agreement, but still snarled with fright when Ulf stepped towards them.

"We are goblins! Goblins have no king!"

Ulf clenched his fists, his mouth twisted so tightly into a snarl that his nose twisted with it, the expression animalistic. "You need a king! You need an Agrokū who can lead our people—"

"These are not my tribe! Not my people! I'm a Beziickt!" one of the other goblins interrupted.

"And I'm a Mizack!"

"A Gurght!"

Several goblins called out from the group, listing their old tribal allegiances.

"You are all goblins to the dwarves!" Ulf bellowed as he pointed to the mountains, his voice so loud it could be heard almost a hundred feet away. "Our enemy knows we are goblins! The humans know we are goblins, but we do not? Gurght, Mizack, Beziickt, they are just names! Languages we use to divide ourselves!"

Suddenly, one of the goblins ran at him, sword raised, and the rest of the group followed suit. Ulf made a small flicking motion with his wrists and thin blades slid down into his hands from behind both of the leather vambraces that covered his forearms. The blades were barely longer than his little finger, their edges serrated with a hundred sharp, teeth-like notches.

As he dodged the first swing, Ulf plunged the knife in his left hand into the goblin's side, just under his lowest rib and straight into his lung. The goblin made a strange sound as he inhaled with shock, a small gasp that was cut short, as if he had suddenly run out of air. His mouth opened and closed as he tried to breathe but no sound came apart from a weak wheeze. His sword tumbled from his hand as he dropped to his knees, both hands pressed over the gash Ulf had cut with the accuracy of a butcher. The second goblin fell to the ground as fast as the first, his throat sliced wide open.

Pulling the blades from his victims, Ulf leapt forward then dropped almost onto his knees between the next two goblins, whose swords were inches away from his face. In one quick jab, like a snake's swift bite, he severed the muscles at the back of their knees. Both goblins dropped to the ground, unable to understand why their legs had given way. The pain that followed a few seconds later forced them to drop their weapons and clutch their legs in agony.

As suddenly as he had attacked, Ulf threw himself back towards Bál. The great dragon horse reared forward and stood over Ulf protectively, like a dog. With its teeth bared, it kicked at every goblin that approached them with its powerful front legs.

The goblins felt the ground shake. The sound of many slow and heavy creatures could be heard behind them, but too afraid to take their eyes from Ulf, nobody turned around.

They should have turned around.

It was easy for Ulf's generals to cut them down. One of the goblins, the youngest, tried to run but there was a dagger in the back of his neck before he'd had even a chance to reach the edge of the pen, thrown by one of Ulf's two female generals.

Ulf got to his feet and observed the carnage for a moment before he pulled himself onto Bál's back. Áki scrambled away as the bison approached him.

"Stop!" Ulf commanded loudly. Instantly, the bison and their riders were motionless as though they had been turned to stone. He turned to Áki. "Why?"

"The dwarves! The dwarves paid us!" Áki quickly spluttered, his eyes so wide the whites of them were visible. "They paid us to kill you!"

"How much?"

"What?"

"How much? I want to know how much an Agrokū is worth to the dwarves!" Ulf shouted. He rode Bál closer to Áki, so close that Aki could feel its hot breath on his face and see just how sharp and long the dragon horse's claws were as they ripped at the grass in front of him.

Áki fumbled with the pouch tied to his belt before one of Ulf's generals snatched it from him and passed it to Ulf, who ripped it open with one of his knives. Six Fé fell into the mud. The crowd that had gathered were disappointed when they saw how few coins there were. Many of them shook their heads, yelling at Áki. "Those aren't even gold!"

Ulf's face turned as black as thunder. "Is that was a goblin's life is worth to you? A few copper coins?"

Áki spluttered in a panic and tried to explain that the coins were worth more than they appeared. The comment only enraged Ulf even more and he turned to face the crowd.

"This? This is what I am worth dead to the dwarves?" he bellowed, the veins in his face protruding. "If I am worth so little, then what is your life worth to them? Nothing! We are nothing more than a spring hunt to them! Game! Rats to cull every spring!"

The goblins murmured and many of them nodded their heads. An angry roar started to build up from the back of the crowd.

"I am your Agrokū! I will see the goblins living in the mountains and the dwarves on the plains! They will struggle, like we have; they will be hunted like we have been! And we will reign over them!"

As the cheers of the crowd got louder and turned into a deafening roar, Áki made a desperate bid for survival and ran, the goblin who had held him distracted by Ulf's speech. He crawled under the pen's fence and scrambled to his feet, facing the miles of uninterrupted plains before him.

The dragon horse did not jump over the fence as Ulf rode after Áki, he slammed through it, and the wood splintered like glass against the powerful animal's frame.

Áki screamed in terror as he heard Bál's heavy footsteps behind him. The loud, distinct snorts of the beast grew closer and he turned, hands raised, and begged for mercy, huddled on the ground with his head bowed against the earth.

From the camp, the other goblins watched in silence. Bál reared and a hollow thud followed. A weak, smothered shriek from Áki's crumpled body sounded with each kick. Bál raised his foot and another thud followed. Ulf barely looked down at Áki. Able to feel each blow shudder through the dragon horse, he looked out over the plains, his eyes on the horizon.

Finally, the goblin beneath him was silent. Bál kicked a few more times, the sound of hoof against soft meat and broken bone echoing through the air.

Thud. Thud.

Ulf looked down at the broken body, silent for a moment. Bál lowered his head and nibbled at the fresh meat before turning to look up at Ulf who shook his head. Bál snorted, hungry, but did not disobey him.

The crowd stood apart to let them through as Ulf rode back to the camp. Bál's front hooves were covered in blood and small chunks of fresh meat were stuck between his front claws. Ulf stopped and looked down at the goblins who remained, most of them dead, some injured but still very much alive. His generals alongside them awaited his verdict.

"Ride the bison over them," Ulf commanded.

A scream rose from the goblins, the pleas and curses of some lost amid the noise.

None of Ulf's generals flinched as they re-mounted and rode slowly forwards, the enormous bison so heavy that the grass beneath them was pressed deep into the mud with each step. Roots creaked and cracked under their terrible weight.

Turning his dragon horse, Ulf rode Bál out of the way as he heard the dull crack of bone and a few gargled shrieks behind him. Like a slow moving cloud, more and more goblins mounted their bison, some with their saddles and others bare-backed. They lined up behind the soldiers to trample over the goblins in turn, their faces set in angry scowls.

Eventually nobody could hear the screams, the sounds muffled by the heavy plod of the animals. Even the sounds of the dull crack of bones was muted as the ground became a slush of blood and ground meat.

Bál sniffed at the air and clawed the earth, agitated. Ulf had not fed him yet and his stomach growled. He had never forgotten to feed Bál before; even when he had been a small foal in the Wyvern Plains Ulf would feed him with whatever small creatures he had managed to hunt, at times even going hungry himself to give him food.

"Shhh!" Ulf whispered, as he leant his head close to Bál's ears. "I didn't forget. I just saved you something special."

POINTS OF VIEW

Astrid was still awake, Jarl's arm heavy around her shoulders. She did her best to stay completely still and pretend she was sleeping, but she couldn't stop herself from fidgeting every few seconds.

It felt strange to be so physically close to another person. With her head against his chest she was able to feel his heartbeat. The sound was oddly calming: slow, constant, and heavy like a drum, but she couldn't shake the intense anxiety either. She battled between wanting to pull away from him and wanting to lie beside him for as long as she possibly could.

She reached towards her lips and ran her fingers over them, feeling the warm flush of colour creeping up her cheeks as she did so. The skin still tingled from when Jarl had pressed his mouth against hers.

Well, now you've done it! the harsh voice cackled. *All these years of being careful and you've gone and thrown it all away! Why would you promise to go with him to a dwarf city? You barely know him!*

Astrid's brows flinched and she curled up closer to Jarl, the quiet voice retaliating in her head.

Don't listen to her! You're in love! That's what it feels like, terrifying and exciting all in one. You've seen it happen to other people, so why not you this time?

"I'm not in love," Astrid whispered under her breath.

She tried to close her eyes and force the voices to be quiet but the noise in her head was impossible to drown out. She felt so horribly confused, like a ball of yarn that had been thrown into a pit of wildcats and was being pulled in every direction until it was just one large, confused knot. A hundred thoughts in her head meshed with the clamour of her two personalities who were shouting like banshees.

Love. Am I in love? Astrid thought to herself. Don't be stupid, how can you love him? You don't know him enough to love him. Love is just a word fools use for mindless infatuation. I don't love him.

The quiet voice laughed as Astrid tried to convince herself. *Not love? How else you would describe it?*

"Astrid, are you awake?" Jarl whispered. She shut her eyes quickly and feigned sleep. For a brief moment even the voices in her head held their breaths as he leaned forward to look down at her for a moment.

Jarl leant back against the tree and gazed out onto the plains, relieved that the only motion was the ripple of the wind over the grass. Not even an animal was in sight.

Astrid's eyes opened slowly and she inadvertently shivered as another cold gust of wind swept across the plains towards them. It was so cold that her joints felt as if they had frozen in place, the tips of her fingers completely numb. Knud was the only one who looked as if he was warm. Astrid's wolf skin was so large he was able to sleep with his arms stretched out on either side of him and not have his foot or hands peek out from under the edges. Even Jarl shivered a little from the wind, despite his thick clothing.

Enjoy this! It won't last! the harsh voice whispered. *We all know how this story ends!*

Astrid flinched a little, her mouth pulled into a grimace, and again she tried to push the voice out of her head.

"I know you're awake," Jarl muttered, and Astrid turned to look up at him. Jarl smiled and, with one arm

30

around her, gently caressed her shoulder. "You think far too loudly. Do you ever sleep?"

"No. Not in the wild. Not unless I'm alone," Astrid replied. "Bad things tend to happen when I'm not watching."

"Don't you trust me to keep watch?" Jarl joked. Astrid smiled and her face relaxed for a moment.

"You? Yes. Other people, no. Besides, I hate this pass. It makes me nervous."

"Why?"

"I lost a little boy I was meant to take care of here." Astrid looked away from him and towards Knud. The fur of her wolf skin draped around his shoulders bristled in the breeze as his shoulders rose and fell in his sleep.

"You've kept him alive so far," Jarl said gently. He stroked her shoulder again and Astrid shivered at his touch.

"I crippled him because I wasn't paying attention."

"Being half elf doesn't help you see under the ground. That trap had been there for months; it was probably there when the village was attacked."

She thought back to the village and the charred remains they had seen. "I hope it wasn't them," she whispered, more to herself than to him. Jarl looked at her, confused. "The people at the stake. There was a child there, it was the right height. It could have been their daughter, Astrid."

"They named their daughter Astrid?"

"Yes. After me. I hope it wasn't them."

Jarl considered saying that he doubted it had been them, but his gut quickly dissuaded him from the idea. He didn't think she would appreciate a lie, even if it was to try and make her feel better. In all likelihood it had been them, and to say otherwise would only make things worse.

"The tattoos. When did you get them?" he asked, taking her right hand in his to look at the intricate patterns inked on her skin, keen to distract her from her current chain of thought.

Astrid, intensely ashamed, tried not to shake but felt her hands begin to tremble. Remembering she didn't like her skin to be touched, Jarl let go of her hand and held her wrist instead, the thick cloth of her tunic separating them.

"These? It must have been about thirty years ago. Aaren's father did them for me. These were my first." Astrid smiled to herself, remembering Aer, with his large smile and warm eyes. He had been dead now for over twenty years but she still missed him. The white and black ink on her hand was a daily reminder of the first human she had met.

"Aaren? Was he the man I saw you with in Ein?" Jarl asked.

"You saw me with Aaren? When?"

Jarl grinned. "Skad told me you wouldn't ride a pony so I went to sell it back to the stable boy and saw you with the inksmith. You were smiling." He laughed.

"Is that so surprising?" she asked, slightly offended.

"Yes, you don't smile much. And when you do, it looks like your face isn't used to it."

"I just forget," Astrid mumbled. "And I don't see the point in grinning like a fool all the time. Seems like your face would get tired after a while."

Jarl laughed again, making his shoulders shake. When he looked back at her he noticed a funny look in her eyes. "What's wrong?"

"Nothing." She forced a smile but her expression dropped back to a vacant gaze as she turned away from him.

It was such a simple little thing, the motion of his shoulders as he laughed. But in that split second, a small part of her memory of being in the Aldwood returned in a rush.

She could recall sitting on her father's lap, her head against his chest and the smell of pine on his clothes.

The image in her mind was so clear. She could remember the feel of his shirt, the fibres rough, one of Sylbil's first early efforts to make clothes. Arnbjörg had complained to Astrid in jest at how uncomfortable it was, but he had not spoken loud enough for Sylbil to hear. He knew how long she had spent on it and, as uncomfortable as it was, he did not want to upset her.

She remembered the smell of the air: late summer; freshly fallen leaves and a plethora of nuts and fruits around the house, drying for winter. Astrid had been told off so many times for helping herself to them but the temptation had been too much to resist. Stacks of food had been laid out on racks along the wall, all within reach of her once little hands.

The food! Suddenly she could taste it again. The redskin peanuts had been so dry. She used to hate them, the skins always peeled off in her mouth and got stuck between her teeth. His laugh though, which was so good to hear again, replayed in her memory.

Well, this surely won't end badly! The harsh voice laughed at her. Astrid snapped her eyes closed to try and block the voice out, but it was no use. *You're comparing him to your father. Yes, that's just perfect! When are you going to grow up and stop looking for them everywhere? They're dead; they have been for forty years! Grow up, you stupid CHILD!*

Astrid sat up with a jolt and quickly shook her hands by her sides before burying her face in them. Her head rolled from side to side.

"Astrid?" Jarl moved towards her, his hand outstretched to rest it on her shoulder, but she flinched and stepped away. "Astrid what's wrong?"

"The voices in my head, they won't stop shouting," she replied, before she had time to think about what she had said.

Oh, perfect! Now he knows you're crazy as well as a cursed half-breed! Keep talking, Astrid! Keep telling him everything that's on your mind! He won't walk away, he'll run! He's going to run! Just wait for it! He should run! You're a damaged little freak who talks to voices in her head! Just wait! Any minute now—

The voices were instantly silenced as, instead, Jarl reached for her hand and pulled her back into his arms. She was reluctant at first but felt relief as soon as she felt his arms around her and his fingers stroking the side of her face. She felt like something precious in his hands. Something valuable. It felt strange, like she had committed some kind of fraud to trick him into thinking she was something he wanted.

"Is that why you always run ahead so much?" Jarl asked, so close she could feel his breath against her. Astrid nodded slowly. She flicked her eyes up at him and felt her cheeks go red as he smiled down at her,

her scars like highlighted silver streaks on her flushed skin.

"Kiss me again," she said, her cheeks reddening even more as she said the words.

Jarl smiled.

This time he kissed her for longer and Astrid kissed him back hesitantly, her heart beating so quickly she could hear it in her ears. Her lungs behaved like they had forgotten how to function while his lips were against hers.

"Don't forget to breathe!" He grinned and opened his eyes. Astrid laughed nervously and found herself leaning forward to kiss him again.

"How do you do that?" she asked. "You kiss me and they can't talk. The voices, I mean."

Jarl was unsure of what to say. He had never seen her so on edge and it was unsettling. To him, Astrid was calm, collected and still. But while he'd kissed her he'd felt her hands tremble slightly as she'd held them defensively against her chest.

In the past weeks he had seen glimpses of how unstable she was beneath her strong and quiet exterior, but the facade had never dropped away this much. She was frightened, and he already knew she had a tendency to run when something scared her. He didn't for even a moment think she would go back on her word; she did not seem the type to do so. But he knew she needed the doubts in her head to stop screaming before they pushed her too far.

"Do the voices talk when I ask you about these?" Jarl said, taking her right hand in his, his fingers running over her tattoos around her fingers and wrist. Astrid nodded. "Will they talk if I ask you about your life?" Astrid nodded again, wincing slightly and bowing her head. She felt deeply ashamed, certain that in his eyes she must appear so strange.

"Then ask me about mine," Jarl said. "Anything you want. Will that make them go away?"

The voices said nothing. Astrid nodded.

"Then ask. Anything."

Astrid didn't know what to say, sure he was just joking until he repeated himself with nothing but sincerity in his voice. Was it so easy for him to speak about himself like this? She stuttered as she struggled to think of something to say, the voices taking advantage of the silence and slowly creeping back into her head.

"Your family," she finally asked. "What were your family like? What were their names?"

Jarl clenched his jaw as she said the words, but forced himself to speak, determined to do as he had promised. "I had two older brothers, Jóð, and Jón. People kept confusing us. To other people we all looked the same. It would really annoy Jón." He chuckled, though his eyes were sad. "We had the same coloured hair and eyes. Jón was in the royal guard and Jóð was training for it."

"Your family guarded the king?"

"Yes. All my family, it was tradition."

"Why?"

"Every year, Bjargtre used to have a summer hunt, the Hætta. On one hunt the king was attacked by goblins. My grandparents and Knud's grandmother protected the king, they saved his life. Since then we have always trained as the king's guards."

Astrid looked up at him, fascinated. It all seemed so strange to her, to know so much about one's family, to remember grandparents and have so many ties to the past.

"I was the youngest," Jarl went on. "I hadn't trained to be a guard yet. You need to train in the army for five years before you can become part of the royal guard. I had only trained for two. He took a deep breath, a pained look on his face. He had not talked about the death of his family for many years now, the last time with Knute, and he wasn't sure which memory was more painful. "There had been a Hætta and some of the kill they brought back had some kind of goblin disease. Within a week half the city was infected. Everyone got sick, my parents my brothers and me."

"And your grandparents?"

"They died quite a few years before."

Astrid watched him intently as he spoke, feeling privileged that he was sharing a clearly painful memory. She was half tempted to stop him, but was morbidly curious at the same time.

"My parents, my brothers, Knud's mother. Two days and they were all dead. A third of Bjargtre died from the Red Plague. They haven't had a Hætta since then."

The sun was fast approaching now, the horizon such a shade of red that it worried Astrid. A red sky meant it would probably rain heavily later on in the day. It was not what they needed but she pulled her attention away from it and back to Jarl, enthralled by his story. "What were their names?"

"My father's name was Jókell, my mother's, Elin."

Astrid repeated the names to herself out loud, determined to remember them. "Hætta hunt...what is that? Deer?"

Jarl looked up at her, surprised. He knew she was a stranger to dwarf culture but he had assumed the Hætta was something she knew about. For a moment he looked away, aware that what he was about to say would, at the very least, horrify her, if not disgust her. "Goblins. We would hunt goblins."

Astrid glared at him, her mouth half open. "Why would you hunt goblins?"

"It's a tradition all the dwarf cities have," Jarl tried to explain. "Bjargtre hasn't had a hunt since the Red Plague, but Lǫgberg still has one every spring."

Astrid pushed herself out of his arms, revolted, unsure of what to say. "You brought back goblin bodies into Bjargtre? Why? What were you going to do with them?"

Jarl tried to think of how to answer her in a way that would not shock her, but found he could not without lying to her. "We used to display them in front of the palace."

"Display?"

"Hang them."

Astrid held her hands over her mouth. Images of Ragi flashed through her head. "Why would you do that?"

"It kept the goblin numbers low."

"Did you ever join one of these hunts?"

"No," Jarl said quickly.

"Did your family?"

"Yes, my brother brought back the kil—the body, which they think carried the Red Plague."

"And you wonder why the goblins hate you?" Astrid muttered, disgusted.

Jarl's face snapped into a furious glare. He got to his feet, angry that he had just told her one of the most painful experiences of his life and all she could think about was the goblins who had been killed. "We are being hunted by goblins! Knud lost his foot because of goblins, my family lost their lives because of a filthy goblin disease, and they are all you can think about?" His voice was low and scathing, the tone much worse than if he had just shouted.

"I didn't mean it like that," Astrid replied.

"How did you mean it?"

"The goblins aren't bad, Jarl."

"Yes they are!" Knud shouted out suddenly.

They both turned to look at Knud, dismayed that he had heard them. Knud tossed Astrid's wolf skin to the floor and kicked it away before he tried to stand up. Jarl moved quickly towards him to offer his support and Knud leant against him before they both faced her.

"They're evil! They're all evil!" Knud yelled.

"Knud, please don't shout," Astrid said, her eyes on the forest behind them, worried he would disturb one of the many Frǫðleikr who she knew lived inside the tree line.

"You like the goblins, so I hate you!" Knud spat. Astrid took a step back and even Jarl was silenced.

Nobody said a word. Knud, red faced and shaking with anger, glared at Astrid, his fingers curled into a tight fist as though he wanted to hit her. Astrid picked up the wolf skin from the floor and pulled it over her shoulders, her eyes dazed.

Say something! the gentle voice whispered, but she ignored it and turned to pick up her bag from where it lay next to Jarl's. She felt something land by her feet and looked down to see the knives she had leant Knud tossed onto the ground.

"I don't want them!" he spat.

Astrid's hands trembled as she reached down for them. As quickly as she could, she tied them around her leg and slung her bag onto her back, deliberately avoiding all eye contact with Jarl and Knud.

In the distance, the sun had only just stared to rise over the horizon, the clouds a brilliant mixture of red, gold and orange.

"We should go then," Astrid mumbled, and began to walk ahead, keen to put some distance between herself and them, with a painful lump lodged in the back of her throat.

I told you! The harsh voice cackled.

BITTER

Halvard shivered and pulled his cloak tighter around him shoulders. He could not believe just how cold it was for late summer. It had been cold a few weeks ago when he had arrived with Jarl, Knud and Astrid, but now it felt almost arctic. Even in Bjargtre he could not remember a single winter that had been this bone-cuttingly bitter. There wasn't much wind; maybe that's what made it worse. That, and the dead silence of the mountains. There was nothing to distract him from the angry thoughts circling in his head.

Far up ahead of him he could see the glow of the Salt Monasteries, several of the upper windows lit with the warm, pink glow of their salt lamps. He swore loudly under his breath, annoyed that it still looked so far away. It had looked just as far away early that morning. A seven hour walk along the path and he still felt like he was no closer to it. His whole body ached and his feet, heavy with tiredness, stumbled over the dusty ground.

With a sharp pang of pain, Halvard tripped over a stone, his leg twisted at a strange angle, and all the muscles along the back of his leg pulled. "Blanda blóð bitch! Curse her! Her and Jarl!"

As soon as the words had left his mouth Halvard was silent, partly ashamed that he had mentioned Jarl's name, but he shrugged the guilt off and continued on ahead, the dull pain from his twisted leg fading a little.

It had been just over a week since he had left Knud, Jarl and Astrid, but he still awoke every day consumed with an overwhelming desire to swear from dawn till dusk.

"Dam Brojóta burðr!"

His nose was broken from when Jarl had struck him, the bridge of it bruised and swollen and now set in a permanent twist. He reached up and touched it gingerly and a stab of pain shot across his face. He screwed up his eyes, waiting for the pain to subside, then snapped them open again when a whiff of hot spice wafted past him. Food, he could smell food! Suddenly, the monasteries didn't look so far away and his stomach growled loudly. An image of grease-covered meat slowly turning on a spit appeared in his mind, the meat red, tender and juicy.

He re-adjusted his back pack and trudged forwards, this time his walk a little faster and more resolute. He was close now. The promise of warm food was so clear in his mind that his mouth was watering, and for the first time in days he forgot about Astrid. The deformed image of her face that he had built up in his mind vanished, and was replaced by apparitions of hot, butter-covered meat. He licked his lips, his thoughts turning to his almost empty food pack.

When he had left the others the last thing on his mind had been rations, and he had been too proud to turn around. Instead, he had tried to search for his own provisions and survive on what little he had. The first plan had failed miserably. He was not a hunter, no matter how hard he tried.

Jarl had been the hunter of the two of them, although Astrid had taken over the role in the past few weeks, her half-elf skills immensely superior to Jarl's. Jarl was good, though. He could patiently stalk prey for hours in complete silence and then scurry through the undergrowth in an instant, barely making a sound.

When he was much younger, Halvard had accompanied Jarl and his parents on a hunting trip in the mountains. The result had left him frustrated, tired and angry, not to mention humiliated.

Jarl had been slow at first, too, and he'd struggled to handle the bow that had been much too large for him. It constantly scraped against the leaves on the ground, or the branches above, each time they got close enough to a target to shoot. The prey, usually young boar or deer, heard him long before he could get close enough to even attempt a shot.

But he had learned quickly, unlike Halvard, who at the end of the third day still could not shoot the arrow properly. The bow would make a strange twanging sound when he released the arrow and he'd watch as it cart-wheeled awkwardly on the ground. Jarl's older brothers, Jóð and Jón, had teased him about it. Spin-shot, they had called him. Even now it made him bristle at the neck. Halvard was not a dwarf who liked to be teased in any way.

Looking up, Halvard groaned. It was still another thirty minutes or so until he'd reach the gate, and his feet felt like they had been skinned at the soles. He was desperate to kick off his heavy, iron boots. He stopped, stretched his legs, and clicked his spine one vertebrae at a time as he straightened his back. Then, reaching into his bag, he pulled out the little food he had left. His fingers shook slightly as he unwrapped

the protective cloth around it and shoved the food into
his mouth. A few crumbs fell into his unkempt beard,
the braids in them now rough and disheveled as it had
been uncombed for days. Halvard scratched at it,
feeling even more frustrated. For a moment he
considered sitting down on the rocks and brushing
through it, embarrassed at the thought that the monks
would see him like this. But the need for food quickly
pushed the idea out of his mind. Besides, why should
he care what a human thought?

He pulled the bag back onto his shoulders, shuffled
for a moment to allow it to fall into place, and
continued up the path. Several large stones splayed out
before him and he grumbled, kicking them away with
his feet.

Finally, he reached the gate and relief washed over
him as his fingers touched the large knocker. He lifted
it and let it slam against the door before, impatiently,
he knocked it again, A gust of wind blew up the path
behind him, the cold so acute that Halvard was sure it
had cut his bones. His face stung and his broken nose
throbbed as he waited.

The door opened a moment later. There was a smile
on the monk's face that was clearly habitual because
his eyes looked irritated as he peered down at Halvard.

"Yes?"

"I need to stay for a few nights," Halvard said.

The monk nodded and pulled the door open to let him through. The hinges creaked as another gust of wind blew up the side of the mountain and caught them by surprise. Halvard simply watched as the monk struggled with the door and tapped his foot impatiently until it was closed.

"This way." The monk smiled, his eyes saying something quite different, and Halvard followed him. The smell of food had become unbearable and he pressed both hands over his stomach to stop it from growling.

"Hungry?"

"What do you think?" Halvard snapped.

The monk led him through the courtyard and past a large pile of packed salt crystals piled neatly in pale, salmon-coloured slabs. There were several monks beside the pile, taking the salt slabs and carefully weighing, counting and packing them in a black cloth, before tying them with a coarse rope and sealing them with wax, the symbol of a Daru flower stamped upon it.

Halvard ignored them and turned his attention to a group of elves loitering in the corner of the courtyard. They all had thick, poker-strait hair, as black as ebony, in stark contrast to their emerald-green eyes. They wore a light elven armour, the woven metal plates making the armour look like leaves. Or, through Halvard's eyes, like petals. He couldn't help snorting loudly. They turned towards him, the ones at the front stepping forward as if they were about to storm up and demand to know what he had found so funny, but the leader of the group called them back. The human monks looked up nervously, hoping they would not have to intervene.

"This way," the monk with Halvard said, taking him down one of the many hallways that led off the courtyard.

"So, business has been bad?" Halvard asked. The monk looked at him, confused, not sure what he was referring to. "The rooms," he went on, nodding at the vacant dormitories either side of him. "They're all empty. They weren't like this a few weeks ago."

"This part of the monastery is over four thousand years old! You can see the bricks on this side of the building are darker. The archives we have talk about there being trees, once, covering the mountains along this part of the Riddari."

Halvard rolled his eyes, aware that he had just set the monk off on a story-telling spree. His stomach growled loudly again.

"After the Three Kings War - I think the dwarves call it Rojóða, yes? Well, after that, I think it was about a hundred years after that, there was an avalanche. It destroyed half the monastery. We had to re-build most of it and the dwarves and the elves had stopped trading with each other by then. You wouldn't even trade with the goblins! So we didn't have as many people passing through the Riddari way."

"We *never* trade with goblins," Halvard snapped. The monk tilted his head, his brows arched, a look of disbelief in his eyes that clearly read 'if that's what you want to believe'.

Halvard, irritated, changed the subject. "Can I get some food? I'm starving."

Clearly annoyed, the monk led him into the kitchens. Several monks were cooking what Halvard assumed would later be dinner for the other monks. Three enormous pots of stew bubbled over the fireplaces lining the walls, massive grates built over the fire pits to hold the huge pots above them. One of the fires had three spits turning over it, the meat on it sizzling deliciously, and Halvard could barely resist grabbing it and tearing at it with his bare teeth.

As he waited by the table, the monk carved him a large slice and handed it to him on a wooden plate. Halvard snatched it up and bit into it, his teeth sinking into the tender and juicy flesh. He closed his eyes as he chewed, a look of immense satisfaction on his face.

"I'll go and get your friend," the monk said, unsure if Halvard had heard him.

It was a few moments later when Halvard heard an annoying tapping sound in the tunnel behind him and then someone cleared their throat. He ignored it, engrossed in clearing his plate.

"Halvard!"

He turned in his seat and faced Skad, who was balanced on a pair of crutches. "You're still here?" he grumbled.

"Of course I'm still here! Where else am I going to go with my leg like this?" He hobbled over to the table, reached over to Halvard's plate and dipped his fingers into the grease.

"How's the leg?" Halvard asked, his tone so uninterested it implied insult more than concern.

"Still broken," he said, then licked at his fingers. "Why are you here? Where's Jarl?"

"He's with Astrid," Halvard growled, his mouth half full but his face as black as thunder. Skad looked at him, a mixture of surprise and amusement on his face.

"What do you mean?"

"I mean Jarl seems to have a weakness for Blanda blóð scum."

To Halvard's surprise, Skad burst out laughing; not a full happy laugh that made the room light up at the sound but a deep laugh that implied a revolted amusement. A cruel laugh. "You should have stayed with them! It would have been entertaining. Astrid has a gift for self-destruction."

"So does Jarl." Grease splattered over Halvard's beard and he tried to wipe some of it away with his sleeve, only to spread the smeared trail further across it. He grumbled and sucked at his fingers. "He's stopped caring about a lot of things that should matter. I still think she bewitched him, he can't be that stupid on his own."

"He wasn't that stupid when I trained him," Skad said, as he sat on the bench opposite Harvard, resting his crutch against the side of the table.

"You left just before the Sótthringr Plague. I think it broke his head a little."

"I was in Lǫgberg," Skad replied, turning away, his eyes tinged with a look that wasn't common on his face. Sadness, regret even. Halvard did not notice.

"Damn goblins!" Halvard spat, before taking a cup of water from one of the monks, not bothering to nod his head in thanks. He gulped it down and dried his mouth. "They should have just burned the bodies."

"There's no point hunting goblins if you can't show off your kill."

"It would have saved a lot of people."

"Well, I never liked Jarl, and his family were worse than him. The boy was far too soft, always had strange ideas." Skad laughed and Halvard's face dropped. He put down the half-eaten meat in his hand.

"You don't know what you're talking about!" Halvard spat, his hand near the hilt of the sword hanging from his belt.

"No fighting or you leave!" one of the monks demanded, stepping forward.

"Yes, I know!" Halvard replied, his eyes still fixed on Skad. Finally he sat down, his fingers flexing as if they wanted to scurry away from his body and murder Skad themselves. The monks turned back to the food, their ears pricked, sure that at any moment they would need to break up a fight. Dwarves were not known for their eagerness to forgive.

"I didn't like his brothers very much," Halvard said, "but his parents were good dwarves. Nobody deserves to die the way they did. Nobody."

"Not even Astrid?" Skad asked. Even Halvard was slightly shocked by his question.

"Astrid? Yes! I would wish it on her. That witch is a curse. What kind of a dwarf had a half-blood child? It's unnatural. It's disgusting."

"Don't ask me. I just knew she was half-blood. I didn't want to know anything else."

"Why in Nida's name would you agree to train a Brojóta burðr?" Halvard asked.

"I owed a debt to Dagmar Eir. You don't break a life debt to a warlock."

Halvard was quiet for a moment before he finally agreed. "No, I guess you don't."

"Three years! Three damned years I trained that Blanda blóð! Dag told me she left the Red Mountains soon after, when some goblin friend of hers died. Started travelling the human lands."

"I'm surprised she didn't catch one of their diseases!" Halvard shuddered and rubbed his hands together as if he were trying to wash them under an imaginary fountain of water.

"The worst thing is, I kept hearing about her. I was the best guide through Ammasteinn for over one hundred years and the little Goðgá had a greater reputation than me within ten. Ten years! The humans talked about her like she was some kind of hero." Skad gritted his teeth and glared at the table. Even now it still irritated him to no end. Three years, three damned years, and a little half-blood runt had become his greatest student. It was insulting.

"She probably used magic," Halvard suggested. He turned to the monks. " Do you have any Daru wine?" One of them nodded and left the kitchen, the scrape of his leather sandals on the stone floor echoing through the tunnel.

"No, she wouldn't use magic. She's terrified of it," Skad replied, matter-of-factly.

"I find that hard to believe."

"Don't believe it then," Skad snapped. "Anyway, it's your useless friend who's fallen in love with her. I could tell two weeks out from Ein he was taking a liking to her. You should have said something to him."

"I did! And I got this for it!" Halvard pointed at his broken and twisted nose. "I told him to let her leave."

"I wouldn't cry about it, you were never a handsome dwarf. Look, I don't like Astrid but she was the only one who was going to get us through the Haltija pass alive. You should have just tolerated her. Trying to get rid of her was stupid."

"He was my friend," Halvard said indignantly. "I've known him since we were boys." Skad sighed and shuffled in his seat, visibly bored by Halvard's conversation. "He's not wrong about the goblins though, they are getting stronger," Halvard admitted. Even through at the present moment he fiercely hated Jarl, he could not deny he was right about the goblins.

"Bah! The goblins are always getting stronger," Skad said, flicking his hand up. "We just need another Hætta and they'll be back to squabbling among themselves."

"King Hábrók won't have another one. Not after the Red Plague."

"Well then, it might just be better to stay here for a bit longer." Skad looked at him intently. "Goblins are like rats - pests in small numbers but dangerous if they're left to get out of hand. That's when they need to be culled."

PILLARS PASS

Astrid had not said anything for the past few hours.

Jarl had tried to calm Knud down but it had not worked. Knud had worked himself up into such a state that it had taken him over an hour just to stop crying. Jarl wasn't sure if it was the trauma of losing his foot, or his rage at the loss of both of his parents finally simmering to the surface. He remembered the terrible day he had told Knud that his last surviving parent was dead. Knud had been so quiet, so calm. He had stared at Jarl, a mixture of denial and shock on his face. For the second time within the space of a few months, Knud's world had crashed down around him. The first time he had cried. The second time there had been no word he could say, no sound he could make, which would express the agony and the anger he had felt inside.

At the time, Halvard had suggested that since Knud's mother had died so recently it was less hard to shock him, but Jarl knew Knud better than that. It would only be a matter of time until he had to vent, and Astrid had just so happened to be the one in the firing line when he did.

Jarl had had time to calm down a little himself, aware of how the Hætta would have sounded to Astrid. But each time he had tried to walk beside her, Knud had deliberately walked slower, and Astrid faster.

They were getting close to the Three Sisters Pass, the forest to their right slowly tapering out. Massive moss-covered boulders were strewn everywhere, their surfaces slippery and slowing them down.

As he stepped over one of the large rocks, Jarl's foot slipped a little and he almost lost his balance. Instinctively, Astrid reached out and grabbed hold of his arm to support him. His eyes connected with hers for a moment and Astrid flinched, quickly letting him go.

"We'll be at the Three Sisters Pass soon," she mumbled.

"Good," Jarl replied curtly.

Knud shook Jarl's arm as Astrid strode ahead. "Please pick me up!" he begged. "I can't walk any more. I'm so tired." Despite being exhausted, Jarl reached down and helped Knud climb onto his back, his bag hanging low enough to act a little like a saddle.

Knud lifted his head from Jarl's shoulder and peered up at the mountains. Instead of a gradual slope that tapered off into a peak like the mountains around Bjargtre did, the mountains on the outside of the Riddari Kviðr were more like jagged walls. Gnarled trees covered the slants at their bases before the massive body of the Riddari Kviðr burst up from the earth with its walls of almost vertical stone, its peeks so high that they pierced several dark clouds hovering above them.

The Three Sisters Pass looked unnatural with a deep cut gouged through the mountain like a giant had struck its way through the stone. The boulders that littered the entrance almost confirmed that the pass had been made by some kind of enormous being. Four soaring stones, three times the height of any man, stood guard at the entrance of the pass with a lintel on top of them that was disproportionately large in comparison.

Knud opened his mouth to ask Astrid who had built the strange stone doorways but he bit his tongue when he remembered that he was still angry with her.

Suddenly, Astrid turned to face the plains, her knees bent slightly and an arrow already pressed against the string of her bow, ready to pull back and release at the first sign of a target. Jarl looked out at the plains but, as much as he squinted in the early morning light, he could not see anything that would raise suspicion. The ripple of wind in the low grass was the only movement he could see for miles.

"Keep walking," Astrid whispered, her back to them. Jarl did as she'd asked and walked briskly ahead as Knud's grip around his neck tightened.

"Is it goblins?" Knud said, shaking a little.

"It's probably nothing. Don't worry," Jarl reassured him.

No sooner had the words left his mouth, a large, gangly Dip wolf burst out of the grass to his left and leapt towards him, its mouth open wide and its long, thin teeth dripping with silver-white venom.

Astrid's arrow struck the Dip so accurately that it entered one eye and emerged from the other. The Dip was dead in an instant, its body pinned to the ground. She had another arrow at the ready almost before the first had left the string and, seeing a ripple trail in the grass, she released it. A loud yelp rung in the air as the Dip tried to crawl forwards on its paws, the arrow lodged in its head.

"Knud! Let go! I can't breathe!" Jarl shrieked, pulling Knud's arms away from his neck. But terror had a stronger hold over Knud than logic, and he clung to Jarl as tightly as he could as they ran ahead.

Another arrow shot past them and the long grass to their left was suddenly brimming with Dip wolves. The animals, realising they had been discovered, stood up and raced through the grass towards them, their heads low.

Astrid looked down at her quiver; she had one arrow left. She had not been able to retrieve her arrows from the village a few days earlier, and taking wood from the forest to make new ones had been far too dangerous to risk. There were worse things to fear than fireflies in the forests along the Riddari Kviðr mountains: creatures that would follow her back to Jarl and Knud if she entered.

Behind them, Jarl heard a loud snarl but did not turn back to look. Holding Knud's hands tightly to prevent himself from being strangled, he ran as fast as he could towards the four stone pillars.

"They're getting closer!" Knud screamed in Jarl's ear, as he looked behind and saw a large pack of Dip right behind them. "Astrid! Astrid!"

The one directly behind them yelped as a huge, clawed hand gripped its hind leg and dragged it back through the mud. Astrid's wolf teeth were around the

Dip's neck before it had time to turn on her, killing it instantly.

As Jarl passed the pillars he reached for his sword and drew it just in time, and a Dip fell to the ground with a large, fatal gash across its stomach. "Knud, get behind me!" he yelled, shaking him off his back.

With a clumsy thud, Knud fell, breaking his fall with his bag. He reached for the daggers he had kept tied to his leg for the past few weeks, confused at first as to why they weren't there. Then he remembered; he had given them back to Astrid.

None of the other Dip followed them past the pillars; they were focused on Astrid who was some way behind them. She had several of them on her back, their curved claws hooked into her wolf skin. Unable to claw them off, she threw herself onto the ground to crush them but, the moment she did, the rest of the pack lunged for her throat and her exposed stomach. She cried out in pain as one of them managed to clamp its jaws around her wrist and a fountain of moss, dirt and blood cascaded through the air as she grappled with it.

Moments passed and the animals fell one by one before the last few admitted defeat and retreated, whimpering back into the grass, their tails between their legs.

Astrid got to her feet. Her wolf skin was covered in deep scratches and there were streaks of bright red blood all over her arms and back. She paused for a moment to catch her breath before she hobbled past the pillars, her head bowed low and both eyes on the ground.

"They won't follow us," she panted. "But goblins will if there are any nearby. I didn't see any torques around their necks; they were probably wild. But we should keep walking."

"You're hurt!" Knud pointed to a large gash across her shoulder blade and a trickle of bright red blood trailing down her arm. Astrid looked up at him for a moment, a hopeful smile on her wolf face. *Had she been forgiven?*

"I'll heal," she said, and walked ahead with an obvious limp, still in her wolf skin. The large lump over her shoulders from where the wolf skin had stretched itself over the bag on her back was evident, as was every scratch and tear from the Dips' claws.

With his sword still drawn, Jarl helped Knud to stand and they both followed Astrid. Despite walking as quietly as they could, every sound echoed up the steep rock face on either side of them. The pass through the mountain was completely devoid of plant life; there was no grass or mud to muffle the sound of their footsteps, it was as if it had been stripped away with a knife. With nothing but stone on either side, the slightest sound amplified against the rock walls. Even the click of Astrid's claws echoed all around them. Even stranger was how the wind had stopped blowing. It was as silent as a graveyard.

Jarl turned to look back every few seconds, his grip firmly on the hilt of his sword, worried that the Dip might try to follow them into the pass. Knud held onto Jarl's free hand as tightly as he could, afraid to let go.

"Are they going to come back?" Knud whispered.

"I don't think so," Jarl reassured him, but still he kept looking behind to make sure they were alone.

Then they heard it: the high pitched whistle of a goblin horn. Astrid's head snapped around, her claws extended instantly. If she hadn't been wearing her wolf skin they would have seen her turn ashen as she recognised the goblin riding ahead of the others.

"Run!" she screamed, the sound of the panic in her voice far more terrifying than the sight of the goblins. Her obvious fear sent a cold shiver of dread down Jarl's spine. He had seen Astrid fearlessly face so many things over the past few months, and if she had been afraid at the time she had never shown it. But now she was afraid, and that frightened him.

Jarl picked Knud up in his arms and ran as fast as he could. Knud held on for dear life, watching the goblins over Jarl's shoulder as they rode past the first set of pillars at the end of the pass behind them.

"Goblins! Goblins!" Knud screamed, and for the second time that day he reached down to his leg where Astrid's daggers used to be tied.

"Get to the pillars! They won't pass the pillars!" Astrid screamed.

Ahead of them they could see a second set of pillars and, a little beyond them, trees. The pillars were close but the goblins were closer.

Astrid ground to a halt, her claws screeching against the ground, and she turned and raced past Jarl and Knud, straight towards the goblins. "Don't wait for me, run! Run!"

The horses were barely one hundred feet away. She flung her wolf skin off and pulled the last arrow to her bow, her eyes fixed on the goblin riding in front of the others. His face was hidden by a grotesque mask that only exposed his eyes - eyes she recognised. Taking a breath she released the arrow, dropped her bow to the ground, and quickly threw the wolf skin back over her shoulders. The arrow hit the goblin and with a horrifying wheeze he toppled backwards off his horse and onto the ground with a loud thud.

Astrid's face dropped. Even with their leader sprawled on the ground, the other goblins did not stop but passed him, riding ahead determinedly. She glanced behind her and saw Jarl and Knud had almost reached the pillars. Provided she held the goblins back for a little longer, they would make it. She knew the goblins would not dare to cross the pass; Frǫðleikr would not tolerate anyone entering who they sensed were there to kill another being.

I wonder if this will be it? both voices whispered in her head.

"No!" Astrid whispered to herself, flexing her back, ready to leap. "You do *not* die before they are safe!"

The first horse rushed past her, so close its skin brushed against hers. She ducked as the goblin on its back swung his jagged sword at her. The tip of the blade swept along the edges of the wolf hairs on her neck but, with one swipe of her claws, Astrid pulled one of the horse's legs out from under it and it fell heavily onto the ground, its rider half crushed beneath its weight. She heard bone break, unsure whose it was.

So, you argue with Jarl over goblins, yet here you are killing them? the harsh voice mocked in her head.

"It's not the same!" she screamed, as she reared onto her hind legs and pulled another of the goblins from his horse, her teeth around his arm. "I'm trying to save them!"

The goblins turned their horses to circle her, none of them interested in the two dwarves who had reached the end of the pass but wholly focused on the enormous wolf with grey and green eyes.

At the end of the pass Jarl and Knud heard a high pitched yelp, shortly followed by another. Jarl froze and his heart stopped mid beat. "Astrid!" He let go of Knud, dropped his bag on the ground and turned back, his mouth pressed into a determined line. Knud panicked as Jarl let go of his hand and he wrapped his arms tightly around him.

"No! No! Don't leave! Please don't leave!"

"Knud, I have to help her! Let go!"

"She'll be alright! She always is! Please don't go!"

The sound of goblins and horses' hooves echoed down the pass, but neither of them were able to see Astrid; she was completely blocked from view.

"Please!" Knud yelled, wide eyed and terrified.

Jarl pushed Knud away and raced past the pillars, back into the pass. He ran as fast as he could, even as he heard Knud pleading behind him to come back. Another half-animal, half-human scream cut through the air as he headed towards the goblins. They were circling Astrid and shouting out in Beziickt, their spears jabbing towards her. He could see three dead goblins alongside her and her jaws dripping with blood.

With a howl, Astrid leapt onto the back of one of the horses and sunk her teeth into the rider's neck. In a panic, the horse began to kick and buck and Astrid and the rider were tossed onto the ground. The goblin's neck snapped on impact and she got to her feet, only to come face to face with the last five goblins, one of them so close that his dagger was just inches from her chest. Astrid was too dazed from the fall to react in time.

Jarl's free hand grabbed the goblin by his long braided hair and he yanked him back onto the end of his sword. He dragged it back through the goblin's flesh and swung it down across a second goblin, killing him instantly, its spine split wide apart. The last thee goblins were too busy grappling with Astrid, who was pinned to the ground beneath them, to notice Jarl as he approached them, his sword raised, ready to kill.

There was a sudden, bright flash of blue light and the goblins released her and scrambled away. One of them fell, screaming in pain, and curled into a foetal position as he thrashed about on the ground.

As the other two goblins retreated, Jarl swung his sword across the back of their exposed necks, carving their heads from their bodies in one swift movement. They were dead before they hit the ground. He stepped over them and towards Astrid who lay slumped on the floor, the wolf skin only covering half of her body. Her pale skin glistened with a cold sweat and both of her hands, swathed in a dim blue glow, curled against her chest.

Jarl looked down at the terrified goblin before her who was barely alive. His eyes were wide open and bloodshot, both of his pupils like needlepoints. For a moment Jarl thought the dust surrounding the goblin was from the ground, but then he saw the goblin's skin had been burned and was crumbling to ash in front of him. For a few seconds the goblin stared at him like a frightened animal, his mouth open in a silent scream. With a horrible shudder his head went limp and half of it disintegrated the moment it touched the earth. He was half flesh, half dust.

Jarl sheathed his sword, crouched down next to Astrid and gently lifted her up into his arms, resting her head against his shoulder.

"Knud? Where is Knud?" Astrid mumbled, her speech slurred from the blood in her mouth.

"He's alright," Jarl replied. "He's by the pillars."

"Put me down," she insisted. "I can walk on my own."

Jarl did as she'd asked but kept one hand across her lower back for support, his other around her arm. Astrid did not object to the support; she felt dizzy. There was a large contusion on the side of her face where a goblin had struck her with the side of his spear.

Slowly, the blue glow faded from her hands and she dropped them to her sides. She had not meant to draw energy from the goblin but, as fear had overtaken her and the goblin's two sharp front teeth had come down towards her exposed neck, an instinct she could not control had taken over - a primal need to survive that overruled any other moral or emotional thought. Before she'd even had time to think, her hand had grasped the goblin's wrist and she'd sucked his life energy from him. Every wound on her wolf skin had healed within seconds, but every nerve in her body had pulsed violently with an energy she knew was not her own.

With her head bowed, Jarl could hear her rapid breathing. The deep puncture on her shoulder was still there, but not as severe as he remembered seeing it, the skin only just broken.

Knud sat huddled on the ground by the pillars. He scrambled to his knees and tried to stand as they both reached him, and wrapped his arms around Jarl's waist as soon as he was close enough, shivering like a frightened bird.

"Knud, it's alright. It's alright!" Jarl crouched down and pulled Knud into a hug as Astrid leant against the pillar, the stone almost as cold as her forehead. Her face was badly bruised, a nasty red gash on her jaw was already turning black, and her upper lip was swollen from where she had been clipped by an elbow. The distinct shape of a fist was imprinted on her skin.

"Astrid?" Knud reached for her hands. "Are you alright?" She peered down at him, relieved that he seemed to have forgiven her. "Are you going to be alright?" he repeated.

"I'll be fine." She smiled, the smile turning to a wince half way through. She reached up to her mouth and pressed the skin with her fingers, her knuckles scratched and bleeding. "I won't even have a scar from this one," she joked.

Her eye caught Jarl's for a second but she turned away when she heard a sound behind them. Jarl and Knud turned to look at what had caught her attention and saw a live goblin still in the pass. Jarl reached for his sword.

"Don't! Don't raise your sword here!" she warned, her hand on his, her eyes on the trees. "He won't pass the pillars."

Exactly as she had predicted, the goblin did not pass but stopped a few feet away from them, his teeth bared, snarling at her. His face was still covered by the horrible, leather mask, moulded to look like the skinned head of a Dip wolf. The arrow Astrid had shot him with was embedded in his shoulder and his hand was clasped around its shaft.

Knud clung to Jarl as the goblin shouted at Astrid in Beziickt, a single name: Moldof. Jarl kept his hand on the hilt of his sword, ready to draw it the moment the goblin attempted to walk past the pillars.

Astrid spoke back to the goblin in Beziickt, her pronunciation understandable to the goblin but shaky after so many years. The complicated clicks and deep words were difficult and painful to speak; her throat was used to the softer sound of the human languages.

"Look!" Knud whispered, awestruck.

By the pillars, the oak roots that stretched out across the path began to move like snakes and slithered forward. The trees moved as though swayed by a strong wind, except there was no wind, the air was a dead calm.

The roots slithered towards the goblin but stopped the minute they reached the pillars. The goblin, with a curved dagger in his hand, was torn between his urge to attack Astrid and his fear of the Frøðleikr. Slowly, he turned to walk back down the pass, but not before he shouted a stream of words at Astrid and made a whipping motion with his hand. Astrid narrowed her eyes at him but did not move. As he walked away, the roots slid back towards the trees and settled around them.

"What if he comes back?" Jarl asked.

"He won't."

The trees around them groaned, almost as if they agreed with her, and Jarl moved his arm protectively around Knud. Astrid swayed a little as she turned around and tried to walk ahead, her head spinning.

"Astrid, sit down," Jarl said. She nodded, leant back against the pillar and slid to the ground, her head against her knees.

"I just need a moment."

Without asking, Jarl pulled her bag off her shoulders, sat down on the ground next to her and slipped his arm around her. As he looked down he noticed a mark on the back of her neck peeking out from under her collar – an old, thin silver scar that stretched from the base of her neck to the edge of her hairline.

Knud pulled out Astrid's flask from her bag and handed it to her. "Do you want some water?" She looked up and took it from him, her hands still shaking.

"That goblin knew you, didn't he?" Jarl asked.

"I met his father," Astrid explained between sips. "Moldof. I would prefer never to meet him again. I was hoping his tribe wouldn't still be near the pass." She paused for a moment and took a large gulp of her drink. "He must have been the one who attacked the village."

Astrid shuddered, though this time it wasn't from Jarls touch as he reached over and held her hand to steady her grip on the flask. She felt cold, exhausted, and in pain. When she had first seen Moldof's son riding towards her, for a terrible moment she had thought it was Moldof himself, the mask he wore was the same. The physical reminders of their last meeting were etched in hundreds of scars across her back.

There were few times in her life when Astrid had feared death was near. Her meeting with Moldof had been one of those moments. She could still remember the taste of cold saliva in her mouth as she drifted in and out of consciousness, remembered her arms tied above her head and her back in so much pain she wished for death just so it would stop.

"We need to move. We can't stay still here."

"You should rest a little more," Jarl replied.

Astrid took another sip from the flask and motioned at the roots nearby. Both of them turned to look and realised that the trees on either side of the path had moved towards them a little while their backs had been turned, the tips of their roots a little closer than before.

"Are all the trees like this?" Knud whispered, worried they could hear him.

"Yes. We can't stop moving. They only move when you're not looking."

"And if they get to us?" Jarl asked.

"They won't let go. Ever."

Jarl helped her as she tried to stand, the colour draining from her face. With her hand on his arm for support, she gripped it as tightly as she could. He reached down and slung her bag onto his back.

"I can take it," she said, reaching for it, but Jarl shook his head.

"I'll take it," he replied firmly, and Astrid did not argue. Her legs were far more unstable than she was ready to admit.

"We don't have to walk fast, we just have to keep moving," Astrid whispered, slightly hunched as she took her first step.

Slowly they all moved forward in silence, Jarl supporting Knud on his left and Astrid on his right.

The path became less cluttered and the trees tapered out the further they went on. The roots no longer stretched out like hundreds of twisted fingers across the path, they stayed closer to the walls of the pass instead. Moss covered everything, even the trees, and there were just a few patches where it had worn away enough to expose the rock underneath.

As Jarl thought to himself that it was unlikely any animals lived in the pass, he heard the sound of something flying above them, and a large shadow blocked out the light for just a few seconds. Jarl and Knud both looked up quickly, but whatever had flown over was gone before they could see it, the clouds above them too thick.

"What was that?" Knud asked.

"It's alright," Astrid rasped, her eyes closed, her head resting against Jarl's shoulder. "It's just gryphon."

"Gryphon?" Knud replied, a tinge of excitement in his voice.

"You don't need to be afraid, they won't come down here," Astrid reassured him.

"Can we sit for a while?" Jarl asked.

Astrid glanced around. The trees were not as close together as they had been by the pillars and the magic in the air was softer, less aggressive. "You should be alright for a few minutes."

"Good."

Astrid did not have the will to fight him as he forced her to sit down and pushed her hair aside to look at her swollen lip and the large bruise across the side of her face. Knud sat beside her, his hand on her knee.

"I'll be fine," she said. "Stop fussing."

Jarl took the end of her veil that hung loosely around her neck and soaked it in the water from his flask to clean the blood on her face. He pushed her hand out of the way as she half-heartedly tried to stop him, and turned her face towards him so he could see the mark on the side of her head better. The skin just above her ear was broken and blood trickled from it down to her jaw.

"I'm sure you will be," Jarl replied, but continued to clean away the blood.

Astrid felt her cheeks burning red as his hand, warm against her face, held her chin. The swell in her chest felt as if she had a hundred butterflies trapped in her ribcage. She could feel him looking at her but she refused to meet his gaze.

"I'm sorry. I didn't mean to upset you about the goblins," Astrid said suddenly. The words were out of her mouth almost before she realised she had said them. "I just didn't...I didn't expect to hear that."

Jarl said nothing and continued to clean away the blood, his mouth pressed into a tight line, his face unreadable. Astrid was unsure if silence was his way of accepting her apology or maintaining his grudge.

Knud, however, hugged her tightly. "Don't leave again!" he begged.

"I'm not going anywhere, Knud."

Sniffing loudly, Knud rubbed his eyes and smiled at her, relieved. "Good. I don't hate you."

"That's good to know." Astrid smiled, a lump at the back of her throat. She coughed to clear it and ruffled Knud's red hair fondly.

Behind them, the trees groaned and all three turned to look at them. The roots were a little closer than they had been a few moments before.

"The crossroads should be about two days' walk from here. We should keep going." Astrid struggled to her feet, her back still in pain but not so much that she could feel a coldness spread from it, like she had before.

"We're going to walk for two days?" Knud asked, horrified at the idea.

"No. We can sleep, but only one at a time. If you have your back to the trees they will try and grab you."

"Why?" Knud asked.

"They're Frǫðleikr. They're still angry about losing their old home. They see everyone as a danger."

"But we won't hurt them." Knud turned to look at the trees, wondering if they could hear him. "Why would they want to hurt us?"

"They've been hurt too much to see the difference, I guess." Astrid shrugged her shoulders. "Dag never told me much about why they lost their home, but it must have hurt them a lot."

She looked at an old twisted oak as they passed it, a deep gash down its ancient trunk that looked as if it had been made by some kind of sword or ax. Time had allowed the bark around it to cover some of the damage but the mark was still visible. It would be another five hundred years before the gash would be covered but, even then, Frǫðleikr would not forget. The mark was etched into its mind as much at its body, and its mind would always remember. Someone had hurt it, badly, and in a small way she understood their anger. The same anger she had grappled with for years.

As they walked on, Jarl inched his arm around her waist and leaned down to gently kiss the side of her face. Astrid turned to look up at him and his gaze caught hers. He smiled at her and she breathed a sigh of relief, leaning her head against his shoulder.

He forgave me.

HUNT

"I still think this is foolish!" Ótama warned Ulf as he mounted Bál. "If I was planning to kill you I would do it now, in the hunt. Why are you giving them another chance?"

Ulf shook his head. "They won't try anything. Bál will see to that." The dragon horse snorted loudly as if it understood and clawed at the ground excitedly.

The air was full of anticipation. Around them, many other goblins were already mounted on their huge bison, their saddles strapped just behind the curved humps of their shoulders. The bison were at least five times the size of their riders, who looked like little dolls strapped to their backs.

The stirrups on the saddles were so short that the goblins had to sit crouched like toads, ready to leap off the backs of the massive creatures at a moment's notice. In the rush of the hunt it was not always possible for the bison and their riders to avoid an animal that had been killed further up in the herd. On every hunt at least one goblin would die after being crushed under their steed as it tripped over a dead carcass. The goblins needed to be able to move quickly. To jump off the back of their bison was extremely dangerous, but to be crushed meant certain death.

The ground shook under the heavy plod of the animals as they moved forward, and the entire group slowly circled Ulf, waiting for him to give the order to ride out.

After mounting her own bison, Ótama glanced back at the camp and ran her fingers across the wolf hair cuff on her forehead, an old, superstitious gesture she made at the start of every hunt. Her general's cuff on the upper part of her right arm pressed against her skin as she leant against her bison's high hunched shoulders, the solid copper arm bracelet held in place only by the thickness of her arm muscles.

She watched Ulf nervously and her eyes flitted every few moments to the other goblins in the hunting party. They had been unable to find any of the other conspirators from the attempted assassination on Ulf; everyone involved had either been killed during the confrontation or had enough common sense to deny any association with the failed attempt.

The unbridled dragon horse reared excitedly. Ulf's hands hung by his sides, holding onto the animal with only his legs. Years of riding Bál bareback had left him with thighs that were almost as strong as the dragon horse's.

The first time he had tried to ride the horse, his inner thighs had been cut to pieces on the sharp edges of Bál's scales. It had been weeks before he had been able to ride again, but now, years later, the skin of his inner thighs were as thick as leather and Bál's scales no longer hurt him.

Ulf looked around him, his head held high, a long thin spear gripped loosely between his fingertips. Everyone watched him, excited, nervous, and hungry. They circled the dragon horse, all eyes on Ulf.

Pushing through the mass of bison riders, Systa and Garðarr approached him, their generals' bracelets visible on their arms.

"There is a herd not far over the ridge!" Garðarr said excitedly, his face flushed by the wind.

Garðarr was the youngest of the generals with very few scars on his body, though not through lack of battle experience. Despite being just fifteen, he had seen more battles than most; he'd had no choice in the matter. As a member of one of the smaller tribes on the plains, to be a great fighter was a matter of survival, not a choice. His lack of scars was testament to his ability - there was even a rumour that the few scars he did carry were self inflicted so as to appear battle hardened.

His likeness to Ulf was uncanny; they had the same sharp nose and jaw, the same rare, cold blue eyes. Garðarr's face was slightly rounder and more youthful but if they had not been from different tribes it would have been easy to assume they were brothers.

Ótama was the oldest general, the braids in her hair flecked with white. She was tall, and the muscles of her shoulders were knotted like an ox's. She was the only goblin who had ever come close to killing Ulf and it was something he respected. Even when her tribe had been defeated in a bloody battle that had lasted the better part of three days, she had been defiant. There was not so much as a fleck of fear in her face when Ulf had stood before her. Even Bál had not been able to shake her courage - and courage, along with loyalty, was something Ulf respected deeply, a trait Ótama's youngest sister, Systa, also carried.

Ulf had been reluctant to make Systa his third general but Ótama had insisted on it as a condition of her loyalty. It was not a decision he had come to regret.

The pairing of the two sisters in battle could not have been more deadly. With their backs to each other as they fought, they were the first to enter the battle field and often the last to leave it. Some of their own soldiers often joked that they would braid their hair together so as to not be separated in the heat of combat.

Despite being sisters they looked vastly different to one another. Ótama's hair gold as corn, streaks of grey laced throughout it, and braided in a tight knot around her hair cuff, with four sharp thick metal pins, which often doubled as weapons in battle, speared through it. Her eyes were a mixture of green and yellow, like most goblins.

Systa also had green and yellow eyes, but that was where the similarities ended. Her hair was so short and her features so androgynous that she was often confused for being a young boy, a mistake she loved to use for her own amusement. Any new recruits in Ulf's army were unaware that their general was a girl until Systa would expose the fact in the most outrageous way possible. She revelled in the bewildered and shocked expressions on their faces.

Ulf raised his spear and the entire hunting party ground to a halt. Bál lurched ahead, his curved claw-like hooves digging into the ground as he sprinted past the bison who parted to let him through. His long black mane was braided in a thick plait and Ulf's fingers were knotted into it. Ulf leant forward as Bál's speed increased, an excited smile on his face and goose bumps on his skin as the wind ripped past them.

Behind them, the hunting party took off, the bison slow to match the athletic speed of the dragon horse at first. Even so far ahead of them, Ulf could hear the ground tremble under the hooves of the massive animals. He glanced back for a moment, a large grin on his face as the party began to catch up with him. Systa, Ótama and Garðarr were spaced out in a line at the front, the riders behind them separated into three different regiments behind each of his generals.

Several of the riders tried to make their way ahead to follow Ulf but Systa and Ótama blocked their way.

"The Agrokū rides alone!" Ótama snapped. Disappointed, the riders retreated and rejoined their ranks.

Ulf looked ahead and the end of the ridge rose up before him, the miles and miles of grass-covered hills like undulating waves in an ocean. He raced over the first hill. Bál snorted and ground his teeth as the colossal herd of elk, deer and wild bison came into sight - hundreds of animals packed together, a trail behind them that stretched for miles.

It took less than a second for the animals to see him, and then their slow plod turned into a desperate stampede. The animals bellowed and yelped, terrified by the sight of the dragon horse. Within seconds the rest of the hunting partly were behind Ulf. Ótama rode her regiment to the right of the herd, Systa to the rear, and Garðarr to the left.

Ulf raced down the ridge towards the animals, the three regiments guiding the direction of the panicked herd. The goblins who were closest to them had their spears raised, ready to deal a death strike to the nearest one.

Ulf raised his spear, the strap at the end of it twisted around his wrist. With one quick jab he tossed it towards a nearby elk that straggled behind the rest, either too young or weak to keep up. Like a scorpion's tail, the tip of his spear pierced the nape of the elk's neck and its spine severed instantly before the strap around Ulf's arm pulled the spear back. Ulf's hand snapped around it as the elk fell to the ground.

Soon, a trail of dead animals - elk, deer and wild bison - began to litter the ground behind them.

Ótama watched worriedly as Ulf rode into the stampede, Bál shoulder to shoulder with two large bison and Ulf with his feet pulled up, crouched on Bál's back like a frog.

Ótama rode as close as she dared to the flanks of the stampede, her spear lowered, uninterested in the animals that were within easy reach of her. Her eyes were fixed on Ulf as he jabbed at the animals around him, each blow expertly struck at the base of their spines. One, two, three, four wild bison fell. The animals that ran behind them tripped and stumbled over them. There was a loud bellow as several deer fell in a tangled mess of hooves and antlers.

Ulf pulled back, slowing down until he was out of the stampede, then turned onto the group of fallen prey. Bál snorted excitedly and pounced on the nearest bison, his long razor sharp teeth slicing through the animal's neck. The bison shuddered and fell to the ground and a long stream of dark red blood spilled around it.

Dismounting, Ulf stroked Bál's neck fondly as his teeth crunched down onto the corpse.

"Happy now?" Ulf asked, a smile on his face. He stroked the hard scales of the dragon horse and watched as the rest of the hunting party rode past him, Systa, Ótama and Garðarr content to ride ahead. They would not hunt for much longer. They did not need more. The animals that had already been killed would last them several weeks. The meat would be smoked and dried, the hides picked clean and tanned, the bones stewed and turned into yurt frames, weapons and needles. Every single carcass would be used, not even the intestines wasted.

They could not afford to waste anything. The earth of the plains was not suitable for farming, the animals that lived on it far from varied. Meat, roots and ground nuts were the primary diet. The plains were not the mountains; there were no trees to burn, no rabbits with soft tender meat to hunt, no fruits to eat, and nowhere to hide from the bitterly cold winters.

Ulf looked up at the mountains in the distance, their peaks a pale blue, several of them piercing the clouds that hung above them. Ulf's lip curled with disgust and he turned back to Bál, his eyes narrowed. He did not know how much longer he could wait. While he had done his best to appear carefree about his attempted murder, in a small way he understood Aki's reasoning. None of the tribes were comfortable being so close to the mountains. Mountains meant dwarves, and dwarves meant the Hætta. Even though Bjargtre had not engaged in a Hætta for several years, it did not mean it would remain that way. Autumn was almost over and, like the spring, the end of autumn was not a season the goblins enjoyed. They were nervous and agitated, their eyes on the horizon at all times. The winter was safe. The dwarves never ventured out of the mountains if there was snow on the ground, but in spring and autumn the Hætta would be in full swing, everyone ready to leave at a moment's notice.

Under Ulf's command none of them had encountered a Hætta in many months, but they could all remember at least one – they had all lost, or knew someone who had lost a loved one to the cull. It was not something they would ever forget.

When he had moved the tribe across the plains towards Bjargtre, Ulf had promised they would have a home in the mountains by winter. That had been two winters ago. In that time his own tribe had grown as it had assimilated the smaller goblin tribes, but the promise of a permanent home in the mountains without the fear of the Hætta had not yet materialised.

They were frustrated and hope had given way to disappointment, disappointment to anger. Their dreams of a better, safer life had been raised and dashed. He needed to act soon if he was to keep their undivided loyalty. Fear would only go so far, and a reign of fear was not what he had envisioned for his people.

QUIET MOMENTS

They had stopped briefly to eat before sunset, their backs against one another, their eyes on the forest around them. The sky was still dark but the stars had become less visible as the faint, golden light on the horizon began to block them out.

Knud had barely managed more than a few bites of food before he had drifted back to sleep and after a few hours they had decided to move on, the roots too close for comfort and Astrid uneasy with the darkness and the Frøðleikr being so close.

They had taken turns to carry Knud, who had slept soundly through the night, Jarl the one who had carried him the most despite Astrid's insistence. Neither of them had spoken much but Jarl's hand was still in hers, his fingers occasionally sliding up and down the side of her hand.

It was such a simple little movement, but it made Astrid feel so unbearably happy each time he did it. The euphoric feeling in her chest was a little like the sensation of being slightly intoxicated, light headed and happy.

Next you're going to say you can't live without him! the harsh voice jeered. *Jarl! I need you! I can't live without you!* It laughed again. Astrid shook her head as the voices started to creep back in little ghost-like whispers. *He forgave you this time, but just wait, you'll say something soon and he'll get angry. He'll get so angry he'll never talk to you again, and neither will Knud. It's just a matter of time!*

"Tell me about your home in Bjargtre," Astrid said suddenly, determined to drown out the voices with conversation, no matter how forced the topic was.

"What do you want to know?"

"Anything. What is it like? The people, the houses, the food."

"The food? Well, that's just going to make me hungry!" Jarl laughed. "We like meat, lots and lots of meat. Drowned in butter, of course. Rabbit is my favourite."

"I hate rabbit," Knud muttered, half asleep, his head on Jarl's shoulder.

"Yes, I know you do. But you should still stop throwing it under the table." Knud didn't answer but, instead, a quiet little snore erupted from his open mouth. "Tell me when he starts drooling," Jarl half-joked, and readjusted his grip a little before he continued to walk ahead. "He's always slept like a drunk cat."

Astrid smiled as she tried to imagine what a drunk cat would look like, the image in her head amusing. "The humans say the dwarves just eat meat. Is that true?"

"No," Jarl replied. "King Hastein used to do that though. That's probably how that rumour spread, but no, we don't just eat meat."

"King Hastein? Was that King Hábrók's father?" Astrid asked, and Jarl nodded.

"He thought that just eating meat would make him stronger."

"Why? Was he weak?"

"All the royal family are."

"I thought all dwarves were strong," she said, surprised.

"King Hábrók married his first cousin," Jarl went on, lowering his voice. "The royal family has always married cousins since the Rojóða wars. I think they're afraid that if they marry outsiders it will cause another great war."

"Is that what the dwarves say caused the Rojóða wars?"

"I've heard so many different stories about what caused it," Jarl muttered. Astrid worried for a moment that she had accidentally stumbled onto another sensitive topic of conversation. "One book says it was the elves trying to take over the mountains to mine the gold; another says the goblins wanted more land. The one most people seem to believe is that an elf queen called Erin wanted to marry a dwarf prince called Galmann. He refused and she accepted the hand of a goblin Agrokū. Galmann changed his mind and Erin left the goblin king on the eve of their wedding. So the goblin Agrokū attacked the dwarves."

"How did the elves become involved though? The humans call it the Three Kings Wars."

"That's probably a better name for it," Jarl muttered. "The more I read about it from the old texts, the more I'm sure it was greedy kings who wanted to get into a fight and dragged all of Ammasteinn into the ditch with them." Irritated, he said nothing more for a few moments.

As a boy, the old texts had been read out to him again and again, his tutor's voice hushed as if she were reading a book of prayer. The texts were so old and, with nobody alive to contest what had been written, of course they had to be true! They even had a feast day every year, Bjartr Dagr, as they called it, to celebrate the end of the Rojóða wars. The feast would last three days at least with effigies of goblins and even a few elves burned in public. It all seemed so mindless to him now, so much meaningless death all for the pride of a few kings and queens.

Astrid tried to change the course of the conversation. "The king, what is he like?"

"He is…" Jarl paused as he thought for a moment, his dwarf sense of loyalty urging him to say something respectful. But he couldn't. "He a fool! He thinks if be buries his head in the mud the danger will pass, and he's too weak-willed to stand up to men like Gull. He thinks the goblins will just leave the city if we bury ourselves deep enough in the mountain."

"Is that what he said to you?" Astrid asked, her voice hushed. They were back to the topic of goblins again and she did not want to get into another argument.

"Yes. I tried to tell him. But Áfastr Gull—"

"Áfastr Gull?"

Jarl growled at the back of his throat, the sound startling Knud, but he quickly went back to sleep. His head rocked a little from side to side as they walked, his mouth hanging open.

"A Hlaupa noble!" Jarl spat.

Astrid looked at him, confused. Hlaupa was not a word she was familiar with. Her Mál was merely at a conversational level and she was not accustomed to the more complex and descriptive words.

"A social climber. He's arrogant; greedy. He managed to get the king to trust him and take his advice. If he had tried the same thing with King Hastein he would have been made an Ósómi. He'd rather make me look like a fool than realise the city is in danger." Jarl's face twisted into a strange mixture of a snarl and a frown, his blue eyes fierce. It was not an expression Astrid liked to see, the kindness gone.

"Why?"

"Why what?"

"Why does Gull hate you?"

"I don't know. I've never asked and he never explained."

"Lǫgberg. Have you been before?"

"No, never. I've only ever read about it."

Astrid looked at him with a new found respect. She had assumed from the air of quiet confidence he always carried that he must have at least seen Lǫgberg before. The fact he had decided to trust her - a complete stranger at the time - to take them across Ammasteinn to a city he had never been to, impressed her. He was either brave or calmly reckless. Either way, she admired it.

"Don't look at me like that!" Jarl laughed. His eyes glinted a little in the low light.

"Like what?"

"Like you can't decide if I'm insane," he laughed.

"I was thinking more brave than insane," Astrid admitted.

"You think so?"

"Yes."

They said nothing for several minutes, the slap of their shoes on the ground the only noise except for the light wind whistling above them, the huge rock walls that rose up on either side of the pass blocking most of it out. Occasionally, an eerie sound echoed around them as if a grand flute was being played deep in the mountains as the wind cut over the chasm that made up the pass. The sound made Astrid shiver, though she managed to hide it well. It sounded too much like horns - dwarf horns - and she hated that sound.

The trees started to thin out until, finally, they had only stone around them. It was only then that Astrid felt safe enough to stop.

"Ok, we can rest here," Astrid said as she looked around, her elf eyes able to see through the dark much better than Jarl's could. There were many more kinds of Frøðleikr than just Leshy in the mountains, together with gryphon, huldra and sylph, and possibly many more species she was not even aware of. She knew better than to not be on her guard.

Jarl lowered Knud gently onto the ground, his mouth still wide open and drooling. There was a trail of slobber covering Jarl's left shoulder and Astrid laughed at the disgusted expression on Jarl's face as he wiped it away.

"He has got to stop doing that," Jarl muttered, as he took the wolf skin from Astrid. No sooner had he placed it over Knud's shoulders, Jarl felt Astrid slip her hand into his. She held it tightly, as if she was afraid he would let go, and he turned to look at her. There was a half-smile on her face, the large bruise on the side of her cheek and lip now several colourful shades of red, blue and black.

"What's wrong?" he whispered.

"Nothing," Astrid replied. Her grip faltered a little and she pulled her hand away, suddenly feeling very awkward. "I just wanted to hold your hand."

Jarl raised an eyebrow, sure she was lying. Something was bothering her, he could tell now. For the past few hours she had not said a word, her expression calm. But then she would suddenly shake her head, scrunch her eyes together in a pained expression and tap her knuckles against her forehead like she was trying to knock something out of it.

It had become more and more apparent to him over the last few days that Astrid had two very different sides to her. One withdrawn and silent, a sentinel who refused to engage with any kind of emotion, and another who was desperate for emotional interaction. Occasionally it rose to the surface before it was beaten back by her dominant personality. The two sides of her were volatile and unstable, each in their own way.

Jarl sat down next to Knud and reached up for her hand. "Come here," he whispered, and pulled her down next to him before wrapping his arm around her shoulders. Astrid curled her hands tightly against her chest, awkward and nervous.

Why? Why do you do that? If you're going to hold his hand, just hold his hand! The soft voice laughed. Astrid pulled her knees to her chest and resisted the urge to get up and run.

Jarl felt every single muscle in her shoulders tense. "Astrid, I'm not going to bite!"

She forced a smile and scrunched her eyes together as the voices grew louder. She needed to talk or, better still, for him to talk to make them go away. It was always so hard for them to torment her when he spoke. "We should be there within a day or two. Bugal might have a pony he can lend you. We would get to Lǫgberg a lot faster," Astrid said quickly.

Jarl nodded. It would cut the time it would take them by a third at least if they could borrow a pony. He turned to look over at Knud for a moment as he snored loudly, his bright red curly hair splayed out around his face, messy and tangled. "I have to tell him soon. He won't forgive me if I wait till we arrive," Jarl muttered. "I don't want him to think I'm abandoning him."

"He wouldn't think that. He loves you too much."

"Just because you love someone it doesn't mean you can't get angry at them," Jarl said. Astrid instantly tensed, sure that the comment had been directed at her, and the harsh voice laughed hysterically.

See? He's still angry at you. He hasn't forgiven you at all!

Hearing her inhale sharply, Jarl turned to look at her. Her eyes were fixed on the ground, her whole body tense.

"I didn't mean you!" he reassured her. Astrid nodded but would not look at him. "Why do you hate horses? And ponies?" he asked suddenly.

"I just do!" she snapped, before repeating herself, trying to sound less angry. "I just don't like them."

Jarl watched her face, practically able to see her dual personalities battling inside her head. Her expression flitted from terror to stoic within seconds. Whatever it was that terrified her so much, she was not ready to share it. Perhaps she would never be ready. Something had clearly happened that had left a deeper scar than any of those on her face, and Astrid was not the type to admit when she was wounded.

"Will you let me guess?"

Astrid glared at him. "Guess what?"

"Nod if I'm right and say nothing if I'm wrong."

Talk to him! the soft voice urged her. *You can't pretend to love him if you won't talk to him!*

Astrid flinched at the world 'love' being mentioned, and her bottom lip curled a little in disgust. I am not in love, he's just important to me, she thought. "Alright," she said, "ask what you want."

For a few moments Jarl was silent as he planned how to say what he had pieced together so far. He started with the question he was sure he knew the answer to. "They're dead, aren't they? Your parents."

Astrid nodded, her mouth twisted into a grimace, her throat feeling as if a large stone had suddenly grown in the middle of her gullet.

Jarl took his time as he thought of another question. He had seen the hammer ax she carried around and recognised the dwarf craftsmanship, though he still did not recognise the thistle emblem etched into it. All he knew was that whomever had owned it must have been important. It was not just any dwarf who could afford such a magnificently crafted weapon. "Your father was nobility?" She half nodded. "From Bjargtre?" Astrid shook her head. "From Løgberg?" Another Nod. He thought for a moment. Løgberg; that worried him. A noble would not have been killed by just anyone. An order like that only came from one place. A horrible thought started to form at the back of his mind. "Do you...do you know who—"

Astrid's head froze half way through her nod. She had never asked Dag outright, but like Jarl, she suspected. "I'm not sure."

"I know your mother was an elf." Jarl took the bow from where it was strapped onto the side of her backpack and inspected the beautiful jasmine pattern carved around it. "It's not any elf who has something as well made as this," he remarked to himself out loud.

Astrid watched him run his fingers over the bow, her thoughts rushing through her head. So many times she had considered trying to find out more about her parents, but each time the harsh voice in her head had pulled her away from the notion. It caused too much pain, the kind of pain she was tired of. Peace was all she wanted, a break from the past, to leave it all behind. She turned to look up at Jarl and studied his features: his kind blue eyes, his thick short beard and warm smile.

This...this could be my future, she thought, the beginning of a smile on her face.

The harsh voice laughed. *Don't be stupid!*

Why? Why is it stupid? the quiet voice snapped back. *He's brave, kind...handsome* — Astrid's cheeks flushed bright red and she smiled coyly. He's handsome; I want to know him, she thought.

A handsome dwarf, with a scarred and ugly half elf, why would he love you? You're a novelty, something exotic to distract him. Astrid squeezed her eyes shut and forced the voice away.

Jarl put the bow down. He could feel Astrid becoming more and more agitated and noticed her fingers knotting together, her brow furrowed. He slung his arm back around her and leant his head against hers. "It's alright, I won't ask you about them again."

"Thank you," she whispered.

ARRIVAL

The Mad Gate was in front of him. Halvard stood for a moment, glancing around at the usual bustle of dwarves moving in and out of the city - farmers, soldiers and civilians – and the large herds of animals carrying huge baskets on their backs, laden with food from the nearby fields.

He thought he would be relieved when he finally arrived but all he felt was an emptiness inside. He trudged forward, his legs tired, but that was not why he dragged his feet. Nobody had noticed him as he had walked through the crowded entrance. Even a few of the soldiers he had served beside for years did not recognise the scraggy haired stranger with the unkempt beard.

Out of habit he walked towards the garrison before he realised he had resigned his post in order to travel with Jarl to Lǫgberg. Where else can I go? he thought, turning around. "Holmvé," he muttered, and made his way back down the tunnel towards the centre of the city.

The past few weeks had left him even angrier than before, though at present is was partly subdued by exhaustion. He had been unable to bear the thought of staying at the Salt Monasteries for longer than a few days, irritated by the presence of the humans but even more so by Skad, whose company was about as pleasant as a daily beating. Half way through his journey he had considered turning back, tired, cold and, though he would not admit it, lonely. But after so many weeks on the road he had decided that his only choice was to go home, back to Bjargtre.

Eventually he reached the front door of Vǫrn hall, polished to a sheen as always. Halvard raised his hand and knocked firmly. He heard a loud crash as something was dropped onto the floor followed by a patter of feet. Several excited voices chattered inside.

"Jarl?" Holmvé threw open the door, Eilíf, Gísla and Hlín behind her. Their faces dropped as they saw only him, and a tinge of terror crept over Holmvé's face.

"Halvard? Please…please don't tell me—"

"No, no. They're alive," Halvard reassured her, his hands raised. "Jarl's probably at Lǫgberg by now."

"Probably? Didn't you go with him? I thought he had sent you back for us?" Holmvé said, confused.

Halvard growled and ran his hands over his face. "Can I come in before I explain?"

"Of course!" Holmvé quickly stepped aside and Halvard strolled ahead to the Great Hall, took off his bag and dumped it heavily onto the table. He pulled out a chair and sat down, his feet so sore that they pricked the moment he stopped moving. Holmvé sat next to him and Eilíf, Gísla and Hlín joined them on the opposite side of the table.

"What happened?"

"A Brojóta burðr is what happened," Halvard grumbled.

"No obscenities!" Holmvé demanded, one white eyebrow raised.

Halvard took a deep breath. "We had passed the Salt Monasteries; Skad had to stay there since he broke his leg. We were a few days away from the Haltija Pass and we got into an argument."

Holmvé rolled her eyes. "I thought you two had grown out of that?"

"I had a good reason!" Halvard protested.

"I'm sure you did," Holmvé replied sarcastically. "So…you just left him? Why would you do that? He's your friend. Your only friend."

"You don't need to remind me of that," Halvard snapped.

"What was this reason?"

"We were travelling with a woman." Instantly, all four women sat up and listened all the more intently, Holmvé with a gleam in her eye. "She was a half elf."

"Half what?" Holmvé said.

"Half elf, half dwarf." They all gasped. "At first I thought he was just being kind. But he started to look at her in this way…it made me uncomfortable. She used magic. Jarl couldn't think straight. He wasn't seeing her for what she was. And she was reckless! She nearly got Knud killed when she got into a fight with some elves!"

Holmvé's mouth fell open and she pressed her hand tightly against her chest.

"Knud! Is little Knud alright?" Eilíf asked.

"He was fine when I left."

There was a collective sigh of relief.

"And Jarl. Is he eating properly?" Gísla asked.

"I don't know!" Halvard snapped. "I was more worried about the Brojóta burðr than what he was eating!"

"Halvard!" Holmvé barked. This time he ignored her.

"He'll get himself killed with that Goðgá! She's dangerous! I tried to tell him but he went wild and wouldn't listen. I think she bewitched him with her elf magic."

Holmvé snorted. "I doubt that. Jarl is no fool!" But her voice was uncertain.

"He is a fool for her. Knud is, too. They think she is some kind of…I don't know what they think she is, but they're infatuated. Jarl especially. He's a fool! He'll lose everything if the queen finds out! This hall, his name— "

"He won't lose the hall," Holmvé interrupted, a small smile on her face. Halvard looked at her, baffled. "He passed it to me before he left. They can take his name and his title, but they can't take his home because it's mine now. Like I said, he is no fool!" She smiled proudly.

"He left it all to you?"

Holmvé nodded. "The hall, his wealth. Everything is in my name now."

Halvard sat dumfounded. Jarl had said nothing about this to him on the road.

"You said you left them at the pass," Holmvé said. "Will this half-elf be able to get them through?"

"I think so," Halvard admitted. "We hadn't seen any goblins. I think they'll make it to Lǫgberg."

Holmvé stood and paced up and down the room nervously before returning to her chair. They sat in silence for a few moments, Holmvé, Eilíf, Gísla and Hlín deep in thought with worried expressions on their old, wrinkled faces. Halvard glanced toward the end of the table and noticed the food that had been laid there: beef, potatoes and some kind of green vegetable that he was sure would taste disgusting. His stomach rumbled.

"Hungry?" Eilíf asked, the question pointless. Halvard was practically drooling like a dog at the sight of it. He nodded enthusiastically and she quickly filled a spare plate and laid it down in front of him.

Unlike at that monastery, this time Halvard did his best to eat a little more politely, though Holmvé still flashed him a look of stern disapproval. "Do you have anywhere to stay?" she asked, and he shook his head. "Then you can stay in the old room and when Jarl gets back you two are going to have a long conversation. It's like you both never grew up! Always fighting over petty stupid things."

"Holmvé, did you not hear me? He's in love with a Blanda blóð!"

Holmvé's mouth pressed into a tight line. "I heard you the first time. I'll talk to him about it when he gets back, but what are you going to do now?"

Halvard chewed slowly on his food and swallowed. "I don't know."

"Perfect! Because I do! You're going to go back to Captain Gauss and ask him for your old position back."

Halvard nodded, his head lowered a little. He had thought she would say that.

"Hey." Holmvé walked over to him and rested her hand on his shoulder. "Don't wear that face. It doesn't suit you. It's not as bad as you think. Eat your food, have some sleep and then tomorrow go and speak to him."

"I'd rather do it now. Get it over with." Halvard got to his feet and walked to the front door. He paused for a moment before he opened it and took a deep breath. His pride was about to take a beating and he knew it.

"Halvard! Don't worry! It will be ok!" Holmvé called out, then smiled at him, her old wrinkled face scrunched up like a walnut. Halvard nodded back at her, his face still glum.

He closed the door firmly and walked out into the street. It occurred to him that he should get cleaned up before going to see his old captain, but he knew that no matter how he presented himself, his re-recruitment would be a humiliating experience.

It took him over an hour to walk to the other side of the city, which was a little quicker than usual. But when he finally reached the garrison he stopped, part of him too proud to enter and the other part resigned to the fact there was no other future for him. Nobody in Bjargtre would hire the nameless son of an Ósómi except for the military or the sewer cleaners, and Halvard knew he would rather take endless insults from Captain Gauss than be reduced to the shame of cleaning the sewers.

He strode through the gates of the garrison and past the two huge dwarf statues on either side of it. There were a few soldiers on guard and one of them immediately asked who he was.

"You know who I am!" Halvard spat. The guard studied him for a moment, his eyes widening with recognition. They let him pass but Halvard heard them muttering behind him, a laugh or two mingled with their conversation regarding their horror at his appearance.

He made his way through the courtyard where several soldiers were training, the clash of steel against steel and the bellowing voice of the garrison trainer all too familiar.

As he marched into the building a second guard, a dwarf he did not recognise, tried to stop him.

"I'm here to see Captain Gauss."

"What do you want with him?" the soldier asked. Halvard did his best not to hit the dwarf, who was at least thirty years younger than him and had a distinct air of arrogance around him.

"I'm here to see him!"

"I need to know more than that."

"All you need to know is that I trained here decades before you, and if you get in my way again I'll show you how a real soldier fights!" Halvard threatened. The soldier held his ground.

"Halvard!"

Halvard, recognising the voice behind him, took a deep breath and turned to face Captain Gauss. "Captain." He nodded respectfully.

"By Hel! I never thought I would see you again!" The captain laughed, his tone unfriendly. It reeked of condescension. The soldier behind Halvard snorted and quickly stifled the sound. "I assume you're here to ask for your position back."

Halvard nodded, not trusting himself to speak. His fists clenched together, ready to turn and hit the soldier behind him with all his might if he heard just one more snort from him.

"Well, you can't be a captain anymore. You'll have to start at the bottom," Gauss said.

Halvard stared at him. "What? I've been a soldier for longer than this little brat has lived!" he said, pointing at the soldier behind him.

"Well, you're lucky to have any kind of position at all. You know the only reason you got your position was because of Jókell. And Jarl's not here to vouch for you, so you get to start at the bottom. The king's funeral is in two days, you can— "

"The king is dead?"

"Yes, didn't you see the black flags in the city?" Gauss shook his head and held his hand up, uninterested in what Halvard was about to say. "You can join the other soldiers lining the way to the catacombs. Oh, and I heard a crazy rumour that Vǫrn went to see the queen and took Knud Villieldr with him."

Halvard was quiet for a few moments before he replied. "It's true."

The captain inhaled sharply and shook his head. "I hope nothing happens to that Villieldr boy. If he dies and Jarl is stupid enough to go and see the queen, she'll have him sent to the Gróf."

"Nothing will happen to him," Halvard said firmly with absolute confidence in his voice. "Jarl would rather lose his right foot than let something happen to Knud."

A LITTLE HELP

Jarl was fast asleep, Knud alongside him, with his arm draped protectively across his waist.

Astrid glanced at them one more time before she reached for her shoulder and pushed aside her tunic to expose it, the moonlight only just bright enough for her to see the full extent of the damage.

When the goblin's spear had pierced it, it had gone in deep. She remembered the acute pain as it had hit her shoulder bone. Once she had inadvertently drawn the energy from the goblin, her wolf skin had healed. Her own body, however, had not. The goblin's energy had been sufficient to heal just one body and, while in her wolf form, the skin had absorbed the majority of it, with only a tiny remainder left to transfer to her real body beneath.

Astrid tried to shake the guilt as she recalled the look of horror on the goblin's face as he had felt his life force being violently pulled from him. She'd had no choice, Astrid knew that. It was not murder, but self defence. But unlike the relatively simple motion of a dagger or a sword imposing death on another being, death by Jakkito was far more involved. She had not just taken his life, she had absorbed it. And in the split second that her skin had touched his she had been able to feel every emotion that had rippled through him, as if the ghost of his soul was trapped in her body as his life had left his own.

It had been self defence, but it had not felt like it.

She shook her head and peered down at her shoulder. The wound looked less severe than it had in her wolf form, but it was painful nonetheless. Not that the pain bothered her; she had endured pain far more acute before, but she knew that it was dangerous to leave her body in such a damaged state. If she had been alone and without responsibility she would have waited, but she could not risk being unable to protect Jarl and Knud.

Astrid got to her feet and searched around for any kind of plant she could draw energy from that was not Frǫðleikr. She spotted a small patch of moss not far away, the cluster no bigger than the size of a small rabbit. It would barely be enough to heal a bruise, let alone the small fracture she could feel on one of her ribs. Her shoulder carried the risk of infection but the rib would prevent her from moving quickly. She needed to heal the rib first.

Without Jarl or Knud awake to watch her, she did not bother to hide her obvious limp. There was a large bruise right behind her knee which was swelling uncomfortably.

She crouched down and hovered her hand over the plant for a few moments, her eyes closed, her fingers splayed out to feel for magic. Relieved that she felt only plant life, she opened her eyes and watched as the moss shrivelled and turned to ash. The cut on her lip healed instantly with the energy she had absorbed but the swelling remained.

A hand touched her shoulder and Astrid jumped with fright. "Jarl! Don't sneak up on me like that!" she hissed, her hands blue with magic.

"What are you doing?" Jarl reached for her face, his thumb over her lip where he could have sworn the skin had been broken just a few hours ago.

"Nothing." Astrid stood up to face him. "I just needed a little bit of energy."

Jarl's eyes moved to her shoulder and he saw, through the rip in her tunic, the large scab that had formed. Earlier, when he had asked her how badly she had been hurt, she had reassured him that the wound was not severe. He had asked her to let him clean it but she had adamantly refused and Jarl had not insisted. If she was too afraid to wrap her arms around him when he held her, he could only imagine how she would feel if he were to touch her bare shoulder. As much as he had wanted to help her he was not about to risk her shunning him for doing so. But when he'd watched her walking away he had seen how bad her limp was and the pained expression on her face as she had knelt down next to the patch of moss, her teeth clenched together in a grimace.

"Here." He took her hand in his. "You can take my energy."

"What? No!" Astrid shrieked, as she tried to pull her hand way, but he would not let her.

"You're hurt."

"I'm always hurt," she tried to joke back. Jarl looked at her silently for a few moments before she was forced to look away, his serious blue eyes too much for her to bear. "You'll be exhausted for days," Astrid said.

"Yes, and I won't have to watch you wince every time you think I'm not looking."

Astrid closed her eyes. "I didn't think you'd noticed."

"Of course I noticed," he scoffed. "You might be able to see further with those half-elf eyes of yours but

I can see what is in front of me just fine.' He held her hand tighter. "Take what you need."

Astrid thought for a moment, then nodded. "Only what I need." She looked up at him, her face solemn. "This is going to hurt," she warned.

Jarl laughed. "With you, I normally just assume that."

Nothing could have prepared him for the feeling that shot through his arm. He could only compare it to how he imagined it would have felt if his arm had had the skin peeled from it before being plunged into boiling water. For the first time in his life he felt a shred of pity for a goblin as he wondered how it would have felt to die in such a way. He inhaled sharply and bit down on the insides of his cheeks. The pain was only focused on his arm and Jarl was grateful for that, unsure if he would be able to stop it from showing on his face if it spread to the rest of his body.

He looked up at Astrid, amazed as he saw the horrible bruise on the side of her face vanish like paint dispelled in water.

"Just a bit longer," Astrid reassured him. Jarl nodded and after a few seconds she let go with a relieved sigh, her face free from the marks the goblins had left. "Thank you."

Again Jarl nodded, but he didn't move.

"Jarl?" She took his hand worriedly. "Jarl?"

Jarl did not say a word. His muscles had seized and his arm was still in a fair amount of pain. He took a deep breath and slowly uncurled his fingers. "I'm fine, I just need a mo—"

Without warning , Knud suddenly screamed in his sleep and reached down towards his severed leg in a panic. Astrid and Jarl jumped with fright and Jarl tried to run towards him but fell as his own leg muscles refused to move. Astrid caught him before his knees hit the ground and quickly helped him over to Knud.

"My leg! My leg!" Knud screamed.

Jarl yanked Knud's hands away from his leg before he could scratch away the bandages. "Knud, Knud stop! What's wrong?"

"My leg! It hurts! Make it stop! Astrid, please make it stop!" Knud looked up at her, his eyes so wide he reminded her of a rabbit caught in a trap; terrified.

"Hold him," Astrid ordered, her hand over Knud's leg so that he couldn't pull at the bandages. "Ghost pain," she explained, and her hands began to glow blue. "This will help."

"No!" Jarl knocked her hand away.

"He's in pain, Jarl."

"Then take it from me and give it to him! You need it, I don't!"

"If I take any more energy from you—"

"Take it now!" Jarl yelled at her, gripping Knud's hands. Knud writhed and kicked, his muffled sobs lost against Jarl's chest.

Astrid took hold of Jarl's hand and placed the other on Knud's face. Instantly, Knud's body relaxed. But just as quickly Jarl gasped with the pain that transferred from Knud to himself as he felt what Knud had been experiencing only a few seconds before. His leg felt as if it had been severed just above the ankle, the bone snapped through, the muscles torn and the skin sliced apart. He gripped Astrid's hand with all his might and bit down on his tongue so that he would not howl in pain.

"Jarl?" Astrid let go of Knud and held both of Jarl's hands tightly.

"It's alright," he reassured her, though he kept his head bowed, his long hair like curtains and hiding how tightly his face was twisted in agony. He breathed deeply and tried to think of anything other than the ghost pain in his leg, which he knew wasn't real. Looking down at Knud, guilt washed over him again. He had done this. He had promised his best friend he would care for his only son and he had crippled him.

He wondered how Astrid could bear to absorb pain so regularly before it occurred to him that after so many years her threshold for it would be much higher than his. The thought disturbed him. How many times had Astrid let the pain she absorbed build up inside until she could feel nothing but a constant dull burn, like an exposed nerve?

Slowly, Jarl's pain began to ebb away and he was able to lift his head. "The pain, is it all gone?" he asked, and Knud nodded. "Good, you should go back to sleep."

Knud, exhausted, pulled the wolf skin back over his shoulders and both Jarl and Astrid sat alongside him until they heard his gentle snores.

"How are you feeling?" Astrid whispered.

"I'm fine. You should sleep, too," he said, and she shook her head almost before he had finished speaking. Her face had transformed - her skin had colour again, the bruises were gone and her eyes were open wide. Jarl smiled and stroked her face where the large bruise had been. "It's gone."

Astrid nodded. "You should sleep, I'm alright now."

He lay down next to Knud and, as Astrid tried to stand, he reached for her hand, pulling her towards him.

"Does it hurt like that for you?" he asked, his hand linked with hers and held tightly over his chest.

"A little bit." Astrid shrugged. "But I'm used to it."

Jarl said nothing for a few moments, his fingers stroking hers and his mind a hundred miles away. "Have you ever had to stop?"

"Stop what?"

"Taking the pain. I could feel everything Knud felt and it wasn't even real."

Astrid's face dropped. "A few times, yes, I had to let go."

"When?"

Astrid looked away, embarrassed and ashamed as she remembered. "The first time I let go was in Einn. There was a house fire and a woman got badly burnt. I tried to take the pain but I passed out. When I woke up she had died from shock." She let go of Jarl's hand and pulled back the wrapping that covered her hands. "She was my first rose."

Jarl sat up and studied the first tattoo on her hand - a black rose that looked as if it had been burned into her skin with a branding iron rather than drawn with a needle. It was only when he looked at it a little more closely, the moonlight not quite bright enough to tell at first, that he realised that was exactly what had happened.

"You burned this into your skin?" he asked, horrified.

"She died because I couldn't take her pain; this wasn't so bad compared to that."

Jarl's gaze drifted back to her hands and he noticed how each rose was different, not just in size but in the way it was drawn. Some were crosshatched, some just outlines, and others made up of hundreds of tiny dots on the skin, which from far away looked like shadows and highlights. The only thing identical about her tattoos were the white ink thorns that connected each rose. Before Jarl could ask her another question, Astrid got up and pulled her hand out of his.

"You should sleep, I'll take the first watch."

LITTLE FOX

Ulf peered down at the map Rakki had drawn, the coarse paper spread out across the low table. Garðarr, Ótama and Systa were seated around it, several of their respective captains behind them. Rakki, with both hands pressed against her stomach, had a scowl on her face as the baby kicked and squirmed inside her belly. With his fingers cradling hers, Ulf caressed Rakki's hand gently, his faced fixed on the map, his brows pressed together in an arch.

The new additions to the map had been painstakingly slow, each new seemingly insignificant shred of information meticulously detailed by Rakki. There was the layout of the gate, the frequent change of the guard, how many dwarves entered and left the city - information that weeks of stealthy observation had supplied them with.

An old woman sat behind Ulf and Rakki, her eyes half closed and her pupils mildly dilated as she swayed from side to side. Her hair was as white as bone, only two strands at the front of her head were dark black and hanging free from the multiple braids the rest of her hair was tightly bound in, the ends of which were tinted with a red paste. Unlike every other goblin in the camp, the goblin woman had no cuff across her forehead. The only metal fixed in her hair were the small clasps securing her braids.

"Is this all you could find?" Ulf asked, clearly frustrated.

"Yes. We could find out more if we could be a little less…careful," Garðarr replied.

Ulf ignored Garðarr's comment and browsed the map, frustration setting in. Their previous presence in the mountains had been a mistake, one he did not want to repeat.

"I can lead a few more scouts," Ótama suggested. "But the Mad Gate is the only way into the mountain and it is far too strong for us to break from the outside, even with fire."

"There are no other tunnels?" Rakki asked. She let go of Ulf's hand and shuffled forward to look at the map. Not that she needed to look to remember what it showed; she had spent more hours studying and working on the map than all of them and knew every single detail.

"No. The only other ways are through the sewers, and the water runs out too quickly for anyone to climb through them. I tried," Systa said quietly.

"She did," Ótama confirmed, a small smile at the corner of her mouth. Systa chuckled quietly. Ulf said nothing.

"Where are the sewers?" Rakki asked, interested.

"Here." Systa leant forward and pointed to the east side of the mountain, not that far from the Mad Gate. "They empty out over a precipice, too."

Rakki snarled and sat back down, groaning as the baby kicked her again. "I swear I'm going to hit you if you don't stop moving!" Rakki threatened in a low voice, glaring at her stomach. She reached for Ulf's shoulder for support and pushed herself back onto her feet again to pace the yurt.

"What about farms?" Ulf asked, one eye on his wife. "They can't feed the entire city from hunting."

"We've seen a few farms, but not many."

"Then how—?" Ulf shook his head and stopped mid sentence, frustrated.

"Maybe they eat mushrooms from the tunnels?" one of Systa's captains joked behind them. Systa turned and flashed the captain a furious look. The captain whimpered under her stare and bowed her head, sure she would pay for her ill-timed quip later.

"The dwarves survive off trade," Rakki snapped, her eyes closed as the baby squirmed. "With all their gold they could barter for enough food to keep the whole city supplied. They must have reserves. Most cities do."

They all turned to look at her. Ulf's eyes gleamed as he saw the familiar look in his wife's eyes that hinted at the bare bones of a plan.

"They would have two or maybe even three reserves. One for the city, one for the royal palace and then smaller granaries run by merchants."

Nobody said a word. Even Rakki was silent for a few seconds, squinting as she thought, her fingers drumming against her belly.

"We have the numbers, but they have an army and shelter."

"And food!" Ulf interrupted.

"Yes, and food. They're not used to hunger. If they lose their food the people will riot. They will become unstable."

"But if they have granaries they could last for months," Ótama said.

"Maybe even years," Garðarr added.

Rakki shook her head, tired. She had been unable to sleep properly for the past two nights, worried for

Ulf after the attempt on his life, and the baby seemed determined to perform acrobatics every time the sun went down.

"They have an army, food and defenses. We need to get rid of at least one, just one, and we can win," she muttered.

"Why don't we just attack the Mad Gate?" another captain asked. He, too, was met with withering glares.

"Have you seen the Mad Gate? Do you even know why it's called that?" Ulf asked. The captain shook his head, worried at the vehemence in Ulf's voice. "Five hundred and eleven steps before you reach the gate, which is made of iron, with a second gate behind it." The captain's face dropped but Ulf was not finished. He stood up, his fierce blue eyes fixed on the captain. "Over the gate there is a parapet with a large chute. I imagine there are several creative things they could pour down on whichever fools tried to attack them. How many goblins do you think would have to die before we could even scratch the gate?"

"My wolf." Rakki walked over to Ulf and took his hand in hers to distract him from the captain. Ulf turned towards her, the residue of a snarl still on his face.

"Mother?" Ulf turned to the goblin woman who sat silently behind them, her eyes still glazed over. She looked up at Ulf and instantly snapped out of her stupor, her eyes pure black from drinking an excessive amount of Honey Root tea. Whatever her original eye colour had been, they had long been stained several shades darker by the Honey Root smoke. "What do you think?"

Gríð snorted loudly and shrugged her shoulders, one of her hands fumbling in her pocket with a piece of freshly dried root. She was desperate to brew it but determined to wait until at least the captains had left the tent. "I was never a soldier, Ulf. Fight your own battles."

Ulf shook his head and looked back at the map, even more frustrated than before. "If we attack them they will hole themselves in and call for aid. We cannot fight both Lǫgberg and Bjargtre, and Moldof would never join us."

Rakki's face snapped around to look at him, an excited gleam in her eyes. Everyone sat up straight, their eyes on her. They knew that look, that gleam in her eyes when all her plans and schemes suddenly fell into place. Rakki bounced excitedly on her toes and paced for a few seconds. Her lips moved but she did not speak; the thoughts that flashed through her mind too fast for her lips to utter.

"We need a spy!" she finally said. "The dwarves paid to have you killed. We can play the same game!"

"We don't have anything a dwarf would value!" Gríð cackled. Rakki ignored her.

"There are still a few traders who cross to Einn, if we can…persuade one of them to tell us more about the city, then—"

"No dwarf would help us!" Gríð interrupted.

"We don't need them to talk. We just need them to go to the mountain." Everyone looked at her with deeply confused expressions on their faces. "In the last Hætta, half of the city died from the Red Fever. Systa, you said they have not had a Hætta since." Systa nodded in agreement and Rakki clapped her hands together excitedly. "If a dwarf is taken by us and… escapes," Rakki paused at the word, a long thin grin at the corner of her mouth, "he would return to the city as fast as his short legs could carry him. It would be hours before he would feel the effects, hours for him to infect the city."

Ulf smiled, a smile that stretched from ear to ear and exposed every single one of his teeth.

"If we waited long enough we could take the gate with just a handful of goblins. They would be unprepared and too weak to fight!"

The captains turned to mutter between themselves; Ótama, Garðarr and Systa were silent but clearly impressed by Rakki's suggestion.

Ulf reached for his wife's hand and squeezed it firmly. "I married a fox!" He smiled proudly. "Garðarr, how do you feel about hunting a few dwarves?"

Garðarr smiled and stood up, a glimmer in his eyes.

Rakki padded over to the low bed at the far side of the yurt and sat down, her face a little pale, one hand over her stomach and the other clutched against the side of the bed.

With his eyes on his wife, Ulf motioned that the others should leave. He walked over to her and sat down on the side of the bed. Rakki smiled and leant her head against his shoulder. "What do you think, my wolf? Will it work?"

"Of course it will work!" Gríð said loudly. She reached into her pocket and pulled out one of the many dried roots she kept inside. "You married a fox, Ulf. A clever, clever little fox." Gríð snarled and twisted and the root in her hand cracked open with a horrible crunch. A sickly sweet smell filled the room and her eyes glazed a little more as she inhaled the aroma as deeply as she could. "Clever, clever little fox."

THE OAK TREE

"Knud! Knud wake up! We have to start walking." Jarl shook him gently and his eyes snapped open. He looked panicked for a moment, his eyes darting around the camp, but as soon as he saw the sun had barely risen and they were in no danger, he closed them again and slumped back onto the ground.

"Can I sleep just a little more?" he groaned, hiding under the wolf skin. Jarl shook his head and wrestled the wolf skin from him before he could fall into another slumber.

Knud shivered. It had gotten a lot colder overnight. The early morning light was warm but the air was as cold as ice. Jarl, however, felt colder than the others and was completely exhausted, just as Astrid had warned him he would feel. It hadn't helped that he had slept very badly; he'd had nightmare after nightmare about Astrid and Knud being in danger. The image of Knud's leg caught in the trap had replayed a hundred times in his head with Knute's shadowy figure nearby every time, watching, disappointed in him.

"Why is it so cold?" Knud groaned.

"It's autumn, it'll be winter soon," Astrid replied. "It's only going to get colder."

"When are we going to get there?"

"Tomorrow, probably. Faster if I carry you," Astrid suggested.

"I can walk though!" Knud said, letting go of Jarl's arm for a moment and trying to stand on his one remaining foot, but he was barely able to keep his balance.

"Let me see your leg," Astrid said gently.

Although he didn't want to admit it, his amputated leg still hurt quite a lot. He had managed to hide his discomfort from Jarl but he knew Astrid could sense his pain. The sensation that his foot was still there was occasionally blocked by an unbearable itchiness, as if ants had managed to creep under the bandages and were crawling over his skin. It was all he could do not to scratch at it with all his might when neither Jarl or Astrid were looking, but after the previous night he was determined to bear it.

He could not decide what was worse: The pain he felt, or the pitying looks Jarl and Astrid gave him, which only reminded him that he was damaged. He looked down at his stump and tried not to cry as Astrid unwrapped the bandages.

The end of Knud's leg was bright red, the cut skin folded over the stump and fused together, the bulge of the broken bone visible beneath it.

"It hurts, doesn't it?" she asked.

Knud nodded. It wasn't like he would be able to lie to her. The minute she touched his skin she knew, able to feel every twinge of pain that he could. With her eyes open, Astrid's hands glowed blue and she gently moved her fingers over the stump. Knud breathed deeply as she absorbed the pain, the cold wash of relief instant.

"Thank you," Knud smiled.

"Will you let me carry you now?" she asked, as Jarl wrapped a fresh piece of Knute's torn cloak around Knud's leg.

Knud got to his feet and scrambled up onto Astrid's back as soon as she had transformed under her wolf skin, the large hump of her bag on her human body like a furry pillow, perfect for him to lean forward and rest his head against.

"Knud! Don't go back to sleep!" Jarl ordered as he walked alongside them. Knud groaned loudly.

"But I'm tired!"
"You'll fall off!"
"No I won't!"

Neither of them had spoken for the past few hours, Jarl surprised by Astrid's lack of conversation. She was calm, relaxed almost, with no flinches of anger or confusion on her face, her mind quiet. She seemed…happy.

The pass stretched on, mile after mile, the sides of the mountain like two walls on either side of them. Jarl thought it strange that they were so smooth, there were no natural faults in them. In fact, everything about the pass gave him the distinct impression that at some point a being other than nature had been involved in its formation.

"How far now to the Aldwood?"

Astrid shook her head. "I thought Knud would be the one asking that question all day!" She chuckled. "It won't be long now until we reach the crossroads, I think. I've never gone through this part. Last time we went over the mountains."

"Last time?"

"With Loba and Bugal."

Jarl wanted to press her for more of what he suspected was a very long story, but decided against it. If it was a story she was ready to talk about she would tell him in her own time.

"What is that?" Knud's voice croaked, still half asleep.

They all looked up and saw a cluster of trees ahead, the sight a little strange since nothing grew around it - no weeds, bushes or even gorse. But suddenly a circle of enormous pines shot up from the stony earth, a stunted oak at its centre. Beyond the trees, a little further on, they could clearly see a crossroads in the path. Jarl looked down at Astrid and saw all the fur along her neck and shoulders was on end. Her teeth were bared.

"What's wrong?" Jarl asked. His hand moved to the hilt of his sword but he did not draw it, worried that the trees would be like the ones they had encountered at the pillars.

"Frøðleikr," Astrid replied.

"How do you know?"

"I can feel their magic."

"Are they going to hurt us?" Knud asked, his hands gripped around Astrid's shoulders a little tighter. She said nothing but looked up at Jarl, her eyes narrowed. His fingertips were on the hilt of his sword. "Don't. Just in case," she warned, and Jarl nodded.

"Can we go around it?" Knud asked.

But there was no way around. The circle of trees was so wide that they grew alongside the walls of the pass. Astrid looked down to the base of the pines, surprised to see there were no roots. The massive trunks shot out from the ground like living pillars, the rock at their bases cracked with dozens of hairline fractures. The tops of the pines curled inwards towards the oak tree, knotting together and casting a shadow directly over it.

"We're going to have to go through," Astrid whispered. "Knud, get down for a moment."

Jarl helped him down and Astrid dropped the wolf skin to the ground along with her bag and weapons, except for Ragi's small knives that were tucked in the inside of her boot.

"Wait here," she ordered, and cautiously made her way towards the trees, her hands held out at her sides as if she were walking a tightrope. With her fingers spread apart she could feel the magic in the air like waves of energy that resonated with each nerve in her body.

"Astrid!" Jarl moved to walk after her but stopped himself. He knew he should not follow her, she knew the Frøðleikr, she understood magic far better than he did. All he could do was watch and pray that it would be alright. "Be careful!"

She nodded and turned back to the trees, her relaxed and confident expression gone the moment they could not see her face, her eyes suddenly wide and wary.

Something was wrong. What exactly, she could not pin point. The trees were Frǫðleikr, she was sure of that. The oak tree was not, yet she could feel a magic that emanated from inside it like the heat from a furnace. Its branches curled in on each other in horrible, contorted positions. They reminded her of fingers that had been broken repeatedly, only to grow back malformed and stunted.

She stepped inside the tree circle and held her breath, both hands raised to the level of her shoulders. The pines were completely still. She walked forward a little more into the shadow the pine branches cast over the oak and felt the air grow colder instantly. Still nothing moved.

Now she was closer to the oak she could see the burns that covered it, the marks unnatural and unlike any she had seen before. Distinct vein-like patterns spiralled around the centre of the tree and there was an old tear down the middle that had healed badly, the edges knotted and covered in tumor-like bumps.

Whatever had happened to the tree was not natural, of that she was sure. It was clear that at some point the oak had been violently split open with a great amount of force, only to be closed again. What was even stranger were the large nodules that covered the repaired split like infected bubbles. The tree had fought to die, but somehow it was still alive.

Knud and Jarl watched with baited breath as she turned to face the trees and spoke in a series of words neither of them understood.

"What's she saying?" Knud asked worriedly.

"I don't know. I think she's speaking in Axtī."

"Why would she speak in elvish?"

"Because she can't speak tree," Jarl replied sarcastically.

Astrid was just about to usher them into the circle when she heard a voice behind her, faint and soft, followed by the sound of knocking. She turned to look at the oak.

"Hello?"

Again, there was a knock from inside the tree.

"Astrid?" Knud called over to her.

"It's alright, Knud," she called back, her eyes still on the tree.

It's not alright! both voices screamed inside her head. *Leave! You can find another way into the Aldwood!*

"I can't!" Astrid hissed back at them. "The Frøðleikr won't let me pass over the mountains with Jarl and Knud. We have to go this way!"

She stepped back from the oak and began to walk around it to the other side. Instantly, the knocks became more frequent, mingled with a muffled voice from deep inside the tree, the words high pitched and frantic. Astrid ignored it, every instinct telling her to stay out of its way.

She motioned to Jarl and Knud to join her in the circle.

"Is it safe?" Knud said, as Jarl slung Astrid's belongings and wolf skin over his shoulder.

"I hope so," Jarl muttered, and reached for Knud's hand. Warily, they stepped into the circle. Astrid had not moved, her feet were apart as though she was ready to run at a moment's notice and both her eyes were on the oak.

"Come on! Quickly!"

The knocks had turned to scratches, frantic and angry like a wild animal trapped in a cage. Knud hobbled alongside Jarl as quickly as he could but he could not move fast enough. Jarl reached down and lifted him up, their bags on one arm and Knud on the other. As quickly as he could, he walked straight through the circle and out onto the other side.

"Astrid!" Knud called back to her. "Come on!"

Jarl quickly slapped his hand across Knud's mouth but it was too late. At the sound of Knud's voice the trees in the circle shuddered. Astrid's knees bent and her back arched. She side-stepped towards them, the tingle at the back of her neck rapidly increasing. The voices in her head were panicked, screaming at her to run.

"You can't outrun Frǫðleikr!" she hissed to herself. "Slowly, just move slowly. You don't want to hurt them, you just want to pass through," she whispered, more to the trees than to herself.

Frǫðleikr were unpredictable. The few she had crossed in the past were calm and could be reasoned with, provided they did not feel threatened. But the Frǫðleikr by the Aldwood had always been different; angrier. She had felt it the last time she had passed over the Riddari Kviðr and she felt it now, only worse, so much worse. There was a heavy tension in the air and every hair on Astrid's neck stood upright.

From the middle of the oak she saw the bark beginning to shake and move. The scream grew a little louder and something inside the tree tried to force itself out.

Astrid ran.

There was a great burst of blue light behind her and she felt an odd sensation run over her, her muscles becoming heavy and stiff as if they were turning to stone. Suddenly, she was catapulted back to one of childhood nightmares where she was running desperately from the red-eyed horses, her parents calling her, their arms outreached. But no matter how hard she tried, her legs would not move fast enough, half frozen in time while the horses behind her ran unimpeded, so close to her she could feel their hot breath on her neck.

Just as she reached the edge of the tree circle and grasped one of the pines, she heard a high pitched whistle. Instantly, there was an intense coldness in her shoulder. Knud screamed as she dropped to her knees, her skin ashen. A long, double ended dagger had torn through her shoulder, the blade so long it protruded through to the other side, the tip red with her own blood.

With a horrifying roar the oak split open and a burst of energy and light emanated from within it, so powerful that Jarl and Knud were thrown to the floor, blinded by its force.

"Astrid!" Jarl let go of Knud and stumbled towards her, the back of his eyes burning as though the light had stabbed them. He stumbled along the ground, unable to see colour, everything a white blur as he reached out frantically. "Astrid!"

His fingers brushed across something warm; a hand. He held it as tightly as he could and reached up to Astrid's shoulder. She was cold, as if her skin had turned to marble, but her shoulder was warm and wet. The distinct coppery smell of blood flooded the air.

Behind them, Knud's jaw dropped as the oak split open with a loud crack, the sound so loud it echoed like thunder against the pass walls. Two hands emerged and gripped the edges of the split tree, followed by a long slender leg. The woman inside stepped out, shaking, and breathed long and deeply. Her clothes, or what remained of them, were in tatters.

She was beautiful. Even from far away Knud could see she was beautiful, though the word could not quite stress just how much. Her skin was a flawless ebony, her figure, though quite gaunt, was tall and poised. Knud stared at her long slender legs, wide curved hips and tiny waist. Every part of her body was a gentle rise and fall, like the plains of a dune. Her long, thick hair was curled so tightly it circled her face like a halo and the remnants of a red, gold and blue sash was wrapped around her head.

With one last, long gasp for air, she opened her eyes. Knud felt his heart stop as she looked at him. Her eyes were not blue, grey or even green. They were gold, the colour of honey or a warm sunlight, the glint of winter sun reflected on a gold coin.

She stumbled forward on the ground and fell to her knees. Astrid, barely a few feet away from her, was also on her knees, the dagger embedded in her shoulder.

Jarl's eyesight had returned a little but he had not noticed the woman. His arms were around Astrid as he tried to help her stand. She was almost completely limp, her hand still pressed against the pine tree beside her.

"Jarl! Jarl!" Knud screamed, and pointed to the woman as she slowly stood up, her movements stiff and pained. Even Jarl was struck dumb as he saw the woman. She turned to look at him, both eyes half narrowed as she straightened her back and smiled.

Astrid screamed in agony as the woman raised her hands, and she felt the dagger draw the life out of her. Instinctively, Astrid drew her own energy from the nearest source that could support such a terrible power, and the pine against her hand creaked and cracked beneath her fingers. The branches further up the tree quivered and began to twist in a contorted spiral. Flakes of ash floated down towards Jarl and Astrid, covering them, the bark on the branches above them consumed by the hundreds of small sparks that rippled up from where Astrid's hand was clutching it.

The woman turned to face the oak, raised her hands and clenched her fingers. In front of her, the gash in the tree shrunk and closed. Splinters flew in all directions as the old wood was forced to buckle in on itself. The pass was filled with the sound of fragmenting timber, cracking like bones.

Jarl reached for the dagger in Astrid's shoulder and, against his better judgment, tried to pull it out of her. The shock that spread up his arm the moment he touched the hilt of the dagger knocked him to the ground. He gripped his chest in pain, the pressure around his heart severe. It wasn't like when he had given Astrid his energy, as painful as it had been his body had not fought it, the energy willingly given. This time it was ripped from him without permission, the sensation unbearable.

The woman turned to face Astrid, a sneer on her face. She raised her hand and, like an arrow from a bow, the dagger was ripped back out of Astrid's shoulder. Astrid's spine arched and her mouth fell open in a silent scream, her voice lost.

Jarl pushed himself to his feet and hauled Astrid up into his arms. Her whole body was weak, the last bit of strength in her diminished the moment her hand had left the pine. The tree was drained of every last piece of its life-force and was nothing but a hollow, charred shell.

"Stay away from her!" Jarl bellowed, his sword drawn. With Astrid half in his arms, her feet dragged on the ground as he pulled her back from the tree circle.

The woman did not even bother to look in their direction. She held the dagger in her hand, Astrid's blood still on the blades. "I told you I would escape!" she screamed at the trees and slowly raised her hands to the level of her shoulders. "You should have listened!"

Jarl did not wait to see what was about to happen. Holding Astrid tightly, he grabbed Knud's arm and hurried as fast as he could down the nearest path. Behind them, they heard the crackle of fire as it consumed the trees, but none of them looked back.

Knud held onto Jarl's arm as firmly as he could and was half dragged along as he tried to keep up. Astrid was utterly limp, a dead weight across Jarl's shoulder.

There was another deafening noise behind them, followed by a wave of heat that ripped down the pass. The screams were terrible; deep voices, inhuman voices, that made the ground shake.

Still Jarl did not stop, the pain in his chest not enough to hinder him. He did not stop until he could look behind him and not see the trees. When he finally turned around he saw a dense blackness rising up to the clouds, the sky thick with the acrid smoke.

The blood from Astrid's shoulder had spread down her arm and seeped through the three tunics Jarl wore. His shoulder and back were saturated. He glanced back down the pass one more time to make sure they had not been followed by the woman before he set

Astrid down on the ground, his left hand under her neck and the other around her waist.

"Astrid?"

She was as cold as ice, her eyes open but blank, a cold sweat on her face. Half of her arm was drenched in the blood that oozed from her shoulder.

"Astrid, please wake up!" Knud begged, crawling towards her.

"Knud stay there! Don't touch her!" Jarl ordered.

He quickly unwrapped Astrid's long veil from around her neck and waist. She hadn't moved since he had carried her away from the tree circle. He leant his head down over her mouth, the relief washing over his face as he heard her breathing, though the sound was faint, barely more than a whisper of air.

Frantically, he pulled off his top tunic and ripped it into two. Ignoring the cold, he folded the pieces into two thick squares and pressed them tightly on either side of her wound, before wrapping Astrid's veil over them and securing her arm in a crude sling across her chest. Still she did not move.

"Astrid! Please look at me!" Jarl begged. He took her face in his hands and shook her gently. Nothing. He squeezed her hand and begged her to draw energy from him. Still she did not move. "Astrid, don't do this to me! Come on! I know you! You're too stubborn to let something like this ki..." his voice faltered, the word 'kill' at the tip of his tongue. "...hurt, hurt you!" he finished.

Astrid shuddered, her eyelids flickered, but she was lifeless. Jarl looked around him, almost as if he expected to see someone nearby who could help.

"The Aldwood," he said, and got to his feet. "We have to get her to the Aldwood!"

HOLMVÉ

Halvard perched on the side of his bed and ran his fingers though his hair, his body so tired all he wanted to do was lie down and sleep for a month, but his brain was wide awake and refusing to let him. He stood up and paced the room, frustrated that while he had been on the road all he had been able to think about was sleep, and now that he was back at the closest place he could call home, he was unable to.

"You're awake."

Halvard turned and saw Holmvé's face peeking around the door, a lit candle in her hand. She walked in and pulled her thick shawl closer around her shoulders. "Well, since you're still awake, maybe you would like some food and wine?"

Halvard nodded and followed her out of the room and down the corridor to the Great Hall. The fire was still lit, a few weak flames fluttering in the hearth. Halvard tossed in another log as Holmvé pottered around the kitchen. She returned shortly with two large flasks in her hand, both filled to the brim with wine.

"One for you," she said, passing him a flask, "and one for me!" She raised hers towards him and took several large gulps before she sat down opposite him at the table.

"I didn't know you liked wine so much," Halvard said, as he drank slowly from his own.

"Only in stressful situations, and the last few months have been stressful." Holmvé shook her head and took another large swig, the flask already almost half empty.

"When did the king die?"

"Barely a few days after you three left," Holmvé replied. "His poor son, Haddr, is king now. I've never seen such a frightened and sick little child. He could barely stand with that crown on his head."

Halvard noticed that Holmvé's face was considerably more wrinkled than when they had left a few months before, the bags under her eyes much larger, and for once in her life she did not sit proudly to attention, her shoulders stooped.

"You look tired."

Holmvé rolled her eyes at him. "You would, too, if your family was half way across Ammasteinn with a half-elf woman." Holmvé stared at her as she realised what she had just said to him. "I'm sorry, I didn't mean that you're not family."

"I'm not though, am I?" Halvard shrugged his shoulders nonchalantly, though his eyes told quite a different story. "I've always been an outsider here."

Holmvé sighed. She had lost count of the amount of times she had had the same conversation with him as a young boy. "You know that's not true. Jóð, and Jón just liked to tease you."

Halvard did not reply, his eyes on his flask as he drank slowly from it. Holmvé was quiet for a moment as she fiddled with her worn nails. The hall was in silence except for the crackle of the fire; the only light from the hearth and the red glow of the embers.

"Halvard, the half-elf; what is she really like?"

He set his flask down on the table. "What do you mean?"

"I know you hate her, and you might be right, but you and Jarl have always had different...tastes."

"A Blanda blóð is not just a different taste!" Halvard snapped.

156

"Shhh! The others are sleeping!" she hissed. "And I can't believe you would use that word after everything you've seen happen to this family!"

There was an awkward silence before Holmvé dared to ask another question, Halvard's face as black as thunder.

"What does she look like?" she eventually asked.

"Ugly. Her eyes are a different colour and she has these scars all over her face."

"What kind of scars?"

"A Dip wolf's claw marks." Halvard dragged his hand down his cheek for effect. "And another one right through her lips. If she opens her mouth too wide her lips look like they're going to split apart." Holmvé held one hand across her face, her mouth open, aghast. "She had scars everywhere," Halvard continued, his eyes on the fireplace. "Even her hands, and she's always wearing this ridiculous wolf skin over her head."

Holmvé nodded and stared down at the table, disappointment etched on her face. "I always hoped Jarl would find a dwarf here."

"He won't ask her to stay with him," Halvard scoffed confidently. "He's just infatuated for the moment because she's something exotic to him."

Holmvé shook her head. "Jarl doesn't trust people easily but when he does he's as loyal as a dog. It wouldn't surprise me if he comes back to the city with her."

"He couldn't do that, she could never stay here." Halvard's voice was less confident this time.

"No," Holmvé nodded sadly. "I don't suppose she could. But if he loves her then I really think he would go wherever she does." She look another long swig from her flask and emptied it, then looked at the bottom disappointedly and set it down on the table.

"He doesn't love her," Halvard repeated, more to himself than Holmvé. "And what about Knud? He couldn't just take him with him."

"Why? Do you think Knud would object?" Holmvé raised an eyebrow, reached across the table and began to drink from Halvard's half full flask, oblivious to his looks of indignation. "He'd be happier than a fed cat to see other places. The boy is a natural traveller."

"The king wouldn't let him. Knud is a higher noble."

"And since when has the king stopped Jarl from doing what he wants before?" Holmvé scoffed. Halvard reached across the table and took back his flask before she could finish it completely. "She will keep them safe won't she? Was she capable?"

Halvard nodded. "Yes, very capable. Skad recommended her."

Holmvé's eyes rolled at the mention of his name before she stood up, a little dizzy as the wine reached her head. "Good, I've lost enough of this family already."

TREACHERY

Rakki groaned and turned over for what felt like the hundredth time that night. Her lower back was aching and her stomach heavy and swollen. She felt miserable, so tired that her brain felt as if it had been removed from her skull. Ulf was snoring beside her, his arm across her.

"Well, I'm glad you can sleep," Rakki muttered, and pushed his arm away. She lay on her back and stared up at the ceiling. The frame of the yurt rattled a little as the wind outside beat against the thick hides that covered it. A few of the carefully packed bags that hung from the domed ceiling rocked back and forth.

Gríð was asleep by the fire, a large fur beneath and over her, and a long thin knife clutched against her chest. A warm glow bathed her face from the fire's embers as she lay curled up like a dog, her knees practically against her chin.

Rakki pushed her fox fur blanket aside and stood up. She paused for a moment before padding over to the fire. Her feet were bare and swollen and the woven mats on the ground rustled under her weight.

"Rakki? What's wrong?" Ulf called out, propping himself up in the bed.

"I'm just hungry! Sleep!"

All too happy to oblige, Ulf slumped back down, but not before he had shifted over to her side of the bed to keep it warm. Rakki hated a cold bed.

Gríð did not wake up, even as Rakki sat down beside her and tossed a large log onto the fire. A burst of sparks rose from the embers and soon several small flames began to lick their way up either side of the log. Rakki held her hands out, rubbing them together, and closed her eyes.

"There you go!" she murmured. "You like fire, don't you little one?" She sat back on her heels and closed her eyes, relieved as the baby finally stopped twisting around and curled up, one of its feet pressed lightly against her belly. She moved her hand down and smiled, her fingertips pressed against the imprint of her child's foot. "Enjoy it in there. It will be cold when you leave."

Rakki suddenly heard a high pitched whistle as several objects pierced through the thick bison hides lining the yurt and impaled the bed where Ulf had been laying only a few seconds before. She screamed and jumped to her feet, waking Ulf and Gríð with a start. Without thinking, Rakki leapt towards Ulf and yanked him out of the bed, blankets and all, just as another three arrows shot through the wall lining.

Ulf pulled Rakki into his arms to shield her while Gríð raced towards the lining of the wall and sliced it open in one swipe with the tip of her dagger. With the daze in her eyes gone, she darted through and into the open air after the attackers.

"Ulf!" Rakki screamed, pointing at the doorway, her other hand clutched firmly across her belly.

A tall goblin girl with bright red hair raced towards them, a long thin sword in her hands. She screamed and swung the weapon down towards them. Ulf was on his feet in an instant and hurtled towards the girl. She did not stand a chance. In one fluid motion he gripped her wrist and twisted her arm around so violently that her whole body was forced sideways. There was the dull sound of a bone being pulled from its joint and he felt her arm shudder as she dropped the sword and crumpled to the ground. Defiant, the girl reached for a small dagger that was tucked inside one of her fur leg warmers. Ulf snarled and struck the girl as hard as she could. She fell to the ground, face down in the dirt.

"Rakki!"

"I'm fine…I'm fine Ulf!" Rakki whispered, crouched down on the floor, a knife gripped firmly in her hand that she had retrieved from beneath the bed.

Ulf could hear Gríð fighting with the attackers outside, her high pitched shrieks like a banshee's. He ran through the open hides, his eyes darting around.

Three goblins lay dead on the floor, the wounds on their bodies inflicted with a hideous accuracy: One directly through the kidneys, one over the heart and a final one through one ear and out the other. There was barely any blood, all the damage internal.

More goblins circled Gríð, swords in each of their hands and veils covering their faces so that only their eyes were exposed.

As Ulf brought his fist down on the neck of the nearest goblin, Gríð slipped through the legs of another in one fluid movement. Before the goblin could turn around his legs suddenly gave way. Gríð gnashed her teeth and pulled the tip of her dagger out of the goblin's spine. He fell to the ground spluttering.

"My legs! My legs!"

Gríð looked down at the goblin Ulf had struck, the blow to his neck lethal. Ulf reached down and ripped the veil from his face.

"Ri?" he gasped, shocked as he saw one of his own captains staring up at him.

The goblin looked even more horrified than before, his eyes fixed on Ulf as his expression changed from shock to fury.

"Why?"

"Your plan is mad! We haven't suffered a Hætta in years, and you want to provoke them!"

"You speak about them like they're gods!" Ulf shouted back.

"They might as well be! They have the mountains! A home they can survive in without leaving for months! And a queen with an army a hundred times larger than ours! What makes you so arrogant that you think you can possibly win against them?"

Ulf snarled like a rabid wolf as he crouched over Ri and struck him repeatedly. Again and again, even as Ri's head rolled back, he continued to hit him with all his might. "I am your Agrokū! You attack me in the night like a coward! With my wife and child beside me!"

"Ulf?" Rakki called nervously from the open yurt wall, but Ulf did not look up. His fist was bloodied and red, Ri's face a pulp. "Ulf!" He dropped Ri's unconscious body to the ground with a loud thud and Ri's fingers twitched as he lay on the ground, his jaw half open at a strange angle. He was barely breathing. Ulf marched up to Rakki and pulled her towards him.

"Ulf, I'm fine," Rakki said, as he ran his hand down her arm and onto her belly. "Find the others! Find them and deal with them!"

Gríð, stood beside Rakki, pushed Ulf's hands away from his wife. "Go! Find them! They won't get past me!"

The expression on Ulf's face changed in an instant from concern to rage, his brows pressed together in a sharp slant. He stormed into the tent and grabbed the still unconscious female goblin by her hair before he dragged her outside. It did not surprise him as he saw his two guards dead on the ground outside; in fact he was relieved. Had they been alive he would have assumed they were either a part of the plan or too careless to do their duty, both of which he would have killed them for.

"Come out! Come out, cowards!" Ulf bellowed at the top of his voice.

From the nearby tents, several goblins peered out, half asleep and frightened. Several of them shuffled out into the cold, blankets of animal hide and grass wool wrapped tightly around their shoulders.

"I know you can still hear me! Come out!" Ulf shouted again. He held the girl up higher. Her body twitched slightly as she began to regain consciousness and her eyes flickered.

From between two of the yurts not far from him, two figures stepped forward, a female and a young male goblin, weapons in each of their hands. The female had been crying, her eyes puffy and tearstained.

Ulf recognised them immediately as Aki's widow and young son. He looked down at the girl and realised for the first time that it was Aki's eldest daughter. His shock gave way to anger within seconds.

"Is this how you repay me?" He snarled and hoisted the girl up higher by her hair. She reached up to her head and tried to prise his fingers open and Ulf kicked her as hard as he could. She yelped in pain, a high pitched whimper like a wounded dog.

"You are not one of us!" You are not one of my tribe! You weren't here when the dwarves would hunt us for the Hætta, and now you want to attack them! You'll bring the Hætta back on us!"

Ulf did not say a word as he reached his hand across the girl's throat and slid the tip of his dagger across the soft skin. Aki's widow screamed as her daughter fell to the ground, her hands pressed to her throat, flecks of blood splattered between her fingers. She raced forwards but, before she could reach her, Ulf plunged the tip of his dagger into the back of the girl's skull. He stepped back as Aki's widow threw herself beside her dead daughter.

Ulf watched, a scowl on his face, as mother and son wailed over the girl's body, her blood covering their hands and knees. He looked up and glanced at the many goblin faces who watched, blank expressions on their faces, unmoved by the violence. Ulf gripped the dagger tighter.

Before Aki's widow or her son could react, he stepped towards them. Two quick jabs in quick succession saw them crumple over the body of the girl, trickles of blood oozing down their backs from the deep puncture wounds in their necks.

Ótama and Garðarr ran towards him, both of them half dressed. Systa was the only one who appeared to have already been awake. Ulf ignored them. He paced silently for a few seconds, his breathing like a bull's, hot and angry and ready to charge at a moment's notice.

He glared at the crowd.

"You would let them butcher you! You would let the dwarves decide when you should be culled like rats!" he bellowed. "If you want to live in fear then so be it! After tonight there will be no mercy! Just like *they* showed no mercy! I promised to protect every goblin who swore themselves to me. Any goblin who breaks that oath will be killed!"

Nobody made a sound as more and more goblins emerged from their tents, shivering either from the cold, or the terrible expression on Ulf's face.

"You wear my cuff! Any goblin who wishes to leave it will leave his head behind with it! Any goblin who attempts to undermine me will be killed! Any goblin who attempts to hurt my family will die, along with every single member of their family! I don't care if you have wives, or children! I will show them no mercy just as these showed no care to the lives of my mother, my wife and my child!"

Ótama, Garðarr and Systa stood silently, completely unmoved by Ulf's outburst.

After snarling like a wild dog for a few more moments, his gaze turned to his generals. Systa was the only one who dared look him in the eye.

"I will have a captain outside my tent at all times! Wherever my wife goes, two captains will escort her at all times! If they fail again I will be the one to cut their throats!"

"What should I do about them?" Systa asked, pointing at the bodies on the ground.

"The Dip can have them," Ulf sneered. "Traitors don't deserve a burial."

LOBA

Jarl was exhausted. He paused for a moment to lean against a tree, his long hair in his face, beads of sweat on his forehead.

The Aldwood was not like the barren pass. Wild plants, trees and bushes were everywhere, together with long grass that caught in his feet as he ran. His knees were scratched from the amount of times he had tripped and fallen, Knud and Astrid's added weight making it all the more painful.

Knud was not much better off, his red curly hair limp and dirty. He had done his best to keep up with Jarl but could not match his long strides. Jarl's entire right side was strained from Knud's weight pulling him down with each hobble.

"Can we stop for a moment?" Knud panted. Jarl shook his head, Astrid's face against the side of his neck, her skin cold and damp.

"No! We have to keep moving!"

Knud began to cry, exhausted. "Please! I can't run anymore!"

"Knud, I can't leave you here and I can't heal Astrid. She needs help, we need to keep moving!"

Knud slumped onto the floor and began to wail. "Please! Please Jarl! I can't! My leg!"

"KNUD! Get up!" Jarl yelled. He reached down and pulled him up to his feet. "Stand!" he ordered.

Still crying, Knud stumbled along beside him, Jarl's hand firmly on his arm. They both trudged along with slow heavy steps. The light of the sun was long gone, only the stars and the moonlight was there to guide them.

Jarl had called out into the forest several times but nobody had replied; he would have been surprised if anyone had. When they had stepped out of the pass, the path down had been on a small rise from which he could see most of the Aldwood - miles and miles of forest and not so much as a puff of smoke in sight, let alone the flicker of firelight.

Jarl looked around him and shouted out the only name he could remember from his earlier conversation with Astrid. "Loba! Loba!"

"Jarl?" Astrid croaked.

Instantly, Jarl dropped to his knees and pulled Astrid off his back as gently as he could, his hand behind her neck to support her head as it fell back. "You're awake!" He stroked her hair from her face, relief washing over him.

"Awake...not quite how I would describe it," Astrid muttered, her lips barely moving, both eyes closed. "Where are we?"

"The Aldwood."

Astrid opened her eyes, both of them alert for a few seconds. "Don't move! Nobody move! Not till morning!"

"Thank you!" Knud muttered, and dropped to the ground in a huddle.

"Why? What's wrong?"

"Vârcolac...the Vârcolac." Astrid's voice began to trail off. "Light a fire, don't leave the fire!"

"No, no, no! You stay awake!" Jarl shook her head firmly and her eyes opened a little before they partly closed again. "You stay awake!"

"Alright! Stop shaking me!" Astrid muttered.

Jarl took her hand and reached for Knud. "Hold her hand and don't let her fall asleep!" he ordered.

"But what if she does?"

"Don't let her! Shout at her if you have to!"

"Just know that if you slap me I will slap you back," Astrid mumbled, a weak smile at the corner of her mouth.

Jarl got to his feet and glanced around. There were plenty of fallen branches and twigs on the ground and he barely had to move from where he was standing to collect a smile pile of kindling. "Astrid! Keep talking. Tell me anything you want. Just stay awake!"

He quickly cleared the ground of anything that could set alight and dug a small pit for the fire. With his fingers caked in mud and dirt under his nails, he stacked up the firewood in a pyramid, the smaller more flammable twigs and leaves in the centre, the thicker branches on the outside. Astrid mumbled but did not say anything coherent, her head rolled to the side.

"Knud!" Jarl said, as he reached for the fire stones in his pocket. "Keep her awake!"

"Astrid! Astrid wake up!" Knud took her head in his hands and shook her face.

"Ah! Don't do that!" Astrid snapped.

"Sorry."

"Knud! Keep doing that! If she falls asleep keep doing that!" Jarl ordered. He struck the fire stones repeatedly until a burst of sparks finally caught on the tinder. The sparks spread across the leaves and a small flame took hold and began to lick its way up the twigs surrounding it. Jarl fed it with dry leaves until the first few large flames emerged. "Knud. Keep an eye on the fire. Don't let it go out."

They switched places, Knud by the fire and Jarl with Astrid in his arms. He pulled her close to him and wrapped his arms around her to keep her warm. "Stay awake, Astrid." He tapped her face firmly and she opened her eyes. "You have to stay awake. Here." He took her hand in his. "Now you're awake you can take energy from me. You need it."

For a moment she looked as if she was about to argue with him.

Don't be stupid! the harsh voice hissed. *How well do you think you can protect them if you're like this? Take the energy!*

Resigned, she reached for his hand and Jarl braced himself. He waited but nothing happened. "Astrid?"

She looked up at him, at first confused and then frightened. "I can't!"

"What's wrong?" Knud asked, scared by the tone in Astrid's voice.

Jarl said nothing, but held both her hands in his tightly. "It's alright. You just need to stay awake."

"Why? I don't understand!" Astrid panicked.

"You don't need it," Jarl reassured her. "We have the fire; you just need to stay awake for a few more hours. Here..." He reached into his bag and pulled out some of the dried food he still had wrapped tightly between his other belongings. "Eat. You need it."

"We don't have much left. You should keep it."

Jarl growled, irritated. "Just for once, can you not argue with me? You need this, now eat!" He tore off a small piece of bread, barely the size of a pebble, and placed it between her lips. Astrid chewed slowly, almost too tired to grind the tiny morsels between her teeth.

"Good, and another."

"I don't understand!" Astrid muttered again, panic on her face. "I've always been able to! Why can't I—?

"Stop!" Jarl pressed his hand over her mouth firmly. "You're alive. You are going to eat, then sleep, and tomorrow we will find your friends."

Astrid could not help herself as a small sob erupted from the back of her throat that would not be suppressed, no matter how hard she tried. Jarl laid the bread on the ground and held her, Astrid's face hidden against his chest.

Knud looked away and poked at the fire with a stick, not sure where to look, embarrassed as Jarl kissed her gently and rocked her in his arms.

"It's alright, Astrid. It's alright."

Exhausted from crying and from the loss of blood, Astrid finally slept. Every so often Jarl leant down to listen for her breathing, afraid that at any moment her lungs would stop. Each breath was heavy and slow.

The sky had turned a beautiful mixture of red and purple and the stars grew fainter by the second as the dawn's light began to drown them out. The sun had not yet risen above the mountains of the Riddari Kviðr, which surrounded the Aldwood.

Knud was also asleep, curled up beside Jarl like a small puppy and using Astrid's leg for a pillow. Jarl leant against the tree behind him and took a deep breath. He was tired, and the early morning air nipped at his skin.

As carefully as he could, he reached for the fire and tossed a few more branches into the red embers. A plume of smoke rose from the branches before they finally caught and he leant back against the tree and looked down at Astrid's face.

Her skin was still cold, but a little of the colour had returned to her lips and scars. He reached for the scar that ran down the side of her face and traced his fingertip over the knotted skin, feeling every rise and fall in it. The lower lid of her right eye pulled down ever so slightly from the puckered scar tissue.

He wondered how many people had looked at those scars and visibly recoiled from her. Even though he had not shown it at the time, he remembered his internal reaction when he had first seen her. Years of maintaining a constant stoic expression had left him with a pretty adept poker face, but internally he had been shocked at the marks, even slightly repulsed. Now, as he stroked the side of her face gently, he realised he barely even noticed them. Exhausted, Jarl lowered his head to her shoulder.

"Don't move!"

Jarl felt the cold tip of a dagger pressed against the nape of his neck and his breath caught in his throat.

"What are you doing in the Aldwood?" a woman's voice asked.

"My friend, she's wounded," Jarl replied as calmly as he could. Astrid opened her eyes, his head so close to hers that his voice had woken her. "Astrid. Please don't move, I have a knife against my neck," he said quickly.

Astrid's eyes snapped open but she remained still. "Please! My name is Astrid Dagmar! I'm here—"

"Astrid?"

The knife against Jarl's neck moved instantly. He slowly sat up, worried the tip of the dagger was not too far away, and a tall skinny woman walked around from behind him. She was not the only one near;

several large animals surrounded them, most of them wolves but a few wild boar, bears, and one huge black fox among them. As they saw Astrid, all the animal skins suddenly fell to the floor like curtains, the people beneath them recognising her.

"Loba," Astrid said, and managed a tired half smile.

Jarl looked at the woman apprehensively. If it had not been for the large wolf skin draped over her shoulders he would have assumed she was human. Her skin was a rich dark brown and long poker-straight black hair fell across her shoulders. Her eyes though, in fact the eyes of all the people around him, were distinctly unusual - the outer iris a dark brown that merged into a vibrant shade of blue and green. The colour was so vivid that it gave the impression their eyes glowed like a cat's in the low, early morning light.

Loba crouched down on her knees and reached for Astrid, ready to pull her out of Jarl's arms. His grip around her instantly tightened, reluctant to let her go to a woman who glared at him and Knud with nothing but disdain.

"Put her down, dwarf!" Loba ordered. Jarl refused.

"Jarl, she's my friend," Astrid begged him. Jarl begrudgingly did as she'd asked and set her down gently on the grass.

178

Crouched next to her like some kind of spider, Loba undid Astrid's veil bandage and winced as she saw her shoulder. She looked up at Jarl for a moment, the blame clearly placed on him, and re-wrapped the bandage.

"It's not far, I can help better there," she reassured Astrid, and smiled at her, her teeth as white as pearls, although two pairs of teeth on either side of her mouth were slightly longer and more pointed than the rest. She reached to pick Astrid up but again Jarl blocked her.

"I'll take her!" he insisted.

All the Vârcolac snarled and their skins instantly slid back up their bodies as if lifted by invisible strings. They were no longer people but wolves, bears, boar and one very large fox. The only thing that remained of their previous human forms were the eyes, though even they had taken on the wild appearance of angry animals.

"Stop it!" Astrid shouted, pain in her voice. "Loba, stop it! They are my friends!" She lifted her hand for a moment before it dropped limply down by her side again.

Loba was shocked to see the tears in Astrid's eyes. She had never seen Astrid cry, and after all that they had been through together in the past, it frightened her. Before Jarl could block her, Loba stooped down and picked Astrid up in her arms. She towered over Jarl and held Astrid as if she were nothing but a small child. Jarl was intensely aware of how much shorter he was than the fierce wolf woman.

"This way," she ordered.

"Wait! Knud! He needs help!" Astrid motioned weakly towards him.

Knud's face turned a bright red. He had wanted to at least try to walk on his own, but before he had even had a chance she had outed him as a cripple. "I can walk on my own!" he protested.

Irritated, Loba glared at Jarl. "Will you pick him up so we can stop wasting time? Let's go!"

Knud looked around, fascinated at the incredible maze of tunnels and domed rooms they had walked into. When they had reached the village he had been surprised at how quiet it was. It had taken him a few minutes to realise that the round stone houses with weeds and moss between the cracks were all abandoned, the wooden doors on several of them half open, the interior of the buildings nothing more than dried leaves and grass.

In the middle of the village grew a large oak that looked as if it had once been two trees, which over time had fused together. One side was decidedly dead;

stumps left where its long branches would have once grown.

Loba studied Jarl and Knud warily as they approached, and spoke to the Vârcolac. Astrid, barely conscious, spoke back to Loba in the same language.

"They don't trust you," Astrid muttered to Jarl, her mouth curling in a small smile.

"I didn't think so," Jarl replied grimly.

Loba stopped and the entire group crowded around the tree, reaching for a severed branch that grew not much higher than her head. With a slight creak the entire side of the dead tree pulled away to reveal a tunnel that led down into the earth. The steps were carved of stone, though as they descended Jarl could not see any sign of masonry. The formation appeared natural, not so much as a single man-made chip on its surface.

Astrid shivered. "I can't feel my arm," she whispered.

Loba walked as fast as she could down one of the multiple hallways at the bottom of the steps and led them into a small domed room. The walls from floor to ceiling held wooden shelves, clay pots on each of them, some marked with a strange script that neither Jarl or Knud could read. Others had images of the plants they contained drawn onto them with meticulous detail.

As gently as she could, Loba set Astrid down on a raised bed in the middle of the room, little more than a mattress on a table with shelves beneath it.

"Out!" Loba ordered Jarl and Knud as they hovered close to the bed.

"No!" Astrid said, and tried to reach for Jarl's hand with her injured arm. A sharp twang of pain shot through it and it dropped down to her side, limp. "He stays! And Knud!" she insisted. Loba did not argue.

"Stay out of my way!" she snarled at them. The other Vârcolac crowded around the entrance outside, curious and worried for Astrid.

"Will she be alright?" one of the older woman in the group asked.

"Prepare a room and some food for her," Loba said, evading the question.

"And the others?"

"I really don't care. The hallway should be good enough," Loba muttered under her breath. Perched on the edge of the bed, Loba carefully unwrapped the bandages. Astrid did not flinch, even as Loba gently pressed her long slender fingers on the side of the wound. The skin was red and inflamed.

"It's not too bad, is it?" Astrid smiled, the colour in her lips gone again.

"Not as bad as last time," Loba replied, and reached for a bottle on the top shelf. "You!" She looked up at Jarl. "Take her hand; this will hurt."

Astrid inhaled sharply and squeezed Jarl's hand as tightly as she could as Loba poured the clear alcohol onto her shoulder.

"Astrid, move your arm," Loba asked.

Astrid turned her head and looked down as she tried to lift it. Her whole arm shook from side to side as she raised it no more than a couple of centimetres from the bed before it dropped back down.

"Will she be alright?" Knud asked, his back to the wall and crouched on the floor.

"I don't know," Loba replied, irritated. "Stop asking me stupid questions."

"It wasn't a stupid question," Jarl snapped. "He's just frightened."

"Well, the world is a frightening place. He'd better get used to it."

"Loba!" Astrid said. "Stop it!"

"What were you thinking bringing them here?" Loba snapped. "This is not their home! None of us want dwarves here!"

"You're right! But it's *my* home!" Astrid said. She opened her mouth to say more but found she could not, too tired to utter the angry tirade that came to mind.

Loba was silent as she cut away the arm of Astrid's tunic then turned her onto her side so she could pour the alcohol onto the entry wound. Astrid's face drained of yet more colour and she bit down onto her finger to stop herself from screaming.

Even from the doorway, Knud could see the edge of the massive patchwork of scars that covered Astrid's back, the side of them visible from where Loba had cut away her sleeve. Jarl was able to see them much better, the marks a combination of deep grooves and knotted clumps of silver skin, like thin tree roots, with hundreds of fine veins dotted across them.

Knud stood up, his arm against the wall for support, and opened his mouth to speak. Jarl shook his head at him and motioned at him to be quiet.

"What was it?" Loba asked. "An arrow?"

When Jarl did not reply, his attention on the scars on Astrid's back, she repeated the question and pointed at Astrid's shoulder.

"It was a knife," Jarl replied.

"A really long knife! It had two ends and it looked like it was made of glass," Knud added.

"Well, that would explain it."

"Explain what?" Astrid asked, confused.

Loba walked over to the shelves and pulled out one of the several wicker baskets that sat there. She moved a mortar and pestle aside and held up a small, double edged dagger, no longer than her hand. "Did it look like this?"

Jarl nodded. "Yes."

"Why would that explain it?" Astrid groaned, her skin paling by the second.

"You can't heal a wound caused by a healing dagger without using the dagger that caused the wound," Loba explained. Jarl and Knud looked at her, even more confused. They had never heard of a healing dagger; the very concept of a dagger that healed seemed quite contradictory.

Loba rolled her eyes and tossed the dagger back into the wicker basket. "Of course, dwarves wouldn't know about that."

Jarl's grip on Astrid's hand tightened, mad at Loba's constant jibes.

None of them spoke for the next few minutes as Loba ground up several herbs into honey and smeared the paste over both sides of the dagger wound.

"What is that?" Astrid asked, the smell of the mixture nauseatingly strong.

"Honey, honey root and garlic for the most part." Loba smiled a little. "The honey root will help the pain but you might be a little disoriented for a while."

"There isn't any pain," Astrid muttered, as Loba wrapped her shoulder with thick brown bandages and laid her arm across her chest. "My hand just feels cold."

Despite the worry on Loba's face, she didn't let the expression work its way into her voice.

"It's just the shock," she lied.

LITTLE KINGS

The armour was new and stiff. Halvard was sure they had given it to him on purpose, another successful attempt by Gauss to humiliate him.

The line of soldiers stretched all the way from the Royal Palace to the entrance of the catacombs. Halvard was stationed a few metres from its great stone door, a spear in one hand and a lit torch in the other. He could feel the crowds pressing up behind him and hissed under his breath at the dwarf closest to him to step back. Although he could hear the funeral procession approaching, he did not turn his head. Every soldier in the line was still, only their eyes moving. They were just as curious as the crowds but with orders to stand to attention they didn't dare move.

As the raised litter that carried the king passed the first soldier, he reached up and extinguished the torch he held in his hand. His leather glove hissed as the flame was smothered, and as the funeral procession moved on, all the soldiers' torches were quenched, one after another.

Every light in the city had been dimmed, at least along the route the procession was taking. The crowds were silent, the only noise the heavy clink of their boots on stone and the tinkle of gold and glass beads from the litter bed.

From the corner of his eye, Halvard could see the servants leading the procession tossing dried, scented flowers onto the ground in front of them, which crunched under their feet as they walked. After the first row of servants came the nobles dressed in their best robes, their faces covered by masks, followed by two burial masters. Each of them carried a large silver burner filled with incense, and an overwhelming scent of musk, pine and frankincense wafted through the air.

Frankincense. Halvard hated that smell, as did half the city, evoking memories of the Red Plague and the loved ones it had taken.

The litter was in front of him now, the body of Hábrók laid out on it. The robes the dead king wore were pure white, which only made the stones embroidered into the hem more vivid. The king's face was covered by a thick gold mask that appeared to be a cast of his face when he was younger, its expression calm for the first time in years. King Hábrók's jaw was so large that it protruded out from beneath it.

Suddenly, one of the soldiers who held up one corner of the litter tripped, out of balance for a second at most. But it was enough for the litter to tip to its side for a moment and for the gold mask to slide from Hábrók's face and clatter onto the ground.

With the litter directly in front of him, Halvard was able to see the king's face clearly. The crowd behind him gasped and recoiled in disgust at the sight of his pale purple skin, a tinge of blue around his lips. Both his eyes were wide open and glazed; even in death they stared up at the ceiling in a panic. His mouth was open in a grimace.

"King's Disease!" someone muttered behind Halvard.

"Not a nice way to go," another voice chirped. "Not nice at all."

Halvard looked at the king's hands and saw they were clenched tightly, no rings on them as there should have been, his fingers too stiff to move. Instead, the rings had been placed around his hand and held there by gold threads sewn into his sleeves.

"Faðir!" a young boy's voice called out, and he rushed over to the mask from behind the litter.

Halvard could not resist the temptation and turned his head a little to see who the voice belonged to, surprised as he saw the young prince Hálfr kneel down to pick up the mask . His older brother, Haddr, still behind the litter, was being carried on a raised gold chair, his legs hidden under a dark red blanket, the hem heavy with gold tassels.

With tears in his eyes, Hálfr picked up the mask and pushed away the servants who tried to stop him. He scrambled onto the litter bed and gently placed the mask back over the face of his father before he climbed back down, walked back towards his king brother and took his seat on the litter.

Halvard looked at the boy curiously, his features and proportions quite unusual for a royal. There was a trace of the distinctive jaw of King Hábrók, but it was nowhere near as prominent as it was in his older, much shorter brother.

Yrsa Gull was alongside them and leant towards them to whisper something. Haddr immediately let go of his brother's hand but Hálfr snatched it back and muttered something under his breath. Yrsa stood up quickly, an annoyed twitch at the corner of her mouth and her face more than a little red.

The litter began to move forward again towards the catacombs. Halvard did his best not to cough loudly as they passed, the thick heavy smoke stuck in his throat. He kept his eyes on the two boys, Yrsa Gull right behind them and her own son, Vard, behind her, his appearance just as ghastly as Halvard had remembered it to be.

When the stone doors of the catacombs closed behind them, every soldier visibly relaxed. It would be a while until they would emerge. The two burial masters stood outside the door, the incense burners still in their hands. Plumes of thick smoke rose up into the air.

"Faðir? Where did they go?" A boy in the crowd behind Halvard asked his father.

"To bury him. All the kings and queens are buried in the catacombs."

"Was the old king buried there?"

"Hastein? Yes, he was buried there too."

"Was Hastein a good king?"

"Yes, I think so," the boy's father replied.

Halvard was glad nobody could see his face at that moment, a revolted expression on it.

"When will they come out?" the boy asked.

"It'll be a while."

The boy taped his foot impatiently on the floor, the sound quite irritating.

"Can you stop that?" the soldier next to Halvard hissed.

The boy pointed his tongue at the soldier and continued to tap.

It was over an hour before the catacomb doors opened again. The young King Haddr was the first to walk out, his pale blue eyes frightened, each of his steps uncertain, but already with the royal crown on his head. The thing was far too big and heavy for the small boy; he waddled slightly as he walked and Halvard noticed that the boy's feet had grown slightly twisted and curled inward. He was followed closely by his brother, Hálfr.

Ignoring protocol, Hálfr walked beside his older brother and took his hand to help him walk. Haddr smiled at him gratefully, relived to have his brother next to him.

"The King!" the two funeral masters bellowed.

Haddr whimpered as the entire crowed bowed before him like a wave. Even kneeling, almost every single dwarf in the crowd was taller than him and he clutched his brother's hand for support and tried to stand a little taller.

For several seconds he opened and closed his mouth, terrified, and his brother leant down towards him and whispered something. Haddr took a deep breath and tried to speak as loudly and clearly as he could, an obvious shake in his voice.

"My first act as king..." he paused for a moment to take another deep breath, "...is to reenate..."

"Reinstate!" Hálfr whispered to correct him.

"Reinstate! Reinstate..." He took another deep breath, "...the Hætta."

Everyone gasped loudly, even the soldiers. Halvard couldn't help but feel sorry for the little boy king as he stepped back a little. Frightened by the crowd's reaction, he gripped his brother's hand even tighter, his mouth gaping open as if ready to say more, but nerves overtook him and he walked, almost ran, away from the catacombs and back along the line of soldiers. The rest of the funeral party rushed after him.

Yrsa Gull, clearly flustered, reached the boy king and whispered in his ear that he should not run and should let go of his brother's hand. He obeyed her first suggestion but completely ignored the second.

Halvard shook his head and followed the soldiers on their way down into the catacombs in a slow, respectful line. Even though the soldiers were meant to remain silent, a great many of them whispered to each other as they walked down the seemingly endless steps that wound down into the roots of the mountain. The word 'Hætta' was tossed around with a great deal of excitement and a good measure of fear.

"It's about time!" he overheard someone say. "We should have had a spring Hætta a long time ago!"

"I think he's mad!" someone ventured to mention, their opinion only met with jeers.

"Afraid of a few goblins are you? Coward."

"If your family had all died in the Red Plague, you would be a coward, too!" the soldier retorted. "The king better pray it goes well or everyone will think his reign is cursed."

UNWELCOME GUESTS

Jarl ate his food as silently as he could, intensely aware that every single eye in the room was fixed on him and Knud. Everyone sat cross-legged on thick, round cushions that had been distributed, but neither Knud or Jarl had been offered one. Their food had been shoved towards them and then they were promptly ignored. To make matters worse, Jarl was sure the Vârcolac were deliberately speaking in a language neither of them could understand.

Knud, though, did not seem to notice their offensive treatment and instead was fascinated by the room. It was much larger than the one they had left Astrid sleeping in. A cluster of luminescent mushrooms hung from the highest part of the domed ceiling, some with a cold pale blue light, but most glowing in a warm orange, like that of a fire.

A good twenty families had congregated in the room, most with four or more children. Some had small animals skins slung over their backs but most did not, their attire simple and made of flax, wool or animal skins. Squirrel was the fur of choice, though Knud did spot one or two fox coats dotted about.

The food was the only thing that did not interest him. He could see a few pots in the centre of the room filled with some kind of cooked meat, but none of it had been offered to him or Jarl. Instead, a large clump of what looked like cooked grasshoppers stared up at him with their dead black eyes. Knud put down his bowl of food as soon as he thought none of the Vârcolac would notice.

Even though he did not show it, Jarl did not appreciate the food either, but he ate it nonetheless, his mind a million miles away and worrying about what he would do now that he had met Loba and the Vârcolac.

He had learned not to make assumptions where Astrid was concerned, but he did not like the Vârcolac any more than they seemed to like him. With Astrid injured he knew it would be a while before they could leave and the thought unsettled him. Although the road to Waidu was reportedly a lot safer than the

Haltija Pass, he knew it would be unwise to travel it alone, and in any case, he did not want to.

As he finished his food, Jarl ran his hands through his hair, worried and unsure what to do, his brows pressed together in a tight arch. He glanced over at Knud and inwardly cursed himself as his eyes fell on the stump that remained of Knud's foot. He wished it had occurred to him to have left Knud with Halvard and the monks in the Salt Monasteries. Knud would still have his foot and he would still have had Halvard as a friend.

"Don't you like the food?"

Knud looked up and yelped in shock at the ugly man who stood in front of him, a wide toothy grin on his face. His skin was not a golden brown like the other Vârcolac, but a sickly shade of almost transparent white with tinges of blue. The colour reminded Knud of a maggot. He was a small man, barely taller than Knud, and he walked with a distinct hunch in his back. He had long, claw-like hands and the skin of his face looked like a melted candle, folding over itself like wax drips. The only thing remotely pleasant about him was his eyes, a warm brown with an almost black tint to them.

"Hehe, I know I'm not much to look at!" the man laughed. "My name is Bugal. Bugal Noz."

Knud just stared, horrified. Jarl, slightly embarrassed at Knud's reaction, introduced himself and ordered Knud to do the same.

"My name is Knud," Knud stuttered.

"Just Knud?" Bugual asked with a chuckle. "Your family can't have been very imaginative if they just called you Knud."

"Knud Villieldr."

"Well, Knud, Jarl, I see you've met my wife, Loba."

Knud's jaw dropped and Loba scowled at his reaction, the questions 'why?' and 'how?' practically written on his face.

"Knud!" Jarl snapped at him, embarrassed again.

"It's alright, I don't expect dwarves to have manners," Loba sneered.

"Loba," Bugal said, smiling awkwardly. "Don't say that, they are our guests."

Loba shook her head and strolled to the far side of the room where Jarl noticed for the first time that two girls had joined her. Their skin tone was a mixture of Bugul's and Loba's, though the second girl had fortunately inherited her mother's a little more than her sister.

"I've made a room for you to stay in near the herb room. I think you'll like it there." Bugal smiled, his teeth more like a crooked line of ivory, all of them a different colour and shape except for his two front ones, which were much larger than their counterparts. Knud could not help but liken Bugal's appearance to a crazed rabbit, especially when he smiled.

"I'm sure we will. Thank you," Jarl said.

"When will you be leaving?" Loba asked.

Jarl's knuckles cracked as he clenched his hands into tight fists. "As soon as Astrid is better."

"Sorry, my wife does not have fond memories of dwarves," Bugual explained quietly, his face flushed with embarrassment, his large bulbous nose bright red along with the tips of his bat-like ears.

"No, we don't!" another of the Vârcolac chimed in. "The sooner you leave the better! You're not welcome!"

"That's enough!" Bugal shouted, and Knud jumped with fright in his chair. The lights in the room flickered. "Loba?"

Loba shook her head and muttered a stream of words in a language neither Jarl or Knud could understand before she strode out of the room along with a large majority of the other Vârcolac. Bugal looked at Jarl and Knud helplessly.

"I'm so sorry. We don't have many guests here, I'm afraid."

"Especially not dwarves, I gather," Jarl joked, but his eyes were as cold as steel. The Aldwood was not at all how he had expected.

* * *

Astrid opened her eyes and gasped out loud. Loba had been right about the pain; the coldness in her arm was gone and instead it felt like someone had placed a burning coal inside her shoulder. She felt hot, irritated and oddly lightheaded, an effect she was sure was the result of the honey-root mixture on her arm. Her head was so warm she could feel the heat radiate from her cheeks and bounce back against her pillow.

She turned onto her side and saw Knud's face propped up on the edge of the bed, his brown eyes wide open and fixed on her like an owl's, dark with tired circles around them.

"Awake?" he whispered. Astrid grinned and nodded.

"Where's Jarl?"

Knud motioned with his head to the foot of the bed and Astrid winced as she sat up to look. Jarl was fast asleep on the chair he had pulled alongside her, his head on the side of the bed, both arms under it to use as a pillow.

"Jarl! Jarl wake up!" Astrid whispered, and gently prodded him with her foot. Jarl didn't move; he was completely exhausted.

"I'll do it!" Knud grinned and poked Jarl's face as hard as he could. Jarl woke with a start.

"What's wrong?" he asked, worried.

"You can't sleep like that," Astrid insisted. Jarl looked up at her groggily and straightened his stiff neck.

"It's fine, it's actually the best sleep I've had in weeks." He looked over at Knud who grinned cheekily at him. "Don't wake me up like that again, Knud." He grumbled and stood up. "They put down some blankets for us in the next room, I'll bring them in here."

As soon as Jarl opened the door and walked out, Knud scrambled up onto the bed and curled up next to Astrid. "I don't want to sleep alone," he whispered. "I keep having nightmares about the goblins."

Astrid nodded. "Alright."

Knud breathed a sigh of relief and dropped his head onto the pillow. He was asleep within seconds with Astrid's good arm laid across him. She turned to look at Jarl as he walked back into the room with two pitifully thin blankets tucked under his arms.

"He's fast asleep." She smiled and motioned at Knud.

Jarl rolled his eyes and moved to wake him but Astrid stopped him.

"It's alright. I don't mind."

"You're the one that needs that bed. Not him."

"Jarl, I said it was fine," Astrid repeated.

Jarl shook his head, too tired to argue with her and Astrid smiled, running her fingers through Knud's red curly hair.

Jarl draped one of the blankets over them both and pulled the last one around himself before he pulled the chair to the head of the bed so that he could sit next to Astrid. He reached across the bed and stroked her cheek, worried when he felt how hot her skin had become. "Can you feel your arm now?"

"Yes, a little bit too much," Astrid admitted. "I don't like honey root but right now I'd do anything for a strong honey root tea, just to make this horrible itching go away."

"Can you move your fingers?"

Astrid nodded and wiggled them a little under the sling to prove it. Several stabs of pain shot down her arm as she did so. "It's strange," she murmured.

"What is?"

"Not being able to heal myself."

"I thought you liked scars," Jarl jibed.

Astrid smiled briefly, but worry soon flooded her face. "We can stay for a few days and then leave. I just need to rest a little while longer," she said, wiggling her fingers again and feeling the pain shoot through her arm.

"No, we're not leaving until you can use your arm. If you don't take care of it now it'll hurt for the rest of your life."

Astrid shook her head, her eyes so heavy she could barely keep them open. She was exhausted but was enjoying the quiet conversation with Jarl too much to allow herself to fall asleep quite yet. "Where is Loba?"

Jarl's jaw clenched at the mention of her name and his eyes narrowed. "Asleep, I think."

"What happened at dinner?"

"Not much, but none of them want us here."

Astrid groaned and rubbed at her forehead. "I'm sorry, I should have spoken to Loba. I didn't want you to meet them like this."

"Don't worry about it. Just rest," Jarl reassured her, and took her good hand in his, both of their arms across Knud who had started to snore loudly.

Astrid nestled her head into the pillow, aware that Jarl's eyes were still on her. She pretended not to notice and waited until he fell asleep too, his head against the side of the bed.

She reached across to move away some of Jarl's long hair that had fallen across his face. She could feel how tired he was from their frantic journey into the

Aldwood, the muscles across his shoulders tense and sore. It took less than a few seconds for her to absorb the strain in them and his face instantly relaxed in his sleep.

Astrid leant her head back down on the pillow and thought quietly to herself, the pain from her shoulder too strong to allow her to sleep. She stroked Knud's hair absentmindedly and her mind wandered back to the pass.

Her hand still burned from the energy she had sucked from the Frǫðleikr tree when the dagger had pierced her shoulder. It had not been intentional, and even though she knew she would have died within seconds had her hand not been pressed against the tree, she could not shake the feeling of guilt. The Frǫðleikr tree, while not as mobile as its Leshy cousin, had still been very much alive. She had felt its bark crack and shrivel under her hand as it was sucked dry of life. Now the enormous amount of energy was trapped in her own body but completely unable to heal her.

Astrid was frustrated, in more pain than she would admit and, although she would not mention it, more than a little afraid. There had been no way to fight the mysterious woman, her magic so strong that Astrid's own undeveloped magic had felt powerless. No, worse than powerless; she had felt completely and utterly insignificant. In all her years wandering Ammasteinn she had never met anyone, except for Dag, who had possessed such an extraordinary amount of magic.

Not for the first time, Astrid felt angry at Dag and his insistence that she never learn to use her magic. "You should have taught me, Mossi," she whispered. "I needed my magic, and I couldn't use it because of you."

Astrid was still awake when Loba walked into the room several hours later.

"You filthy little runt!' Loba growled as she saw Knud on the bed, curled up in Astrid's arms, her blanket over him.

"Don't yell!"

"You need to rest, not them!" Loba argued back.

Slowly, Astrid got up from the raised bed, careful to not pull the blanket away from Knud or wake Jarl.

"What are you doing? Go back to sleep!"

"I can't sleep," Astrid replied. She arched her back and stood up, stiff, cold and sore.

Loba took her arm, worried at how pale Astrid's skin was. "You're mad. You need to lie down."

"You already knew I was mad." Astrid smiled. "I need to move, I can't stay lying down any more."

Loba led her out of the room into the one beside it, which was mostly bare except for a small low bed and several small stools.

"Sit there and don't move." She pressed the palm of her hand against Astrid's forehead, the skin hot and dry. "You're an idiot, Astrid.'

"I know!" Astrid smiled again, her grin infectious. Loba shook her head and suddenly reached out and hugged her tightly.

"It's good to see you," she admitted, careful not to touch Astrid's bad shoulder. "You should have come back sooner."

"I was busy."

"You mean you just didn't want to see the forest again."

Astrid shrugged her shoulders. "That too."

"Sit. I'll make you some honey root."

Astrid grumbled but could not refuse Loba's offer. As much as she hated the light-headedness the tea gave her, she needed the pain in her shoulder to stop before it built to the point where she'd be unable to hide it.

Loba left the room for a few minutes and returned with a small cauldron of hot water. A strong, sickly-sweet aroma filled the room and Astrid's headache eased slightly just from the smell.

"Does it hurt?" Loba dipped a large drinking horn into the cauldron and passed it to her.

"Just a little," Astrid lied. She peered into the drinking horn and then sipped at the tea, a relieved smile on her face as the pain began to dim.

"You would never drink that before." Loba shook her head. "Even last time."

Astrid held the horn tightly against her chest, her hands cold. "Last time I was stupid. I should have asked for help."

Loba snorted in agreement. "Yes, you should have." She sat down next to Astrid as she drank the tea and her face dropped from a smile to a frown. "How can you be friends with a dwarf?"

"Why shouldn't I be? My father was a dwarf!" Astrid snapped back, irritation in her voice. She put the drinking horn down, annoyed at herself for having drunk it so fast. While it had made the pain go away it also made it a lot harder for her to stop her thoughts from slipping out of her mouth before she had time to hold them back.

"I just don't understand," Loba said.

"I know, and I'm sorry you had to meet them like this."

"It doesn't matter how I'd have met them, I will always hate dwarves," Loba muttered.

"I thought that too, once."

Loba let out an irritated growl. "It's not the same, Astrid!"

"How is it not the same?"

"We lost everything, you only..." Loba stopped herself quickly, but the damage had been done. Astrid's eyes flashed, her mouth pressed into a thin line.

"I only lost my parents?" Astrid finished.

Loba clenched her fists together and held her ground. "It was harder for us."

There was silence for a few seconds.

Oh I see! the harsh voice sneered in Astrid's head. *You only lost your parents, you only had to leave the Aldwood to live with a warlock who wouldn't even bury Ragi when he died, let alone teach you how to use magic so you could protect yourself! You only nearly died to save her and now she is trying to make you feel ashamed of them!*

If the honey root tea had not impaired her thought process, Astrid would have questioned why the harsh voice was suddenly on the side of Knud and Jarl. But between the numb pain in her shoulder and the lightness in her head she did not pause to question the voice's motives.

Astrid shouted at Loba with all her might. "No! No it wasn't harder for you! I lost everything! Every time

I look into a mirror I have to remember that! You still had your family, your friends! I had nothing!"

"Astrid! What's wrong?"

Loba's wolf skin instantly fused to her body and she bared her teeth at Jarl who was standing in the doorway. "Get out, dwarf!"

Jarl did not move. "Astrid?"

Astrid's hands were bright blue, the crackle of magic in the air. She glared at Loba who looked back at her a little frightened.

Jarl strode into the room and held Astrid by the wrists, afraid to hold her hands while they glowed with magic. As soon as his skin touched hers, Astrid turned to look at him, her eyes a little unfocused, her head ringing with the angry words she wanted to scream at Loba.

"Let's go outside," Jarl suggested, and Astrid nodded.

Loba watched silently as they left the room, surprised and even a little amazed at how Astrid's face had softened when he'd spoken to her. She had never seen her eyes light up the way they just had, the guarded blank expression gone, like a mask he had managed to lift away.

Nobody followed them up from the tunnels and Jarl did not ask what had happened to make Astrid so angry. He tried to look at her face as they climbed the steps but she turned away from him so he would not see the angry tears in her eyes.

As soon as they were out in the fresh air, Astrid walked away from him, her head bowed as the first few tears escaped. She held her hand firmly over her mouth to muffle the sound of her sobs, but she could not stop her shoulders from shaking.

You know you are feeling this way just because you're in the Aldwood, the soft voice whispered in her head, barely able to finish its sentence before the second voice interrupted.

Oh, poor pathetic little you! it sneered. *You're so predictable; just a few silly little words and you're crying like a baby. It's laughable.*

Jarl watched her for a few moments as she kept her back to him and cried silently into her hands. He knew she hated for anyone to see her crying but he could not bear to just stand by and watch.

Astrid flinched as he came up behind her and rested his hand on her uninjured shoulder, afraid he would try to make her turn to look at him. Instead, his arm moved around her and he held her gently against his chest, his chin against the back of her head. She took a deep breath, both her eyes swollen and red from crying.

"I'm sorry," she whispered. "I'm being stupid."

"Don't be sorry. If you need to cry, just cry."

Astrid took another deep breath and brushed her hair away from her face. "I don't know what to do, Jarl. I didn't think Loba would be like this." She turned to look up at him. "I'm sorry, I didn't mean to get you into this mess."

Oh look at you! the harsh voice whispered. *Worried you've disappointed him? Worried he'll leave because everything didn't go as planned? You're pathetic! Stop groveling!*

"It's alright," Jarl reassured her, recognising the tell-tale flinches her face made when the two voices battled it out in her head. "We'll think of something."

212

OLD TRADITIONS

Ulf glared down at the dwarves before him, all three of them on their knees, snivelling and hunched over. He studied them slowly, his upper lip curled into a sneer, disgusted by how weak and pathetic they looked.

Their clothes were fine and heavy: thick leather boots, dark wool trousers and several layered tunics that were a hundred times finer than the white dress Rakki wore. Fur trim embellished their heavy coats. But their hands were soft, not so much as a single callous on them.

They whimpered as Ulf strode towards them and tried to crawl back, but were roughly pushed forward by the goblins behind them.

"Systa!" he barked. "You can speak Mál?"

Systa shrugged her shoulders and stepped forward. "A little."

"Ask which of them is the youngest."

Systa turned to the dwarves and did her best to speak in Mál to them, pausing every few seconds as she spoke, her memory of the language rusty, the words difficult for her to pronounce. The dwarves clearly struggled to understand her thick Beziickt accent.

Finally one of them replied.

"That one!" Systa pointed to the dwarf in the middle. "They said he is the youngest."

"Good. Kill him. And that one." Then he pointed to the oldest dwarf. "This one we'll keep for later."

Systa nodded towards one of her captains who dragged the two dwarves out of the yurt by their long hair. They kicked and screamed but could not shake themselves free of her grasp. The oldest dwarf, his beard a silver grey, crawled towards Ulf and begged.

"The dwarf says he has gold!" Systa laughed. "Lots of it!"

Ulf sneered down at the old dwarf. "You think gold is what I want?"

Outside the yurt there were shouts of anger, the young dwarves' screams drowned out by the crowd.

"He says he'll give you anything if you let them go."

"Tell him..." Ulf paused deliberately so that the old dwarf could hear the commotion outside. "Tell him I want to know about Bjargtre."

"What do you want to know?" Systa translated.

"Anything! Is there another entrance to the city? How many people are in the city? How large is their army?"

Systa conveyed the message and for a moment the old dwarf just stared back at her. Systa repeated the question, this time with an additional threat at the end. They heard the young dwarf outside start to scream, the roar of the crowd growing louder. Goaded by the horror of his companion's pleas, the old dwarf let out a garbled string of phrases.

"He says...he says that the Mad Gate is the only way he knows. There are rumours of three other entrances but..." Systa asked the dwarf to repeat himself more slowly. "He says only the royal family know where they are."

"The army? How large is the army?"

"He says he's not sure. Twenty or thirty thousand."

Ulf paused for a moment as he thought. Hearing the young dwarf screaming again, the old dwarf begged to be let go.

"He says he'll give you anything. Just let the young dwarf go," Systa translated, her face dropping a little. "He says the youngest dwarf is his nephew."

The screams of both the crowd and the two dwarves had become so loud that Systa had to shout in order to hear herself. They could hear the sounds of objects being thrown and the dull thud on impact. Then in a wave, the entire crowd were silent.

The old dwarf's mouth hung open, his eyes wide, as he realised his nephew was dead. Suddenly, his fear turned to rage. He swore at Systa and let out a stream of threats, spitting as he did so. Systa gasped out loud suddenly.

"He says the king has died!"

"What?"

"King Hábrók is dead. His son is now king." Systa's face visibly drained of blood as the dwarf repeated himself over and again, his face bright red as he spat out each word amid the wails for his dead nephew.

"The Hætta...they will have a Hætta to celebrate the new king's coronation."

Ulf's face turned ashen and his eyes flitted along the ground as he thought as quickly as he could. The old dwarf laughed; a hollow, spiteful laugh.

"Agrokū, if the people find out..." Systa walked up to Ulf and whispered quietly in his ear, her back to the rest of the goblins in the yurt, "there will be a panic!"

"Ulf?" Rakki stepped out from behind the screen that had been set up to divide the yurt in half. He turned to face her, Rakki's hands over her stomach, her face pale, dark circles around her eyes. She should have looked miserable, except she had a huge smile on her face and a gleam in her eyes.

"You can use this, Ulf! This, this is good news!"

Worried for her, Ulf strode towards her and held her gently. "Go back to bed," he whispered, his touch on her hands gentle but firm. "You shouldn't be standing."

"I'm with child, not dying," Rakki snapped at him. "Aki's family, they will never forgive you for what you did," she said matter-of-factly. "And your threat will not stop all of them from trying to kill you again." She paused for a moment and leant her head against the frame of the screen, her lips dry and her breathing heavy.

"Rakki, sit," Ulf urged her, but she ignored him.

She had not been the same since the attack on Ulf's life and both the baby and her nightmares had kept her awake. The daggers she usually kept within arm's reach under the bed had been relocated to a discreet sheath tied around her lower leg. He had tried to convince her not to wear it, the daggers clearly uncomfortable for her, but she had refused.

"Tell them we're leaving, the whole tribe is leaving, and Aki's family can remain. We are the only ones who know about the Hætta. If they stay, the dwarves will take them and infect their city again!"

Ulf took her arm firmly and led her back past the animal hide screen and to her bed.

"You!" he barked over at one of the two guards who was sitting in the sectioned off part of the yurt. "Next time she stands, you help her! Do not let her walk on her own!"

"Ulf listen to me!" Rakki gasped, exasperated.

"I am listening, fox. I am." He held her face in his hands. "It is a good plan."

Relieved, Rakki sank back on the bed and let Ulf pull the blanket over her. "We should leave soon," she murmured, and nestled her head against her pillow. "I just need to sleep…I just need to sleep…"

Ulf knelt down next to her and stroked the side of her face until she finally closed her eyes. From the other side of the room, through the screen, he could hear his generals and their respective captains muttering loudly, Garðarr and Ótama the loudest of all of them, Systa completely silent.

He stood up and looked down at Rakki, her breathing more of a pant. Her plan was a good one, the best they had at the moment, but the very last thing he wanted to do was see his heavily pregnant wife anywhere else other than on a bed. The ride would be exhausting; even on one of the crude carriages it would be uncomfortable for her. He clenched his fist and cursed the dwarves under his breath, his sharp front teeth pressed down against his lower lip like snake fangs.

The panicked whispers of his generals and captains diminished as he stepped back around the screen and took his place in front of the fire.

"Systa, make an announcement. We will be leaving the camp. Anyone who no longer wishes to follow me can stay. Tell nobody about the Hætta. Nobody."

ACCEPTANCE

Astrid sat down at the edge of the hot spring pool and began to untie her boots, her left arm still useless and strapped across her chest in a sling. She grumbled under her breath, the knots almost impossible to untie with just one hand. As soon as she had managed, she kicked off her boots, desperate to clean off the filth from the road. Her long hair, unwashed since the Salt Monasteries, was thick with dirt.

It took her more than a few minutes to remove the several layers she wore, her improvised veil bandage one of the first things to fall onto the floor, exposing her open wound.

With a contented sigh she stepped into the water and perched on the steps that had been cut into the rock around the pool, holding her shoulders just above the surface of the water. Closing her eyes she leant back, the sound of running water echoing around the large underground room and relaxing her.

Every few seconds the steam that collected on the ceiling pooled together and a cold drip of water plopped back down to the ground. When one of the drops splashed on Astrid's shoulder she looked up. Dozens of stalactites hung down from the ceiling like little daggers, providing a constant rain-like drizzle throughout the hot spring cave.

"Need help?"

Astrid turned to look at Loba, a spare change of clothes draped over her arm and an apologetic expression on her face. "I brought you these," she said. "I don't think you can wear those filthy things again until they're cleaned." She pointed at Astrid's dirty clothes, which lay where they had been dropped by the poolside.

Astrid nodded but turned her back, still angry, but not angry enough to refuse Loba's peace offering. Loba sat down next to her on the steps and was silent for a few moments until she felt Astrid's shoulders relax a little and the tension in the air loosen.

With her feet in the water, Loba pulled a long lock of Astrid's hair into her lap and retrieved a bone comb from her pocket. "I don't know how you could let your hair get like this, it's filthy!" she grumbled, as she scooped water from the pool onto the end of it and began to brush the dirt out. "You're worse than my daughters."

Astrid said nothing, her knees against her chest with her arms around them, staring blankly at the wall opposite.

From where she sat, Loba could see the hundreds of scars that marked Astrid's back, line after line layered over another in a horrible patchwork of twisted skin. "I haven't forgotten, you know, what you did for us," Loba finally said. "I know if you hadn't come we would all be dead...my children wouldn't be alive today."

"It's not a debt, Loba." Astrid turned her head but would not look her in the eye. "I'm not asking you to repay me. I'm just asking for help."

Loba brushed through Astrid's hair a little less carefully as she replied. "Don't ask me to help dwarves. What if I asked you to help elves? What would you do?"

"I would help them," Astrid said. "If you asked me and they were your friends, I would help."

"You know what your problem is? You like trouble!" Loba argued back.

Astrid grinned. "I wouldn't know what to do with myself if I wasn't in trouble."

Loba had reached the middle of Astrid's hair and a small cloud of dirty water gathered in the pool around them, the gentle current slow to wash it away. She took a deep breath. "You need them to stay here, don't you?"

Astrid nodded. "Knud, the little boy. I don't want to risk taking him with his leg the way it is."

"And the other dwarf?"

"I'll be going with him to Lǫgberg."

Loba put down the comb and moved further down the steps so she could see Astrid's face. She didn't care that she was still clothed and half of her wolf skin was submerged. "You love him, don't you?"

"It's not love," Astrid said quickly. "I don't know him enough to love him."

Loba snorted loudly and picked up the comb again. "It didn't look like that to me. Your whole face lights up like a firefly when he touches you. You shouldn't be so afraid of that word."

"I'm not afraid of the word, I'm afraid of not meaning it." Astrid paused for a moment and looked down at her hands through the muddy water. "I don't want to get hurt."

Loba looked over Astrid's back and raised an eyebrow. "Really? I always thought you had a bit of an addiction to pain."

Astrid laughed half-heartedly before her face returned to her usual, distant expression. "Moldof's men were by the pillars. They nearly caught us."

Loba stiffened at the words. "Moldof is back in the Haltija Pass?" She stepped out of the pool and paced the edges, nervous and agitated, her wolf skin half over her so that her hands had taken on the shape of wolf's paws. The claws flexed in and out as she thought. "They can't make it over the mountains, can they?"

"No. Not with the Frǫðleikr there. They were too scared to follow us past the pillars."

"That's good, that's good," Loba mumbled, and bit at her claws nervously. "But what if they try?"

"Then they'll die," Astrid replied without a second's hesitation. "Even Titus wouldn't be able to cross over the Riddari Kviðr. The Frǫðleikr would destroy him."

"Who is Titus?"

"A human king, his army is the largest in Ammasteinn."

"I thought Vígdís had the largest army?"

Astrid shook her head. "No, compared to Titus's or Maxima's, Vígdís's army is small."

Loba sat down on the edge of the pool again and pulled her knees to her chest, excited to hear more of

Astrid's stories. "Have you seen them? Titus and Maxima?"

"I've seen Titus, not very well though. He was up on the palace balcony."

"Well, with those elf eyes of yours, I'm sure that wasn't a problem." Loba laughed.

Astrid took the comb from Loba and began to brush out the dirt from the roots of her hair, but as soon as she raised her arm higher than her waist it began to shake violently and the comb fell into the water.

"You shouldn't move your arm!" Loba reached into the pool and plucked the comb from the steps, despite Astrid's protests. "Here, I'll do it."

"I can do it myself."

"Well I want to do it. Stop arguing." She glanced at Astrid's arm, which was still shaking slightly. "You know, you really should just cut your hair. It's really impractical having it this long."

"No. I like it long."

"Why? It just takes up time and energy to keep it clean. You don't have to cut much, just enough so you can't sit on it. Just a foot or two."

Astrid sighed. "I like it long, Loba." She didn't say that the reason she liked it long was because she had never cut it since she had left the Aldwood the first time. In a strange way, her hair kept her connected to her past and to cut it would just feel wrong, despite the amount of times she had been tempted to do so. Loba was right, though. It was impractical and it would be easier to have it half the length, but she just could not bring herself to do it.

Loba put the comb down on the side of the pool and took a deep breath. "Alright, the boy can stay." Astrid turned to look at her, one eyebrow raised disbelievingly. "Don't look at me like that, Astrid! I'm trying to help."

"You sound like you'd rather kill him than let him stay."

"Well, I won't say it didn't cross my mind," Loba growled. "But they are your friends, I can't say no to that. Besides, how much trouble can a little boy cause?"

Astrid could not have looked more uncomfortable if she had tried, the Vârcolac clothes far too big for her. Her left arm had been wrapped in fresh bandages but they felt coarse and uncomfortable against her skin. She did her best not to scratch at the material, but already there were bright red marks around her elbow and her neck. Her sleeves barely touched her elbows and every tattoo on her arm was visible, as well as every scar.

Knud looked up at her as she crouched next to him, a bowl of warm water in her hands and a cloth draped over her arm. Carefully, Jarl unwrapped the bandages and Knud did his best not to wince as Jarl's fingers accidentally brushed against what remained of his lower leg. The skin was red and irritated, though not red enough to worry Astrid. As much as she wished she had not, she had seen similar injuries and she could tell the difference between healing tissue and infection. Nevertheless, she could feel his pain as her fingers hovered over the leg. An acute itching mimicked on her own leg as she absorbed the same sensations he could feel.

"It will be alright," she reassured him. "It's healing." Her fingers began to glow blue for a moment and Jarl instantly pulled her hand away.

"What are you doing?"

"I just want to take some of his pain away."

"You've been stabbed! You need all the energy you have!"

Astrid ignored him and gently cupped her hands around Knud's leg. "Right now I have the life force of a Frǫðleikr in me. I feel like I'm going to explode if I don't use it and I can't use it on myself. This won't hurt me," she reassured him, and this time Jarl did not argue with her.

After a few moments, Knud breathed a sigh of relief and Astrid smiled contentedly.

Noticing a movement on the far side of the room, Jarl turned and saw Bugal hovering in the doorway.

"I came to see how our guest is doing, Loba told me that Knud would be—"

Astrid flashed him a frantic look to silence him and Bugal quickly changed topic. "Loba told me I could find you down here. How is the little dwarf doing?"

"I'm not a little dwarf!" Knud replied indignantly. "I'm taller that you!"

"Knud!" Jarl frowned at him.

"Yes, yes you are. But at least I'm pretty to look at, eh?" Knud's eyebrows rose so high they were halfway up his forehead. Jarl shook his head.

"I'm sorry, he doesn't know when to keep his mouth shut."

Bugal laughed. "Neither did I at that age, but then that was a very, very long time ago," he said wistfully.

"How long?" Knud asked, before Jarl could glare at him to stay quiet.

"Oh, goodness, I'm not sure. So long I can't really remember. Time seems irrelevant when you have nothing to measure it by." Bugal looked over at Astrid. "Though I wasn't as handsome then, was I?"

Astrid laughed as she remembered the day she had fallen through the roof of Bugal's house and landed face first onto the floor in front of him, both of them terrified by the unexpected sight of each other. "I think you were just as frightened of me as I was of you," she said fondly.

"Well, I'd stopped taking care of myself, you see?" Bugal explained to Knud. "After a few centuries it didn't seem to matter what I looked like. At least until I met Astrid."

Knud tried to visualise an uglier version of Bugal but found he could not, a revolted expression on his face. Still, Bugal did not seem to notice, let alone mind, quite used to the reaction.

"Astrid had been following goblins." He turned to Jarl to explain. "She thought she had been spotted and ducked behind a tree, but she fell right through the ground into my little house."

"You had a house?" Knud asked, the idea that such an ugly creature could live in anything other than a hovel quite strange to him.

"Yes, we stayed in it, remember?" Astrid reminded Knud. "The house with the faces."

"That was yours?" Knud asked. "Why did you paint all those faces on the wall?"

"Well, I never saw many real faces, so I drew them." Bugal shrugged his shoulders as if it was the most natural thing in the world to do.

"How did you get here, though?" Knud asked.

"He's a talkative one, isn't he?" Bugal chuckled.

Jarl smiled. "Yes. He doesn't know when to stop."

"Ah well, age will surely cure him of that." Bugal turned to waddle away before Astrid stopped him and pointed at the bandages he had in his hand. He slapped his head loudly. "My poor old brain isn't too good at remembering." He laughed and passed the bandages to Astrid who began to wrap them around Knud's leg. Her hands glowed blue as she did so, and Knud realised that he could not feel a thing, his leg completely numbed. "You should come up to the surface before night time," Bugal suggested before he walked away. "You are probably sick of the dark by now."

Knud shuddered and turned to look at Jarl with a cheeky grin on his face. "He's so ugly!" he whispered, barely before Bugal was out of earshot.

Jarl's face dropped faster than a heavy stone. "Knud! Don't say that! What does it matter if he's ugly? He was kind to you."

"I just thought—"

"No, that's the problem, Knud, you didn't think!" Jarl snapped, more than a little embarrassed. "Don't ever do that again."

Knud bowed his head, embarrassed and ashamed, and didn't say a word as Astrid helped him to his feet.

"We should go outside," Astrid suggested awkwardly, unsure of how to react to Jarl's outburst. She'd never heard him shout at Knud before.

Silently, they walked out into the passage and down towards the steps, Knud with his crutch under his arm and his eyes on the ground. Jarl's face was as black as thunder as Astrid stood between them like a barrier.

The moment they reached the surface, Jarl noticed that Astrid seemed to shrink back slightly, her eyes darting around as though she expected to see something terrible, the tell-tale flinch across her face as the voices in her head began to taunt her.

You thought it would be ok, didn't you? the harsh voice laughed at her. *Maybe you should just pass out again so you don't have to go into the forest and behave like a frightened little child. What, are you afraid the elves will come? Or the dwarves? What are you afraid of, little girl?*

"Astrid?" Jarl reached for her hand but she pulled away quickly, her eyes out of focus as though her mind had been detached from them momentarily.

"I think I'll stay underground," Astrid whispered, and tried to go, but Jarl would not let go of her hand.

"Just stay for a while?" Jarl asked. Reluctantly, she allowed him to pull her away from the oak door.

The rest of the Vârcolac were already above ground, a large group of them in the clearing not far from the empty village, their skins beside them on the grass, their eyes closed as they absorbed the last warm rays of sun before it disappeared behind the mountain ridges.

Knud was surprised to see just how many of them there were. In the tunnels, the Vârcolac had been able to avoid Jarl and Knud, and as such they had never seen more than twenty of them at a time. But now he saw that they numbered at least two hundred, many of them young children and hardly any of them more than middle aged.

Knud sat down heavily on the grass, all three of them far enough away from the Vârcolac for them not to be noticed.

Loba and Bugal were in the middle of the Vârcolac group, their two daughters beside them. In the light, Bugal looked even stranger, the blue and red veins under his skin more visible. Loba was undeniably beautiful in stark contrast to his hideousness.

Knud did his best to not look over at them, worried that Jarl would get angry with him again if he did, but when he looked up at Jarl to try and apologise, Jarl's attention was entirely on Astrid.

"Jarl, stop looking at me like that," Astrid muttered through gritted teeth.

"What's wrong?"

"Nothing."

Don't you remember when Faðir would take you hunting? the quiet voice whispered. *Remember how excited you were? Mātīr got angry with you because you wouldn't sleep and then in the morning you said you didn't want to go because you were so tired?*

"You're lying, I know you are," Jarl replied.

"How would you know?" Astrid snapped, the voices in her head so loud so she had to raise her voice in order to hear herself.

"You bite the sides of your mouth when something's worrying you, and you won't look me in the eye."

Knud did his best not to pull a disgusted face as Jarl leant his head against Astrid's forehead, sure that he was about to try and kiss her. He quickly scrambled to his feet and made an excuse about wanting to explore the abandoned stone village. In his hurry to get away he didn't notice the end of his crutch had managed to get caught in the long grass. As he tried to move forward, the crutch was pulled out from under his arm and he fell to the ground with a loud thud.

The Vârcolac children looked over at him and laughed, their parents quick to scold them, but the damage was done. Red-faced, Knud hobbled off, annoyed at himself and hurt by the children's laughter, which he was sure had been directed at the stump that remained of his leg rather than how he had fallen. Jarl immediately stood to help him.

"I'm not a cripple! I can walk!"

Jarl watched as Knud wandered off towards the empty buildings. He looked down at Astrid, unsure if he should follow him.

"He'll be alright," Astrid said. "I can still hear him."

Jarl sat back down on the ground and Astrid curled up next to him, her knees against her chest and her head against his shoulder.

"Tell me what's wrong."

At first Astrid considered lying to him, an idea the harsh voice greatly encouraged. Instead she opted for a distraction.

"Loba agreed to take care of Knud."

Jarl stiffened. "Why would she agree to that?" He glanced over at Loba who was smiling at one of her daughters as she made a long daisy necklace.

"She wouldn't ever hurt Knud, you know," Astrid reassured him. "I told her about you, and Knud. She's just angry, but once I spoke to her she agreed."

Jarl sighed and ran his fingers through his hair, unsure of what to say. "He'll hate me if I leave him. And he'll hate you, too, because he'll think you made me pick you over him." Astrid flinched and looked away, hurt by the idea.

"I can't protect him; I've only been to Waidu a few times, but each time I had to run from goblins. And if Moldof is by the Haltija pass then he will be near the plains. With his leg the way it is I don't know what will happen. And you said you'd planned to leave him in Waidu with Halvard."

Jarl leant his head against the tree behind them and closed his eyes. He knew the only real option was to leave Knud behind for his own safety, but the very idea made his gut curl.

"I've never left him alone before," he finally said, a resigned tone in his voice. Astrid held his hands tightly in hers. "I knew it would be dangerous bringing him, but I didn't want to leave him in Bjargtre in case Ulf attacked the city. And now I've gone and crippled him for life because I couldn't just leave him there."

Astrid leant her forehead against his. "You couldn't have predicted what would happen. Don't blame yourself."

Jarl smiled half-heartedly. "That sounds like something I would say to you."

Astrid curled up closer to Jarl and closed her eyes contentedly, her head against his chest and with both his arms around her.

Loba turned away, her ears having heard every word that passed between them.

"It's about time," Bugal said, smiling. "I thought she might have had to wait as long as I did to find the one I loved."

"Loved?" Loba joked, a happy little smirk on her face as she looked back at her husband. "Are you trying to tell me something?"

Bugal grinned, all his jagged teeth on display as the last rays of sunlight disappeared over the mountains. "Of course not, my love."

SACRIFICE

A small crowd still remained inside the confines of the camp. Most of the yurts had been disassembled and packed tightly onto the backs of the bison. Only a dozen or so yurts remained upright, though quite a few of them had been relocated so that they were in a huddled circle in true goblin fashion.

The animals were nervous, as were the people. Only the occasional worried shout of a parent who had misplaced a child broke through the hushed whispers. The animals pawed at the ground, a new patch of grass under their feet.

As the stable yurt was dismantled around him, Ulf ran the grass hair brush over Bál's scales out of habit. He was worried, partly for the tribe but mostly for his wife. She had been unable to sleep again, her skin so pale that even the green-undertone had turned ashen and the dark circles under her eyes a deep green-blue. His mother had tried to convince her to have honey root tea, a concoction she assured Rakki would help her sleep, but she had refused.

"I don't want it to hurt Ulf's son," she had insisted.

"It won't! It will help you relax!" Gríð argued, and inhaled the mix she had just made deeply, as if she could drink it through her nostrils if she breathed in hard enough.

"No!" Rakki snapped, exhaustion making her irritable. "I will not drink it!"

Ulf had tried to convince her, too, but the look she had flashed in his direction at the suggestion warned him not to ask again. She was ready to attack the next unfortunate soul who dared to question her resolve.

Her mood more than her distressed appearance worried him the most. Rakki rarely got angry and she shouted even less, she was simply not the type. But in the last few days she had become more and more agitated, restless and, at times, even nasty. She would apologise almost instantly as soon as she realised what she had said but nobody blamed her. Ulf especially.

"You're going to carry my wife today," Ulf muttered to Bál as the grass hair brush scraped over the dragon horse's scales making a horrible sound like pointed nails against polished slate. "And you're going to walk carefully."

Around them, the stable yurt was quickly taken apart. First the roof, then the skins that covered the bone frames, and then finally the frames. The only evidence that the yurt had ever been there was the trampled circle in the earth.

Ulf passed the brush over Bál's back one more time before handing it to a nearby goblin girl, who packed it tightly away with the yurt. Bál snorted loudly as Ulf picked up the unused saddle from the ground and walked towards him.

"Aii! Don't start!" Ulf said gruffly, and placed it firmly on Bál's back as he tried to side step away from it. "If you're going to carry my wife you'll just have to bear it." Almost as if he understood, the dragon horse shook his head and stood still, his sharp teeth grinding together as he pawed at the ground.

Systa helped him to tie down the saddle, the leather straps stiff, almost new. Able to smell her fear, Bál turned to look at her, his red eyes fixed on her. She did not run, but her fingers shook as she tightened the last strap.

Ulf smiled at her and ran his hands through the dragon horse's wiry mane. "Not everyone is afraid of you," he whispered. He walked around Bál to face

Systa who stood to attention, one eye on the horse and the other on Ulf. "Is everyone ready?"

Systa nodded. "Ready. Apart from those who want to stay." She sounded pleased.

Ulf clenched his jaw. "How many?"

"Thirty families and a few loners."

"Thirty families." Ulf repeated the words slowly, his tone angry.

"Traitors," Systa suggested calmly. "But at least they will serve a purpose even if they won't serve you."

"More goblin death," Ulf muttered, and tightened the bridle around Bál's head a little too tightly. Bál snorted and turned to face him, his sharp teeth bared. Ulf quickly loosened the strap.

"They deserve it, Agrokū," Systa replied unsympathetically.

"Are you sure nobody knows about the Hætta?"

Systa nodded confidently. "Only the other generals and our captains."

Ulf leant his head against the dragon horse for a moment.

"The Kelic worms. Are you sure that will be enough?" Systa asked.

"It's all we can do," Ulf replied, and glanced at Rakki as she waddled towards him, Gríð next to her for support. Systa watched quietly as he helped his wife up onto the saddle before he climbed up behind her. With her skin grey and her hair disheveled, she leant her head against Ulf's chest. He wrapped one arm around her and knotted his right hand into Bál's mane.

"Systa?" Ulf looked down at her, a question clearly on the end of her tongue. For a few moments her eyes flitted over the ground before she shook her head and looked up at him.

"When are we leaving?"

"Now."

With a snort, Bál trotted ahead and instantly the others began to follow, bison after bison with massive packs piled onto their backs.

Ótama pulled up next to Systa and reached down to help her up into the second saddle strapped to the bison's back. Systa shook her head.

"I'm going to stay with Skógi," she replied.

"Finally decided to ride with him, have you?" Ótama laughed.

Systa smiled before her face dropped a little. "Something like that." She took hold of the edge of the saddle and reached up to hold her sister tightly in a hug. "I'll see you later," she promised, a slight panic in her voice.

"You don't need to be so afraid. He's loved you for a long time." Ótama looked at her, confused. She had never seen her sister behave in such a way.

Systa forced a large smile and stepped back down to the ground. "I'll see you soon," she repeated, and watched as the rest of the tribe rode slowly past.

Another bison pulled up next to her and Systa looked up at the young goblin in the saddle, his long black hair with only three cuffs wound into it.

"Ready?" she asked, as she sat down in the saddle in front of him and took the reins.

"Ready," Skógi replied.

Systa took a deep breath as the last of the stragglers passed her, then, with one last glance at them, she turned the bison around and rode in the opposite direction.

* * *

As night fell, the entire caravan huddled together in a tight circle, every weapon drawn, every eye on the horizon. Ulf, Ótama and Garðarr, along with a few of their captains, stood at the front, facing the direction of the camp they had left, the torches that surrounded it only just visible in the distance.

Everyone shuddered as they heard the distinct low howling of dwarf horns shatter the silence and a loud whimper of fear rose up into the air. Even the animals were agitated by the sound. Ótama lowered her head as the first screams were heard, the sound so far away none of them could be sure if it was just the wind. That was until more screams joined the first, layer after layer of high pitched terror.

"Where is Systa?" Ulf asked, noticing his third general was absent.

Ótama smiled. "She mentioned something about Captain Skógi."

Next to them, Garðarr squirmed and looked in the direction of the camp, his face riddled with guilt. He gripped the handle of his sword and waited for a few minutes before he spoke.

"Ótama, Systa didn't come with us."

Ótama and Ulf looked at him.

"Where is she?" Ulf asked.

Garðarr looked back at the camp in the distance and motioned towards it, unable to say the words at first, the sky above the camp red with the glow of flames, the yurts on fire.

"She wanted to make sure the city was infected. She made me promise I wouldn't tell you until the dwarves had attacked," Garðarr said quickly. Ótama's face dropped like a stone as she realised just what Garðarr was implying. "She's in the camp with Skógi."

For a moment Ótama did not move, frozen like a statue, before she suddenly sprinted towards the camp as fast as she could. Ulf glared at Garðarr, just as shocked as Ótama was, and ran after her before she could get too far.

"Ótama! Ótama stop!"

She ignored him, her face white with panic, desperate to reach the camp even though she knew it was too far and that it would be too late.

"Ótama!" Ulf threw himself into her and pinned her down to the ground. Blind with rage, Ótama punched him as hard as she could across his face and kicked him away from her. Before she could get back to her feet, Garðarr pulled her back only for her to turn on him in fury.

"How could you?" she screamed as she swung her fist, so irate that she did not even feel her knuckles hit the hard leather breastplate he wore. "She's my sister! My only sister!"

Ulf tried to tear her away from Garðarr but she was too incensed to be held back. She kicked at Ulf with all her might and turned her attention back to Garðarr who barely put up a fight. The rest of the camp watched in silence as Ótama beat Garðarr till he knelt in a crumpled ball in front of her, his hands over his head to protect himself but otherwise completely submissive to her rage.

Finally she stopped, her face red, tears streaming down her cheeks and a disoriented look in her eyes. She got to her feet and stumbled in the direction of the camp, the screams long since silent, the sky still red. "My sister, my little sister." She dropped to her knees and wailed in pain, her hands knotted into the grass. "My sister! You—" She turned to face Ulf, her eyes bloodshot. "You let her! She would never have done this if you hadn't asked her!"

"No!" Garðarr spat out a mouthful of blood as he stood up to defend Ulf. "She told me not to tell anyone; Ulf didn't know anymore than you did."

"I don't believe you!" Ótama spat, and turned to Ulf. "You must have known!"

"Ótama, I swear on my daughter's life she told me nothing," Ulf promised, his hand close to the dagger on his side, worried that at any moment she would attack him.

In the distance they heard the last of the dwarf horns sound and with it Ótama fell to the ground, her arms limp by her sides.

"She'll be alright," Garðarr mumbled, his mouth swollen from where Ótama had managed to punch him more than once, his upper lip split open. "She said she was sure she could make her way out of the sewers."

Ótama did not reply, her eyes fixed on the distance. "My sister, my only sister," she whispered over and again, her eyes closed even as tears ran down her cheeks in a constant stream.

"My only sister."

HÆTTA

Relieved, Halvard strolled away from the gates and into the garrison, his head hung low out of habit, and made his way to the smaller mess room where he knew there would be less soldiers. The much larger mess room opposite was filled with sound and laughter, the captain's mess quiet beside that.

Halvard sat down on one of the benches, straddling it so he could lean his back against the wall. His foot tapped nervously against the floor and the one soldier in the room looked over at him.

"Would you stop doing that?"

"Doing what?" Halvard snapped.

"That! With your foot!"

Halvard grumbled but did as he was asked, only for his fingers to do the same thing without him realising.

"You're doing it again!"

"Look, if you don't like it, get out!" Halvard snapped, insulted that the much younger dwarf would talk to him so rudely.

The young dwarf studied him and Halvard could tell he was trying to decide if he would fight him or not. Halvard stood up and approached the soldier. In a way he hoped he would rise to the challenge; he needed a good fight to get his mind off things. Threatened, the soldier stood up and glared at him. Halvard cracked his knuckles together. Take the bait! he mentally begged the soldier.

Idiot! Halvard thought, as the solider tried to swing an inexperienced punch at him. The soldier was so off balance it would have been very easy for Halvard to sweep his feet out from under him in one quick move and end the fight there and then. But he didn't want to. He was agitated and needed to hit something. With his palm flat he blocked the soldier's fist while his other arm swung a punch into his stomach with a loud, gut-crushing thud.

The soldier doubled over, winded, his fingers crushed and his wrist twisted.

"Never punch with your thumb on the inside, you fool!" Halvard shouted down at him. "And never throw a punch like that, either! You'd be dead in a minute if you tried to fight like that!" The soldier could not reply, he was gasping for air on the floor.

Halvard shook his head and strode out of the room.

"Halvard!"

He winced as he heard his name being called and turned around, standing to attention. The captain, with his eyes on a scroll, did not even bother to look up as he spoke.

"The Hætta will be back soon. You need to get over to the Great Hall and help with the displays. Rakel and Rúna will help you." The captain called for the two dwarves he had mentioned and they appeared in an instant. Halvard rolled his eyes as he saw them, both of them clearly young and inexperienced. Their uniform looked new and stiff. Even the traditional, thick, guard braids in their hair were tied incorrectly.

"Why don't you ask me to take fresh born babes with me? They would be more experienced!" Halvard said.

"Well, in that case, you can take Vakri with you too!"

From the mess hall, the young dwarf Halvard had punched stumbled out, obviously still in pain.

"Vakri?" Halvard asked, and the young winded dwarf nodded.

Halvard swore and turned to go, the three dwarves following him. The two girls looked over at the young dwarf, concern on their faces, but he quickly waved them away.

"I take it you're related?" Halvard asked, not that he really cared but the similarity between the three dwarves was too much to ignore. Their hair was the same shade of bright orange and they had the same button noses and pale brown eyes.

"Yes," the eldest girl said.

"Then if you're wondering who hit your brother, it was me. I hope you two know better than to try and punch with your thumb in your fist."

Neither of them spoke and Halvard let out an exasperated sigh. "Well, let's hope you know how to string up dead goblins."

They walked out of the garrison and into the Great Hall, the smell of frankincense overpowering them the moment they stepped in.

"Why do they keep using that horrible incense?" Vakri asked his sisters quietly, worried that if he asked Halvard he might receive another punch.

"It helps keep the Red Plague away," Rakel replied under her breath.

"It does nothing of the sort!" Halvard scoffed. "Jarl's entire house was smoked out with the stuff and every single one of them caught the Red Plague."

"Who is Jarl? Did he die?" Rúna asked.

"No, but everyone else did."

"But if it doesn't work then why do they use it?"

"Because nothing sells faster than false hope," Halvard replied.

Outside, the streets were busy. Dwarves rushed by, the entire city infected with an air of apprehension. The city plaza was heaving, people pouring in and out of the long tunnels. In the centre of the plaza a tall platform had been erected, a huge frame on top of it built into the shape of a dwarf. Several large incense burners surrounded the platform and massive plumes of smoke coiled up into the air and collected like a cloud against the ceiling.

"What's that for?" Vakri asked.

"It's to hang the goblins on," Rakel said excitedly.

Hearing a commotion in one of the tunnels, people scrambled away from the entrance, intrigued to see the hunting party but afraid to get too close.

Several nobles walked ahead. They smiled and laughed, goblin weapons in their hands as trophies, as a large cart followed them with the bodies of dead goblins piled up on it. They made their way to the platform. Several guards were there already, keen to string the bodies up on the colossal wooden frame.

The three young dwarves ran forward, intrigued.

"Don't go near it!" Halvard yelled.

"Why?" Rakel asked. "We're going to have to string them up anyway."

Halvard was not the only one who seemed wary of the dead goblins. The older dwarves in the crowd all stood at what they thought was a safe distance away, while the younger dwarves rushed forward with a morbid curiosity.

"I'll take them off the cart, you keep your gloves on," Halvard insisted. The three siblings grumbled loudly but followed him to the platform. The cart was already there but none of the guards stepped forward. Frightened, they looked at each other as the crowd looked on.

"Oh, for Nida's sake!" Halvard snapped. He marched forward, hauled one of the bodies onto his shoulders and tossed it up onto the platform. "There! Now start tying them up!" he barked at the siblings.

None of the other dwarves followed his example, instead they hung back and took the bodies from him, afraid to approach the cart itself.

"Aren't you afraid you'll…get sick?" one of the guards asked him as he took a goblin body from him.

"I didn't get sick last time. I don't see why I would catch it now," Halvard replied, and continued to haul the bodies off the cart. "Stop messing around and tie them up!" he yelled at the siblings as he saw one of them push back the gums of the dead female goblin they were supposed to tie to the frame. Her yellow eyes were wide open, her neck broken from where she had been stuck from behind with a club.

"He has fangs!" Rakel laughed.

"That's a she," Halvard corrected her.

"Wow...they're so ugly! Why isn't their skin greener?"

"Stop messing around and tie them up!" one of the older guards yelled.

From one of the tunnels, a second hunting party arrived. Less apprehensive, the dwarves approached the cart as soon as it emerged. Even the older dwarves who had lived through the Red Plague stepped forward, some of them beginning to cut small mementos from the bodies - a strand of hair, a scrap of clothing. The more morbid among them cut away the tips of their long pointed ears. Even Halvard could not help but be disgusted at the desecrated bodies he hauled up onto the platform.

"They have red blood!" Vakri exclaimed, staring at the goblin he was tying to the frame with its ear tip severed, a long trickle of blood down the side of its face.

"Don't touch the blood!" one of the guards yelled. "It has goblin diseases!"

Halvard finally hauled the last body from the cart and turned to help the guards to tie up the rest. Some of them climbed up the frame so that the bodies could be strapped to the top while others paused to stare at them, intrigued and disgusted by their appearance.

"They're so ugly!"

"What are these rings in their hair?"

"Pass me that! My husband would love me to take that home!"

"I can't get it off! It's tied into his hair!"

"Just cut it off then! It's not like they're going to mind!"

Halvard stepped back and looked up at the frame, most of it covered, dozens of bodies strung up like animal skins at a tannery. One of the goblins in particular caught his attention – a tall female goblin with a single tribal ring tied in her short black hair. It hung down across her forehead, a simple band with a beautifully crafted wolf's head in the middle. Her arms were tightly tied above her head, suspended half way up the frame. The three siblings stood beside him, Vakri with a lock of goblin hair in his hands.

"Put that down!" Halvard said, tossing it away. "You're here to help, not to collect trophies."

"But we've finished!" Vakri protested.

"I don't care. Leave it."

The plaza was full. People heaved out of the tunnels and pressed up against the edges of the platform. The sounds of hundreds of chattering voices filled the air. Halvard had never seen the plaza so full, even for the king's funeral.

Behind him, the captain called out his name and Halvard turned his head away from the frame for a moment.

"Halvard! You and Ríkvé's lot will keep watch. I don't want anyone trying to take pieces of goblins home with them."

"It's a bit too late for that," Halvard mumbled. "Some of them had bits missing before we even got to tie them up."

Suddenly, there was a loud scream from the crowd as one of the bodies moved and dropped down from the frame, a long thin knife between her teeth. Halvard turned and saw it was the same goblin he had observed just moments before. Her yellow and green eyes fixed on him.

With one quick movement she reached down to one of the pouches that hung from her belt and tossed it out over the crowd, a plume of black dust falling from it. Another goblin shook himself free from the frame and fell down next to her. The crowd panicked, even some of the guards threw themselves away. Shrieks and screams echoed through the hall and the massive body of people pushed and shoved against each other in a panic, desperate to get as far away from the platform as they could.

The female goblin dropped her knife into her hand and shouted to the other goblin in a language nobody could understand before they both leapt from the platform. The crowd did their best to back away from them, but with so many people crammed into the hall there was very little space, or at least not enough to move anywhere quickly. The dwarves were packed together so tightly that the two goblins could run over them.

Halvard was the first to react.

He pushed the three siblings away from him and ordered them to remain by the platform. With his heavy sword drawn, he pushed his way through the crowd towards a third goblin, who was about to throw himself after his companions. Halvard brought the tip of his sword down his spine with all his force.

The siblings turned ashen as they saw the goblin cleaved open from the nape of his neck down to his tail bone. Rakel looked like she might even be sick. The goblin toppled over the edge of the platform and into the crowd, dead, his blood splattering on more than one dwarf. The other two goblins were half way towards the nearest tunnel and Halvard raced after them, trying his best to catch up.

It would have been easier to run through a stampede of wild ponies. Dwarves pushed and shoved past him, shouting and screaming hysterically. Halvard was grateful that he was quite a stocky dwarf and was not easily toppled over; the same could not be said for many of the dwarves around him. He stopped for a moment to help an old dwarf who had been knocked to the ground and was on the verge of being trampled to death, and when he turned to chase after the goblins again he could no longer see them. Still, he raced ahead and trusted that wherever dwarves ran from, that must be where they were.

He turned into a narrow tunnel, the crowd only more panicked in the constricted space. Shoulder to shoulder, Halvard pushed his way through the crowd, yelling at people to let him pass, his progress painfully slow. Very few of them heard him and even less did as they were asked.

Ahead, he saw one of the goblins force their way into one of the homes that lined the edge of the tunnel.

"Move!" Halvard bellowed, pushing his way violently through the crowd. It was another minute until he was able to reach the house and, with the front door forced open, he scrambled up the steps and went inside.

Everything was silent. Too silent. He raced into the hall and saw two dwarves on the floor, one clearly dead, her throat cut open, and the other with a deep gash across his stomach, his hands pressed tightly over it and his mouth wide open in shock.

"Where did they go?" Halvard said. The dwarf stared at him. "Where did they go!" he repeated. The dwarf nodded at the passage which led downstairs and Halvard dashed down it, following a small trail of blood.

The room was empty, the kitchen table shoved onto its side and half-prepared food scattered on the ground. He glanced around, confused, then spotted a splatter of blood leading to a latrine in the far corner of the room, its stone seat nudged to the side. He grabbed a torch from the wall, kicked the lid off the latrine and lowered the torch inside, surprised to see how much space there was below. He heard a loud commotion above him and the captain's voice calling his name.

The smell made his stomach heave but he clambered over the edge and dropped down into the small tunnel with a splash as his feet hit the floor.

"Halvard!" the captain's voice bellowed from the stairs to the kitchen.

With the torch gripped firmly in his hand, Halvard stooped and made his way down the tunnel, following a trail of footprints in the sludge. He did his best not to breathe through his nose, each inhalation like acid fumes in his lungs. The thick excrement squelched under his boots. Ahead, he could hear voices, the guttural sound of goblin words. He picked up his pace and jogged as fast as he dared, worried that if he ran he would slip.

Just as he was about to turn the corner a goblin lunged, his thin dagger passing centimetres from Halvard's nose. As Halvard jumped back to dodge it, he tripped, and the goblin pounced on top of him. They grappled in the sludge, Halvard the stronger of the two despite being much shorter. The goblin did his best to cut him but Halvard grabbed his wrist and turned the knife back on him, and he exhaled sharply as his own blade pierced his throat. He looked down at Halvard in horror for a few seconds, a dribble of blood between his teeth, before he went limp and slumped on top of him.

Halvard pushed the goblin roughly to the side, got to his feet and plucked the torch from the ground, the horrible smell of smouldering excrement wafting around him. He pulled the dagger from the goblin's neck and left his own sword on the floor, the tunnels too narrow to be able to use it well.

He could hear the sound of running water nearby and a loud roar at the end of the tunnel. *We must be near the aqueducts,* he thought.

Snarling, her two sharp front teeth exposed, a female goblin lunged from a small hollowed out space in the edge of the tunnel and a brief pang of fear ran through Halvard. This goblin was quick, every muscle in her lean limbs flexed. Even worse, she seemed to have some kind of experience with the dwarf style of fighting.

Halvard managed to dodge her first attack but, as he did, he felt a blade tip drag itself over his arm, the leather vambrace he wore just barely protecting him. Thrown off balance for a moment, her foot swept underneath him and knocked him to the ground. The back of his head hit the floor and his long thick hair mashed into the muck beneath him. Before he could react, her food slammed down on his wrist. Halvard bellowed in pain and let go of the knife. He looked up and saw her head above his and both her hands on the hilt of her knife, raised and ready to plunge it into his chest.

Halvard reached up and grabbed her wrists as the knife came down towards him. With her eyes wide and her mouth pressed into a furious contortion, her hands shook as she tried to push the dagger down. There was a trace of worry on her face as she realised she was not physically strong enough to kill the dwarf beneath her.

I'm doing to die, Halvard thought. *I'm going to die in the sewers and nobody is going to look for me.* He screamed and allowed her to push the knife down towards him with her entire body weight on top of it. There was a smirk on her face, the look of victory, but just as the dagger tip was about to pierce his stomach, Halvard twisted it and turned it back on her.

She gasped as the blade entered her abdomen. Her pupils instantly dilated and she stumbled back, both hands clutched over the dagger's handle.

Halvard scrambled to his feet and plucked his knife from the ground, but when he turned around she had vanished. He quickly followed the distant sound of footsteps down the tunnel, only to see it drop off into a large vent when he reached the end. He glanced around at several other tunnels, all of them dropping off into the same vent, then peered into it and saw the strong current of an underground stream below.

There was a faint glow above him and he looked up to see what appeared to be small bugs on the roof of the sewer, their outer shells a luminous blue and producing just enough light for Halvard to be able to see a little of what surrounded him.

Peering down over the precipice again, he could not see anything but water and the massive pipes in the walls around him which drained into it. The smell was even worse than it was in the tunnel. Angry, he turned back and retrieved the partly extinguished torch, noticing the dead goblin nearby, his eyes still open, a shocked expression frozen on his face. He looked down at it for a few moments, vaguely curious.

He reached for his sword and cut through the hair that held the cuff over the goblin's forehead. The wolf's head was beautiful, even to his aesthetic standards, and he held it up and studied it closely. The cuff was smooth without a single pattern, until it reached the wolf's head. The eyes glinted in the dim light, the metal over the eyes more polished than the metal on its face.

Halvard sighed as he heard Captain Gauss's voice echo towards him.

"He'll want proof, won't he?" he remarked to the corpse. "And I want to keep this, so—"

In the room above, Captain Gauss heard a loud grunt and the dull sound of steel against flesh before a goblin's head suddenly flew out of the latrine and landed on the floor in front of him.

Halvard breathed a loud sigh of relief as he clambered out of the sewers and up into the clean air of the kitchen. The guards in the room instantly stepped back and covered this noses, the stench stomach-churning.

"Well?" Gauss asked. "Are they dead?"

Halvard looked down at the head at his feet and kicked it like he was playing ball.

"Yes, all dead."

HATE

Jarl was fast asleep, his head buried in the pillows that had unexpectedly been left in their room, along with much more comfortable bedding. Astrid had explained to him that they were Loba's attempts at reparation without actually apologising to them directly.

"Loba will never actually say she is sorry," Astrid had laughed. "She'll only show she is."

It was an apology Jarl happily accepted. He was asleep almost before his head hit the pillow, worried about the inevitable conversation he would have to have with Knud in the morning and sleep a temporary escape from it.

Astrid was still wide awake, her eyes on the ceiling, her thoughts a jumble of voices and memories. She could not wait to leave the forest and escape the horrible images it forced her to see each time she closed her eyes. She shivered as the sound of elf horns rang in her ears followed by the sound of horses' hooves on the ground.

"No, no. Get out!" Astrid whispered, and held her hands over her ears, both her knees pulled tight against her chest. "Ragi," she said under her breath, and for a brief moment the images changed and she was transported to Dag's hut in the Heilagr forest, Ragi's food over the fireplace, the warm, comforting smell of berry pies.

Astrid smiled, even as her eyes began to water. She had re-played this image so many times and even now, almost forty years later, it still had the strength to chase away the memories that frightened her.

"Astrid?" Knud looked over at her, his eyes half open. "What's wrong?"

"Nothing," Astrid lied. "It's just the shoulder."

"Then why were you covering your ears?"

She shook her head and shuffled over to lie next to him. "Your leg. How does it feel?"

Knud lifted it slightly from the pillow that had been placed beneath it, so as not to irritate the stump. "I can still feel it. I was dreaming and I could feel my toes move."

Astrid moved the curly, red hair from his face with a sad smile. "Don't worry, it will go soon. Soon you won't even feel it."

"But I want to feel it," Knud admitted. "Is this why you let yourself get scared? So you can still feel?"

Astrid looked at him, surprised. "No, it's not like that. I just don't mind the scars."

"That's strange."

"I know."

Next to Knud, Jarl snored loudly and Astrid did her best not to laugh. She had never heard Jarl snore before.

"He only does that if he's really tired," Knud giggled, looking at Jarl face down in his pillow, his long dark hair splayed around his head in a dishevelled mess.

"He's not as bad as you." Knud looked up at her indignantly and she grinned. "I've heard bulls bellow more quietly than you!"

"I don't snore!" Knud pouted, his arms crossed, and Astrid laughed at him. "Yes you do."

"I don't, I can prove it!" Knud screwed up his eyes for a few minutes and pulled his blanket tightly around his shoulders. Astrid just watched him with an amused smirk as he tried to force himself to fall asleep. Finally he admitted defeat and sat up. "I can't fall asleep now." His eyes lit up as a thought crossed his mind and he looked up at Astrid. "Do you know any songs?"

"Songs?"

Knud nodded enthusiastically. "To help me get to sleep?"

Oh go on! the quiet voice purred. *You haven't sung that song in such a long time. You don't want to forget it, do you? You love that song! Someone else should know it, not just you.*

Finally, Astrid nodded. Curled up next to Knud, she whispered the song at first, afraid she would wake Jarl, before she was forced to sing a little higher so that the lump in her throat would not make her voice croak.

> *Sleep and be happy, the moon is awake*
> *There's light in the darkness*
> *Smile dear, you're safe.*

> *Don't think of the howling,*
> *The wolves are long gone*
> *No matter your fears, you're safe, you are strong.*

Astrid felt the lump rise in her throat and she did her best not to let it be heard but, as much as she tried, her voice wavered a little more with each word. Knud did not notice at first, completely spellbound by the song and the unusual way in which she sang it.

> *The clouds hide the moonlight,*
> *Don't worry, don't fear.*
> *The moon is still there,*
> *Will in time re-appear.*
> *There's light in the darkness,*
> *Don't fret, we are here.*

Before she could finish her voice broke and she held her hands over her mouth to stop the lump in her throat from becoming an audible sob.

"Astrid?"

"It's just my arm," she lied. "I...I need to go outside."

As she got to her feet she felt a wash of cold pain run through her and was overwhelmed by a need to run and never stop. Suddenly, she felt small, helpless, and utterly terrified. With her eyes wide open, her mouth seized in a silent scream.

As soon as Astrid had left the room, Knud shook Jarl until he awoke.

"Knud! I'm trying to sleep!" he said, groggy and irritated.

"Something's wrong with Astrid, I think her shoulder hurts. She was crying."

Jarl groaned into his pillow for a moment before he forced himself to stand up and walk out into the passage, desperate to get back to bed.

"Astrid?" he whispered, worried he might wake a Vârcolac who would be equally as upset about being woken as he was. He felt a breeze rip through the maze of tunnels as the door to the outside was opened, followed by a quiet 'thud' as it closed again.

Jarl ambled down the hall and up the stairs to the tree door, easily able to open it despite the heavy weight that kept it closed at night. He stepped outside just as Astrid disappeared into the forest, her long black hair loose over her shoulders.

Quickly, he followed her, surprised that she had not heard him. He trailed behind her as she walked through the forest, noticing the flinching of her head from side to side, her hands over her ears.

After a while they reached a glade and suddenly Astrid dropped to her knees on the ground and huddled into a ball with both her hands pressed down over her ears, and screamed as hard as she could. The sound sent a cold shiver down Jarl's spine and woke a large flock of blackbirds in the nearby trees. For a few seconds the light of the moon was blocked as the birds rose up in unison like a dark cloud, screeching as they flew away in a panic.

"Astrid?"

She jumped with fright and turned to look at him before quickly turning away so he could not see her tear-stained face. She rubbed at her eyes and stood up. "My arm, it's just hurting a little," she muttered, as she pulled her hair out from behind her ears so that it hid her face slightly. "What are you doing here? You should be asleep."

"You're lying again." Jarl walked up behind her and wrapped his arms around her waist, his beard prickly against the side of her neck, his chin on her shoulder. Astrid's whole body tensed, her hands held against her chest and her chin against them. "What's wrong?" Jarl whispered.

Astrid turned and buried her head against his chest so that he still could not see her face. Jarl couldn't help but wish that just for once she would wrap her arms around him rather than clench her fists against her chest. Her body language was nearly always defensive, afraid to hold him or to let him hold her properly.

Astrid did not say a word, the voices in her head so loud she could barely think.

"Talk to me!"

"What happens, Jarl?" Astrid said suddenly. "After this? After Lǫgberg, and Bjargtre?"

Jarl knew that it was not this that had really upset her, but he answered anyway. "I don't know, why?"

Astrid's eyes squinted together as she tried to think over the clamour the voices were making in her head. "I just wanted to know what happens if people discover I'm a Blanda blóð. If they see you with me, what happens to you?" Jarl's grip around her tightened.

"Nothing will happen."

Astrid scratched at the scar down the centre of her lips as the voices got louder. "Would anyone hurt you if they discovered I'm half elf?"

Jarl wished he could look into her eyes and truthfully tell her that that would not happen, but they both knew it would be a lie. "I'm sure some people would try," he finally replied, his voice deep and serious. "But if they don't find out—"

"Someone always finds out," Astrid muttered under her breath. "You think you're safe, and you're where nobody can hurt you, and then they find you and—"

"Astrid," Jarl interrupted her. "What's really worrying you?" Her whole face was red from crying, her eyes especially, the scars down her cheek even more pronounced than usual, silver streaks surrounded by red.

"I'm just afraid. I'm always afraid. I hate it here!" Astrid tried not to shout the words but the sob in her throat had built up so much she could not stop it.

Every few words were interrupted by a sharp intake of breath. "Each time I think it might feel like home but it just feels like a nightmare! I…I keep thinking I can come back and I won't feel like a useless, weak child! And with you... I'm so, so happy when I'm with you. But all I can think about is that something might happen to you. I might not be strong enough again." Astrid tried to keep talking but couldn't speak between the sobs and the desperate breaths for air. Jarl held her and did his best to calm her down, her whole body shaking.

"Astrid, stop. Nothing is going to happen to me. You're not weak, you're the bravest woman I've ever met." She began to breathe more slowly and let her hands drop down to her sides, Jarl's arm still around her and his hand repetitively stoking the back of her head.

It was then he noticed the ruin, and the white jasmine flowers that covered it like hundreds of little lanterns in the dark shade of the pine tree, the moonlight particularly reflective on the flowers' silver petals. The entire bottom half of the pine tree was covered in the wild plant, which carpeted the ground around the ruins. The little masonry that could be seen was clearly dwarven and it did not take Jarl long to figure out why the sight of it had upset Astrid so much.

Taking a deep breath, Astrid stood and stepped away from him, rubbing at her eyes. Embarrassed at her sudden outburst, her jaw was clenched in an angry scowl and both cheeks were bright red. "I'm being stupid, I'm sorry. Let's go back. You need to sleep."

Jarl held her arms and did not let her turn away. "Just wait a little, we don't need to go back yet."

Astrid rubbed at her face even harder, determined to scratch away the tear stains if she had to. Before she could scar herself, Jarl lifted up her chin so she had no choice but to look at him. He tried to think of all the things he could possibly say that would calm her, but he knew as well as she did that he could make no promises.

The road would be dangerous, he knew that, and he also knew that in Løgberg especially, his association with Astrid could be very dangerous. With her height, provided her ears were covered, the chance that they would be discovered was small, but there was a chance nonetheless.

He leaned down to kiss her, one hand against her neck and the other around her waist. Astrid kissed him back, the voices in her head instantly silent. Jarl suddenly pulled back and smiled as a thought occurred to him.

"I didn't tell you I love you, did I?" Astrid inhaled sharply and looked up at him in shock "What?" Jarl laughed. "Why are you surprised?"

Astrid's mouth opened and then closed before her face dropped. She looked down at the ground. "Do you want me to say it, too?"

Jarl shook his head. "No. You can say it when you're ready."

Astrid noticed he did not say the word 'if'.

* * *

Knud rolled over and opened his eyes, rested but still sleepy. For once he had not had any nightmares about Dip wolves or traps, or woken in the middle of the night in terrible pain. He'd had a completely dreamless sleep.

Next to him, Jarl's bed was empty, the blanket gone. Worried, Knud turned around to look for him and saw Jarl and Astrid fast asleep behind him, Astrid's hands held tightly against her chest, her head against Jarl's shoulder, Jarl's arm around her. He rolled his eyes and pulled a disgusted face.

"I saw that!" Jarl mumbled. Careful not to wake Astrid, he set her down on the floor, stood up and walked over to Knud. He sat quietly on the bed for a few moments as he ran every possible way he could break his decision to Knud through his mind. Finally, he took a deep breath and spoke.

"Knud, I need to leave the Aldwood, and I need to leave you here with Bugal and Loba for a few weeks while I go to Lǫgberg." Knud's face dropped and he said nothing for a moment as he tried to take in what Jarl had just said to him.

"You're going with Astrid?" His lips trembled as he spoke, both eyes already full of tears.

"Yes."

"But I can come with you!" Knud pleaded. "Look!" He tried to stand up, his hand against the wall for support. "I can stand! And I'm better now, my leg didn't hurt last night. Please, please don't leave me here!"

"Knud, please, I don't have a choice. I can't have anything else happen to you because of me."

"Nothing will happen! Astrid can take care of us, she's done it before! I'll be alright, please don't leave me here!" Knud begged.

Behind them, Astrid opened her eyes but did not turn to look at them.

"I will come back as soon as I've seen the queen, Knud. I'm not leaving you here."

"But you are!" Knud wailed. "They hate dwarves! I can't stay here, I want to go with you and Astrid!"

"You remember what I said when Knute died? I said I would take care of you, that I wouldn't let anything bad happen to you. I promised Knute I would never let you get hurt and I've already broken that promise. I won't risk breaking it again."

"You also said you wouldn't leave me like he did!" Knud screamed. "You're leaving me but going with Astrid!"

"I have to leave you, Knud, just for a little while."

Without warning, Knud turned and threw himself at Astrid. He kicked and hit her as hard as he could. Astrid held up her arms to protect her face but otherwise did not try to stop him. "You did this! You're making him go because you're not strong enough! I hate you! I hate you!"

Jarl tore Knud away but he kicked and flailed around like a wild animal until Jarl was forced to let him fall to the floor.

Outside in the hallway, Loba and a few of the other Vârcolac listened, Bugal with a concerned expression on his face.

"Should I do something? Loba whispered.

Bugal shook his head. "You'll only make it worse if you do."

"If Astrid is going, I am too!" Knud screamed.

"No, you are not!"

"I hate you!" Knud said, tears streaming down his face. "I *hate* you!"

Jarl flinched at the words and Knud's face fell as he realised what he had said. Ashamed of himself but too angry to apologise, he picked up his crutch from the floor and stormed out into the passage way.

The Vârcolac quickly scattered into the nearby rooms, but Bugal remained in the hallway like a startled owl.

"And I hate you too!" Knud shouted at Bugal, before hobbling as quickly as he could down the tunnel.

DANGEROUS PREDICTIONS

Gríð jumped down from her bison and began to pull up the honey root weed she had spotted. The vine-like plant lay flat against the ground, its long tendrils weaving between the grass, almost completely hidden and visible only to the trained eye.

Ulf watched his mother as she feverishly dug it up. She did not even clean the mud that stuck to it as she broke off the top part of the plant and chucked in carelessly to the side. The roots were ten times the size of the leaves, and she quickly snapped it into several pieces, the sickly sweet smell from it overpowering.

"This is a good one!" Gríð smiled. "Not too old, not too young, just right." She got up and dusted the mud from her knees. "Here! Take it!"

Rakki was in no condition to argue, the desperate need to sleep overriding any other thought. She took the root from Gríð and began to chew on it, the effects almost instantaneous. Ulf felt her whole body relax, with his arm around her waist and the other across her stomach.

He had waited until morning before he had given the orders for the caravan to make camp, and the yurts had been erected almost as quickly as they had been taken apart. At first Rakki had been relieved to be back in her own bed, but no matter how many times she had tossed and turned, she still could not find sleep. The baby was as restless as she was.

The relief she felt from the root was almost instant, the dull pain from her lower back washing away within seconds. A calmness followed and she was asleep before she had barely finished it. Ulf breathed a sigh of relief and pulled the fur blanket over his wife.

"It won't hurt the child, will it?"

Gríð scoffed. "No! It never hurt you, I don't see why it would hurt the child."

Ulf nodded but he still looked worried. Gríð sat down beside Rakki's bed and took Ulf's hand in her own, all the while chewing a large root in the side of her mouth.

"What's wrong?"

Ulf looked up at his mother and leant his head against her shoulder. He suddenly felt very tired, desperate to just lie down on the bed and sleep. Every single worry that had built up in his head over the past few days was tormenting him. As much as he was happy that Rakki was finally able to rest, he could not wait until she was awake and able to talk with him as she always did when he was worried.

"I promised I would protect them," Ulf muttered, too tired to enunciate properly. "Ótama will never forgive me for Systa. What if she turns on me? We can't run again, not with Rakki like this."

Gríð suddenly slapped his face as hard as she could. "Stop it, Ulf! You cannot worry about what might happen. Ótama is loyal. If you are worried she might turn on you, give her someone she hates even more. You will take the mountain and you will give her the boy king to avenge Systa."

"I want to trust them," Ulf replied, irritated. "I want to trust my own people!"

Gríð shook her shoulders and spat out the pulp that remained of the honey root onto the floor, popping another fresh piece in her mouth. "Ulf, you can't trust people. How many times do I have to tell you? Expect the best but always plan for the worst! It's the only way you survive."

Ulf pulled his head away from her shoulder and looked down at Rakki, her face no longer pressed into a grimace bit calm; relaxed. "I don't want my daughter to just survive, I want her to live."

Gríð groaned and stood up. "I don't know how Rakki puts up with you! You're a fighter, so fight. Let Rakki and me do the worrying."

Ulf sat beside his wife for a few minutes more before he got up to leave the yurt. As soon as he passed the two guards at the doorway, his face changed back to the mask-like grimace he normally wore.

He could feel the eyes of every goblin in the camp on him as he walked and he wondered if, at any moment, he would feel the sharp tip of a dagger in his back. Most of the families that had deserted had taken their entire family to the grave with them when the dwarves had attacked, but he was sure there would be a friend or two in the camp with more than a thought for revenge.

"Ulf!" He turned and saw Ótama at a nearby yurt, blood on her fists.

"The dwarf?" Ulf asked, and Ótama nodded but would not make eye contact with him.

"He'll live."

"Good, we might still need him."

"He doesn't know anything else."

"I didn't think you could speak their language?"

"I learnt a little from Systa." Ótama glared at him and wiped her hands down the side of her tunic to remove the blood. "But I wasn't there to ask him any questions."

"Still, he might be useful." He paused. "The Hætta. Did they take all of them?"

"All of them." Ótama did her best to control the shake in her voice as she spoke. "There was nothing left, the tents were burned to the ground."

Before she could leave, Ulf called her back. "I swear to you, I did not know." Ótama nodded but turned away.

"I'm leaving for the mountains with Systa's captains. I want to wait till I am sure."

Ulf could not help that there was no question in her tone, but nevertheless he nodded in agreement. "She will survive. She's strong."

"She'd better," Ótama muttered under her breath as she walked away.

* * *

Ótama had not moved from the sewer's edge for hours, despite the rancid smell. Her eyes were alert as she crouched over the ridge of the river, ready to jump in at a moment's notice.

They had not lit a fire, despite the cold, but had pulled their cloaks tightly around them to stay warm. The early morning air bit at their skin and long clouds of vapour blew from their mouths with each breath. They all stood alert watching the sewage tunnel that led into the river, polluting the water with thick brown sludge.

Suddenly the water stopped, the flow blocked by something further up. Ótama jumped down and stood next to the pipe, the filthy water up to her thighs. For a few seconds everyone was silent, Ótama with her heart in her chest as she crouched down to peer inside the pipe. With a rush, a large blockage of sewage was pushed out of the tunnel along with a body encased in the thick excrement. She gasped as she saw her sister's face and pulled her into her arms.

Systa shivered and tried to stand, her hands clamped over a dagger that protruded from her side. She had not removed it, the dagger the only thing preventing the sewage from entering the wound and from bleeding to death.

"Ótama?" She opened her yellow eyes and smiled at her sister, the movement more of a flinch. Ótama held her tightly, tears in her eyes.

"You did it! You did it, you crazy fool!" She kissed Systa's filthy forehead repeatedly, the smile on her face dropping as soon as she noticed the dagger in her little sister's side.

Without waiting to be told, the other goblins jumped down into the water and waded towards them. One of them pulled off her cloak and passed the corners to her fellow goblins who gently pulled it under Systa. With two goblins on either side of her they held the edges of the cloak and lifted her to the height of their shoulders and out of the water before wading out of the river.

As gently as they could, they set her down by the riverside and two more goblins pulled off their cloaks to drape over her. Systa's lips were colourless and contorted into a pained grimace.

Ótama gently moved Systa's frozen fingers aside and looked at the wound, the skin around it surprisingly free of blood, the handle of the dagger acting like a plug.

"This, it's your dagger," Ótama said. Systa nodded. Ótama reached for the second cloak that covered Systa and began to tear it into long thin strips. "Hold her hands," she ordered.

With her eyes on her sister's face, Ótama clasped the dagger hilt. Slowly, she pulled it out and a rush of blood spurted from the wound. Next to her, one of the goblins took the rough bandages she had made from the cloak and pressed them down tightly over Systa's gushing side. Systa groaned in pain but otherwise did not move.

When the wound was covered, the other goblins lifted Systa up so Ótama could wrap a bandage around her waist.

"I...I'm the only one," Systa managed to mutter. "They're dead. Skógi, Skógi is dead. The dwarf who followed me killed him."

"We'll get you back home," Ótama reassured her, as they picked up the edges of the cloak and carried her towards the bison who were tethered to the nearby pine trees. Systa nodded but still did not say a word, her hand pressed over her side. Ótama mounted her bison first and reached down for her sister. "Put her behind me," she ordered. "And get me a rope! I don't want her to fall off."

As the goblins tied the two of them together, Ótama reached for her sister's hands and pulled them around her waist. "Stay awake little sister," she whispered over her shoulder.

Systa made a faint sound, somewhere between a groan and a mutter, and her fingers moved slightly against Ótama's hands.

As soon as the other goblins had mounted their bison they slowly rode out, Ótama afraid to ride too quickly incase it aggravated Systa's injury.

"Ride ahead!" Ótama ordered half of her group. "Let Ulf know that Systa is alive!"

* * *

As Ulf entered the tent, Ótama turned to look at him. Systa lay on the ground, cleaned and in fresh clothes but, even so, the smell of the sewers still permeated the air.

"She's alive," Ótama said, but her tone was grim.

Ulf nodded. "Good."

Gríð appeared with a large bowl of honey root soup. "Here, it will help." Ótama took it from her and gently lifted Systa's head so she could drink from it. She slurped at the soup at a painfully slow rate, her lips barely moving. Eventually, Ótama had to resort to pouring it into her half open mouth a drip at a time.

The tono had been blocked with a hide covering, the fire in the middle of the yurt the only source of light, the embers red and hot.

"Did she manage it?" Ulf asked quietly. "Is the city infected?"

Systa opened her eyes and looked at him. "Yes," she croaked, her eyes lighting up for a moment. Ótama, with her back to Ulf, did not turn around but continued to help Systa drink the soup, kneeling beside her.

Ulf watched her silently, a nervous worry in his gut. While he had prepared himself for the possibility of Systa's death, he had seen the vengeful expression on Ótama's face. He hoped that her anger would focus on the dwarfs, but if her sister died, he knew he would have to prepare himself for the possibility that his most powerful general would turn on him in anger.

"Gríð? Will you read the bones for Systa?" Ótama asked suddenly. A quick look passed between mother and son and Ulf nodded.

Gríð reluctantly reached into her pocket for a small bag, untied the string around it and poured out several bones into her open palm. She extended her hand to Ótama who took them and held them in her clasped hands tightly against her chest.

"Now drop them on the ground."

Ótama did as she was asked and the bone pieces splayed out haphazardly on the grass mats that covered the floor. Gríð crouched over them, a piece of honey root in her mouth and her brow furrowed in concentration.

There were no symbols on the bones, only deep lines carved into them, some with a single line, others with several. Gríð spat out the chewed piece of root and reached into another of her many pockets for a fresh piece, her eyes out of focus. Finally she looked down and, barely able to crouch, swayed slightly from side to side.

"I see…I see…" Gríð slurred, and her eyes flickered slightly. "A wolf leads our people across the plains to the mountains. The city will burn and fall before the wolf. I see you, Ótama, by its side."

"Systa. What about Systa?" Ótama asked anxiously. "Will she be saved?"

Ulf watched his mother, the nervous worry in his gut gone. He knew as well as Gríð did that her 'visions' were false; lucid dreams brought on by the honey root she loved to consume at a dangerous pace. It had not been the first time Gríð had convinced other goblins to follow her son without question through her false predictions. This would doubtlessly end as it always did, with a blind faith in the carefully constructed visions of his mother.

Suddenly, Gríð shouted as though she had been stabbed and stood up, her eyes wide open and wild. She flailed around theatrically for a few seconds and gasped, her performance so convincing that even Ulf felt slightly unsettled.

"The wolf will come to you, Ótama! The wolf will ask for your protection, and unless you protect you will lose everything you hold dear." With a groan, Gríð slumped onto the floor, panting like an animal. She opened her eyes and looked up at Ótama, sweat on her temples and both her pupils dilating and contracting at a frightening speed. She reached for the bones on the floor and scooped them into her hands.

Ótama looked down at Systa and held her hands, only the faintest trace of hope on her face.

Ulf walked towards his mother and helped her stand, her old body so light he could have picked her up in one arm. Without a word they both stepped out of Ótama's yurt, the sunlight blinding after the darkness inside.

"Thank you, Mother," Ulf said, as soon as they were out of earshot.

"You shouldn't encourage people to ask that of me!" Gríð snapped, as she walked into Ulf's yurt. "It's a dangerous thing to play with, superstition."

Ulf waited until the guards inside had left before he replied. "They're only bones, Mother, and you tell them what they want to hear. What harm is there in that?"

"No, Ulf, they hear what they want to hear and that is what is dangerous," Gríð argued, as she huddled in front of the low fire. "If I'm too specific they get suspicious, if I'm too vague it's open to interpretation, and interpretation can work against you."

Ulf shrugged his shoulders and his mother shook her head, reaching again into her pocket. "Good thing you married brains," she grumbled. "The sooner

Rakki is awake, the fewer stupid decisions you can make."

LIMITATIONS

Astrid scrubbed her tunic up and down the washboard as hard as she could, the dirt long gone, but still she ferociously dragged it up and down, the repetitive motion cathartic. The ends of her fingers were bright red and wrinkled from the cold river water.

Jarl had gone to try and calm Knud down, but Astrid could not find it in herself to follow him. The look Knud had given her was far worse than any scar she had earned over the course of the last few months.

The great outsider, Astrid, crying over the tantrum of a silly little boy! the harsh voice laughed. *He'll get over it. When you return he'll realise you were right.*

You're still angry at Dag. What if he does the same? the soft voice chimed in unhelpfully.

Astrid rubbed her tears away and tossed her tunic onto the dry rocks. Her veil was next. She snatched at it with her left arm and winced as a twinge of pain shot from her shoulder. Her hand shuddered for a second, her fingers curled into her palm, but still she ignored it and pushed the veil under the water. Just before she lost all control of her left arm she took her veil in her right hand and threw it onto the washing board. Her eyes closed and her face lifted up to the warm sunlight. She leant back on her heels and waited for the pain to pass.

Further down the river she could hear several of the other Vârcolac setting up their own washboards alongside the large flat rocks that littered the riverside. Sensing their gaze, Astrid untucked her hair from behind her ear to hide her tear-stained face. She had barely resumed control over her arm but she threw all her weight into the veil and pushed it up and down the washboard. A cloud of mud and blood squeezed out of it into the water.

She could feel the rips and burns in the cloth stretching but she ignored them until she heard the material rip loudly, and she peered down at the large tear half way down the veil. She cursed as loudly as she could and tossed it across the river where it fell with a loud 'spat' on the dry dirt.

Further down the river the Vârcolac muttered amongst themselves but none of them dared approach her, her hands bright blue with the glow of magic.

"If one of my daughters ever said that to me I would smack them to Nida and back!" Loba said, as she sat down next to her with Astrid's bow and a quiver of Vârcolac arrows in her hand.

"Knud isn't my son," Astrid muttered quietly.

"He's not Jarl's son, either." Astrid looked at Loba, confused. "I heard everything," Loba went on. "What he said was cruel, to both of you."

"He was just angry."

Loba scoffed. "If I said and did what I wanted when I was angry, a lot of people would be dead."

Astrid smiled, but her face quickly resumed a blank expression, both eyes on the ground.

"Here." Loba placed the arrow and full quiver into Astrid's lap. "We don't have many arrows but I thought you could use these when you leave."

Astrid took her bow from Loba and pulled one of the arrows back onto the string, the nock a little different to the human arrows she was used to, far less smooth and the arrow shaft far shorter.

"Will they do?" Loba asked.

Astrid straightened her back and pulled back on the string, the nock of the arrow against it, her eyes set on a tree across the river. With a jolt her entire left arm dropped to her side and shuddered uncontrollably. She gasped, her face contorted with pain, and the arrow bounced off the ground and into the river. Loba held Astrid's shoulder and tried to calm her as she curled up in a ball, her head against her knees, waiting for the pain to pass.

"Astrid, it's going to take a while for your arm to heal," Loba warned her.

"I don't understand! Why can't I heal myself? I have all this energy inside me just waiting to be used and I can't even shoot a damned arrow!"

"You can't trick magic. That wound will have to heal on its own or not at all."

"If Dag had taught me to use my magic this wouldn't have happened!" Astrid groaned, her teeth clenched as another spasm ran down her arm.

"This world would be a better place if warlocks just did what they were supposed to," Loba agreed, her hand gently rubbing Astrid's back. Astrid moaned in pain as several particularly vicious spasms wracked her arm. She bared her teeth, both eyes closed, ready to cry with frustration.

"I can't use the bow," she whispered through gritted teeth. "I can't lift my arm higher than my elbow."

"I'm not surprised. You need to wait for your shoulder to heal completely and then you will probably have to re-train every muscle in that arm."

"What?"

"Don't look at me like that! I'm just saying how it will be."

Astrid sat up and glared down at her arm, angry that for the first time she could not heal her own body. She felt trapped, stuck in a shell she could only partly control. The pain she could bear, but the helplessness was intolerable. "Knud, he must feel like this," she whispered under her breath.

Loba rolled her eyes and picked up Astrid's bow from where it had fallen, grumbling about how Knud's behaviour was hurtful and unjustifiable.

"Loba, please don't be harsh with him. He's afraid, he didn't mean what he said."

"If he didn't mean it then why did it hurt you so much to hear it?" Loba snapped, before taking a breath and calming herself. "I'll treat him exactly how I would my daughters while he's here," she reassured Astrid.

"That's what I'm worried about," Astrid replied, only half joking.

"I'm not that bad!"

"No, you're worse."

Loba got to her feet and waded across the river for Astrid's veil, the water barely reaching her calves. Astrid tried to take it from her as Loba sat back down but she would not hear of it.

"I wash, you talk!" Loba ordered, as she began to scrub the veil down the washboard, her method far less abrasive than Astrid's.

"The woman in the pass, is she still—?"

"She's gone," Loba interrupted. "Bugal searched the entire Three Sisters Pass. She wasn't there."

Astrid nodded and sat silently, lost in her own thoughts.

"You are terrible at talking, you know that? I'm going to die of boredom. Talk!"

"About what?"

"The dwarf...he seems—"

"No!" Astrid said. "I don't want to talk about him."

"Why not?"

Astrid shrugged her shoulders and Loba let out an exasperated sigh. "I just want to know a little bit more about him. I thought you would be happy about that."

Astrid raised an eyebrow and looked at her blankly. "No," she repeated.

"I'm not asking about both of you, I'm just asking about him. You said he was from some dwarf city but you didn't tell me anything else."

"He's from Bjargtre, it's in the west."

Loba smiled and pounced on her small window of opportunity, another question out of her mouth almost before Astrid had finished speaking.

"How old is he?"

Astrid shook her head. "If I tell you that you'll just say he's old."

"I'd say he's…thirty? Forty?" Loba guessed out loud. Astrid's face was still blank. "Fifty?"

"He's younger than Bugal," Astrid replied, before Loba got close to Jarl's real age.

"All of Ammasteinn is younger than Bugal!" Loba scoffed. "Now come on, tell me his age, I won't make a face, I promise."

"He's one hundred and twenty five," Astrid said quickly and Loba's face twisted into a revolted frown. "See?" Astrid held her hand up and pointed at Loba accusingly. "You said you wouldn't make a face!"

"He's so…old!"

"Dwarves age differently, you know that."

"I know, but still, he would have white hair if he was a Vârcolac. Not black hair. He looks barely past thirty."

"Well, he's a dwarf."

"I know!" Loba laughed out loud. "You look so strange together!" Astrid looked at her indignantly and Loba quickly explained her meaning. "You always looked like an elf, you move like an elf and he, well, he looks and moves like a dwarf."

I wonder if people thought that about Mātīr and Faðir? the quiet voice thought. Instantly, the harsh voice chuckled back.

I'm sure they did, right before they killed them.

Astrid's face twitched and she shook her head to try and silence the voices.

"Astrid?" Loba asked, worried that her arm had begun to hurt again. "Do you want more honey root?"

"No. I've had enough of that."

"If you need it for the pain you should take it," Loba urged, but Astrid shook her head.

"I don't like what it does to my mind."

Loba shrugged her shoulders and pulled the veil off the wash board. Not so much as a single grain of dirt remained on the silky black material. "Fine, but I'm going to put some in your bag before you go, just in case."

"There's no point. You can find it all over the plains."

"Yes, all over the plains where some Kelic probably pissed all over it. I'm packing you some of mine and I don't care if you don't like it," Loba insisted, as she picked up Astrid's wet clothes from the rocks and slung them over her shoulder.

"Fine," Astrid conceded, aware that there was no point in arguing with her on the merits of honey-root. "I'll take some."

As they left the river, Astrid reached down with her good arm to pick up the her bow. Loba watched as she ran her fingers over it with a sad expression on her face. "You're not going to take it with you, are you?"

Astrid shook her head. "No. There's no point. I can't shoot with my arm like this."

Loba took the bow in her spare hand. "I'll keep it safe until you come back," she said. "Then you can take it, and the boy, back."

BAD OMENS

"Halvard! Halvard, wake up!"

The first things he noticed as he opened his eyes were the overwhelming smell of garlic and incense assaulting his nose, a bright light held not far from his face, and Eilíf next to the bed.

"Eilíf?"

"You need to get up! The captain is outside!"

Halvard dragged himself to his feet, his head still foggy from sleep. "What time is it?"

"Dawn."

He groaned. It had taken him three baths to get the smell of the sewers off his skin and he was sure his hair still carried some traces of it. "What does he want?"

Eilíf was silent and Halvard noticed the frightened look on her face. "It's back," she whispered.

"What is?"

"The Red Plague."

It was only as she said the words that Halvard realised he could hear the wailing outside. The city bell echoed through the tunnel outside the house, a low deep 'clang' which vibrated with each strike. As quickly as he could, he dressed and rushed outside, his hair uncombed. Captain Gauss was waiting for him, his face ashen.

Halvard took a moment to observe the chaos. From every building, small plumes of smoke trickled out of the windows and doors. Anything remotely fragrant had been piled into incense burners in an attempt to keep the disease at bay. There were hundreds of people in the street, all standing apart from fear of infection. Some shouted, others shrieked. They were terrified.

"We need to get to the palace. Now!" Captain Gauss ordered.

Halvard followed him and did his best to braid his still damp hair as they ran through the city but after a few minutes he gave up; his appearance would be the last thing on anyone's mind.

The atmosphere was frightening; there were screams in every corner. He saw a young dwarf stumble and fall to the floor, her shoulders shuddering violently as she threw up a mixture of blood and vomit. Most ran from her, others threw dirt at her.

"Stop!" Halvard shouted, and raced up to the woman.

"Halvard! Leave her!"

Halvard ignored the captain and placed his arms around her. Her head hung to the side and she threw up again as he lifted her from the ground. The captain recoiled.

"What are you doing? She's sick!"

"I'm not leaving her in the street! She'll get trampled!" Halvard insisted.

"You'll get infected! Put her down! That's an order!"

"I didn't get sick last time! I won't now!"

The woman shook violently, the whites of her eyes bloodshot, almost completely red. He held her tighter as she nearly rolled out of his arms.

Before Captain Gauss could bellow at him, there was a loud crash in the plaza and a great fire lit up the platform that held the bodies of the goblins. They both ran as fast as they could towards it and looked on in horror at the crowd that had gathered. The air buzzed with loud, angry voices. Fists were raised in the air. Nobody bothered to put the fire out, even the guards watched as it burned, the dead bodies on it roasting like meat on a spit. The entire frame was consumed within minutes.

"Filthy monsters!"

"It's an Omen! The boy king brought this on us!"

"We need to get to the palace," Halvard said, turning to run. The dwarf in his arms jostled as he ran but he did not slow down.

When they reached the palace they saw a line of soldiers in front of it, though they were spaced out far too much, everyone afraid to stand too close to each other. Scarves, clothes and even old rags were tied across their faces to cover their mouths. Huge streams of smoke rose up from the multiple burners that had been placed along the steps.

In front of them an old dwarf stood, one eye completely white, blinded from an injury earned decades previously. His white hair was twisted into several long braids that hung down his back. Heavy armour covered him, every piece with the mark of a spear or a sword on it.

"Stand closer!" he barked. The soldiers did as he'd asked but only by a little; there was still a clear space between them all. Halvard laid the dwarf on the steps of the palace before he turned and took his place in the line.

"Soldier! What are you doing? Put that woman somewhere else!" the general barked.

"She's sick, sir!" Halvard replied, standing to attention.

"So is half the city! Move her somewhere else!"

Before Halvard could obey, there was a loud roar behind them as a massive wave of people burst out of the tunnels towards the palace with torches and weapons in their hands. Wide eyed, they shrieked like rabid animals as they approached.

"Hold your ground!" the general ordered and turned to face the crowd, his sword drawn. Halvard spotted the three siblings not far from him, their faces pale and frightened, though Rakel did her best not to show it.

"Heads up!" Halvard hissed over at them. "Don't let them see you're frightened!"

Rakel nodded and did as he'd said before she began to cough a little. The soldier to her right looked over nervously and shuffled away from her. Even her two siblings moved a little.

"You!" Captain Gauss shouted, pointing at her. "Are you sick?"

"No!" Rakel exclaimed, before she began to cough again.

"Go! Now! Straight home!"

"But sir..."

"Now!"

With her head bowed, Rakel left the line and pushed her way through the people, who separated like a curtain to let her through.

Screams of "the king...where is the king?" rose up in the crowd. The soldiers lining the steps did their best to appear unmoved, but from the corner of his eye Halvard was able to see more than one hand around the shaft of a spear that was shaking.

"The king brought this on us! It's an omen!" a woman shrieked, her shrill voice ripping at the ears of those close to her.

"Go back home!" the general yelled, his powerful voice carrying to the very back of the crowd. "The more people in the streets, the faster the Red Plague will spread!"

A few of the dwarves turned to leave but for the majority that remained, his demand only enraged them more.

"The King! Bring him out! He brought this on us!"

The noise increased, the sound echoing off the rock-face walls and down into the marble courtyard of the palace.

"The king! Bring the king out!"

There was a loud commotion and suddenly every eye in the crowd looked up at the palace balcony. A small frightened little face peered over it, barely tall enough to prop his chin on the ledge. Prince Hálfr stood beside him, his arm around his older brother's shoulder.

With a roar the crowd surged forward and the soldiers locked their spears together in an attempt to hold them back.

"He'd better get back inside," the soldier next to Halvard muttered. "He's just going to make it worse!"

From up on the balcony, the young boy king stared out, terrified. Several thrown rocks clattered against the palace walls and the king stepped back, startled. Hálfr quickly helped him back inside but the crowd only screamed louder.

"Come out! See what you've done to us! Come out, boy king!

Halvard felt the back of his foot hit the first step of the palace and he pushed back at the crowd with all his might. A reinforcement of soldiers from inside the palace rushed out and lined up behind them.

From far back in the crowd there was a horrible shriek, the sound so high pitched Halvard thought his ears might bleed. The crowd in front of him suddenly parted and stumbled back from the figure who had made his way through.

Every soldier stared in horror at the young dwarf who approached. Blood ran like tears from his eyes and he dropped to his knees and coughed up a pool of red, fleshy vomit.

"A wolf! A wolf!" he screamed. "A wolf will take the city!"

There was a horrible silence. Halvard looked back at the palace for a moment and saw the small frightened face of the boy king look over the balcony edge, his brother beside him, and Yrsa Gull skulking in the background, clearly terrified and half hidden by the thick red curtain that hung behind the balcony.

The man threw up again, more blood than vomit. He screamed and writhed in pain, his hands over his ears he clutched at his head in agony. "The wolf, the wolf is coming!"

There was complete hysteria in the crowd and Halvard turned to the captain.

"Shut him up!" Captain Gauss hissed.

Halvard laid his spear on the ground, worried that if he approached the dying dwarf with it in his hands the crowd would only become more enraged, and he slowly walked towards him.

The dwarf fell into a huddle on the floor, both arms limp, his chest convulsing violently. Halvard had seen enough of the Red Plague to know there was nothing to be done. He would be dead within a few minutes. He knelt beside the young dwarf and held his head gently to the side so that he would not choke on the blood he was coughing up from his lungs. "It's alright," he whispered. "It will all be over in a moment."

"The wolf! The wolf!" the dwarf gargled.

"The wolf isn't here yet," Halvard said gently, and pulled the dwarf's long hair out of his face. "Just breathe. It will soon be over."

The man's eyes closed a little. He was somewhat calmed by Halvard's presence, but still he struggled. Horrible gargled breaths caught in his throat several times, only to be followed by trickles of blood from his mouth. Halvard closed his eyes for a moment. A steam of terrible memories flooded back to him.

Jóð and Jón had died like this, just minutes after their parents. As much as he had disliked Jarl's older brothers, he would not have wished the way they had died on anyone. He remembered the look on Jarl's face when he had come round, dazed and in pain. He was alive, yet his world was crumbling around him.

The dwarf's breaths became longer and less frequent; his eyes and hands twitched. "Not long now. Don't worry, the pain will soon be gone."

With a small shudder, the dwarf's head curled back and arched with his spine. Both hands curled in on each other, a goblin cuff gripped tightly in one of them, the wolf head only just visible between his fingers.

"There." Halvard laid him down on the ground and stood up. "No more pain."

COME BACK SOON

Knud had not spoken to Jarl for the past few days, and Astrid he would not even look at. The atmosphere was awkward and tense. He would not even apologise for the bruise he had left on the side of Astrid's face when he had hit her, and Astrid did not heal it or ask him to say sorry, even when Jarl had insisted he did. It was an order Knud had deliberately ignored. His angry words burned into Astrid's mind every time she looked at him.

Loba, despite her initial reservations, did her best to lighten the mood. She even went so far as to insist her two daughters invite Knud to play with the other children, an order that had backfired spectacularly. With his crutch, Knud could not keep up with the other children and eventually, at the first chance they got, they left him on his own in the middle of the forest. Knud had returned in tears a few hours later, angry at himself and even angrier at Astrid who, in his mind, was the one to blame.

But when Knud woke a few days later in an empty room and walked outside to see Jarl tying his bag to the back of a pony, he ran up to him and hugged him as tightly as he could.

"Come back as fast as you can!" Knud begged, and Jarl knelt down in front of him, a relieved smile on his face. He had not wanted to leave without saying goodbye.

"Of course I will. Now you be good," he warned him, and ruffled Knud's red hair fondly.

Knud sniffed but managed a smile. "I will."

Jarl laughed and hugged him, reluctant to let go. "You'd better be!"

Astrid's Vârcolac clothes were gone and instead she wore her own black clothes, which had been cleaned and patched. Numerous stitches held her veil together where it had been torn and burned. Her hair was tied into a bun and covered by the veil and the wolf skin, though her face was visible. She waited quietly, hopeful that Knud would have a goodbye hug for her too, but her face dropped as he glared at her over Jarl's shoulder. She quickly pulled her veil across her face to hide her sadness.

Most of the Vârcolac had come out to say their goodbyes to Astrid and they crowded around her, though all the children stayed away. To them she was still a stranger and, as ugly as Bugal was, they had grown up with him and were used to the sight of his face, whereas Astrid's scars frightened them. Even Loba's daughters looked at her suspiciously.

"You'd better hurry back," Loba warned Astrid and she held her hands tightly. "I've packed enough food on the pony for you to get there and back."

Astrid smiled and pulled her into a hug. "Thank you. And thank you for lending us the pony."

"Just bring it back alive," Loba joked. "I'll need him for the harvest."

Astrid turned to Bugal, crouching down so that she was at his height. "Take care of him," she whispered, so that Knud could not hear. "Don't let him do anything stupid."

"If he's been around you then it is really not my fault if he does," Bugual laughed back at her.

Jarl mounted the pony and, used to much taller and heavier riders, the animal shook its head as though it were surprised, though it quickly realised its new rider would not allow it to misbehave. Jarl's grip on the reins was firm.

Astrid stood in front of Knud for a moment before they left, hopeful that Knud would at least look at her, but he did not. Both his eyes were on the ground. Crestfallen, she turned away.

As Jarl and Astrid left, Loba approached Knud who looked up at her suspiciously. "You should say goodbye, it's bad luck not to," she warned. Knud ignored her and hobbled back down into the tunnel.

Neither of them spoke as they journeyed out of the Aldwood, their minds back with Knud and Loba. Desperate to be out of there as quickly as possible, Astrid took the form of her wolf skin and ran as fast as her injured arm allowed, though after a few minutes she was forced to admit defeat and run in her human form. The pony, quite used to the Vârcolac and their various animal transformations, was completely unfazed by her transformation and easily kept up with her.

They reached the pass out of the Aldwood within a few hours, just as the sun had risen over the mountains.

Despite Loba's reassurances that the woman was not in the pass, Astrid could not help but feel apprehensive as they walked through it, her hammer ax in her hand. But nothing could prepare her for the sight of what remained of the Frøðleikr trees. Even Jarl was shocked as he saw their charred remains, the pines burned to a cinder, the branches consumed, only the lower part of the trunks left. Astrid shivered, the magic in the air so strong she could feel it tingle between the ends of her fingertips.

"What's wrong?" Jarl asked when he saw her eyes widen with fear.

"I've never felt magic like this before," Astrid explained. "Dag's magic felt a little like this. We should go." Jarl did not argue with her suggestion.

Their journey through the rest of the pass was uneventful. The Frǫðleikr trees on either side of the pass shifted a little as they walked through, and Jarl could have sworn he saw one or two of them slowly turn, watching them like sentinels.

Eventually he dismounted the pony so he could hold Astrid's hand as they walked. Even now she would not walk close to the creature and would flinch each time it came too close to her. With a smile, he reached up to her veil and pulled it away before placing a kiss on her surprised lips. Astrid shook her head and smiled at him before her expression returned to the worried frown she had worn for the past few hours.

"He didn't mean it, you know," Jarl said eventually. "He's just afraid. He did the same thing with Knute when his mother died."

"What, he said he hated him?" Astrid replied.

"He blamed Knute for it, then he blamed me. Eventually he stopped blaming anyone."

Astrid nodded but the frown did not leave her face. "After all this, after Lǫgberg, we could take him to Dag. Maybe he could help?" Astrid suggested. "With his leg."

"Would he help?"

Astrid clenched her jaw. "He will, I'll make sure of it."

"What are you going to do? Fight him?" Jarl laughed.

"No, I'm going to tell him if he won't help I won't come back to the Heilagr forest. He wouldn't help me with Ragi, but he will help me with Knud."

"Astrid, I don't think there's any kind of magic that will grow Knud's foot back for him," Jarl replied, a little surprised that Astrid would think to threaten a warlock.

"He can try. It would be the least he could do." She looked at Jarl and noticed his apprehensive expression. "Dag and I, we haven't been on very good terms for a while," she explained. "Each time I go back he keeps asking me to stay with him and I try to tell him of the people I've helped, but he never listens. This glaze goes down over his eyes and I can tell his mind is miles away. I've asked him to teach me magic so many times so that I can help people but he won't listen! And when I ask him to use his own magic to help people like he should, he always says: 'it's not my place to fix the world.'" Astrid growled, kicking at the ground. "He's a warlock. All he does is complain about how broken Ammasteinn is, but he never tires to change it!"

"What if we meet him and he hates me?" Jarl said, a grin on his face. Astrid laughed out loud as she imagined how Dag would react, then the smile faded as she predicted the outcome.

"I don't think he would do anything. I think he would just shrug his shoulders and tell me it's a mistake, like he always does."

"So if a warlock won't like me, why do I get the feeling I might not survive a visit to the Heilagr forest?" Jarl joked, and Astrid barely grinned.

"Jarl, why did you get so angry with Knud? I've never seen you talk to him like that before."

Jarl shook his head and scratched at his beard. "I don't know. I just thought I'd raised him better than that."

"Better than what?"

He reached into his cloak and pulled out a rectangular tablet which he passed to Astrid. It was made from what appeared to be pure silver and gold with an emblem sealed on the front and a scrawl on the back, which Astrid assumed was Mál, though she could not read it. Her knowledge of the dwarf language was limited to speaking only.

"Every noble family has one of those," Jarl said, his face set in a grim frown. "If you become an Ósómi you lose your family name and they take that from you. I nearly lost my family name before because of my mother. When the Red Plague infected the city, people became desperate, they were buying from anyone who claimed they had a cure and paying everything they had. My mother sent for a human healer from Einn she had heard of and smuggled her in."

Jarl took the plaque and held it in his free hand. The gold and silver was polished smooth in the middle from the countless times he had run his fingers over its surface.

"A neighbour spotted her and insisted the healer saw her son first or she would tell the guards. My mother refused and the healer saw me before the guards came and threw her out of the city. I had caught the plague first and she was sure I was going to die." Jarl cleared his throat and paused for a few moments. "The healer, her face was disfigured. She had these burns on one side of her face. People kept saying she couldn't be good because she was ugly, but they were happy to buy from any dwarf on a corner who said inhaling frankincense would help!"

He stopped for a moment and looked at Astrid, his face as hard as stone but his eyes deeply hurt as he replayed the events in his head.

"Because my family died in the plague, the king decided we had been punished enough and didn't take my name from me. But I've always remembered how they looked at that woman when they took her away. She saved my life, but because she was ugly they treated her like filth. I've always remembered that, and Knud, he was talking like they did. I don't want him to grow up like them."

Astrid did not know how to respond at first. She was sad for Jarl but not at all shocked by his story. "Is that why you're not afraid of losing your family name?"

"I am afraid," Jarl admitted. "I was still ill when I got the summons to see the king, that was after..." Jarl cleared his throat, a lump in the back of it. "They'd all died the day before. I remember being so angry. My mother was just trying to save her family, and if we'd just had more time then the healer might have saved them, too. I wanted them to take it at first - the plaque, my name - I thought it couldn't get any worse. But it's my family's name, too, and it's all I have left of them now." Jarl forced a smile and put the plaque back inside his tunic. "I gave my family home to Holmvé before I left, so they can't take that from me at least."

* * *

They reached the end of the pass close to nightfall and made camp between the thin tree-line and the plains. Astrid had warned Jarl about the the plains past the Riddari Kviðr, but he had not been prepared to see such a stark and barren wasteland. The few trees past the mountain pass were battered by the cold winds that ripped at the mountainside.

"Well, at least the pony won't go hungry," Jarl joked, looking out over miles upon miles of long grass. He dismounted and undid the reins. "Is it safe to start a fire?"

Astrid glanced around . "The trees here aren't Frǫðleikr…but it's probably safer if we don't. We don't want to draw attention to ourselves."

"How can you tell?" Jarl asked.

"I can feel it. You know that feeling you get at the back of your neck when someone is watching you?" Jarl nodded. "I get that at the ends of my fingers."

Jarl led the pony out into the plains to allow it to eat. Astrid was alongside him, her eyes like a hawk's. She could not see anything for miles other than the wind blowing ripples through the grass, but she knew that did not always mean there was nothing out there.

"You said you went to Waidu before?" Jarl asked. Astrid nodded, her back to him, both eyes looking out.

"A few times. There used to be a lot more trade between the humans from the Gold Coast and Waidu."

"And you helped them travel there?"

"Yes." Suddenly, a thought occurred to her and she turned to look at him, a smile on her face. "Jarl, would you want to see the Gold Coast?"

"What?" He laughed, surprised by her unexpected question.

"The Gold Coast, or Bayswater, would you want to see them?"

Jarl thought for a moment. "Yes, I think I would."

Astrid smiled, an excited look in her eyes as the beginning of an idea began to form in her mind.

"Why?" Jarl asked, a grin at the corner of his mouth.

"You would like it, I think. It's warm. Knud would love it, too."

Jarl faked a loud sigh. "The heat and me don't mix, especially with a beard."

"Oh," Astrid replied, a little disappointed.

" I was joking!" He laughed and Astrid's smile returned.

As soon as the pony had had its full of grass they walked back into the forest and huddled together under one of the larger trees, the pony tethered not too far from them.

"I'm taking the first watch," Jarl insisted, his arm around her, careful not to put any pressure over her injured one. "How's your shoulder?"

"It's fine." Jarl raised an eyebrow at her. "It hurts a little," Astrid admitted.

"You should sleep. And if it still hurts by morning you should let me have a look at it."

Astrid nodded and leant her head against him. "It doesn't hurt much. I'll be fine by morning."

A TRICK OF THE LIGHT

The dwarf glanced around, his face battered, barely able to see through the blood that trickled down into his eyes from the large cut along his hairline.

He knew he was in some kind of tent. His hands were tied behind his back around a pole, which had been hammered into the ground just for him. Nobody had come into the tent for hours, even though he could see the shadow of guards outside and a large fire burning nearby.

For the hundredth time he tried to break through the ropes that held his hands behind him, his face bright red as he pulled with all his might. But all he succeeded in doing was leaving an even deeper rope burn around his wrists. The ends of his fingers were slightly blue, the blood trapped in them for far longer than was safe.

Mad with pain and fear, he looked through the open doorway at the fire that burned outside and wondered what horrible fate awaited him. As much as he was afraid of death, now he just wanted it all to be over, the waiting a slow form of torture.

Suddenly, a cold hand touched his arm. Before he could scream a second hand covered his mouth firmly.

"Shhh! I'm here to help you!" a woman's voice whispered in his ear, her voice slow and slightly slurred.

The dwarf held his breath, his heart in his chest, as he felt a knife cutting at the ropes behind him. As soon as the last thread broke he crawled away towards the doorway but the woman quickly pulled him back, the knife she had used to cut the ropes pressed tightly against his throat.

"Not that way, fool! Go through the back!"

The dwarf glanced behind him and saw that a large hole had been cut through the lattice and hides. "Why are you helping me?" he gasped, afraid that at any second the knife would slice its way across his neck.

"Because Ulf is a madman! He destroyed my tribe and now he has his army there's nothing to stop him taking Bjargtre."

"Nobody can take Bjargtre!" the dwarf scoffed. The woman pressed the knife down a little harder.

"With a hundred thousand goblins, he can take what he wants!" she warned, and the dwarf's eyes opened so wide they threatened to fall from his head.

"A hundred thousand?"

'Yes, you see now? He must be stopped!"

The woman let go of him and he turned to look at her. Her face was old and haggard and she had two distinctive black strands of hair that ran down the sides of it, the tips dyed by some kind of red pigment. The rest of her hair was pure white. She pointed with the knife at the opening she had cut at the back of the yurt.

"Go that way! I will distract the guards and then you must run south towards Bjargtre. Don't stop until you get there; I can't distract them forever."

The dwarf did not need to be told twice. He ran out of the tent so fast he did not see Ulf in the shadows, his blue eyes glinting in the moonlight. Ulf watched as the dwarf stumbled through the abandoned camp, not a soul in sight.

"I am a madman, am I?" He laughed quietly as his mother walked out of the yurt and stood next to him.

"If I tell him the truth he's more likely to believe me."

The dwarf did not turn around until he had passed the very last yurt, too afraid to consider why there had not been more guards around. When he did turn around though, he gasped with shock and fell to the floor in horror.

The camp seemed to stretch out for miles along the horizon. Torch after torch was burning in the night, the line so long that he could not see where it ended. From what he saw before him he knew that the army at Ulf's disposal was at least two, if not three times larger than any in Bjargtre.

With a renewed sense of terror he scrambled to his feet and ran, this time fuelled not only by fear for his own life but for the life of every dwarf in Bjargtre.

Ulf watched from the camp line and smiled.

In the darkness, the dwarf had been unable to see that the camp had been laid out in a line for a mile. Beyond that, hundreds of flimsy grass men had been constructed to create the illusion of an army ten times the size of his own, a torch hammered into the ground every fifty yards.

Ulf watched in silence until the dwarf's figure could no longer be seen, with his mother beside him. Gríð tilted her head to the side and grinned. "I wish I could see them, the fear in their faces," she said.

"We will have to attack the city soon," Ulf replied.

"If they send for help from Lǫgberg, we may only have three months to take it." Gríð smiled up at her son.

"Fear and sickness can do a lot in three months, and we should only need one to break through the Mad Gate."

GHOST

Knud scraped the knife under the apple skin, turning it slowly in his hand. After having peeled what must have been at least two hundred apples, the motion had become quite natural to him. A pile of apple skins collected at his foot, next to his crutch that was propped against the back of his chair.

Several other Vârcolac sat along the long, rough table that was not much more than a series of long boards propped up by several wooden poles thrust into the earth.

Knud was at the far end of the table, a pile of unpeeled apples in front of him. Earlier that morning there had been other Vârcolac children to help: Lina, Nos, Trid and Riik. They had spoken to him for a little while but, as soon at the other adults had turned their backs, they had run into the forest. Knud had been unable to follow them as he wasn't fast enough to keep up.

Beside him, the other Vârcolac laughed and talked among themselves as they sliced the apples into thin strips and laid them on large mesh-like cloths strung up on a wooden frame. As soon as one frame had been covered with the thin slices, one of them would take the tray from the table and out into the sun to dry them. A few Vârcolac stood guard nearby with long willow brushes, which they whisked over the mesh frames every few minutes to keep the wasps and the flies away.

Every half hour or so, a large group would approach the table with baskets full of freshly picked apples. The pile of apples in front of Knud grew faster than he could peel them and eventually hid did not try to keep up, his face lost, lonely and bored.

He had slept dreadfully the last few days, ashamed to admit to himself more than to anyone else that he did not like to sleep alone. To make matters worse, Astrid was no longer there to absorb the pain from his leg. More than once he had woken up screaming in pain, only to scream again when Bugal would rush in to ask what was wrong. Bugal's ugly face was the last thing he wanted to see while his head was still half trapped in a nightmare.

Knud reached for another apple but the man beside him, noticing it was rotten, took it and tossed it into a nearby basket.

"That be for the Pyre!" he said.

"The what?"

"The Pyre. Tomorrow we burn all the bad fruit for the Autumn Offering."

Knud looked at him, confused.

The Vârcolac man shook his head at him. "Don't worry. You'll see it soon enough."

Knud took another apple and peeled it, his mind a million miles away. He wondered where Astrid and Jarl would be, but most of all he wondered how soon they would return. Absentmindedly, he looked out into the forest. The sun was high up in the sky and light beams trickled their way through the trees. The air was pleasantly warm, though the wind carried the early touches of late autumn on it. Some of the leaves on the trees were already speckled with shades of gold and red.

Not far from him he noticed something move, a pale outline like a puff of white dust. Curious, he put down the knife and reached for his crutch. The other Vârcolac were too busy to notice him leave the table, most of them deep in conversation. Slowly, he hobbled over to the tree and the shape up in the branches moved again. He was sure he could see the outline of a face, except it was pale, as transparent as glass. He stared up into the branches and the face stared back.

"Hello?" Knud whispered.

The shape moved again, this time further into the forest through the treetops. Knud followed it as quickly as he could. "Hello?" Knud repeated, the Vârcolac so far behind him now he could barely hear their laugher.

After a few minutes he could not hear them at all and he turned to see if the table was still visible from where he stood. But when he turned back to look up into the treetops, the face was gone.

"Hello?" a small voice whispered behind him, its voice barely a foot away.

Knud jumped in shock and nearly lost his balance. The shape moved towards him to help him stand, and Knud felt a pressure on his skin for a few seconds before its fingers passed right through him.

"Are you a ghost?" Knud said, stepping back, frightened.

"I am no ghost!" the creature snapped.

Knud stared at it, or him or her, he wasn't sure which. He suspected it was female from the tone of its voice, an odd sound like a crystal flute, but otherwise he could not tell.

She was tall, a good foot taller than him, and whatever she was made of he doubted it was flesh and bone. She did not stand in front of him, instead she hovered on her toes. With each light gust of wind her whole body lifted from the ground and then floated gently back down. Her long, knee-length white hair was so thin and light it looked like the silky threads of spiders' webs. Her whole body was translucent.

"I'm a Sylph!"

"What's a Sylph? Is that like a ghost?"

"What are you?" she asked back. "Some kind of dwarf?" She pushed her toes against the ground and hovered up onto the branch of a nearby tree.

"Yes," Knud nodded. "I'm from Bjargtre."

"Oh, Bjargtre." The Sylph stepped off the branch and floated down to the ground where she sat cross-legged on the grass in front of him, her hands knotted into the grass beside her like anchors so that she didn't float away. "I've never seen a dwarf before."

"I've never seen a...Sylph before. What's your name?"

"What's yours?"

"Knud."

"Knud," she repeated, her head tilted to the side. "Mine's Vivilla."

Knud sat down and studied her curiously. Vivilla did the same.

"Wh...why can I see through you?" Knud asked.

"Because I'm not Knāto yet."

"Knāto?"

"Flesh. I'll grow my skin when I'm seventeen."

"How old are you?"

"How old are you?" she asked defensively.

"I'm twenty two."

"What? You look like a baby!"

Knud glared at her. "I'm a dwarf! We don't age as fast as humans."

"I'm fifteen." She laughed at the indignant expression on his face.

"You're the baby!" Knud grumbled.

"At least I don't look like one!"

"Well at least I don't look like glass!"

Vivilla stepped back, Knud not able to make out the expression on her face, but he guessed that he had offended her. She looked as though she was about to float away.

"But you have both your feet, so I guess I lose," Knud said quickly, and lifted his stump up so she could see it.

Vivilla stat down again and stared at him, shocked and then morbidly interested. "Can I touch it?"

Knud shrugged his shoulders and Vivilla moved her hand across the end of his leg. Her fingers felt cold as they touched the severed limb, and one by one each finger passed through his leg. The idea of a body which could be hurt enough to lose a limb was fascinating and frightening to her all at once.

"What happened?"

"A bear!" Knud lied, a grin on his face. "A huge bear! It was two...no three times bigger than me! It attacked our group but I held it off!"

"With what?" Vivilla asked, a transparent eyebrow raised in disbelief.

"My leg!" Knud improvised quickly. "It had eaten my sword and..."

"It ate your sword?"

"Yes! Everyone else was frightened, so I attacked it with my bare hands! It bit on to my leg and swallowed my foot so I strangled it to death! But by then my foot was gone!"

Vivilla burst into a fit of laugher, the sound like dozens of crystal bells. Had she been a dwarf, Knud would have been insulted by her reaction, but after a week with the Vârcolac he was desperate for any kind of social interaction. He was relieved to have an audience who would listen to him. "What really happened?" she asked.

"I got caught in a trap."

"A bear trap?" Vivilla joked.

"A goblin trap."

"Does it hurt?"

"Sometimes," Knud admitted. "Sometimes my foot feels like it's still there, too."

Vivilla reached out again and swept her hand over the stump.

"Can you feel anything?" he asked her.

"Of course I can!"

"Then why does your hand go through my leg?"

"It just does."

Knud reached out for her hand and passed his fingers through hers, the sensation as if he had run his hand through a vent of cold air. "You're so cold!"

"I'm a Sylph. We're meant to be cold."

"Can…can you walk through a tree?"

Vivilla looked at him, Knud vaguely able to make out an unimpressed expression on her face. She pushed past him and floated towards the tree beside them, her feet barely touching the ground. Slowly, she pushed herself through it with a sound like ice breaking. As she came out the other side she turned to look at him triumphantly. "I can go through almost anything!"

"Almost?"

"Stone is a little hard to pass through. It used to be easy."

"Why?"

"I was more air when I was younger. I become more Knāto each year. Soon I should have my wings!"

She smiled proudly, her face shimmering like water ripples.

"You get wings? Can't you fly now? It looks like you are."

"No," she said sadly, and shuffled her feet. "I just float for the moment."

Knud looked around as he heard one of the Vârcolac call for him. Vivilla looked up, frightened, but she did not leave. "Are you going to go?"

Knud looked at her. *She's lonely,* he thought, a little relieved to see someone as lonely as he was. "No." He picked up his crutch and hobbled further into the forest. "They can find someone else to help."

Vivilla floated alongside him as he made his way further through the trees. Knud did his best to move as quickly as he could but he still found the crutch heavy and hard to use, not to mention mildly uncomfortable as it was a little too tall for him.

"Do you need any help?"

"No," Knud replied. "I'm just getting used to this stupid thing."

Vivilla suddenly ran up behind him and pushed his back with all her might. For a few seconds Knud was lifted into the air as though a strong gust of wind had swept him off his feet before he gently landed on the ground.

"Wow!' Knud laughed. "That was amazing!" Vivilla smiled proudly.

"Come on, it'll be faster this way!"

It wasn't faster. In fact they covered far less ground, but Knud didn't care to point it out. The weightless feeling for the few moments that he was lifted from the ground was quite addictive and he was able to forget he was a cripple for a few seconds before he landed again. "If I jump off something, would you be able to catch me?"

"I don't know, we can try."

Knud looked around and saw a large rock not far away. He hobbled over to it and managed to scramble on top, wobbling slightly as he balanced on his one foot.

"Jump!" Vivilla said.

Knud threw himself forward into the air and Vivilla rose up to catch him. For a few seconds he hovered, his stomach in a knot at the strange sensation. With his arms outstretched he laughed, a huge smile on his face for the first time in days.

When Vivilla was not able to hold him up any more, he fell down onto the ground with a thud. The ripe plums that covered the ground crushed beneath him.

"Wow! That was amazing!" Knud laughed. "Can we try again?"

Vivilla shook her head. "I can't do it for long. I'm not strong enough."

As Knud leant over to pick up his crutch, he noticed a ripe plum on the ground by his feet. A cheeky grin spread across his face.

Vivilla gasped as the fruit half-hit half-passed through her. The stone hit the floor but the flesh slid down her face leaving a trail of bright purple plum juice.

"Why did you do that?"

Knud shrugged his shoulders and grinned. "I wanted to see what would happen." He laughed and pointed at her head. "The stone went right through you."

Vivilla glared at him and reached down to the ground to sweep as many ripe fruits into her arms as possible. A few of the heavier ones instantly fell through her arms, but the rest teetered perilously in her hands.

Knud grabbed hold of his crutch and tried to scuttle away as he realised she was about to retaliate. Vivilla, now armed, threw them as hard as she could, but most of them slid through her arms and fell to the ground. She stooped to pick up more, unable to hold anything for long.

"It's not funny!" She tossed an apple after him but missed.

"It is!" Knud cackled. "I hit your brain!"

Vivilla reached into her head and pulled out the plum stone that floated inside before throwing it back at him.

For a moment Knud forgot about his leg, his crutch on the ground. Vivilla was covered in rotten fruit remains, her outline more visible. Knud did not look much better.

"Knud!" a worried voice called from the forest behind him. It was Loba. She did not sound happy.

"I should probably go." He reached for his crutch but before he could do his best to run away, Vivilla floated up into the branches above him and shook them as hard as she could. A shower of ripe and rotten fruit pelted down on top of him.

"I win!" she laughed.

"Well, I'll get you back later," Knud replied, disgusted, his curly red hair sticky with plum juice.

"You'll come back?" Vivilla asked, surprised. Knud looked up at her, perched above the tree like a cloud.

"I'll be back here tomorrow." He smiled and Vivilla smiled back, floating down to the ground like a feather.

"I'll wait here!" she said, bobbing up and down a little with excitement. "See you tomorrow."

KELICS

"Astrid?" As gently as he could, Jarl shook her shoulder and she woke with a start, looking around her. It was still bitterly cold but from the pale pink light in the west she could tell dawn was not far away.

"Morning?"

Jarl nodded.

"Why didn't you wake me? You needed to sleep."

"I'll be on the pony all day, I'll be alright."

It only took a few hours for lack of sleep to take its toll. Astrid watched as she ran alongside the pony, Jarl's eyes half closed. She said nothing until they stopped for midday to allow the pony to rest and, sore and tired, Jarl dismounted and sat down heavily on the grass.

She had pretended not to notice, but during the last few days they had spent in the Aldwood Jarl had been unable to sleep well. He was worried about Knud, worried that Loba would fall back on her promise but, most of all, worried that Knud would not forgive him.

Astrid's sleep had not been much better, but being numb with exhaustion was not so alien to her. After so many years of guiding traders and travellers across Ammasteinn, the numbness from lack of sleep was standard to her and not a hindrance as much as it was for Jarl.

Astrid unpacked some of the food Loba had given them - more grasshopper pies, dried fruits and only a few pieces of cured meat. Jarl did not even look at the food as he ate it, so hungry that the taste of it did not kick in for a few moments. He grimaced at the taste of grasshopper pie but did not throw it away.

"I guess I'll be eating that in future," Astrid laughed. "Grasshopper cakes."

"Not my favourite," Jarl admitted. "Is there any meat?"

"Some." Astrid unwrapped some tightly packed cured meat. She pulled out her knife and smoothly cut away a small chunk and passed it to him.

"Now this, this I do like." Jarl smiled and chewed on it happily as he lay back on the grass. As soon as he had finished it he closed his eyes for a moment and took a deep breath. Astrid watched him and counted down the seconds before she was sure he would fall asleep. She could already hear his heart beat begin to slow.

The wind was still bitterly cold but the clouds had begun to pass a little and, as weak as it was, the midday sun did provide a little warmth.

Astrid stood up and pulled the blanket off the pony at arm's length so she did not risk touching it. The pony shuffled a little, agitated by her obvious animosity towards it, but otherwise did not cause trouble. Jarl was too tired to notice as Astrid pulled the blanket over him.

Behind her in the distance, Astrid heard a deep rumble and turned to see several dark clouds on the horizon moving towards them. "Oh no," she muttered.

For a few moments she watched as the clouds rolled towards them, hopeful that the storm would change course. The storms on the plain were notoriously unpredictable, able to change direction within seconds, and the last thing she wanted to do was wake Jarl.

As the first few flecks of rain hit her cheek, Astrid admitted defeat. The storm would be on them in a matter of minutes. Reluctantly she woke him. "There's a storm," she explained apologetically.

"Where?"

Astrid pointed to the clouds and Jarl's face dropped. In Bjargtre, no matter how severe the storms were, they were never really felt so far under the ground. And the winter storms were quite different to the clouds that rolled towards them like a black wave.

"We'll have to weather it out. It's dangerous to walk through a storm like this," Astrid explained.

"Why?"

"Kelics."

"Kelics?"

The wind had picked up speed, the storm clouds less than a half a mile away, and already they could see the massive stream of water that poured down beneath it like a grey curtain.

"They live under the ground and come up when it rains. They'll attack anything that moves."

Jarl looked down at his feet nervously and Astrid laughed. "Don't worry, I've only seen them a few times before. They probably won't bother us, most of them are further out in the plains."

The rain didn't arrive with a patter but with a roar. Within seconds they were drenched through, huddled together near the pony that had sat down on the ground as soon as it had felt the storm approach. The rain beat down like hundreds of little stones, and even with his cloak held over his head for protection, the rain still dripped through it and a stream of water ran down

Jarl's arm and neck. Next to him, Astrid had taken her wolf skin form to protect herself and her clothes from the downpour.

"How long do these usually last?" Jarl yelled over the sound of the rain.

"It could be an hour, it could be five minutes," Astrid yelled back in her deep wolf voice. She looked up at the clouds and then to the horizon, but there was nothing to imply it would be over soon. "I don't think this will pass quickly."

Jarl didn't think he had ever felt so cold before. The rain was freezing, but paired with the wind he felt as though his ribs might break at any moment from shivering. Astrid lay on the ground next to him, her wolf ears flat against her head. The entire plain was under two inches of water. The only warmth came from Astrid beside him and the pony behind him, its side against his back. Even Astrid did not seem to mind the pony being so close. The need for warmth was greater than her repulsion of the animal.

"Now I'm so glad I didn't let Knud come!" Jarl laughed, a shiver in his voice.

Astrid suddenly sat upright, both ears raised, her eyes wide and alert. At first Jarl couldn't see what had caught her attention, the rain was so heavy it was like a mist. Then he saw it: a mound of earth rising from the ground, the shape similar to that of an enormous molehill, except what emerged from it was very far from a mole.

Remembering their earlier conversation, Jarl did not move but fixed his eyes on the snake-like creature as it slithered out of the hole. For a few seconds it remained motionless at the bottom of the mound, its mouth open towards the sky to catch the rain as it fell, its eyes closed and covered with a semi-transparent film. An enormous head with two lizard-like arms next to it was attached to a long tail. Its claws were long, thick and dangerously sharp.

As it drank the rain that filled its large basin-like mouth, Astrid reached behind them for the pony.

While she was sure that Jarl would not move she could not say the same of the pony, and as much as she hated the animal she knew that without it their journey to Lǫgberg would take at least twice as long. She had promised Knud that they would return as quickly as possible and it was not a promise she intended to break, let alone the fact that it would be a great inconvenience to the Vârcolac who needed as many ponies as possible to help with the harvest. She could not risk the pony bolting.

The pony did not have time to react as she sucked most of its energy from it; it barely made a sound as it slumped to its side in a deep sleep.

With a snarl, the Kelic opened its enormous orange and green eyes and turned to face them, then bared its thin, razor-sharp teeth.

Jarl didn't move, and neither did Astrid, the Kelic unable to see them as long as they remained utterly still. Its nostrils flared as it sensed a presence nearby.

From the grass behind the first Kelic, a second, much smaller one crawled up, its front legs dragging through the water and the mud, half swimming and half slithering.

With its eyes fixed on Jarl and Astrid, the first Kelic did not notice the second, and before it had time to react, the second Kelic leapt onto its back and buried its fangs into its neck.

Even with the fatal poison in its bloodstream, the first Kelic fought as though its life depended on it. It writhed frantically on the ground, desperate to throw its attacker off, the Kelic's claws embedded in its back like meat hooks. With a shudder, the first Kelic dropped to the floor, and submerged beneath the pool of water that covered the plains. With a snarl, the victorious Kelic began to slice it up into pieces with its claws.

Jarl watched, fascinated and horrified, as the first Kelic was cut up and ingested by the victor, a process that lasted barely more than twenty seconds.

With a contented snort, the Kelic slithered off slowly into the grass, its belly full and heavy, but it was another few minutes before either Astrid or Jarl allowed themselves to move.

"A Kelic?" Jarl asked, even though he already knew the answer.

"Yes," Astrid nodded.

Almost as quickly as the rain had arrived, it left, and within minutes the puddle of water that covered the plains was absorbed by the earth.

Astrid looked worriedly at Jarl, his lips slightly blue from the cold and completely wet through. He breathed a sigh of relief as the sun shone down, the tiny bit of warmth it provided enough to stop him shivering so violently.

"We'll move when you're warm," Astrid insisted, and shook off her wolf skin and handed it to him. Jarl wrapped it around himself gratefully. "Sit down next to the pony and wrap your arms around your chest," Astrid ordered him. Jarl did as she'd asked and, between the warmth that the pony emanated and the wolf-skin, he began to shiver a little less.

"The Gold Coast," he said. "I suddenly really want to be there! You said it was warm?"

"Sometimes it's a little too warm," Astrid admitted. She sat down facing him and rubbed her hands down his arms to get the blood flowing.

"Too warm sounds good," Jarl joked. "Snow I don't mind, but this? This is miserable."

Astrid laughed out loud. "You won't be saying that when it's so hot you can't step outside during the day."

Jarl tried to imagine what she described but could not, the idea of a place where the sun burned the ground to sand was completely alien to him.

"But the water is always warm," Astrid added, her eyes lighting up. " And there are so many ships there. The ports are always busy with traders from Bayswater over the desert and from the Narcissus Isles!"

Jarl smiled at her excited expression. "Are there many dwarves there?"

Astrid shook her head. "No, none. Everywhere I went people looked at me. At first they thought I was a child and then they saw my skin and thought I was a witch or that I had some kind of disease because I was pale." As she spoke, Astrid carried on rubbing his arms and slowly the colour returned to his face.

"How old were you when you left the Red Mountains?" Jarl asked.

Astrid squinted a little as she thought. "I can't remember. Fifteen, I think."

"Fifteen!"

"You don't have to sound so surprised! I'm only half dwarf. I don't mature as slowly as you do." Jarl raised an eyebrow and pretended to be offended but Astrid did not notice. "Besides, I couldn't spend any more time with Dag after what he did to Ragi," she said, clenching her jaw as she always did when she was angry.

"Weren't you scared?" Jarl asked, avoiding the topic of Ragi, determined to not discuss anything that involved a goblin.

"Very," Astrid admitted. "The first human I saw was riding a horse. He thought I was a child."

"I can't imagine that ended well!" Jarl laughed through a shiver.

"It did, actually. He gave me work in Einn, and then later in the year I travelled with him to Bayswater. He was a good friend."

"Was?"

"He was human; they all die too soon."

Jarl said nothing for a moment and then shuffled to his feet. "Shouldn't we start walking?"

"You need to get warm."

"I'm warmer now," he reassured her. "I'll dry faster if we're moving."

Astrid nodded and reached over to the pony. As soon as her hand touched its hide, the pony leapt onto its feet with a snort, the energy Astrid had taken from it returning the moment she touched it. Astrid shook her head at it and pulled her bag over her shoulders.

"Are you sure those things won't come out of the ground again?" Jarl asked.

"Yes, I'm sure. They only come out with the rain."

BROKEN FALLS

A cold hand touched his shoulder and Knud shrieked as loudly as he could. "Don't do that!" he snapped at Vivilla, his heart pounding in his chest.

Vivilla looked at him sadly. "You said you would be back in the morning. I waited all morning."

"Loba made me help with the crop," Knud explained. "They're getting ready for a feast and they made me help. I'm sorry." Vivilla drifted backwards and for a moment he thought she was about to leave. "Please don't go!" he begged.

"You said you would be back."

"Yes…but I didn't say when," Knud said, a small grin on his face. Vivilla repressed a smile at his reply.

"Ok. What do you want to do?"

"I don't know," Knud said, shrugging his shoulders.

"Have you been to the lake?" Vivilla asked. Knud shook his head and her face lit up with excitement as she clapped her hands together. "I'll show you the Broken Falls!"

"How far is it?"

"Only five or six miles."

Knud's face dropped. "I can't walk that far."

"Of course you can!"

"No! I can't!" Knud shouted. "I'm a cripple! I can't walk properly anymore!"

Vivilla stared at him, her hands curled together nervously, and Knud stared at the ground, ashamed that he had yelled at her.

"What if you made a new foot?"

"What?"

"Make a foot for your leg. Tie a stick to it or something."

Angry, Knud turned his back on her and stormed off. He was in such a hurry to leave her behind that the long grass caught the bottom of his crutch as he walked away and he nearly toppled over as he tried to pull it free.

Just as the village came into sight, he heard the sound of hooves and turned to see Vivilla with a pony, a bemused expression on her face.

"Can you ride?" she asked.

Knud recognised the pony as one of the ones the Vârcolac used for the crop, two large baskets on either side of it and half filed with apples. Before he could reply there was the sound of shouting in the distance.

"Ride it or run!" Vivilla said quickly.

Knud clambered onto the pony's back, Vivilla dong her best to help him. As soon as he was upright he tucked his crutch into one of the baskets. "Go! Go!" Knud urged the pony, the shouting getting closer. Vivilla laughed excitedly and led the pony away as quickly as she could.

* * *

"It's beautiful!" Vivilla smiled. Knud looked up, his mouth open slightly. The sun was close to the mountain tops, the light already a warm sunset yellow.

Not far from the edge of the lake, a long plume of water fell from the mountain ledge a couple of hundred feet above them. Small rainbows of light floated around the mist that surrounded it. The lake itself was beautiful with the warm light shimmering on it and the shore a vivid green. But the fall took his breath away. The sound of the crashing water was incredible but it was the base of the falls that fascinated him, the rocks beneath it sparkling as if they were made of shattered marble and crystal.

Knud turned on the pony's back to reach for his crutch but to his horror he saw nothing but an empty basket. "It's gone!"

"What is?"

"My crutch! It's gone!"

Knud grabbed the reins and moved to turn the pony back. "I need to find it!"

"Wait!" Vivilla darted off into the forest, the sunlight catching on her skin like glass, and returned with a long stick she had found on the forest floor. "Would this work?" Knud glared at her. "We'll have to come back tomorrow if we look for the crutch now and I want to show you the gryphon eggs!"

Knud's face lit up and he climbed down from the pony's back. Vivilla did her best to help him and passed him the stick. Knud leant on it a little before he hopped forward with Vivilla close by in case he toppled forward. Her wind-like body pushed enough to make sure he didn't fall over.

Slowly they made their way along the lakeside and approached the water fall. Knud stopped for a moment and stooped down, so close to the waterfall that his clothes were already damp from the spray. It collected on Vivilla like dew on a glass window.

He picked up one of the rocks and looked at it, horrified as he saw a small little shape curled up inside it. It was a baby gryphon, its wings not much more than skin over a bone frame. Its large eyes were half open, glazed and cold.

Knud pulled it out of the eggshell and held it in his hands protectively, its body as cold as ice. Gently he moved his finger over its chest. Even though it was clearly dead, he could not help but hope that he would feel a tiny heartbeat. He glanced around and suddenly realised that all of the rock space under the fall was littered with broken eggs. Some of them were shattered into several pieces but a few were still intact with huge cracks around them.

From above the falls, something hurtled down towards them and crashed through Vivilla. She screamed in shock and clutched her head in pain. The egg that had hit her exploded on impact into several pieces and a tiny body lay on the ground among the fragments.

Knud scooped the little body into his hands and held it against his chest. The hairless creature fluttered in his palm, frail and cold. The skin over its large eyes was practically transparent and one of its legs was clearly broken from the impact.

"Are you alright?" Knud asked Vivilla, who had both hands on her head where the egg had crashed through her. She nodded, though her face said otherwise.

"It's cold. I'm going back to the shore," Knud said, and picked up his stick. Vivilla didn't help him as he hopped along the shore line until he was out of the waterfall's spray. As soon as he was back in the sunlight he opened his hands. The baby gryphon shuddered but otherwise barely moved. Knud leant towards it, fascinated. It was so small, completely helpless, its claws and beak barely more than tough skin.

In the distance the sun finally dropped over the mountains and the cold set in instantly. Knud closed his hands to keep the baby gryphon warm.

"It won't survive," Vivilla warned him.

"Maybe if I keep it warm?" Knud replied, even though he knew she was right.

"I think they throw all the runts of the waterfall. They're a bit like eagles; they don't want any weak eggs."

"But it could survive!" Knud said, clearly upset. The baby gryphon lay motionless in his hand, its heartbeat slowing.

They sat there for a few more minutes, Knud with his cupped hands to his chest. The gryphon's heartbeat was so weak it was barely more than a patter. Finally he felt it shudder and when he opened his hands he burst into tears. The dead gryphon was curled up tightly into a ball, its webbed wings curled around it like wet paper.

"You should bury it," Vivilla suggested.

Knud nodded and dug a small grave with his fingers, tears running down his face as he placed the dead gryphon into the hole and covered it up with the soil. "Do they all die?" he asked, his voice shaking a little.

"If they hit the ground, yes. The eggs are strong but if they fall from that high they all die."

"Do all the gryphon do that?" Knud asked, and rubbed the tears away roughly with his sleeve.

"I don't know. I've never been up there."

"Why not?"

"I'm scared," Vivilla admitted.

"Why would you be scared? You can't get hurt."

Vivilla glared at him. "Yes I can! That egg hurt when it hit me. I might not die but it still hurts!" She struck his face as hard as she could. Knud winced, the attempted blow like an ice cold winter gale.

"That's how it feels!" Vivilla snapped.

"That actually doesn't hurt that much," Knud said.

"Well just you wait till I get my wings!"

Knud glanced over at the waterfall and up at the great peak it poured over. There were several large shapes that he could not quite make out in the sky above it. Faint shrieks, which sounded like eagles, echoed down the mountain. His face dropped as he saw another egg hurtle down the falls and smash into a million pieces on the rocky ground. Another tiny pink body flew into the lake and floated on the surface for a while before it sank beneath the water. Knud looked like he might cry again and he reached for his stick and stood up, the sky dark already, the first few stars visible.

"I should go back."

"Will you come back tomorrow?" Vivilla asked, her hands pressed together nervously.

Knud pulled himself onto the pony. "Will you be near the village tomorrow?" Vivilla nodded, a large smile on her translucent face. He managed a small smile back. "I'll see you tomorrow then."

Vivilla floated away over the lake, her laugher a little ghost-like as it echoed over the water, and Knud rode the pony back through the forest. The clatter of another egg hitting the ground behind him made him wince, and he was relieved when he was far enough away to not hear them anymore.

He loosened his grip on the reins and let the pony take control, unsure of the direction he should go in to get back to the village. The pony seemed to know where it was going though, and confidently plodded ahead.

They were only about fifteen minutes into the journey when Knud spotted his crutch on the ground, lodged between two small bushes. He clambered down to retrieve it, nestled it firmly in one of the baskets and remounted the pony, this time keeping a firm hold on the crutch. The palm of his hand still tingled where he had held the dying gryphon, the coldness from its little body soaked into his skin.

In the distance he could hear someone calling his name, the voice unfamiliar. Knud turned the pony a little to the left and deliberately skirted around the figure in the dark, not ready to talk to someone he didn't know. Several more voices ahead of him called for him.

Suddenly, something brushed against his face and Knud panicked and hit out at it. The large net suspended under the apple tree shook as he hit it, as did the ropes attached to the branches. A flurry of ripe apples tumbled down from above and were caught by the net, one or two of them hitting his head.

The pony snorted loudly and lowered its head to eat the smaller apples that had tumbled through the net. There was a loud crunch as the pony ground up the fruit between its strong flat teeth.

Knud looked at the net, a small excited grin at the corner of his mouth and his eyes glinting with the spark of an idea. He looked down at the ground and noticed a large pile of apples had collected under the tree, except for where the net had been hoisted. All of the apples inside the net had been spared the bruises they would have collected had they hit the ground. Knud smiled. In the dark they did not look much like apples, in fact they almost looked like eggs.

"Knud!" He turned to look and saw Loba, a mixture of worry and fury on her face. "Didn't you hear us? And what are you doing on that pony? Radu has been looking for it all day!"

"I found it wandering around by the lake," Knud lied. Her face softened a little but not by much.

"Don't wander off like that again!" She walked up to the pony, took the reins and plucked several large apples from the net to coax the animal away from the windfall on the ground.

"Do you have those nets there during the day, too?" Knud asked.

"No. Those are just for the night. We'll take all the fruit in the morning which, by the way, you're helping with!" Loba said. "We need all the help we can get for the autumn crop."

Knud groaned loudly and Loba flashed him a reproachful look. "If you want to eat, you'll help with the food. Or do you have somewhere more pressing to be?" she asked.

Knud said nothing more. He knew Loba would wake up early, an hour, maybe two before dawn. If he got up before her then he might have a chance to borrow both the pony and a net before anyone would realise he was gone.

BAD LUCK

Jarl swore as the first raindrops hit his head, passing the wolf skin back to Astrid. "There's no point in both of us getting wet," he insisted, and pulled his partly dry cloak back around his shoulders.

Once again they sat down on the ground and huddled together to keep warm, his back against the pony with Astrid curled up in his arms.

"If I didn't know better, I would say that cloud hates us," Jarl grumbled, his long hair so wet it looked like seaweed across his shoulders and back.

Astrid chuckled and curled up to him a little more. "It won't last long."

"You said that last time."

With her eyes closed, Astrid listened intently for any sounds that were not caused by the rain. They had managed to walk four more miles before a second storm cloud had made its way towards them, this one even darker than its predecessor and coupled with a storm.

The pony whinnied as a bright flash lit up the sky, followed by a crash of thunder that made the ground shake. Even Jarl jumped a little from the sound.

"Close your eyes!" Astrid ordered him.

"Why?" Jarl asked.

"Because it's going to get worse!"

A second flash of lightning followed, then another, everything illuminated by the bright white light. The crashes of thunder were so loud that Jarl had to cover his ears. Behind him, the pony shivered with fear, completely unused to the violent storms of the plains.

The onslaught continued for the next fifteen minutes and, by the time it finally passed, Jarl was not sure if his hearing would ever be the same.

In his arms, Astrid suddenly stiffened. "Don't move!" She turned slowly, her eyes on the band of goblins she could hear not far from them. Through the rain neither Jarl or the goblins could see each other but Astrid could see them: A small group of five, most of them young except for the large goblin who led them, her shoulders so broad they were bigger than the pony she walked alongside.

Not far from the goblins, a Kelic dug its way out of the ground and one of the goblins' Dip wolves instantly pounced on it. The Kelic was completely unprepared to fight back, groggy from weeks buried underground.

Jarl could hear the Dip yelp loudly, but still he could not see through the rain. He moved his hand to the hilt of his sword. "How close are they?"

"Fifty feet," Astrid whispered back. "Just don't move."

For a second she considered draining the pony of its energy again in case it made a sound, but she decided against it. If the goblins did see them they would need to run, and quickly. A half dazed pony would take too long to pick up a decent pace.

"We might need to run," she warned Jarl, and he nodded, reaching for the pony's bridle.

The goblins were so close by then that even Jarl could see a hazy shape through the rain of five wild ponies, five goblins and the gangly shapes of several Dip wolves.

Slowly, Astrid moved away from Jarl and crawled along the ground, ready to attack them the moment they came too close. As they approached, Astrid stopped and lay flat against the ground, half submerged in the muddy water. In her wolf skin she was hard to distinguish from the thick long grass that surrounded her. Her green and grey eyes were the only things that did not blend in with her surroundings.

The goblins were so close to Astrid that one of the Dip nearly stood on her hand as it slunk by. Jarl was ready to draw his sword, his heart in his throat, sure that they would notice her at any moment.

With a loud crack, a bolt of lightning struck the ground and the sky illuminated with bright white light before the thunder followed.

The pony panicked. With a shriek it tried to bolt out into the plains but Jarl managed to restrain it. Startled, the goblins looked over in the direction of the sound and saw Jarl as he leapt onto the pony's back.

"Run!" Astrid screamed.

The goblins drew their swords but stopped as Astrid rose from the ground, her hackles raised and teeth bared. None of them moved, shocked as the large wolf's front legs began to glow a bright blue.

With a snarl, Astrid spread her fingers apart and pulled every piece of energy from the grass around her. Even submerged under water, the ground lit up in with a brilliant trickle of blue and orange flames and everything was burnt to a cinder. The heat from the charred plants was enough to turn the water above it into a thick cloud of steam, which blinded the goblins for several seconds.

Astrid ran after Jarl and quickly caught up with him. "Don't stop!" she yelled, as she ran alongside him. "Don't stop until the rain does!"

The goblins did not follow them but still Jarl and Astrid ran until they had passed the storm cloud. Cold and exhausted, they collapsed on the muddy ground. Astrid rolled over onto her back and looked up at the sky, the first few stars visible as the sun began to set.

Under her wolf skin she could feel her wounded shoulder burning with pain, the tissue raw and inflamed from the run. She looked down at her hand and saw that the fingers of her left hand were shaking again.

With one last flash of light, the sun disappeared over the horizon and the cold set in. Jarl got to his feet and reached down to help Astrid up, confused when she offered him her opposite hand.

"The shoulder?" he asked.

"Fine," Astrid lied. "It hurts a little but I'll be alright."

"I think the pony needs a rest. I don't think it's used to so much running."

"Loba uses them for farming," Astrid explained. "It's used to pulling carts, not carrying dwarves."

"The poor thing!" Jarl laughed. The pony looked up at him and snorted loudly as though it understood him. "How many days will it take to reach Waidu?"

"If we keep going, two days. If we rest, four."

"Keep going? What, till we reach Waidu?"

Astrid nodded. "Rest for two hours every six and keep walking. I couldn't see the cuffs the goblins wore, but if they were Moldof's they will be back."

Every muscle in Jarl's body begged him to ignore her suggestion but instead he nodded in agreement.

"You should rest for a while, though." Astrid held her hand against his chest before he could try and walk ahead. "You need the rest and so does the pony."

"I thought you said the goblins would follow?"

"If they do I can take care of them, and if they go back to their camp for more reinforcements it still gives you a few hours. You're no use if you're too tired to run."

* * *

Astrid unwound her veil from around her neck so she could push aside her tunic and look at the wound on her shoulder. Jarl was fast asleep, her wolf skin around him.

She shivered as she lifted the side of her tunic and undid the bandages that were tightly wrapped across her chest, shoulder and upper arm. An angry red sore glared up at her, the skin around the large scab a bright, irritated pink and flecked with streaks of red from where the scab had been scratched away. She swore under her breath and pulled her tunic back down over her shoulder. Quietly, she crept back over to Jarl and rummaged through her bag, searching for a small clay flask of honey wine at the bottom. Before she poured it over her shoulder, she walked far away enough so that Jarl would not hear her if she cursed.

She bit down on her lip hard as she poured some of the honey wine over the wound. Her left hand shook like a leaf, but she did not scream. For a moment she paused to breathe and then she reached over her shoulder and poured the wine over the wound at the back.

"Breathe! It doesn't hurt!" Astrid whispered to herself.

Before she wrapped her shoulder in the bandages again, she drenched them in the honey wine. With her head spinning slightly, Astrid did not notice the little black worm that had managed to crawl up onto the bandages while they were propped on her knee.

It took her a few minutes before she could stand and be sure that the dizziness in her head would not make her drop back to the ground. Her shoulder cooled slightly by the wind as it blew on the wet bandages, the wound hot.

With the half empty flask still in her hand, Astrid crept back to Jarl and curled up next to him under the wolf skin, his beard prickly against the back of her neck.

"Is it time to leave yet?" Jarl mumbled, half asleep.

"No, not yet."

"Good," he said, his eyes still closed, and moved his arm across her back. Astrid flinched as he touched her shoulder and Jarl opened his eyes.

"Astrid, why is your shoulder wet?"

"It was just the rain," she said.

Jarl would have ignored her obvious lie if it had not been for the strong smell of honey wine that surrounded her. "Don't lie to me," he snapped, too tired to restrain his annoyance. He sat up and noticed Astrid's left arm was shaking.

"It's just hurting a little. I wanted to put some honey wine on it. It's fine, I promise." Jarl's face relaxed a little and he looked down at the flask.

"Any of that left?" he joked, and Astrid passed it over.

"I thought you might need it."

Jarl smiled and took a small sip, the wine so strong his heart jolted a little before the blood rushed around his body at a frantic pace, leaving a burning sensation in his chest.

"Don't you want more?" Astrid asked, surprised. "I remember you liked the Daru wine quite a lot."

Jarl grinned. "We should probably keep the rest, I'm sure they'll have wine in Waidu."

"They do, but it's foul," Astrid warned him, and Jarl's face dropped.

"Well, one more sip won't hurt," Jarl replied, and took one last mouthful before returning the flask to Astrid.

Another gust of wind ripped past them but this time Jarl did not feel it, his blood warm with the honey wine. "We should probably go." He got to his feet but Astrid was far less enthusiastic. "You should ride the pony for a while," Jarl suggested. "You're tired."

Astrid laughed. "No," she said flatly. "I'm not riding that thing."

Jarl mounted the pony and reached down for her hand, his jaw set in a determined frown. "Get on or I'm not going anywhere." Astrid looked up at him slightly dumbfounded. "I'm not joking, Astrid, get on!"

For a few moments they just glared at each other, Jarl with his hand outstretched towards her and Astrid refusing to budge. At first she walked ahead, only to turn and see he had not moved, his lips pressed together.

"Jarl, I'm not riding that thing!"

"It's a pony, Astrid, not a dragon. Get on."

Astrid glared at him and then glanced around as if she were looking for someone else to agree with her. Finally, when she realised he would not back down, she stepped forward and took his hand hesitantly. In one quick motion, Jarl pulled her up onto the pony in front of him, one hand on the reins and the other around her waist. Astrid took a deep breath, her whole body tense. Jarl's grip against her stomach was firm enough to stop her from jumping down.

"I hate you," Astrid whispered half-heartedly.

Jarl shook his head. "You're lying." Slowly, he urged the pony into a slow canter and Astrid closed her eyes, both the voices in her head terrified and screaming at her to get down.

"It's alright!" Jarl reassured her, the side of his face against hers. "It not going to hurt you."

Astrid held his hands as tightly as she could, her grip on him slightly painful, but Jarl bore it and did not complain, aware of just how hard it was for Astrid not to jump down and run.

The voices in her head screamed at her and her shoulders shook, but after a few minutes she relaxed a little, though her grip on Jarl's hand was just as firm and her eyes remained closed.

In her head, a series of images flashed in quick succession: the horses as they had first come into the glade, the sound of their hooves like thunder, all of them so much taller than her. There was no clear image of how they looked, the only thing clear to her was the fear that gripped her heart each time she remembered.

Her head flinched a little as they rode and Jarl urged her to open her eyes a little, aware that the voices in her head were fighting against him.

"Astrid, open your eyes. Please?"

Astrid shuddered and opened her eyes slowly, a terrified expression on her face. She was not prepared for the rush of excitement as Jarl rode the pony into a fast canter, the wind against her face. It was a sensation that felt a little like flying.

Jarl smiled as he felt her shoulders relax and he kissed the side of her neck, "See? It's alright."

With her left hand still holding Jarl's grip across her stomach, Astrid reached down with her right hand and knotted her fingers into the pony's mane. As her fingers began to glow blue with magic she closed her eyes, and for a brief moment she could feel every muscle in the animal's body as it ran. It wasn't a monster; it had no malice towards her. And try as she might, she could not see it as the terrible creatures of her nightmares as it carried her.

"Can I try?" Astrid reached for the reins and Jarl passed them to her.

"Don't pull on them," he instructed, his hands lightly over hers to guide her. "If you pull back you'll hurt him and he'll stop."

Astrid nodded, but as she readjusted her grip on the reins her left hand began to tremble, the nerves in her arm on fire. She quickly passed the reins back to Jarl and made an excuse. "I don't know what I'm doing, you should do it."

"I can teach you," Jarl suggested.

Astrid leant back against him, her head against his shoulders. "Maybe one day."

REDEMPTION

Halvard sat down at the edge of the table, exhausted. Eilíf, Gísla and Hlín sat down opposite him. They were all tired; emotionally drained.

He ripped the bread beside his soup into tiny pieces and dropped them inside the bowl for them to soak. He had barely had four hours sleep, most of the night having been spent outside the palace until finally the captain had seen fit to let him leave to rest. It had been left to him and a few other soldiers to cart the bodies of the dead off the streets and out of the city where a small group of dwarves had already started to dig mass graves, which were filled faster than they could be dug. Many soldiers and even sergeants refused to touch the bodies of the dead and dying, despite the threat of demotion.

"Where's Holmvé?"

"She's asleep."

"Is she alright?" Halvard asked.

"She's just tired."

There was a loud knock on the door and Halvard got up to open it, grumbling as he did so. A middle aged dwarf woman stood at the door, a scarf held over her face and the strong aroma of garlic and lavender around her.

"Holmvé Hjort?" she asked, her voice muffled through the scarf.

"Do I look like my name is Holmvé Hjort?" Halvard said.

"I need to speak with her."

"She's resting. Come back later."

"I need to speak to her! I heard she knows a cure!"

Halvard glared at her. "I don't know where you heard that but it's simply not true." He tried to close the door but the woman jammed her foot between it and the door frame.

"Please! I won't tell anyone! I just need her to help my son!"

The expression on her face was so similar to the one Halvard remembered seeing on Elin. She was a mother who would do anything to save the life of her children, just like Jarl's mother had when she had thought her sons were about to die. *And remember how that ended,* Halvard thought to himself.

"She's not here!" Halvard roughly pushed her away and closed the door. The woman did not give up though, she threw herself against the door and shrieked that they could not leave her on the doorstep.

"Please! Please I'll do anything!" she wailed. "I have gold! I'll give you everything I have! Please, just help my son!"

Halvard closed his eyes and held his head in his hands, his back against the door as the woman continued to throw herself against it on the other side.

"Halvard! Let her in!" Holmvé said. He looked up to the stairs and saw her, her face drained and tired, her eyes red with exhaustion.

"Holmvé, you need to sleep. You've been up all night," Eilíf said.

"I can sleep when I'm dead. I can't just leave her outside like an animal." She walked towards the door and stumbled slightly. Eilíf, Gísla and Hlín rushed forward and took her hands to steady her.

"What are you doing? You need to rest!" Hlín said uneasily. Outside, the woman hammered on the door even harder. "No! No, you stay and rest. I can help her," Hlín reassured her.

Holmvé did not argue. Hlín passed her and walked out the door and as soon as it had closed Holmvé sat down on the stairs in a huddle and burst into tears. Halvard stared at her, unsure of how to respond, while Eilíf and Gísla sat down next to her on the step.

"I'm sorry, I'm just tired," Holmvé snivelled. "I can't believe this is happening again. What was the king thinking? Didn't enough people die last time?"

"He's a young boy. And with the likes of Yrsa Gull around, I don't say I blame him. The poor thing looked scared out of his wits after the funeral," Halvard replied.

His reply did not help Holmvé who just buried her head against Eilíf's shoulder, sobbing like a banshee. Halvard had to turn away and walk back into the hall, worried that he might break down at any moment.

"It's ok to cry," Eilíf's quiet little voice called over to him.

"I'm not crying," Halvard snapped. "I'm tired."

He strolled back to his place at the table and sat down, the bread in his soup now completely disintegrated and nothing but a gloopy mess. He dropped his spoon in it and leant his head in his hand as another wave of tiredness hit him. He was cold on the inside, despite the multiple layers of clothing he wore, his body too tired to generate any kind of heat.

There was another loud knock on the door. Before Halvard could say a word, Holmvé stormed up and threw the door open, a wave of curses escaping her mouth even as she saw who stood on the doorstep.

"What in Hel's name do you want, Captain Gauss?"

"I'm here for Halvard," the captain replied, a little frightened of the old woman who stood before him with her bloodshot eyes.

"You wouldn't give him his old position back but now you're walking all this way for a soldier? Go away!" Holmvé shouted furiously, and tried to close the door on him.

"The general asked for him specifically," Captain Gauss replied just as angrily, and shoved his foot in the doorway.

With a sigh, Halvard scooped one last spoonful of cold soup into his mouth and got up, grabbing his cloak. Before he walked out of the house he turned to Holmvé and laid his hand gently on her shoulder. "It's alright."

Halvard didn't bother to talk to the captain as they both walked in silence to the garrison. The streets were deserted. There was rubbish everywhere and crumpled heaps were scattered on the floor, feet peeking out from beneath the rags. With not enough soldiers brave enough to touch the bodies, many had been left in the streets until they could be taken outside the city. Passersby brave enough to approach the bodies had left cloaks or rags over them so they would not become a spectacle, giving them one small shred of dignity.

"What does the general want with me?" Halvard asked flatly, too tired to really care, but the tiny part of his mind that was still awake was curious.

"He was impressed with how you dealt with that boy in the plaza."

"Is that all? You couldn't have just told me and let me sleep for a few more hours instead of dragging me across the city?" Halvard snapped.

"He wants to thank you in person."

The captain sounded angry and would not even turn to look at Halvard. Halvard was too tired to pick up on what normally would have sent alarm bells ringing.

A small group of dwarves walked by, their hands bright red, but it wasn't blood. One of them quickly hid something behind his back as they passed them.

"Go home!" the captain bellowed, and they scurried away. He muttered to himself as they turned into one of the larger tunnels towards the plaza and noticed a large scrawl on the wall.

'The wolf is coming,' Halvard read out loud to himself.

Above the words a large icon had been drawn of a wolf in white chalk, its likeness almost identical to the one on the goblin cuffs they had taken. There was a block of discarded chalk on the ground.

"Bloody fools," Halvard scoffed. The captain said nothing.

They reached the garrison, the entire front of the building concealed behind a thick fog. Massive plumes of incense trickled from every window. Halvard did his best not to cough, the smoke so thick his eyes watered.

The first thing he noticed as he entered the mess hall was the huddle of soldiers at one side of the room, the general and another dwarf at the far end. The dwarf was slumped over on the bench, his clothes torn and ragged, with one of his boots missing.

The general looked up as they entered. "Is this him?" he asked Captain Gauss, who nodded. Halvard strode up to the general and bowed respectfully. Even after so many years in the army he had never been in the same room as the general and he was surprised at how alert the old dwarf's face was, his eyes bright and able.

"He's coming," the dwarf next to the general muttered, and turned to look at Halvard, his eyes bloodshot. Captain Gauss quickly retreated as soon as he saw the dwarves eyes, frightened that it was the first stages of the Red Plague. Halvard, however, stood his ground, unfazed. The general smiled at his reaction.

"I like this dwarf! More guts than the lot of you!" he sneered at the others in the room. "You survived the Red Plague last time?"

"I never caught it."

"Well…you'd be one of the few!" The general turned back to the dwarf with the bloodshot eyes. "Tell him what you told me."

The dwarf looked up at Halvard. Still seated on the bench, he rocked back and forth a little as he spoke. "I was returning from Einn and I was caught by a swarm of goblins. They…they killed my friends, my nephew." The dwarf looked like he was about to wail with grief but the general urged him to continue. "The goblins, they're led by someone called Ulf."

Halvard couldn't stop the twinge of cold superstition run down his spine at the mention of his name. The image of the wolf icon painted on the pillar they had passed earlier flashed through his mind.

"He has more goblins than I've ever seen! When I escaped I could see their torches. Everywhere I looked, there were so many of them! At least one hundred thousand goblins!"

Halvard inhaled sharply. "One hundred thousand? Are you sure?" he asked. The dwarf stared at him, a deranged look in his eyes.

"Yes, I'm sure! Do you think I would make that up? There were thousands of them! I saw them! And I heard Ulf... they're going to attack the city! They're going to attack and there's nothing we can do to stop him!"

The dwarf got to his feet, his arms flailing and both eyes so wide they almost protruded from his head. He was pushed roughly back onto the bench.

"Why are you telling me this?" Halvard asked, confused.

"You've been promoted to captain again." Halvard's mouth dropped open a little and he quickly closed it, unsure if he had heard correctly. "You will be taking Captain Gauss's position," the general continued. "He has been demoted."

"Why?" Halvard asked before he could stop himself. *Don't ask why, you fool! You've been made captain!*

"Because Captain Gauss is a coward!" the general sneered, glancing at the captain. "He should have been the one to calm the crowds and stop that dwarf in the plaza. Instead he stayed skulking behind his men! I won't have dwarves like that in charge."

Captain Gauss scowled, his head bowed, avoiding the general's icy stare.

"Can you remember everything he said?" the general muttered, turning back to Halvard.

"Goblins, a lot of them, and he thinks we're all going to die," Halvard summarised before he could think about what he had said, still dazed by his unexpected promotion. The general looked at him, both eyes squinting, and Halvard was sure he had offended him for a moment. *Well done Halvard, you've been promoted and demoted in less than a minute!*

Instead, the general chuckled loudly. "I like this dwarf! He has backbone!"

Halvard turned to look at Gauss, unsure of what to do next, partly sure it was all a dream.

"I need you to go to the palace and tell the king everything he has just said. The palace will not allow anyone to enter who might have the plague. If you were going to catch it you'd be dead already, so you're going to take the message."

Before he could embarrass himself any more with the incredulous look on his face, Halvard managed to pull himself together. He turned to go.

"Wait!" The general strode up to Captain Gauss and pulled away the large breastpin that held up his cloak. "This is yours now," he said, and pinned it onto Halvard's shoulder.

"Thank you, General." Halvard's face was blank, not sure how to process what had just happened.

"Well, what are you waiting for?"

Still dazed, Halvard asked the first thing that crossed his mind. "Why am I going to the palace? I'm not a general."

"No, you're not. But I am leading a patrol to see just how close this Ulf is to the city."

Halvard nodded and left the room passing Gauss, huddled in the corner, his eyes on the ground. Halvard could not stop the little smile which crept up his face as he saw how humiliated Gauss looked. *Now you know how I felt!* he thought.

Once he had left the garrison, Halvard stopped for a moment to let what had just happened sink in. He leant against the wall they had passed earlier, the graffiti of the wolf still there, the drips of red paint dripping down to the floor. This time he didn't even notice it, he was euphoric. He looked down at the breast pin on his shoulder and admired it, his large clumsy fingers holding it like it was made of glass.

"I'm a captain…I'm a captain!"

THE IRON KING

Everyone was asleep.

He got up, pushing his blanket away, careful to be as quiet as he could. With his crutch under one arm he crawled away, grateful for a moment that he had only lost his foot and not his knee, too. He crawled out of the room,, every tiny sound amplified in the silence. He could hear his heart beating like a drum in his chest as he made his way down the hallway. A few loud snores coming from the many rooms that led into the passage made him jump with fright a couple of times, and he was half tempted to peek past the curtains that covered each doorway to see if any of the Vârcolac slept in their animal skins, unable to believe the noises had been made by humans. But the thought of an angry Vârcolac waking to see him staring at them pushed the idea out of his head.

He finally reached the spiral stairs and, concerned that the crutch would make too much noise on the stone steps, he crawled up them. The door to the outside was closed.

Knud got to his feet and placed his hand on the lever. Slowly he pressed down on it. The weight that held the door closed grated up the inside of the tree and Knud winced, pausing for a second. Nobody seemed to have been woken by the sound so he tried again. The weights scraped on the door some more and his face twisted into a grimace, terrified that at any minute he would see an angry face glaring at him, or worse, Loba's.

As soon as the door was open enough for him to slip past he tossed his crutch outside and dived through after it. He landed heavily on the grass outside and the tree door closed behind him with a hollow thud. The grass beneath him was wet with early morning dew and the sun had barely risen over the mountains, the first few rays only just visible over the peaks.

He looked up and saw Vivilla perched at the top of a nearby apple tree, her eyes closed as she faced the approaching sunrise, her body an odd grey colour like a rain filled cloud.

"Vivilla!" Knud hissed.

Startled, she toppled from the branch and floated to the floor. "What are you doing up so early? I didn't think you would be out for a few hours yet!"

"Loba was going to make me help with the apples," Knud replied. "If I see one more apple I'll throw it at someone."

"So long as that's not me, then that's fine." She floated back up to the tree and closed her eyes. The sun was nearly over the peaks and a thin line of yellow glowed along the mountain tops like they were on fire. "Are you going to get the pony?" Vivilla asked, still with her face to the sunrise.

Knud grumbled and hobbled over to the five ponies that were penned in a small paddock nearby. He was surprised the Vârcolac did not have more of them. Three of them were so old he could see their ribs, their coats grey and thin. It took him several minutes to chase one of them down and, when he finally caught it, he mounted it.

He rode the pony back to the tree and looked up at Vivilla, the first rays of sun dazzled on her face. An expression of pure joy was spread across it and her body shimmered from the rays that warmed her, turning her from grey to a clear silver.

"We have to go," Knud hissed. "I have an idea to save some of the eggs!"

"Oh?" she said, but did not move from her branch, her palms extended in front of her towards the sun.

"The nets the Vârcolac use to catch apples...we can borrow one and use it to catch eggs instead."

Vivilla smiled and opened her eyes excitedly. "That should work!"

"Yes, but we have to leave now. I don't want anyone to see me take it."

She rolled her eyes and pushed herself off the branch. Like a cloud, she floated down onto the back of the pony, her body instantly turning grey the moment she was no longer in the sun's rays. She wrapped her arms around her legs and brought them up to her chest.

"Are you cold?" Knud asked, surprised.

"Of course I'm cold! The moonlight isn't exactly warm," she growled at him. "Please hurry up and get this net! The sunrise is always the best time to eat!"

"You eat the sunlight?" Knud said, as he led the pony in the direction he thought the net had been.

"Do I look like I can eat anything else? I'm made of air!"

"You don't need to be so grumpy," Knud snapped back at her. "I was just asking."

"I'm sorry," Vivilla muttered. "I'm just hungry, I get grumpy when I'm hungry."

"Why don't you stay with the Vârcolac? It's warm in the tunnels."

"I'm scared to ask them," she admitted. "Every time the children see me they run away screaming. You're the first person to actually talk to me."

After a few wrong turns they reached the apple tree Knud had seen the previous day, the net now filled with ripe fruit. He reached up to untie it, trying to lower the side of the net down as carefully as he could so the fruit would not be bruised. A little of the pile that had collected over the night tumbled onto the ground. Vivilla tried to help him but with the slightest bit of pressure, her hands just passed straight through the knots as she tried to undo them.

"Ugh! I can't wait till I become Knāto. I'm so tired of not being able to move things."

Knud finished untying the net and draped it over the pony before he urged it on towards the lake, the pony contentedly crunching on some of the apples.

"When will that happen?"

"What?"

"Your wings? When will they grow?"

"In a few months. I'm not sure exactly," she said, a small tinge of fear in her face. "Sometimes I can feel a weird tingle on my back like there's something crawling on it, but there's no wings yet."

"Will your wings be big?"

"Very big!" she said proudly. "Bigger than a gryphon's!"

"I thought you hadn't gone up the mountains to see them?"

"I haven't. I've only seen them from down here, but I still think my wings will be bigger!"

"Are there any other Sylph here in the Aldwood?"

"No," she replied sadly. "My egg landed here. I haven't met any of my other siblings."

Knud turned and looked at her, confused, as the pony continued to plod on ahead. "Your egg landed here? What do you mean?"

For a moment she looked like she might snap at him again, but instead she pulled the irritated look from her face and took a small breath before she replied. "Sylphs lay their eggs just before they die. My mother's memories are all in my shell. It landed on the other side of the lake. The eggs float on the clouds till they land and then they..." She stopped mid sentence as the sun rose enough over the mountains to reach her face. She smiled, raising her hands and palms to the sky. Her skin glistened and turned silver again and her hair, which had lain flat against her skin as though it was weighed down, instantly lifted and began to float around her head.

They reached the edge of the lake. Another loud crack echoed from the falls and Knud winced at the sound. Quickly, he pulled the net from the pony's back and Vivilla did her best to help him.

With his crutch under one arm, Knud hobbled along, the net tucked under his other arm and dragging along the ground behind him, twigs and bracken caught up in it. They reached the stony shore that led under the waterfall and Knud did his best to pick the net up so it would not catch on the jagged rocks.

"How are we going to hold the net up?" Vivilla asked.

Knud's face dropped. "I didn't think of that."

From above them, another egg hurtled to the ground. Vivilla pushed Knud out of the way and the egg hit the ground barely three feet away from him. Shards of rock-like shell ricocheted everywhere. A few of them bounced against Vivilla as she stood in front of Knud, but did not pass through her.

"Thank you," Knud muttered, his face sad as he dropped the net to the floor.

Vivilla floated over the water and looked up at the falls, her face lighting up. "I think I see a ledge!" She floated up the waterfall a little more, the force of the water stronger the higher she went, but not strong enough to push her down. "There's a tunnel, I think. It must lead up to the mountain!"

Knud hobbled closer. The waterfall was weak, barely more than a thick mist after having fallen from so high up, but thick enough to drench him within a few seconds. Mist swirled everywhere. His face lit up as he saw grips and small footholds in the wall, which led up to the platform Vivilla had seen. "Do you think you could go up it?"

"I'm not going by myself!" she said, clearly scared. "It's dark in there!"

"What, you're scared of the dark?" Knud laughed. "Why would you be scared of the dark? You're made of..."

"If you say air, I swear I'll push you under the next egg that falls down," she snapped. "I'll go up if you come with me."

This time it was Knud's turn to get angry. "I can't! I don't have a foot!"

"You could climb that!" Vivilla insisted, and floated over to the rock face. "It's not that high up, just a few metres."

Knud clutched his crutch nervously. "What if I fall?"

"You won't," she reassured him, but he did not look convinced.

"Look, the net won't work. But If we get to that tunnel then maybe we can save some of the eggs at the top."

Knud gulped and stared at the grips in the wall, all of them wet from the mist. Vivilla clapped her hands together excitedly as Knud put his crutch down, took a deep breath and reached out for the nearest grip. Slowly, he reached up for second one and managed to slot his foot into the first hole. His heart pounded. *What if I fall?*

He managed to pull himself up a few more feet, the pace painfully slow for Vivilla as she floated up behind him, but she did not criticise, able to see how terrified he was. His hands shook more each time he let go of one of the eroded grips and pulled himself up a little further.

As he was about half way up, he looked down and felt his muscles seize, terrified at how far down the ground was. "I can't do this!" he shrieked, and pressed himself against the rock face, his injured leg shaking as much as his hands. Vivilla was sure for a moment that he was about to slip.

"You're almost there! Just keep going!"

"I can't!" Knud bellowed. "I only have one foot! I can't do it! I can't!"

"The Iron King did it!" Vivilla blurted out, and Knud looked at her, both eyes wide open like a terrified bird, his face pressed against the cold rock.

"Who?"

"The Iron King!" Vivilla said again. "He was a dwarf king from…um…Lǫgberg! Yes, he was from Lǫgberg! He lost all his leg, not just his foot, and one arm… and part of his face! So..so…they made him an iron leg, and one for his arm and a mask to cover his face. And he climbed the Riddari Leggr and built Lǫgberg *before* they made him the leg and the arm. If he could do that then you can climb this rock! Look it's not that far! Just a few more feet!"

Knud took several quick breaths and nodded, still scared but encouraged by her story. Vivilla continued to talk as he climbed to distract him.

"He lost his leg in a bear fight. He survived, but only after the bear had swallowed his leg and he had to strangle it to death with his bare hands."

Knud pulled himself up a little further. He was so close to the ledge that Vivilla could have sat down on it and reached down to touch his head. He paused for a moment and took several more deep breaths.

"He dragged himself seven miles across a desert till he reached his camp! He had lost almost all the blood in his body but he carried on! When they made him his new leg he had it made so the tip looked like a hammer. When he reached the mountain where he wanted to build Lǫgberg, he pulled his iron leg off and used it to break open the mountain because none of the other dwarves had remembered to bring a hammer."

Knud shouted with relief as his hands reached the edge of the ledge and Vivilla joined in, shouting at him to pull himself up.

"YES! Yes! I did it!" Knud laughed as he pulled himself over the edge and collapsed on the ground, his eyes alight, both arms raised above his head, the sound of his voice echoing across the fall. "I did it!"

Vivilla floated to the ground, picked up the crutch and managed to float back up to the ledge before it slipped through her hands. It fell with a loud clatter next to Knud.

The sun had completely risen by now. The entire valley was bathed in its warm light, the air was fresh and new and birdsong echoed over the lake. Knud took a deep breath and smiled from ear to ear, his eyes closed. "What happened to the Iron King?" he asked, panting on the rock.

"He climbed up the rest of the mountain and saved a few gryphon eggs," Vivilla smiled down at him.

WAIDU

Astrid breathed a loud sigh of relief as she saw the tall red walls of Waidu ahead of them, the miles upon miles of plains around it a rich, vibrant green.

Under her clothes she could feel the heat radiating from her infected shoulder and an unbearable itchiness under her skin. The tremors in her hand were becoming more and more difficult to hide from Jarl. "We need to hurry. They won't open the gate past sunset."

Nodding, Jarl rode the pony faster, Waidu not much more than a large cluster in the distance, the red walls at odds with their grass green surroundings.

They reached the walls just as the horns sounded to warn that the gate would soon be closed. Now that they were upon it, Jarl could see that they were not red as they had appeared in the distance but, for the most part, stone grey. At the tops of the walls the stone had been replaced with clay red bricks, which over time had stained the rocks below them, dripping onto them like trickles of blood.

They both dismounted and joined the steady line of people who were queuing at the gate, Astrid quick to cover her face with her veil. Before they reached the guards she reached into her bag and pulled out a small charm from one of the side pockets, the image of a hawk stamped upon it. Jarl noticed her left hand was trembling slightly and she had an obvious limpness in three of her fingers.

"What's that?" Jarl asked.

"A trader's coin. It should help with any problems," she explained.

The two dwarves at the gate stopped them as soon as they saw Astrid, her green and grey eyes completely out of place among the crowd.

"I have a trader's coin," Astrid reassured them, her voice muffled through her veil, and passed the small gold coin to one of them.

"Wow, I haven't seen one of these in a while!" the first dwarf laughed, the large belly that bulged over the top of his belt shaking. "Alright, in you go."

Jarl followed but a firm, grubby hand stopped him. "I didn't see a coin from you, and I haven't seen you before."

"He's with me," Astrid explained to the second guard.

"He doesn't have a coin though, and he doesn't look like a trader. Not with that hair. Far too pretty to be a trader."

Jarl smiled coldly at the guard and reached inside his tunic, his eyes narrowed. "Would this count?"

At first the guard did not recognise the crest on the round silver and gold plaque, but after a quick nudge from his fellow guard he looked back down at it and quickly passed it back to Jarl. "Alright, go in," he said, his eyes on the ground.

Behind them, the gates closed with a loud thud and three wooden beams were lowered across it into metal slots. Up on the walls, one of the guards passed a torch along to the other soldiers and, one by one, the beacons that lined the walls - large metal basins filled with dry wood - were lit.

"You'd think they were preparing for war," Jarl muttered to himself.

"It wouldn't be the first time," Astrid replied. "Moldof has tried to attack the city before."

With her veil drawn tightly around her face, Astrid led Jarl through the busy city streets. Traders on either side of them were packing away their goods, which had been displayed along the street throughout the day. Shutter after shutter closed as baskets full of goods were taken inside.

It did not take them long to reach the nearest inn. It was a tall building, two floors taller than the ones surrounding it and much, much uglier. Astrid strolled to where a group of humans were gathered outside.

"Astrid? Where are you going?" Jarl asked.

"To the inn." Astrid pointed at it before she realised what he had meant. "I've never stayed anywhere else before," she explained. "It's not safe for me."

Jarl nodded, looking up at the ugly building. "Do you want to stay there?"

Astrid nodded. "It would help if you stay with the dwarves over there," she said, pointing across the street. "You'll need to find out which caravans are leaving soon for the Kaito Passage."

Jarl stepped towards her, smiling, and removed her veil to kiss her. "See you tomorrow then." Astrid smiled back and turned to go, both her cheeks red as a few of the humans made several remarks that she clearly understood. They watched in surprise as she strode into the inn confidently, making comments among themselves that she obviously couldn't read the sign, completely unaware that she understood them.

The inside of the inn was packed full. Unlike Jarl, Astrid did not find the height difference between herself and the humans intimidating, though she did not appreciate having to forcefully push her way though until she reached the innkeeper, who stood behind the counter at the edge of the room.

"Apsu!"

The innkeeper looked around, confused, when he could not see the face the voice came from.

"Apsu!"

"Alright! Which one of you bastards asked for me?" he yelled, a dirty flask in his hand.

"I did," Astrid said, her head barely over the edge of the counter.

Apsu stared at her before he burst out laughing. "Erin!" He put down the flask and reached over the counter to pull her into a bear hug. Astrid inhaled sharply as he pressed down on her shoulder, the brief pain so acute her vision was blurred for a moment. "I was wondering when I'd see your short face around. Are you alright? You look…wrong."

"I missed you too!" Astrid laughed back at him. "Do you have a room for me?"

"You know we don't have any beds for children," he joked, and Astrid raised her eyebrows at him. "A normal bed will do, Apsu."

He grinned at her and passed her a key from the wall behind him. "Need help opening the door?" he teased. "You might not be able to reach."

"No! I'll be just fine, thank you." She jumped down from the counter. "The fifth door?" she asked, and held the key up, a pattern printed on the leather strap that hung around it.

Apsu nodded. "Still can't understand human numbers, can you?"

Astrid shook her head. "No, and I don't intend to. Far too confusing!"

The other humans in the room watched curiously as she walked up the stairs. Reaching her door, she stood on the tips of her toes to turn the key in the rusty lock.

As soon as she was inside, she closed the door and locked it. Within seconds she had torn off her tunic and looked at the angry, red wound on her shoulder, the heat from it so strong she could feel it bounce against her cheek. She reached into her bag and pulled out what remained of the honey wine. "Ok, don't scream," she said out loud, and poured what remained of the alcohol over her bare shoulder.

Jarl could not have enjoyed his food more if it had been covered in butter and honey. The plain bread and lean beef slices were like the finest meal after the food

Loba had provided them with. He bit into the meat and slowly chewed it, a contented smile on his face.

Despite all the worries that were crammed inside his head, Jarl had been too tired to not sleep deeply. He barely remembered reaching the bed and was asleep almost before his head touched the pillow. Had it not been for the loud sound of a horn that ripped through the city to announce the opening of the gates, he was sure he could have slept several hours more.

As the innkeeper brought him a large flask of mead, Jarl asked when the next caravan would leave for the Kano Passage.

"Kano? You mean the Kaito Passage, right?" he asked, and Jarl nodded. "One is leaving tomorrow at midday. After that you'll have to wait another week, unless you want to pay for passage." Jarl nodded his thanks and finished the rest of his food in silence.

Part of him wanted to leave as soon as possible, but the tremor he had seen in Astrid's arm worried him. It had been too soon for her to travel, and he was sure that to embark on another trek so soon would only invite trouble. But he also knew that part of him wanted to delay his audience with the queen for as long as possible.

He ran his hands through his hair and wondered for the hundredth time what he would feel when he would inevitably lose it, though the shame of it was not his worst fear. He reached into his tunic and pulled out the plaque to look at it.

He remembered the day his father had taken him to the palace to have his own plaque made and how excited he had been. Jóð and Jón had been given theirs years before and they teased him about how long it had taken for him to get his. He remembered how thrilled he had been when he had seen his name carved onto the back, but now the cold piece of metal in his hand was all he had left of that part of his life.

Jarl put the plaque back into his tunic and reached for the mead. The flask was halfway to his mouth when he saw a face he did not expect to see.

With his clothes filthy and the large fur coat he wore covered in mud, Gull looked as content as a wet cat. Jarl's stomach dropped as he saw Skad behind him, who looked equally as bedraggled and sour. A small convoy of dwarves were behind them, the insignia of the royal family of Bjargtre on their cloaks.

Jarl got up, clutching his bag in his hand, and leaving his full flask of mead on the table he walked to the opposite side of the room. He hid behind one of the wooden pillars, close enough to be able to hear Gull as he ordered the finest room.

When the innkeeper laughed at him and said all the rooms were the same, Gull flamboyantly reached into his tunic and tossed his family plaque onto the counter. The innkeeper just laughed at him as Gull stared incredulously at his reaction.

"You can flash that around all you want. This isn't Logberg; you get the same room as everyone else. Here—" He pulled two keys down from the wall behind him. "These should have been cleaned today. It's the best you're going to get."

As Skad and the rest of the inn were distracted by Gull's loud protests, Jarl left before anyone could notice him. He ignored the strange looks as he crossed the street to the human inn, and the muttering in the room as he walked up to the innkeeper and asked for Astrid.

"Who?" Apsu asked, amused by the dark haired dwarf's persistence. "Look, I know your kind like to drink and you're probably just having a laugh, but you're wasting my time. I don't know anyone called Astrid here."

"Erin. Do you have a dwarf called Erin here?" Jarl asked, remembering the name Astrid had used in the Salt Monasteries. Apsu's face twitched slightly but otherwise his face was unreadable.

"She's about my height—"

"All your kind are your height!" Apsu scoffed, and the other humans in the room laughed with him.

"She has one grey eye and one green eye," Jarl said, ignoring them. "She has a scar down her lips and three on the side of her face."

"Ok, so you know who Erin is. What do you want with her?"

"I'm her friend."

"Friend? She never has anything to do with the dwarves."

Jarl gritted his teeth and tried not to get irritated with the innkeeper who was as at least twice as tall as him and not the kind of human he wanted to get into a fight with. "She made an exception."

"Look, if you want to see her you can wait, until then—"

"She hasn't left?" Jarl said, relieved, and Apsu nodded.

"No, not yet. But she could have slipped past me. Wouldn't be the first time."

"Can you ask her to come down? It's important."

With a loud sigh, Apsu trudged out from behind the counter towards the stairs. "Who should I say is asking?"

"Jarl."

"And your second name?"

"Vorn."

As slowly as he could, Apsu climbed the stairs and Jarl waited impatiently by the counter. Apsu had barely been gone more than a minute when he raced back down. "You'd better come up."

Jarl did not need to be told twice and he followed Apsu to one of the rooms on the first floor.

With her back against the wall, Astrid looked at Jarl, her skin a sickly shade of grey and both her eyes rimmed red. The whole of her left arm was exposed, the bandages partly unwound and the wound completely visible. The angry, open sore was clearly infected.

"Jarl, I think I'm sick."

SKY STABLES

By the time they reached the top of the stairs, Knud had already had to stop several times to take a breath as step after step stretched on for what seemed like miles.

Exhausted, he sat down, his crutch beside him. Vivilla floated nearby, the tips of her toes occasionally touching the ground but otherwise remaining airborne. Her long white hair floated behind her as she looked around the room. As he caught his breath Knud looked up, fascinated, the smell of dust, mould and feathers heavy in the air.

"Wow!" he whispered, his whole face lighting up."It's so big!" Several large tables ran down the length of the room, the wood decayed and broken in several places. There were feathers everywhere, especially where the tables had been broken, as if a large creature had smashed through them and left a trail of them behind. Massive webs hung across the beams above them like blankets.

"How old do you think this place is?"

"I don't know. Five hundred? Maybe a thousand years old?" Vivilla floated over to the table and touched the surface gingerly, the wood crumbling instantly beneath her airy fingertips.

"Wow!" Knud pressed his face against the table surface leaving a perfect mould of it in the crumbling wood. Dust covered his face and hair and he laughed, brushing it away. "Now I look like you!" Vivilla slapped him, her hand little more than a strong gust of wind against him.

From the corridor they heard a loud screech and they both felt their breath catch in their throats.

"We should be quiet," Vivilla whispered. Knud nodded but crept towards the sound.

"What are you doing?"

"The sound came from over there. I want to see the gryphon."

"No! Let's just look around this side," Vivilla begged.

"You're the one they can't hurt! Stop being such a weakling!"

"I'm not a weakling!" she hissed. She stood up and floated ahead of him, but reached out to put her hand on his shoulder.

The hallway was dark and cobwebs hung from the ceilings and walls.

"You go ahead," Knud insisted, spotting several large spiders, their hairy bodies scuttling up the webs, disturbed by the noise they had made.

With her hand still on his shoulder, Vivilla did as he'd asked, her eyes wide and frightened, though the webs and their occupants did not bother her at all. Soon she was covered in them and small black spiders dropped from her and scurried away as their webs wrapped themselves across her like a dress.

They turned several corners and soon Vivilla was so covered in webs she looked like she was made of them. One spider sat comfortably on her shoulder and stared at Knud, its dozens of little eyes glinting at him. Knud walked a little slower, scared it might jump towards him.

The hallway ended and opened out into a large hall, the staircase in front of them broken, the wood long since decayed. But what impressed them was not just the size of the hall but the hundreds of old abandoned nests that covered the floor and the stone rafters of the roof. Each nest was a good three metres wide and feathers of almost every colour were strewn around, most of them with a plain base colour of brown but flecked with vivid teals, oranges, reds and blues.

Vivilla floated forwards a little, worried that a gryphon would be nearby, but she saw none. Surprised, she floated a little further and looked down over the edge of the balcony to the ground.

Far below them, a woman lay in one of the smaller nests, curled up like a child. She was covered in feathers, which was fortunate since whatever had once passed as clothes had long since been reduced to ribbons. A few useless threads clung to her body. Her perfect ebony skin glinted in the low light and she clutched a long, thin double-ended dagger in her hands like it was a doll, the tips red with blood.

Vivilla couldn't move, she was so frightened, but both were transfixed by the sight of the woman. Her eyes were closed and Knud assumed she was asleep. She looked so peaceful curled up at the bottom of the nest with a few gryphon feathers caught up in her tightly curled hair.

It took them a moment to notice the shapes in the ash that surrounded the nest - the shapes of beaks, claws and large powerful wings, feathered creatures in the throes of death. Only some parts of the beaks and bones were still solid, but all of them charred.

As quietly as he could, Knud stepped back and made his way back down the hall. Vivilla followed, her hand on his shoulder. Knud did not even recoil from the spider that ran from her hand onto his arm, more frightened of the woman for reasons he could not explain.

It took them several minutes to walk back down the stretch of corridor they had just come from but finally they turned the corner.

"I want to go!" Vivilla whispered. "She scares me!"

Knud was about to interrupt and point out that, as it was, Vivilla could not physically be hurt, but he did not. Even he felt frightened, and a strange coldness spread over him like dozens of ice cold fingertips pressed against his skin. "We need to find some of the eggs," Knud insisted, though he sounded far less confident than earlier.

"Knud, please! I don't want to be anywhere near that woman!"

"Then we'll go another way."

"No! I don't want to! I want to go back!"

"Fine! Stay here!" Knud replied, exasperated, and walked past the entrance to the stairs towards one of the many hallways that led from the first room. Vivilla did not follow him but huddled by the door, her knees against her chest, hovering a few feet from the ground.

Knud made his way down the hallway and through several smaller rooms. He walked slowly, worried he would turn a corner and come face to face with a gryphon. He was a little glad of the cobwebs that blocked his way, sure that they implied nothing large had passed down the corridors recently. He held his crutch in front of him, his hand against the wall for support, and swept the cobwebs away. Most of the spiders scuttled away as soon as they felt their webs being touched but a few held on for dear life.

Ahead of him he saw a door blocking his way. When he reached it and pressed his hands against the wood, the surface instantly crumbled. It only took a few gentle shoves for the entire thing to break apart and a swarm of wood lice and spiders scampered away from the dust.

Slowly he stepped through, crutch first. He was more frightened than he cared to admit, his curiosity a little less fervent and his weak sense of self preservation a little more acute.

A hand touched his shoulder and he yelped and slipped. The door crumbled under his weight as he fell on it.

Vivilla hissed at him to be quiet. Just as terrified as Knud, she leant down and tried to help him up, and her hands slipped through his several times before he was able to stand.

They both looked around, terrified that the commotion would attract one of the gryphon but the old courtyard was completely abandoned. There were a few wild fig trees with their roots twisted into the cobblestones but barely a feather in sight. Wherever the gryphon were, they clearly had not visited the courtyard recently.

Knud walked forward, happy to have Vivilla back with him.

"Please say we can go soon?" she begged.

"I just want to find some eggs. Look, I can hear water, we can't be far!"

The old cobblestones were rickety, most of them loose, pushed up by centuries of tough weeds and fig tree roots. They walked ahead through a low archway, the sound of running water getting closer.

Knud breathed a loud sigh of relief when he saw the glint of water in the sunlight ahead of them, but the smile on his face disappeared as soon as he saw several large creatures reclined near the small river bed, their massive wings curled beside them.

Vivilla looked at him, terrified, her eyes so wide Knud could see right through them into the back of her head. "We should go!"

"Don't leave now!" a soft, silky voice laughed behind them.

They turned around slowly.

With the dagger still in her hands, the woman they had seen earlier stood before them, her golden eyes hypnotic. Neither of them noticed that she was still essentially naked, the tattered rags over her barely more than strings with feathers and straw tangled in them. They were captivated by her beautiful golden eyes.

"Did you climb all the way up here?" she purred. Her fingers caressed the blade of the dagger like it was a pet as she spoke.

Knud nodded, the horrible cold sensation he had felt earlier in her presence a hundred times worse. Vivilla's hair wrapped itself around her and her hand gripped Knud's shoulder like a vice.

"Well, that was brave of you! Especially with that leg!" The woman laughed, the sound too sweet, to melodic, a carefully perfected sound with no genuine emotion in it. She looked them up and down, both of them unable to pull their gaze away from her face. Vivilla tried to step back but found she could not move.

"My name is Ragana." She murmured her name as if it was the most beautiful sound in the world to her. Her perfect teeth flashed like pearls against her flawless black skin as she smiled. Knud opened his mouth and tried to speak but she cut him off. "I don't want to know your name! I don't care, and you…" she turned to Vivilla. "A sylph? Too young to even get your wings and you thought you would come here?"

"We just wanted some of the eggs," Vivilla spluttered.

"Eggs?"

"The ones they throw off the cliff," Knud finished, his voice hardly more than a whisper.

"You want the runts?" For a moment she toyed with the dagger tip. "Well then, go ahead! They won't hurt you. Take as many as you want." She smiled again.

Like an invisible chain had been released from around them, they both stumbled back. Ragana stepped slowly towards them and they scrambled back towards the river.

The gryphon looked up as they approached, but instead of advancing towards the two small figures they too recoiled from Ragana's presence, just as frightened as Knud and Vivilla.

"Go on, pick up the eggs!" Ragana laughed, and strolled after them into the sunlight.

Embarrassed almost as much as he was frightened, Knud turned to the river and looked around. He had no choice but to do as she'd said, and the gryphon were too afraid to approach. Several eggs lay in the water where they had been tossed out of the nests that littered the riverbank. Knud hobbled forward and stepped into the river, the water barely deep enough to pass his ankle. He reached out to the nearest egg and picked it up, feeling a weak heat emanating from within it, then quickly tucked it inside his shirt.

Knud waded through the river, the current strong enough to slowly push the abandoned gryphon eggs towards the waterfall, which was only a few feet away. Two eggs hung perilously close to the edge, ready to topple over, a small wobble from inside both of them clearly visible as if the babies inside could sense the danger they were in.

Already with three eggs tucked in his shirt, Knud rushed forwards and reached out for them. Vivilla scratched at him to leave them, but he ignored her. He picked up the first and finally the second egg, so close to the edge that the smallest slip or a strong gust of wind would have pushed him over the edge too.

Vivilla could feel her heart pounding in her chest. Knud's attention had been on the eggs, but her eyes looked out over the Aldwood and how far down the ground was. The roar of the many streams that poured over the edge of the cliff was amplified by the bare rock face on the way down.

They both turned to leave the cliff edge but Ragana blocked their way, the dagger in her hands held at the height of their eyes.

"You can't go back! You must never go back!" She laughed. "If you want to leave then you go that way." She motioned to the edge of the cliff.

"No! Please! You can't!" Vivilla begged.

Instantly, the expression on Ragana's face changed and her brows dipped into a cruel curve. "I can do whatever I wish! The dagger or the cliff, air spirit!"

"Why are you doing this?" Vivilla begged. Knud did not say a word, one arm on his crutch and the other against his chest to hold the eggs. Between his shirt and his skin he could feel the eggs shaking slightly, five tiny little heartbeats inside, weak but alive.

Ragana stepped forward and they both stepped back, the back of Knud's boots alongside the edge of the water fall.

"Please!" Knud begged. "I won't tell anyone you're here! I just wanted some of the eggs!"

Ragana rolled her eyes, a disgusted expression on her face, and raised the dagger to strike him. Knud did not know if he himself had jumped or if Vivilla had pushed him, but suddenly they were both in the air.

The ground hurtled towards them. With his heart in his mouth, Knud screamed, both arms wrapped around his chest protectively, his only instinct to make sure the eggs did not slip out from under his shirt as he fell.

Vivilla screamed as she held on to him, Knud's weight the only thing that made her fall at the same speed as him. She pulled at his shoulders as hard as she could, desperate to slow their rate of decent. It barely made a difference. The water below grew closer and closer.

Desperate, Vivilla did the only thing she could think of before they both hit the water. She pulled herself under him, her arms and her hair spread out like wings. Instantly, Knud noticed a difference, like a large blanket of air was pushing itself against him. The ground was getting closer but the speed of the fall was no longer going to be fatal.

Villella pushed Knud upwards with all her might, Knud only just able to straighten out his body so he fell feet first before they hit the water, Vivilla beneath him like an air cushion, the brunt of the fall absorbed by her. She crumbled like wet paper on impact. Knud shot through the water right through her, a cloud of bubbles behind him.

He swam up towards the surface with all his might but his heavy boot held him down like an anchor. With the last bit of breath in his lungs, Knud reached down and fumbled at the metal clasps down the side of his boot before he kicked it off as quickly as he could.

Above him, Vivilla floated on the surface. With a loud gasp Knud burst towards the surface, even more panicked now that he was in the water. He reached for Vivilla and wrapped his arms around her waist, the shore at least a hundred feet away from them.

"Vivilla! I can't swim! I can't swim!" Knud panicked.

Vivilla looked at him, dazed, both her eyes half closed. Knud readjusted his grip around her and kicked as hard as he could for the shore, his injured leg not much use but still enough for both of them to slowly move through the water.

It took several minutes for them to reach the edge of the lake. Vivilla still dazed, floated like a leaf on the water's surface while Knud dragged himself out, tears streaming down his face.

"We're alive!"

OUT OF TURN

The row of guards outside the palace had not left since the riot. In fact, the line had gotten thicker since he had last been there. Hundreds of stones and small rocks littered the foot of the palace wall, there were chips on the marble where they had struck and several of the beautiful statues had been damaged.

At first they had looked at him warily, despite the captain's badge on his shoulder. With their faces covered they had studied him, searching for signs of the plague. Halvard was surprised they could even breathe with the large clouds of incense smoke surrounding the palace. Finally, two of them stepped aside to let him pass.

As he walked under the massive palace gate passing hundreds of intricate carvings in the marble around him, he felt a wave of insignificance overwhelm him. *I am the son of an Ósómi, the son of a dwarf who murdered his family. I'm not a captain.*

He straightened his back and held his head high, determined not to show how he felt inside. His boots clicked loudly on the marble floors as he approached another set of guards in the middle of the large corridor.

"I have a message for King Haddr." He tried to muster as much nerve as he could, afraid that he would say something wrong or inappropriate. The guards looked him up and down, a little confused by his soldier's clothes, though they could tell from the badge pinned over his cloak that he was a captain.

"Are you infected?"

"Do I look infected to you?"

"Are you infected?" a second guard snapped.

"No, I'm not."

"This way."

The multiple halls and rooms seemed to stretch on forever. Huge murals decorated the walls, a mixture of mosaics, paints and stones depicting the history of Bjargtre.

The guard stopped for a moment to talk with another outside the throne room and a few glances flashed in Halvard's direction.

"What do you mean he's not there?"

"Lady Gull insisted the royal family and the court stayed above until the plague has gone," the guard replied. The first guard let out an exhausted sigh.

"This way!" he grumbled, and led Halvard up the steep staircase opposite the throne room doors. The stairs were so wide that twenty men could have climbed them shoulder to shoulder. When they reached the top, two enormous oak doors greeted them with six guards stationed outside it. Their uniforms were far more elaborate than the ones worn at the front of the palace, yet they still wore wraps on their faces. The air was filled with the fragrance of orange blossom, mint and pine, though the heavy smell of frankincense still permeated the air.

The guards opened the door and Halvard walked through. The rooms here were less tall, though still tall enough to emanate spectacular grandeur. Instead of murals on the walls, multiple tapestries hung down over them. The air was warmer than in the rest of the palace as numerous fireplaces stretched along the length of the walls, the coals red hot and smokeless. Halvard was struck by how empty the rooms were, just a few token pieces of furniture were in each, emphasising the vastness of the space. He couldn't shake the feeling that he was walking through a tomb.

Finally, the guard opened a pair of doors and he saw a group of dwarves in the room inside. The king sat at a large stone table at the far end of it, so short that his head barely reached the top of it. His brother sat next to him at the corner of the table and Lady Gull was nearby, as well as a few old dwarves Halvard did not recognise. A few servants stood silently by the walls.

They all looked up at him.

Be polite and think before you speak! Halvard thought to himself as he walked up to the end of the table and bowed, unsure if he should approach the king or if he should wait at the end of the table until he was called closer.

There was an awkward silence as they waited for him to speak, Halvard unaware that he did not need to wait for permission.

"I have a message from the general for the king," Halvard said in his clearest voice, worried his voice might falter. His brain was blank for a moment as he thought of how to word the message. *Think Halvard! Think!*

The boy king nodded and his hand reached for his brother's under the table and held it tightly. Lady Gull shook her head at them and began to cut up the food a little more, she did not even bother to look in Halvard's direction as he started speaking.

"A dwarf trader made it to the city a few hours ago. He reported that a goblin Agrokū named Ulf commands an army of over one hundred thousand goblins and that he plans to attack the city soon."

Lady Gull shrieked and her knife and fork clattered loudly onto her plate as she held her fingers over her mouth, each finger with a large gold ring forced around it. "One hundred thousand!" The young King Haddr jumped with fright at the sound of her. "So many goblins! Why are there so many goblins? And why would they want to attack the city?"

Halvard did his best not to visibly wince at the horrible sound of her voice or her stupid question.

"What do I do?" the boy king asked quietly, his frightened pale blue eyes looking down at the row of dwarves lining the right side of the table as they bickered among themselves with obvious fear in their faces. As their voices grew louder, two got to their feet, on the verge of a fight. The boy king looked to his younger brother who did his best to remain calm, though he was clearly just as frightened.

"We have to attack them! Yes…yes, that is what we should do!"

"One hundred thousand goblins, Lady Gull! We can't win against that!"

"We are dwarves! They are just goblins! Of course we'll win!"

"We should close the gates! Seal the city!"

"And what? Wait for them to starve us out?"

"We should have listened to Vǫrn! He saw this coming!"

"We need to send for the Queen! The Queen can save us!"

"She would never get here in time. It would take her a month, maybe even two to reach us."

Halvard ignored them, his eyes on the boy king who's face began to visibly crumble with fear, completely overwhelmed. His brother moved his arm around him, the young boy king on the verge of tears.

"What would you do?" Prince Hálfr suddenly shouted over the other voices in the room, his eyes on Halvard.

"Prince Hálfr...that is for the king, your brother to..." Lady Gull interrupted, but Hálfr shouted at her to be silent. She stared at him, at first shocked and then visibly angry, but she did as she was told nevertheless.

"Me?" Halvard spluttered. The boy king nodded. Halvard did not say a word for several seconds as everyone had their eyes on him.

I'm going to be made a soldier again, or worse! Halvard thought to himself, but he held his head high and replied.

"Send for help, now. Even with the plague, we can still bar the gates of the city and hold out for long enough."

"They have one hundred thousand goblins!" Lady Gull scoffed. "We can't fight against those kind of numbers!"

"Well, then I hope you're prepared to die," Halvard replied, his irritation getting the better of him. Lady Gull looked at him as if he were mad.

"What?"

"Are you ready to die? Because that is the choice you have: fight or die. I don't want to die and I'm sure you don't either, so we must fight."

"You cannot speak to the king like that," Lady Gull warned him.

"I was speaking to you, Lady Gull."

Lady Gull looked like she could not quite decide if she was about to explode from shock or anger.

"You're very outspoken for the son of an Ósómi," she smiled cruelly, fully aware of how much her jibe would hurt Halvard's pride. "Son of an Ósómi and probably the friend of one, too. I believe there is a pattern with you."

Yes, I'm going to be a soldier again, Halvard thought as his eyes narrowed at her.

"Jarl Vǫrn was right though, wasn't he? He may be an Ósómi, but he may save this city. You won't be anything else than hlaupa."

Lady Gull's mouth hung open and Hálfr grinned.

"Why was your father Ósómi?" Haddr asked curiously.

There was a few seconds of silence before Halvard replied. "He disobeyed the king's orders."

"Seems to run in the blood!" Lady Gull laughed.

"Lady Gull!" Hálfr shouted again, frightening his smaller older brother. "Everyone leave. Now!"

At first everyone looked at each other, unsure if the king's younger brother could command them to leave but slowly they got to their feet, red faced, and no one more so than Lady Gull. There were several loud grumbles before the door closed behind them and Halvard was left with the two boys.

Hálfr let go of his brother's hand and they both walked down the length of the table to stand in front of him. Halvard stood completely still, afraid of saying or doing something wrong. As they stood in front of him, Halvard thought how strange the two boys looked next to each other. The younger brother, Hálfr, so much taller than his older brother that anyone could be forgiven for thinking their ages were reversed.

Hálfr looked up at Halvard. "Your friend, Jarl Vǫrn, would he reach Lǫgberg before the crows... if we do send crows?"

"If he survived, then yes, I think he would. But you should send crows," Halvard quickly added. "The queen might not believe him and, even if she does, it will take a while for her to send a scout here. We need to send for help."

From outside the city they heard a large crash and the ground shook.

"What was that?" Hálfr asked.

Halvard listened and after a while was able to hear the sound of people from outside the palace and the unmistakable scream of an enraged mob.

"Can they get in?" Haddr said.

"No," Halvard lied. "The guards will hold them back."

Another loud crash sounded outside the palace, this time the floor even shook with the ferocity.

"Should I go outside?" Haddr asked.

"I don't know," Halvard admitted. "It might just make things worse."

Haddr looked up at his younger brother who shrugged his shoulders.

"What if they hurt me?"

"I won't let them!" Hálfr replied, a protective arm around him.

Haddr took a deep breath. "I should go outside."

Both brothers walked to the door, though Hálfr had to open it as Haddr was too weak. Lady Gull was the closest to the door, her ear almost against the key hole.

My King, the people..."

"I'm going to talk to them," Haddr interrupted her.

"I don't think that would be..."

"Halvard?" Haddr turned to look at him. "Would you speak for me? I...I don't think they'll hear me if I talk."

Halvard nodded and followed them quietly, Lady Gull's expression revolted at the king's request, though she did not dare question it. The rest of the councillors were clearly confused at who the soldier was that merited such an unexpected honour. They all followed silently but were instantly ordered to remain behind.

"What is your name?" Hálfr asked.

"Halvard."

"Just Halvard? What about your family name?"

"My father was an Ósómi. My family name was not allowed to pass to me."

Both boys stopped and looked up at him. "What was your father's family name?"

"Byström."

"Can I give you back your family name?"

Halvard's breath caught in his throat and he had to take a few seconds to be sure he had heard correctly before he nodded. Haddr smiled, a large toothy smile, a few of his milk teeth gone.

"Then I give you back your name," he said.

Halvard had no control over the sound that escaped his throat, a mixture of a gasp and a sob. He cleared his throat several times before he could talk clearly and even then his voice shook.

"Thank you, My King." He didn't care that the boys saw him cry. "Thank you!"

DEFIANCE

SICK

"I know what you're going to say," Astrid mumbled, her voice slurred. "You're going to tell me I should have asked for help."

Jarl rolled his eyes. "Not exactly the words I would have used." He had pulled her blanket from the bed down in front of the fire and put several logs in the hearth. Her shoulder was wrapped in fresh bandages and a compress of honey wine and various herbs Apsu had insisted would help was pressed against both sides of the wound.

What had surprised Jarl the most was that her shoulder did not look as bad as he had expected it would. The wound was a little red and still healing, but nowhere near as bad as he had assumed it would be. In a way that worried him even more. Astrid was completely exhausted and every word she tried to say was spoken in barely a whisper.

"When does the caravan leave?" Astrid muttered, both her eyes closed.

"In a week," Jarl lied. "Enough time for you to get better."

There was a quiet knock outside the door and Apsu walked in, a large bowl of soup in his hands. "How is she?"

"I'm just tired," Astrid mumbled, her voice barely strong enough to carry over the doorway.

"She needs to eat." Apsu crouched down next to them and passed the bowl to Jarl, its size too small for humans but perfect for them. "I don't have a spoon small enough, I'm afraid," Apsu explained. "She'll have to drink it from the side."

"Thank you," Jarl said, before Apsu could leave the room. He just shrugged his shoulders at him.

"She's my friend. A short friend, but still a friend."

Apsu left the room and quietly closed the door behind him before yelling at someone down the hall.

"Can you sit up?" Jarl asked. Astrid nodded and tried to sit up without his help but could barely lift her head from the floor, her head spinning. Gently, Jarl helped her and propped her back against him for support. With his arms around her and the bowl of soup in his hands, he carefully held it to her lips.

"When is the caravan really leaving?" she asked between sips.

"It's leaving tomorrow," Jarl admitted, and Astrid swore under her breath.

"I'll be fine, I just need to have a good sleep and we can leave tomorrow," she reassured him.

"You're not going anywhere!" Jarl told her firmly. "You're not leaving this room until you're better!"

"I'll be better by morning," Astrid insisted.

* * *

At first Astrid seemed to have improved, the infection in her shoulder a little less red and irritated when Jarl changed the bandages again a few hours later. She did not speak to him much, partly too tired but mostly too humiliated. She felt ashamed that she had allowed herself to get so sick and embarrassed that Jarl was once again the one who had to help her.

The silence did not help Jarl's growing nervousness as he thought about what he would say when he reached Lǫgberg. That was until Astrid began to toss and turn in her sleep, her forehead burning up.

"Astrid?" Jarl tried to wake her, but no matter how hard he shook her she would not open her eyes, her left arm now permanently convulsing.

446

Worried, Jarl pulled her into his arms and tried to wake her again. Her eyes were half open but glazed over and she began to mutter a stream of words Jarl could not understand, though he could only assume they were Axtī.

There was a quiet knock on the door before Apsu opened it and walked in. "How long has she been like this?"

"A few minutes. It doesn't make any sense! The wound is healing!"

"I have a friend, a healer who can help," Apsu offered. Jarl nodded, his whole face twisted with worry. Apsu quickly left and closed the door behind him, leaving the room in virtual darkness. Only a faint red light from the hearth remained, the logs long since burned into embers.

Below their room, a loud group of noisy revellers shouted and Astrid flinched, muttering in the language Jarl could not understand again.

"You're a fool, you know that?" Jarl whispered, kissing her forehead. "You should have let me help, you stubborn idiot."

When Apsu returned, it was with a surprisingly small human and it took Jarl a moment to realise that he was a young boy, even shorter than Jarl. At first Jarl was angry at the idea that a human child would be able to help Astrid, but the boy ignored his objections and carefully unwrapped the bandages around Astrid's shoulder.

"It's infected—"

"I knew that," Jarl replied sarcastically. The boy ignored him.

"How long has she been like this?"

"An hour. She was getting better and then she suddenly got worse."

As the boy turned Astrid over onto her front he noticed her ears as her hair fell away from them.

"She's an elf?" the boy exclaimed and Apsu's mouth fell open, just as surprised as the boy was.

Jarl decided not to elaborate on the boy's assumption and nodded.

"That's not right. She shouldn't be like this if she's an elf. They heal fast or die quickly." Jarl's breath caught in his throat at the boys words. "What was she like in the plains?"

"How do you know we were in the plains?" Jarl asked suspiciously.

"You're a dwarf, I doubt you came from the forest. Was she like this on the plains?"

"No, she was fine at first, her arm started giving her more trouble the closer we got to Waidu."

"Well that I'm not surprised by. With an injury like this it'll be a long time before she can use her arm properly again. But this..." he unwrapped the bandages that covered the back of Astrid's shoulder, "this doesn't make sense."

For a few seconds he prodded the skin around the wound and Astrid flinched, her arm shuddering with each prod.

"Do you have to do that?" Jarl snapped.

"Hey, be quiet little man! My nephew knows what he's doing," Apsu replied.

Suddenly a large smile crossed the boys face. "It rained, didn't it?"

"Yes, it did," Jarl confirmed, confused as to how the boy could have known.

"Do you have a knife?"

Jarl nodded.

"Can I have it?"

Jarl hesitantly passed it over and the boy took a deep breath, an excited look on his face. "Hold her arms. I've never done this before so I might not be able to do it quickly."

Jarl knelt down in front of Astrid and held her arms. With her back to the boy, the knife was poised above Astrid's left shoulder. He prodded some more until suddenly the skin just under the inflamed edges shuddered and a small bump protruded.

"Got it!" With his fingers pressed down on either side of the bump, he sliced firmly into her skin. Astrid woke with a start and screamed into the blanket as the boy cut into her back. Jarl held Astrid as tightly as he could, her wide panicked eyes on his.

"It's alright! It's alright! It'll be over soon, I promise," he said, as she struggled weakly.

From the corner of his eye, Jarl saw the boy press down around the cut and dig something out from under her skin. A trickle of blood spread down Astrid's back as he did so.

"I've got it!" the boy laughed excitedly.

Jarl stared, horrified, as a long thin black worm was pulled out of the cut the boy had made, its body fat with Astrid's blood, its head nothing more than a set of teeth that pulsated between the boy's fingers.

"A Kelic worm," the boy explained, as it squirmed between his fingers. "Normally harmless, except if you have an open wound and it's rained. The nasty little things can smell blood a mile away."

"But Astrid had her shoulder covered the whole time," Jarl said, confused.

"I'll bet she tried to change the bandages and it had enough time to crawl into the wound," the boy replied confidently. "They can be surprisingly fast."

He tossed the worm into the fire with a flamboyant flick of his wrist and pressed around the incision he had made. A trickle of bright red blood speckled with small black grains of Kelic worm venom oozed from her skin and Astrid bit down onto the blanket beneath her so that she wouldn't scream out loud.

"Done!"

The boy stood up and smiled triumphantly before he walked to the other side of the room and cleaned the blood off his hands in the basin.

"She should heal quickly now. They can only really cause trouble while they're under the skin."

Apsu cleaned away the blood that dripped from the fresh cut. With her eyes half open, she muttered under her breath in a garbled mix of Axtī and Mál as Jarl wrapped her arm up again.

"I'll need to get some sleep. I'll be back in the morning though," Apsu said, and got to his feet.

"Thank you!" Jarl said quickly, then looked over at the boy. "I didn't ask your name." "Ishum," the boy replied.

The door closed behind them and Jarl sat down next to Astrid, his face in his hands, exhausted. The bandages Apsu had used to clean away the blood on Astrid's shoulder were still on the floor.

"You need to stop doing this to me," Jarl laughed dryly. "You're going to give me grey hair."

* * *

Jarl awoke with a start. The fire had completely burned out, just a few embers were barely alive in the ash, and outside the sky was completely black. Other than the whistle of a few birds that darted around the rooftops of Waidu, anxious for the sunrise that was only a few hours away, there was silence.

He groaned and straightened his back as he stood up from the chair he had pulled next to the bed. Astrid was still fast asleep on the bed, the human blanket large enough to fold in half and lay over her like a normal dwarf blanket.

"We missed the caravan, didn't we?" Astrid looked over at him from her bed, disappointment on her face. Jarl nodded.

"Don't worry about it. There's another one in three days."

Astrid nodded, still slightly groggy, but the shine in her eyes had come back, the dull film over them gone. "Three days? They only have a caravan every week."

"You've been asleep for a while."

"How long?"

"Four days, almost five."

Astrid turned in the bed and reached for her shoulder with her good arm to undo the bandages, relieved as she saw the dagger wound had all but completely healed, the skin knotted together with the remains of a large scab still in the middle. She twisted her head around to see the entry wound on the back of her shoulder, a neat little scar left where Ishum had cut into it. Not that it stood out much compared to the patchwork of whip marks that could be seen peeking out from her tunic.

"Pretty enough to add to your collection?" Jarl asked, as he stepped from the chair onto the bed beside her. "Can you move your arm?"

Astrid looked down at her left hand and tried to lift it, but before she had even managed to lift it more than an inch from the bed, her arm began to shake and she was forced to let it drop back down.

"Can you close your hand?"

Astrid winced with frustration as her fingers trembled, only just able to curl her fingers into the palm of her hand.

"Ishum did say that would happen for a while," Jarl tried to reassure her.

"Who?"

"The boy who helped you."

"I can't remember much," Astrid admitted. "I just remember you holding me and then this pain in my shoulder."

"Does it hurt anymore?" Jarl asked as he re-wrapped the bandages.

"No. The pain is gone."

"Can you walk?"

Astrid sat up, glad that the horrible light-headedness had gone. She took Jarl's hand and stepped down from the bed, the human bed so much bigger than her that her feet did not reach the ground when she sat on the side. Her legs were stiff, every muscle in her body heavy and weak, but not weak enough to prevent her from taking a few steps forward.

Jarl smiled at her before a concerned frown crossed his face. "Skad is here."

"What?" Astrid stared at him.

"He arrived a few days ago with Áfastr Gull."

"Skad's leg was broken, he couldn't have made it here on his own."

"He didn't, Gull had a royal escort with him."

"Áfastr Gull? I can't remember if you ever told me about him," Astrid said, as she tried to remember back to her first conversations with Jarl. "Who is he?"

"A noble."

"Like you?"

Jarl laughed. "No. He's nothing like me."

"Why would he come to Waidu?"

"I don't know. But the only reason I can think of is that that Bjargtre is under siege," Jarl replied, and Astrid was surprised as she saw a relieved look on his face.

"Jarl?"

"If Gull is here then we don't have to go Lǫgberg! We won't get there any faster than they will now, so we can go back to the Aldwood for Knud."

"If Bjargtre was under siege he would have taken the first caravan. He wouldn't wait so long in the inn," Astrid pointed out. Jarl's hopeful expression faded.

"I can bribe the innkeeper, ask him what they've been saying," he suggested.

Already tired, Astrid leant against the bed for support and nodded in agreement. "I've bribed that innkeeper before, you only have to give him a couple of Fé and he'd sell his family secrets."

EGGS

Vivilla had hardly moved since they had fallen over the cliff edge; she lay on the ground, her arms wrapped around her chest, her face more transparent than usual.

"Are you alright?" Knud asked, resting his hand on her shoulder.

"That hurt!" she whispered.

"I thought you couldn't get hurt."

"I can! I'm not completely made of air!"

From inside his shirt one of the eggs wobbled a little. "It moved!" Knud exclaimed.

"What did?"

"The egg!"

Vivilla turned towards him and Knud took the eggs from inside his shirt to lay them out on the ground. They both stared at them, the eggs like perfectly smooth oval marbles without a single crack. The shells were slightly opaque in the sunlight and faint foetal shapes were visible inside.

"They're beautiful!" He reached out and lifted one of them up in the air so that the sun shone behind it, making the shape inside a little more visible. He smiled at the tiny body with its wings wrapped around it, its head barely bigger than a plum pip. "They're so small!"

"You need to keep them warm," Vivilla said.

"I need to hide them. I don't think Loba would let me keep them." Knud scratched his head and looked around. He did not want to leave the eggs alone for a single minute. One of the eggs shuddered, the motion more of a shiver, and Knud picked them back up and tucked them in his shirt, a little worried his wet clothes were not much help against the cold. Inside his shirt the tiny little bodies inside the eggs shuffled again and Knud wrapped his arms around his chest. "They're mine."

Vivilla got up, the front part of her body where she had hit the water more transparent than before, her face almost invisible expect for an eye. She turned to face the sunlight and spread out her arms to absorb every single ray that reached her.

Knud was excited but worried, keenly aware of the massive responsibility he now had for the tiny creatures that now relied on him. "They're birds, so I have to keep them warm…" he muttered to himself. "I can pretend I'm cold and wear my cloak to hide them."

"And when they hatch?" Vivilla asked. Knud bit his lip.

"I don't know. Do you know somewhere I could hide them?"

Vivilla thought for a few moments. "The abandoned village. We can hide them there."

"Would someone be able to hear them?"

"They might, but I can keep watch. I normally stay there during the night anyway."

Knud looked at her. "Aren't you lonely?"

"No!" Vivilla said, a little too quickly. She lowered her arms and turned to look at Knud, her face less transparent than before. "The woman, you should tell the others about her."

His expression changed instantly from worry to anger. He got up and reached for his crutch, then looked around the lakeside and noticed that the pony was long gone.

"What are you doing?"

"I'm going to tell them about the woman."

"But what about the eggs?"

Knud tapped at his shirt and smiled. "They'll be fine."

Vivilla did not stop him, instead she hovered behind as Knud walked back through the forest as quickly as he could, one arm over his crutch and the other across his chest to keep the eggs as warm as possible. He could feel the little creatures wiggle more and more inside their shells.

"Knud! I'll wait here!" she whispered, frightened as she saw one of the Vârcolac in the distance in the shape of a large boar.

Knud stopped and looked down at the eggs tucked under his shirt. They would notice, he was sure of that, and the last thing he wanted was to have them taken away from him. He glanced around and spotted a nearby gorse bush. Carefully, he pulled the eggs out one by one and laid them next to each other under the sharp prickly leaves.

"They'll get cold," Vivilla protested, crouched next to him.

"They were in a river before. They'll be alright for a bit longer," Knud replied. He reached around the bush and dragged some dry leaves and dead grass over them. As he got up, Vivilla crawled under the bush and curled around the eggs to protect them.

"I'll wait here."

Knud nodded and hobbled in the direction he had seen the Vârcolac walking. "Wait!" he called out.

The Vârcolac turned to look at him, the large boar skin slipping off his back as he did so.

"The woman, the woman who hurt Astrid!" Knud panted. "I saw her!"

"You saw a stranger?"

Knud nodded.

"Where?"

"By the falls!" Knud paused as he thought of how to point them in the right direction without telling them about where he had been. "I saw her up in the tunnel behind the falls."

With a loud snort the Vârcolac's skin slid back over him and he darted off into the forest, trampling over anything in his way as he charged through it.

Vivilla hovered above the bush she had been hiding under and motioned at him to go. "Find the wolf girl!"

"But the eggs!"

"The eggs are fine!"

It took Knud several minutes to reach the clearing and by the time he got there he was completely out of breath.

"Knud?" Loba put down the large wicker basked packed full of apples and walked over to him. "Why are you wet? And where have you been? I told you that—"

"The woman who stabbed Astrid, she's by the falls!"

"What?"

"The woman! She's in that tunnel behind the waterfall. I saw her!"

Loba's eyes widened. "The Broken Falls?" Knud nodded.

If she ordered a command to the others Knud did not hear it, but in almost perfect unison every Vârcolac in the clearing dropped down onto all fours and took the form of the animal skin they had slung over their backs. Bugal clung onto his wife as she led the pack out of the clearing, his legs too short to be able to keep up with the Vârcolac. The clearing was deserted within seconds.

Knud looked around the clearing for anything he could use to keep the eggs warm, but other than several piles of peeled fruit skins there was nothing. He walked back to the bush where Vivilla was still curled around its base and pulled out the eggs.

"Are they gone?"

Knud nodded and tucked the eggs into his shirt along with some of the dried grass and leaves from under the bush. Nervously, they both got up and walked as quickly as they could to the deserted village. Impatient at how slow Knud was, Vivilla darted ahead of him every few seconds only to float back, each time more irritated.

"Hurry up!"

"I can't, one foot remember?" he argued.

By the time they reached the village, Vivilla was ready to tear her long white hair out, sure that at any minute the Vârcolac would return despite Knud's reassurances that it would take them a while just to reach the falls, let alone return.

"Here, this one will do." Vivilla floated into the smallest of the deserted buildings, pushing away the bracken that had grown across the front of the doorway. Knud sat down on a large pile of leaves at the far side of the hut and looked up at the holes in the roof.

"You live here?"

Vivilla nodded.

"Aren't you cold?"

"No." She shrugged her shoulders. "I don't get that cold," she lied.

Knud reached into his shirt and pulled out one of the eggs to look at it, fascinated by the hundreds of colours that covered it like threads of pigment trapped in marble. As he wrapped his hand around it, the egg shuddered, and from inside the hard shell he could feel a tiny little body shuffle around so that it lay above the palm of his hand.

"It's alive!" Knud smiled and looked at Vivilla who was just as excited. She reached out to touch it and laughed as the egg shuddered again.

"What do we do now?" Knud asked her.

"Keep them here. At least till they hatch," Vivilla suggested.

"They need to keep warm though."

"Well you can't keep them in your shirt all the time. Someone will notice."

Suddenly, an idea flashed across his mind and he looked at Vivilla excitedly. "If they're all gone, I could hide you both in the caves!" Vivilla looked at him as though he had suggested they fall off the cliff again.

"No!"

"Why not?"

"I don't like dark places, I need sunlight."

Knud sighed, exasperated, and pushed himself up. "I can't leave the eggs out here. If you don't want to come then don't, but I'm taking them down into the tunnels."

Even though he was sure most of the Vârcolac were gone, he looked around just to make sure. As he approached the tree stairs, Vivilla called for him to wait for her and rushed to catch him up, putting her cold hand on his shoulder.

As quickly as he could, Knud walked down the stairs and into the tunnels, Vivilla's touch on his shoulder suddenly a lot colder the moment they walked out of the sunlight. She shuddered but did not turn around to leave.

"It smells strange in here," she whispered.

Knud ignored her and carried on walking, his crutch a little too loud on the stone floor. Both of them worried that at any moment a Vârcolac would appear from one of the rooms and see them.

"In here."

As soon as he reached his room, Knud ushered Vivilla into it and pulled the curtain across the doorway.

"Why isn't there a door?" Vivilla asked, surprised.

"They don't have any doors down here."

"Why?"

"I don't know." He walked over to his bag that was propped against the wall, reached in and pulled the contents onto the floor.

"What are you doing?"

"If I make a vest I could still keep them under my shirt without too many people noticing," Knud suggested.

"Knud, they're too big for you to hide under your shirt. You'll look like a pregnant woman."

"Well, what else can I do?"

Vivilla looked around, the room almost completely bare except for the bedding in the middle of the room and Knud's bag.

"What if you carry them in the bag? Wrap them up and keep them in the bag?"

Knud nodded and shook the bag upside down until every last item had fallen out of it.

"Here, why don't you use this?" Vivilla picked up the bandages Jarl had been forced to make from Knute's cloak. Knud took them from her and held them tightly in his hands.

"What's wrong?" she asked, his expression difficult to read.

"Nothing." One by one he wrapped up the eggs, first in the cloak and then in the clothes that had been in his bag.

"No, wrap them up together," Vivilla suggested.

"Why?"

"They'll be lonely otherwise."

"They're in eggs, they won't notice."

"I was in an egg once and I noticed," Vivilla replied. "They should be together."

Reluctantly, Knud unwrapped the first two eggs and placed them inside the nest he had created in his bag before the rest of the eggs followed.

"We should wrap them up more, do you have any more clothes you can use?"

Knud shook his head and Vivilla darted off down the tunnel only to return a few seconds later with a bundle of dry leaves and grass in her arms. "Will this do?"

Knud nodded and stuffed the dried leaves and grass into the bag until all the eggs were mostly covered, only the very tops of them exposed.

"There, they're safe now." Knud grinned at Vivilla who grinned back excitedly.

THE WOLF OF WAIDU

Astrid had not been wrong. With only one Fé in his hand, the innkeeper listened for, goaded and outright asked for every piece of information he thought would be relevant. With enough flattery and more than enough drinks, Gull let slip the secret he had been meant to keep until he reached Lǫgberg.

Jarl stared at the innkeeper in shock and then dismay. "So, the king is dead."

The innkeeper nodded. "You're from Bjargtre, too, aren't you? Is that why you came here?"

Jarl shook his head. "No, I came for something else."

Jarl passed the innkeeper one more Fé to stay quiet about what he had heard and walked back around to the front of the inn and into the street. He kicked at the ground as he walked, angry that he had allowed his hopes to pick up so quickly. This is it, he thought, there's no escaping this.

"Is the Brojóta burðr still with you?"

He turned and saw Skad behind him, leaning against the wall of the inn, a splint over his broken leg and the same old scowl on his face. Jarl glanced around, worried that Gull would also be close, but saw that they were almost alone in the street.

"No, she left," Jarl replied coldly.

Skad looked at him, both eyes narrowed, unsure if Jarl was telling the truth. "I thought you liked that Blanda blóð."

"She didn't feel the same as I did," Jarl replied convincingly.

Skad snorted loudly. "Yes she did! She was always watching you when you thought she wasn't looking, the silly bitch." Jarl scowled at him, his fists clenched into a tight ball. "You really fell for that Goðgá, didn't you? How did you think it would end falling for her? That girl is a witch's Fé—"

Jarl punched Skad so hard in the stomach that the old dwarf doubled over, despite the thick leather chest plate he wore. Just as quickly Skad retaliated, hitting back, and Jarl stumbled to his side but regained his footing, able to block Skad's fist as he swung back at him. Jarl was faster and younger but Skad was infinitely more experienced.

Finally Jarl struck Skad so hard across his face that the old dwarf was knocked out of balance and, with one firm sweep of his leg, Jarl knocked him to the ground. He landed heavily on his back, winded.

Jarl towered over him, a revolted sneer on his face, a large bruise surfacing on his cheek and both his knuckles red and bruised.

Skad glared up at him. "It's a good thing for her she didn't decide to go with you to Lǫgberg! I might have trained her but I also trained Vígdís; it would have been easy to make her disappear!"

Jarl stepped back, horrified. "That's why you put up with her? That's why you convinced her to come?"

With his eyes narrowed, Skad turned his head and spat a mouthful of blood onto the ground. "Do you honestly think there weren't other people who could have taken you? Astrid isn't special. There would have been plenty of humans who would have taken you, and they wouldn't flirt with death as much as she does! The sooner she disappears from the face of Ammasteinn the sooner I can forget I ever trained a Blanda blóð!"

Jarl saw red. He stormed up to Skad, his fist raised, so angry he could feel his heart pound in his chest like a drum.

As Jarl's fist came down towards him, Skad kicked him as hard as he could in the face. With a loud grunt Jarl stumbled back, his nose broken, blinded for a few seconds. While still doubled over, Skad stood up and kicked him again, the force of it enough to throw Jarl backwards onto the floor.

Before Jarl had time to pick himself up, Skad's boot slammed into his stomach with the force of a mad horse. Jarl gasped in pain as Skad kicked him again and again as hard as he could. He was unable to retaliate, still blinded from the pain of his broken nose, and unable to breathe properly, though that did not stop Skad from kicking him repeatedly without mercy.

As a metal tipped boot came into contact with his jaw, Jarl felt something large and furry step over him, followed by the sound of a loud snarl and Skad's scream. He turned onto his side, his hand over his broken nose, and spat out a mouth full of blood. It took him several seconds for his vision to return and to regain control of his breathing.

Above him, Astrid dragged her jaws down Skad's arm as he frantically tried to push her away, her teeth sharp enough to tear through his tunic and slice several deep grooves into his skin.

As Skad tried to reach for his sword Astrid let go of him and reared onto her hind legs, her claws flexed, ready to attack. She was almost twice the size of him.

"Ylva!" Jarl scrambled to his feet and pulled Astrid away. She looked at him, confused at first, but when she saw how battered his face was her lip curled back to expose her sharp white teeth, lines of Skad's blood between them, and she turned back to Skad.

"No! No, don't!" Jarl pulled her away and knelt down in front of her, his arms around her neck. "Don't, Astrid, go back to the inn! I'll follow you," he whispered into her ear. Astrid growled and walked away, her hackles raised.

Skad stared at Jarl from the ground, his hand covered in the blood that dripped down the tears in his arm. Jarl roughly rubbed at his face to wipe away the trickle of blood which ran from his nose, his beard already wet with it.

"A wolf! A wolf!" Skad muttered horrified. Revolted, Jarl spat a mouthful of blood at him in disgust and he smiled as it hit Skad's face.

Still severely winded, Jarl walked slowly back to the inn, his hand pressed over his ribs where Skad had kicked him repeatedly.

Apsu looked up at him as he walked through the door and put down the several flasks he had managed to hold in just one hand. "What in Hel happened to you?"

"I had an argument," Jarl mumbled, the entire side of his face already so swollen each word was a struggle.

"I take it you lost?"

"No!" Jarl laughed and managed a bloodied smile. "I think I won." He made his way up the stairs, his hand on the wall for support.

As he was half way up Astrid rushed down, her wolf skin gone, and pulled his arm across her shoulders to help him walk. Slowly they made their way back to her room and closed the door behind them.

"How did you get in without anyone seeing you?" Jarl slurred, a large amount of blood in his mouth, the side of his tongue bitten open from when Skad had kicked him in the face.

"I climbed in through the window."

Jarl looked over to the window and saw it was wide open. There were a few deep scratches on the wood of the windowsill, and the wolf skin lay on the floor in a crumpled mess, Skad's blood covering the snout and teeth.

Astrid reached for his face, careful to be as gentle as she could, and turned it towards her. He winced as she touched the large bruise on his cheek, the skin already a faint shade of dark blue. She growled at the back of her throat as she looked at the damage. "I

473

should have ripped his arm off!" she hissed, and moved her fingers to either side of his nose where the break was. "This will hurt," she warned. As quickly as she could she pushed the broken bone back and there was a loud 'crunch' as it slotted into place. Jarl grunted in pain, his hands clenched into a fist. "It won't hurt for long," Astrid reassured him, as her hands began to glow bright blue.

"No! I'm fine!" Jarl gripped her wrists quickly to stop her touching his skin.

"This won't hurt me, I have more than enough energy for this," she reassured him.

Jarl let go of her hands and his shoulders relaxed a little as her cold fingers touched his skin. He breathed a loud sigh of relief as the pain from his injuries disappeared as if they were being washed away.

He reached up to his nose and tried to wipe the blood away with the side of his hand. "I've always wanted to do that." He laughed and walked up to the basin by the window.

"Do what?"

"Hit Skad." He smiled as he picked up a wash rag and wiped the blood from his face and beard. "And it feels just as good as I thought it would!" His face dropped as he remembered what Skad had said to him and he turned to face Astrid. "Skad told me he was going to have you killed in Logberg."

Astrid's lack of emotion at his information surprised him. She looked at him blankly, almost bored, and shrugged her shoulders.

"You knew?" Jarl asked.

"No, but I'm not surprised. I knew he hated me," she replied calmly. "He only put up with me because he couldn't say no to Dag."

"He's an idiot if he thought he could get away with killing a warlock's daughter!"

"No, it makes sense. Lǫgberg is far away enough from the Red Mountains. It would take months or even years for Dag to hear anything about it, that's if he ever bothered to leave the place."

"Skad wouldn't risk it. He would have to be mad! Dag would kill him."

Astrid rolled her eyes and shook her head, the animosity heavy in her voice. "Dag wouldn't do anything. He would just say that it's not his place to fix the world, like he always does. He would be sad for a while and then he would never talk about it again. He doesn't get attached to people, he's a warlock. Besides, Ragi raised me more than Dag did."

Jarl looked at Astrid's eyes, glazed and distant as they always were when she did not want a strong emotion to show in them. Her jaw clenched. "Ragi would have come to Lǫgberg, he would have—" She quickly cleared her throat and changed the subject.

"What did the innkeeper say? Did he find out why Gull came?"

"The king is dead. Gull came to give the news officially to the queen."

Astrid looked at him, his face downcast. *He doesn't want to go,* she thought to herself.

"What if you sent a message? Pay someone to take it to the queen from here?" she suggested. Jarl shook his head.

"They would never take it seriously. All the dwarves see the goblins as a nuisance, not a threat."

"So you have to lose everything for them to take it seriously?" Astrid snapped.

"Yes. They will either think I'm mad or telling the truth if I go. Either way, Vígdís will at least send swallows to Bjargtre." He looked at Astrid, her hands clenched tightly into fists, a slight glow around them. He took them in his, the glow instantly fading. "Would you stay here in Waidu? If Skad is in Lǫgberg it will be dangerous for you. If he sees you he could try and get you killed." Astrid snorted loudly. "It's always dangerous for me! I'm going with you! We'll just take one of the human caravans before Skad and Gull can leave and get there before him."

"And if Skad sees you..." Jarl said, slightly annoyed at how lightly Astrid took Skad's threat, "he'll kill you."

"He'll try. I could beat him when I was fourteen years old. He'd have better luck trying to kill a Leshy. I can always hide, pretend to be a wolf. It's worked before, there's no reason why it shouldn't work now."

Jarl was silent for a few moments as he looked at the determined frown on Astrid's face. He knew that she would not stay behind and, if truth be told, he did not want her to. She smiled and leant her head against him, her hands curled against her chest.

"I'm going with you."

Jarl closed his eyes, relived and troubled at the same time, his arms around her.

"We'll have to pay though, the human caravans will only take elves or dwarves with them if they pay."

"How much?" Jarl asked.

"It depends on the caravan. Some will ask for three Feoh, others for thirty."

"I only have Fé," Jarl said worriedly.

Astrid stood up and reached into her bag by the bed. She rummaged around for a few seconds before she finally pulled out a small pouch from the bottom. "I have a hundred and eighteen Feoh. I doubt they'll ask for more than ten."

"I thought you never carried money?" Jarl laughed, surprised by just how much she had.

"I do!" Astrid smiled. "I just don't carry dwarf money." She paused for a moment and took the wet rag from next to the basin to wipe away a streak of blood Jarl had missed from his nose. "Jarl, why did you call me Ylva before?"

"I didn't think it was a good idea to call you Astrid," Jarl replied.

"But why Ylva?"

Jarl scratched at his head, aware that what he was about to say would not necessarily be taken the way he wanted it to be. "Ylva was the name of my brother's dog." To his surprise, Astrid burst out laughing.

"You named me after a dog?"

"Ylva means wolf."

Again Astrid laughed. "Ylva, it's a nice name."

"I don't think you need any more names, it's hard enough for me not to call you Astrid in front of Apsu."

"Well, if I have to pretend to be a wolf while we're in Løgberg then that will be my new name," she said.

* * *

Apsu stared at Jarl. "I could have sworn your face was a bit more broken when you came in?" he said, cleaning the flask in his hand.

Jarl shrugged his shoulders, his expression completely unreadable. "It looked worse than it was."

"Doesn't the human convoy leave before the dwarves do? They did last time," Astrid said, worried that Jarl's miraculous recovery would prompt more awkward questions.

"Yes it does. They won't take dwarves though, at least not him. They might take you."

"Not even for a few Feoh?" Jarl asked, one eyebrow raised. Apsu laughed.

"If there's Feoh on offer, then of course! But you should go now or you might miss them. They leave today, just before the gates close for the night."

Jarl exchanged a quick look with Astrid and walked back upstairs to retrieve their bags, his own bag the only one which was unpacked, Astrid's already by the door with her wolf skin.

Astrid turned back to Apsu and reached into her pocket. "Thank you..." she placed several Feoh onto the counter, "for letting me stay after..."

"What, did you think I would throw you out just because of those?" He motioned towards her covered ears and Astrid nervously looked around, but everyone was far too preoccupied with their food to notice them. "You brought me and my sister here alive. That's all that matters." Apsu shrugged his shoulders. "But is there anything else I should know?" he joked. Astrid laughed and shook her head as Jarl came down the stairs with their bags.

"No, nothing else," she lied.

They reached the human caravan just as it was about to leave Waidu, the gates already half closed as they rode through them.

She was surprised at how quickly she had grown accustomed to the pony, even the voices in her head had stopped panicking when she rode it, and the pony would no longer snort at her when she approached it, though she wondered how much of that was down to Jarl more than her newfound trust of the animal.

As they approached the caravan, Astrid jumped down from the pony and ran up to the two guards flanking it. Jarl watched as she spoke in a language he couldn't understand to the tall slender woman whom the guards had called over. At first it looked as though the woman would refuse them passage; she shook her head firmly and Astrid pleaded, pointing towards the gates. Again, the woman shook her head. Finally Astrid reached into her pocket and passed the woman what Jarl assumed was several Fé. The woman smiled and nodded.

Astrid walked back to Jarl and he pulled her back up onto the pony.

"She'll let us stay?"

She nodded, mounted the pony, and held onto Jarl's waist as they rode ahead.

"Did she say how long it would take to get there?"

"No. I know it takes three days to reach the Kaito Passage, but after that I'm not sure. It's a long way through the forest. It could take up to two weeks."

Jar's face dropped as he realised the only food he had with him was what Loba had given them. His stomach groaned at the thought of the grasshopper pies that he would inevitably have to eat.

"And Gull won't catch up with us?"

Astrid shook her head. "Not unless he organises his own caravan. We should reach Logberg long before them."

A LITTLE FAITH

The loud howl that ripped through the tunnels woke Knud with a start. He clutched the bag in his arms tightly, Vivilla next to him, her eyes as wide as saucers.

"What's wrong?" she whispered in a panicked voice.

"I don't know." He crawled over to the doorway and peeked through the small crack between the curtain and the doorframe.

In the opposite room, Loba sat beside Bugual, her hand crushed in his grip. The little man's face was scrunched up in a painful grimace as his other hand was being wrapped in a bandage by one of the other Vârcolac. The skin over his hand was raw, as though the top layer of it had been burned away.

Around them, the other Vârcolac sat huddled on the floor, some of them inside their skins. There were several large bruises on some of their faces and one Vârcolac - the one with the boar skin Knud recognised from earlier in the day - had a large gash just above his eye, his arm tied in a sling.

"What's happening?" Vivilla asked behind him.

"Shhh! I don't know!" Knud whispered back, worried one of them would hear her.

"Aren't you going to find out?"

"No."

"Why not?"

"Because they don't like me."

"So?"

Knud growled and stood up, ready to do anything if she would only stop talking. With the wall as his crutch, Knud hopped forward until he stood in the doorway.

"What happened?"

Loba looked over and for the first time she smiled at him. "She's gone," she said.

"Who was she?"

"I don't know, but she's gone now," Bugal snapped. "And if I see her again I'll bury her in the earth myself." Knud was surprised to hear the malice in Bugal's voice. "Filthy murderer!"

"Murderer?"

"You should go back to sleep," Loba urged him gently. "It's late."

"Who did she murder?" Knud insisted.

"Fróðleikr. You could smell it on her!" Bugal spat. "She sucked the life out of them!"

Knud was about to press for more answers but Loba flashed him a look that warned not to push his luck. He walked back into his room, pulled the curtain across the doorway behind him and looked at Vivilla who had her hands protectively over the bag. "It's alright."

"They're not going to come in?"

"I don't think so." Knud sat down and pulled the bag back into his arms. Inside, the eggs shuddered.

They both listened intently, worried that one of the Vârcolac would walk into the room, but none of them did, and eventually the small crowd dispersed. The tunnels were silent again.

"What are you going to call them?" Vivilla asked.

"What?"

"The eggs. What are you going to call them when they hatch?"

"I'm not sure." Knud opened the bag and looked down at them. "I think we should wait till they're here."

"I want to name some of them!" Vivilla insisted.

"Alright."

"I want to name three of them."

"Two," Knud argued back at her.

"No, three," she insisted. "If it's wasn't for me you would be dead."

Knud's mouth twitched as he thought, reluctant to give up the naming rights to three of the eggs. "We can draw for it!" he suggested.

"Draw?"

Knud reached into the bag and pulled out a long blade of dry grass. Vivilla watched as he broke it into two uneven pieces, shuffled them in his hand and held up the ends in his fist. "Pick one, the person with the shortest straw gets to name two eggs."

"If I pick the longest straw I get to name three?"

Knud nodded. Vivilla rubbed her hands together and looked at the straws for a few moments. Her hand dangled over them and Knud squirmed impatiently.

"Just pick one!"

With a deep breath, Vivilla pulled one of the straws and held it up, a triumphant smile on her face, until Knud opened his hand and they both saw that the straw he held was longer.

"No!"

"I win!" Knud smiled.

Vivilla was about to protest when they both heard footsteps in the tunnel outside, so she said nothing until they had passed.

"Not fair!" Vivilla hissed.

"It was fair, you just lost!"

* * *

Ever since the night he had warned them about the woman, Knud had noticed the Vârcolac treated him differently. If he walked into a room they no longer ignored him and occasionally he would even get a smile, though none of them really made an effort to talk to him. For once Knud was glad of that, terrified that someone would find the gryphon eggs he carried around with him at all times in the bag on his back.

Vivilla had deserted the caves as soon as she could, and even Knud had to admit she was better off for it. The lack of sunlight for even a few hours had left her skin even more transparent than usual and her hair, which usually floated around her head as though she was underwater, had begun to lay flat against her face like a second skin.

They had waited until the second night when everyone was asleep and, to make up for the fact she was still angry with him for winning the draw, Knud stayed with her in one of the abandoned stone huts on the surface until morning.

As soon as the sun rose, Vivilla darted from the hut and hovered above the nearest tree, her face to the sunrise. With his bag on his back, Knud walked out and watched her. The effect of the sunlight on her skin was quite beautiful, especially after so many hours underground. First her hair lifted up and began to float around her face and then the glass-like look returned, her skin no longer so transparent that he struggled to see her.

Over the next few days they took it in turns to care for the eggs, Vivilla during the day and Knud during the night. He couldn't help but notice that each time he took the bag away from her for the night it seemed a little heavier, and it was a relief since the eggs had started to move less and less. Vivilla assured him it was because they were close to hatching, but he couldn't shake the worry that maybe he had not kept them warm enough, and each night he would make sure that his blanket covered the bag, too.

If he'd had his way he would have quite happily spent the days with Vivilla in the forest with the bag slung over his back, but Loba seemed determined to not let him out of her sight any more, and it had become more difficult for him to slip away unnoticed. For the past few days he had been woken by her, only to be ordered to eat with the other Vârcolac in the hall and then help them with the crops until midday.

Knud tapped his foot against the chair and tried not to think about the eggs. His hands clumsily wound together the dried grass and flowers in front of him on the table into a misshapen wreath. The other Vârcolac at the table had already made several wreaths, each of them a lot neater and more elaborate than his.

The Vârcolac were excited and the children who normally played out in the forest ran over to the table every few minutes to take the new wreaths to a second clearing not too far away. The wreaths were strung up on the trees around the large bonfire that had been set up in the middle of the clearing and a basket of fresh fruit was placed at the top of the pyre.

"Smile!" Loba demanded, as she sat down next to him and took his mangled wreath from him. "That's not how you do it. First you need to twist the grass into a braid and then weave the flowers into it."

"Why? Riik just told me that you're going to burn them."

"Only at the end of the day; we want them to look pretty before then."

Knud sighed and took another large handful of hay from the pile in front of him.

"You miss them don't you?" Loba asked quietly. "You miss your father and Astrid?" It took Knud a second to realise that she meant Jarl and not Knute.

For a moment he nearly corrected her honest mistake, but instead he just nodded.

"He'll be alright, Astrid's with him," Loba reassured him.

"But Astrid's hurt. What if she can't protect him?" Knud whispered, a small trickle of fear in his voice.

Loba smiled confidently. "She will."

"What if she can't though?"

Loba looked at him and thought for a moment about how she could convince him not to worry. She put down the wreath in her hand and sat a little closer to him. "Did Astrid tell you how she saved me?"

Knud shook his head.

"Have you seen the scars on Astrid's back?"

Knud nodded.

"When I met Astrid she was tied to a pillar in the middle of a goblin camp with her back whipped to shreds. She did that just so that Bugal could dig a tunnel under the camp without anyone noticing, and even then she still managed to get us over the mountains to here. She can keep your father safe."

"He's not my father."

Loba looked at him, confused. "I thought—"

"He was my father's best friend." A surprised look crossed Loba's face.

"And your mother?"

Knud opened his mouth but found he could not say the words and he swallowed the lump at the back of his throat. Loba nodded her head understandingly and took his hands in hers.

"You don't need to worry about them."

Knud pulled his hands away and rubbed at his eyes before the tears could spill down his face. "I just want him to come back." His shoulders had begun to shake and Knud could feel the suppressed worry in his gut start to worm its way up to his mouth. Loba quickly got up and passed him his crutch.

"I want to show you something."

Knud gulped and forced another lump at the back of his throat back down into his stomach. "What?"

"You'll see when we get there. Actually, leave the crutch, it'll be faster if you just climb onto my back."

A little hesitant, Knud clambered onto Loba's back, his hands on her shoulders. He noticed that Loba's wolf skin, which as usual hung down over her shoulders, had a different feel to Astrid's. The fur was a lot smoother, each hair fine and supple. "Your fur feels different," he remarked.

"I wear it more," Loba replied, and walked out into the forest.

"Is this your fur?"

"Of course it is!" Loba said, offended.

"It's just, Astrid said hers was given to her."

Loba stiffened slightly but did not ignore his question, her eyes sad as she replied. "Una gave it to her."

"So if you gave your fur to someone, could they wear it?" Knud asked.

"You know little dwarf, if you were a Vârcolac I would slap you for asking such a rude question," Loba replied icily.

"Sorry."

Loba took a deep breath. "I suppose you're not a Vârcolac, so I can't expect you to know that. No, if I gave someone my fur they could not wear it. For someone to wear your fur you have to give all your energy to them. Una was dying and so was Astrid. Una gave her the last of her energy to save her."

"Astrid saved all of you, didn't she?" Knud said proudly. Loba shook her head sadly.

"No, should couldn't save all of us. Even she can't save everyone."

Loba was surprised when he did not ask any more questions. "What, no more questions, little dwarf?"

"I was going to ask about the fur," Knud mumbled.

Loba sighed and shuffled her grip around his legs. "What did you want to know?"

"Do you grow this fur? Were you born a wolf?"

Loba raised an eyebrow so high it nearly got lost in her hairline. "No, of course I wasn't born a wolf!"

"You said I could ask!" Knud argued.

Loba growled before she replied. "We are born without our fur. Some of us are given our furs from our passed grandparents, but before seven years old none of us can take the skin until we have chosen our animal."

"How do you choose?"

"Do you ever stop asking questions?"

Knud smiled and shook his head. "No. Jarl says I was born asking a question."

"It wouldn't surprise me."

"Well?"

"Well what?"

"How did you choose?"

"That's also considered rude if you were a Vârcolac."

"But you said I'm not a Vârcolac," Knud replied with a cheeky grin, and even Loba could not help but laugh at his audacity.

"I just did. My parents, when we lived in the Riddari Leggr, both had the skins of large white cats. But a few days before my seventh birthday I saw a wolf out in the forest and…it's difficult to explain! It's like I saw my own eyes in his." Knud didn't need to see Loba's face to know she was smiling. "And when my birthday came I took my own wolf skin. My parents were surprised," she chuckled.

"So you grew the skin?"

"Yes."

"Wow!"

"It's quite painful, actually."

"Oh." Knud's enthusiasm died for a bit but it quickly returned for another question. "Can you take the skin of another Vârcolac?"

"No. Well, some people can—"

"Really?" Knud interrupted her excitedly.

"It's rare—"

"How rare?"

"Will you stop interrupting me?" Loba snapped, and Knud bowed his head. "It's very rare," she continued. "It only happens once every few generations. Una could do it, but I've never met anyone since who could."

"So could Astrid take other skins if she wanted to?"

"No, I don't think so. She isn't a Vârcolac."

Knud looked up over Loba's shoulder and saw that they had reached a large clearing. There was an abandoned building at the side, a pine tree in the centre and ivy over the rubble.

"What is that?"

"That is where Astrid was born."

Knud climbed down from Loba's back and walked towards the ruin, the aura around it similar to that of a graveyard. His attention was instantly drawn to the mound not far from the doorway. The thistle bush that grew there was smothered in a thick layer of white jasmine flowers which, not content to cover the thistle, had spread across the ground and partly covered the ruins in a blanket of green and white.

Without his crutch, Knud was forced to hold Loba's hand as he walked forward, the wild grass almost too thick for him to hop. Loba offered to carry him but he proudly refused.

After a few clumsy steps Knud noticed that the ground around the thistle bush was covered in tightly packed stones, the pattern they formed far to intricate to be formed naturally. The air of magic around the house was so strong he could feel it tingle at the ends of his fingertips.

"That's where her parents are buried." Loba pointed towards the thistle and picked one of the prickly red flowers from it, a small jasmine tendril wrapped around it so tightly she was forced to snap it off with the thistle bud.

Knud looked at her, shocked.

"What?" Loba asked when she saw his horrified expression. "It's just a flower."

"Shouldn't you leave it there?"

"Why? Is that what dwarves do? Bury their dead and just leave their graves alone under the rock?"

"It's bad luck to take something from a grave," Knud muttered.

Loba shrugged her shoulders. "For the Vârcolac it's good luck to take a flower and help it grow somewhere else." Knud nodded but his face still looked superstitiously at the flower.

"Did you plant the flowers?"

"No." Loba held the thistle and the jasmine up to her nose and inhaled the sweet smell. "A warlock did." Knud noticed that she almost spat the word 'warlock' out, her lip curled with disgust.

"You don't like warlocks, do you?" Knud smiled but Loba did not smile back.

"You wouldn't either if you were me."

"Why, what did they do?"

"Nothing, absolutely nothing!" Loba's wolf skin shivered with anger at the words. "Just like a warlock, all the glory but never the responsibility."

"Do you mean Dagmar Eir?"

"Do you know any other warlocks?" Loba asked sarcastically.

Knud looked at her, confused. "Why did you bring me here?"

Loba shook her head. "Astrid survived this. Elves and dwarves attacked them and she survived. She was only a little girl, so imagine how safe Jarl is with her now. You don't have to worry, if she could survive this she can survive anything."

RAGANA

The wall was not like anything Jarl had seen before. They both stared up at it in wonder, the wall made entirely from living trees, and Astrid felt a pang in her chest as she wondered if her mother had ever walked through the Kaito Passage like she was about to.

"Have you ever seen anything like that?" Jarl asked her, impressed by the sheer height of the living walls.

"As tall, yes. Like that? No," Astrid replied, just as impressed, more so though by the magic that radiated from the forest.

The sun had only just set and they were both anxious to sleep for the night, though Shaala, the guide leading the caravan, had insisted they pass through the gates first.

Astrid squirmed uncomfortably in the saddle behind Jarl, both afraid and excited.

As Shaala spoke with the elves at the gate, Astrid saw two of them start to walk down the caravan line to inspect the goods. Jarl felt her grip around his waist tighten as she watched them, their hair black and long and pulled back into braids, their eyes a bright green.

She suddenly remembered the questions her own bright green eye could raise and quickly unwound her veil from around her neck.

"What are you doing?" Jarl asked, able to feel her fumbling behind him. He turned in the saddle and saw she had wrapped the veil so that it covered half her face but mostly covered her right green eye. She considered covering the lower half of her face too, as she usually did, but decided against it, worried that it would raise too many questions.

"Tell them I'm blind in one eye if they ask," Astrid replied.

As one of the elves approached them, Astrid couldn't help but stare at him, a lump in the back of her throat. Jarl let go of the reins and held her hands, both of them wrapped tightly across his stomach.

"You're dwarves?" the elf asked, surprised, at first only interested in Jarl. Astrid huddled behind him, her face buried into his shoulder. "Why did you come with the Keiwo?"

"We needed to get to Lǫgberg."

The elf's eyes turned to Astrid, shocked as he saw the deep scar running down the centre of her lips, which was still slightly visible from under the edge of her veil. "She's blind in that eye," Jarl said quickly. "Goblins," he lied. The elf nodded and waved them on.

Jarl rode the pony quickly after the caravan until he was right behind the last cart. Astrid looked up at the massive gates as they went through, their hinges built into the trees on each side of them. With a loud rumble the gates began to close behind them and Astrid's mouth dropped as she saw that the trees themselves were the ones pushing it shut. As soon as the gates were closed they lifted back up into the canopy, completely motionless as if they had never moved.

"Have you ever seen magic like that?" Jarl asked. Astrid shook her head, as awestruck as he was and slightly intimidated when she realised how feeble her magic was in comparison.

"Never!"

Not content with creating a tree wall around the forest, the road on either side of them was also lined by a wall, only this one was only half the height at most. An elf guard stood every one hundred yards on top of it.

In front of them the caravan drew to a halt.

"We have an early rise tomorrow," Shaala's voice carried over from the front of the caravan. "So sleep while you can."

Astrid jumped down from the pony, relieved to feel her feet on the ground.

"Sore?" Jarl laughed and Astrid nodded.

"I thought riding was meant to be comfortable."

"It isn't if you're not used to it." He smiled at her proudly and she looked back at him with a puzzled expression.

"What?"

"Did you ever think you would ride a pony?"

Astrid laughed. "No, never!" She froze as the guards by the wall looked down at her and she pulled her veil a little further across her face. A strange sensation washed over her and for a moment she panicked, the feeling of being trapped all she could think about. Inside her chest she could feel the Frǫðleikr energy pulse with her nerves. By the gate, two of the guards looked up, able to feel a surge of magic in the air but unable to explain where it came from.

They'll find you! the harsh voice whispered. *Your magic can't save you here! They'll kill you, and him, just for knowing you! Get out, get out now while you still can!*

Astrid clenched her hands together and tried to breathe slowly, the tingle of magic in her fingertips desperate to escape and engulf her hands in a blue glow.

You should have stayed in Waidu! Mātīr left and she was fully elven. What makes you think you can come back? It's not your home, nobody wants you here!

"Astrid?" Jarl laid down the blanket he had unpacked from his bag and walked up to her, concerned by the frantic look in her eye.

Without a word, Astrid buried her head against his chest and let him hold her until the panic had passed, the harsh voice unable to speak while she was in his arms.

Jarl did not ask her what was wrong, able to guess well enough. He sat down next to the pony with Astrid in his arms and pulled his blanket around them. "It's alright," he whispered, and kissed the top of her head.

Astrid closed her eyes and her breathing began to slow, the panic ebbing away. Out of the corner of his eye Jarl looked up at the elves who watched them from the walls, his arms tightening around her protectively. "You're safe with me."

Jarl ran his hand down the side of her face as Astrid slept beside him, her right arm wrapped through his as though she was afraid he would disappear in the middle of the night. With half her face covered he could almost picture what her face would look like without the large scars on the right side of it, though the deep scar down across her lips was still visible.

He lay back down on the ground and stared up at the sky, confused as he realised that he recognised none of the stars, the constellations completely different to those he knew.

Reaching into his tunic, he pulled out the plaque to look at it. The silver and gold glinted in the little light that shone down from the guards' torches high up on the wall, the moon mostly hidden by a large cloud.

Astrid suddenly sat up and propped her chin on his chest, completely wide awake.

"The queen, she can't hurt you can she?" she asked worriedly. "I know it's not easy to lose your family name, but she wouldn't imprison you, would she? I've heard rumours about Vigdis, she sounded a little…mad. I heard she executed dwarves for trying to travel into the forest."

Jarl put the plaque back inside his tunic and moved his hand to the side of her neck. "Don't worry about me. The worst that can happen is I end up with a little less hair on my head. Whoever told you that was lying. It's against the law for a dwarf to be executed." Astrid looked relieved at first and then confused. "It's an old law," Jarl explained. "I was told that after the Rojóða, so many dwarves died that the king decided to make it a crime for a dwarf to be executed by another dwarf."

"But what if a dwarf kills another dwarf or murders someone? Wouldn't they punish them?" Astrid asked, surprised by the seemingly harsh judgment Jarl expected for simply disobeying orders compared to what she considered punishable offences.

"That's what the Ope Gróf is for."

"What's that?"

"Doesn't matter," Jarl quickly said, as he realised it would only make her more worried if she knew. Astrid clenched her jaw stubbornly.

"Jarl, what is the Ope Gróf?" she insisted.

"It's a prison in the Black Basin."

"The Black Basin? Why would the dwarves have a prison there?"

"They don't want it near Lǫgberg," Jarl said.

"Don't lie to me."

"It's run by Ope, demons and trolls."

Astrid's eyes opened wide, horrified at the idea, but before she could ask another question they heard a loud screech in the sky directly above them. Startled, they both looked up, the elves on the wall just as startled as they were.

Jarl was unable to see anything and Astrid could only just make out the shape of what looked like a large bird. Up on the walls the elves shouted out to each other and Astrid became suddenly aware of how broken her Axtī was, able to understand only a little of what they said.

There was another loud screech before a large gryphon flew down and settled on the top of the gate behind the caravan. At first the gryphon stared down at them, its eyes bloodshot, and then with a shudder it arched its back and knelt down.

Jarl pulled Astrid closer as he saw the beautiful woman on the gryphon's back.

"What's wrong?" Astrid asked, and tried to look behind her. Jarl quickly turned her face back to him.

"That's the woman who tried to kill you!" Jarl whispered, his eyes flitting around as if another creature was about to fall from the sky.

The woman did not notice them; she did not even look down. Her focus was entirely on the elves who rushed along the walkway at the top of the gate towards her.

Slowly she stepped down from the gryphon, her arms around her shoulders to hold up the torn tunic that barely covered her, each step deliberately titillating. The tunic was pulled a little too tightly around her so that her breasts were half exposed.

As she walked up to the elf guards, all of whom had lowered their weapons, Jarl noticed the gryphon slowly slump onto its side and saw a long double ended dagger sticking out of its back. Slowly it closed its eyes and let its wings drop down by its side with a shudder, the life behind its eyes gone.

"What are they saying?" Jarl asked Astrid, who had her back to the gate in case the woman happened to look down and recognise her.

"I think they're asking who she is."

Even from so far down, Jarl was able to hear the woman's voice - a soft tone that somehow managed to carry a lot further than was natural, her enunciation slow and purr-like.

"Ragana. My name is Ragana."

The elves glanced at one another, shocked. Astrid looked confused as the elves spoke to Ragana and one of them quickly offered her his cloak to cover herself.

"They asked her where she's been all these years."

Up on the platform, Ragana suddenly toppled forward and was caught by one of the elves who ordered his men to take her to the palace. There was a relieved smile on her face as they carried her.

"She asked if Tyr is still alive. He said that Tyr Jīkkā is now the king."

READING THE WREATH

Knud tried to pretend to be interested as the children tossed their wreaths into the pyre but he just could not. The trip to the ruins had not eased his nerves, if anything it had made them worse. Images of elves and dwarves chasing Astrid flashed through his head, and in all of them Jarl was always the collateral. He couldn't even distract himself with the eggs, which he had been forced to leave behind with Vivilla who had been more than happy to accept the responsibility.

"I'm tired, I just want to lie down," he lied.

"No, you'll enjoy this. Just toss your wreath into the fire," Loba said, and forced the wreath he had made earlier into his hands.

Knud looked down at it with disgust, the straw and flowers so badly woven it barely held together. All the other Vârcolac had beautiful wreaths and suddenly Knud felt ashamed of the sorry mess he had made.

"Can I make another one?" he asked.

Loba shook her head. "No, you'll just have to work with what you have."

"But it looks terrible!"

"Then fix it!" Loba argued. "You have to work with what you have in life. You can't just throw things away."

Knud couldn't help but feel that her comment was directed more towards his leg than the wreath. Angrily, he pulled the wreath apart to reconstruct it but Loba stopped him.

"Stop, don't try and make it the same size. Make it smaller."

"But everyone else—"

"It doesn't matter about everyone else," Loba snapped. "This isn't their wreath, it's yours. Now make it again."

Knud did as she'd said, his mouth pursed into an angry pout, though by the time he finished twisting the wilted flowers and straw together he had to admit it looked a hundred times better than before.

"There, see? Much better!" Loba smiled at him.
"Now, toss it into the fire already, will you?"

Knud stood up, his crutch under his arm, and
hopped over to the fire, everyone's eyes on him.

"Go on!"

"Throw it in!"

"And don't forget to look at the flames!"

Knud looked back at Loba, confused. With an
exasperated sigh, Loba got up and stood next to him.
"Throw it!"

With a heavy thud the wreath landed at the top of
the pyre and began to be eaten by the flames; the
straw crackled loudly as it began to burn, the flowers
the first to wither. The Vârcolac all cheered loudly
and crowded around, their eyes on the wreath.

"What are they looking at?" Knud asked.

"The fire. If you look at the flames you see your
future," Loba replied matter-of-factly.

Knud raised an eyebrow, a small smirk at the
corners of his mouth, but still he turned to look at the
flames. The wreath was almost completely
consumed. At first the only thing he saw was smoke
but, as the last flame licked across it, Knud could
have sworn he saw a small shape - wings, several
wings clustered together before they floated up and
disappeared.

"Did you see it?" Loba asked excitedly.

"I saw wings, and a wolf," Knud stuttered, not sure if what he had seen had been a trick of the light. He felt something small hit the back of his head and turned to look behind him, the Vârcolac's attention still on the fire.

In the tree line, Vivilla motioned at him to follow her and Knud shook his head. But when she held open her hand to reveal eggshells, Knud's stomach jumped with excitement. Loba did not stop him as he darted away, her attention still on the fire.

"I never thought I would see a dwarf read their wreath," Bugal said to his wife.

"I never thought I would let one," Loba growled, and Bugal laughed as he moved an arm around her.

"What did your wreath show?"

Loba walked back to her place by the trees and picked it up.

"Well come on, throw it in."

With a strong flick of her wrist, Loba tossed it into the fire. The wreath crashed into the flames and lay embedded between two large pieces of wood as the flames ate at it. Loba held Bugal's hand, her more superstitious side nervous that she would see a future she did not want. A smile spread across her face as the last flame consumed the wreath and she looked down at Bugal.

"I think we have another cub on the way, my love," she grinned.

Knud picked himself up from the ground, his knees and elbows bruised. In his hurry to reach the abandoned village his crutch had caught on some weeds and he had fallen heavily. But it barely slopped his pace.

"Have they all hatched?" Knud asked, his eyes wide and excited, a massive grin on his face.

"No, just the red egg."

"The one with the blue dots on the top?"

Vivilla nodded.

"That's the biggest one. Have the others moved?"

"The gold egg—"

"Brown," Knud corrected her.

"Well it looks gold to me!"

Knud tried to appease her. "What about the gold egg?"

"It hasn't moved."

"Not even a little bit?"

Vivilla shook her head and they both exchanged a worried glance.

"Maybe it's not ready to hatch yet?" Knud suggested, but the hopeful tone in his voice did not reach his face and he hobbled even faster.

As they reached the abandoned house, Knud dropped his crutch and crawled in beside the nest they had made. One of the eggs had broken open and a small trail of slime led to the tiny black griffin that lay huddled at the edge of the nest.

Knud scooped it into his arms, able to feel every tiny bone in its body under the downy feathers. He stared down at the gryphon as if he had seen gold for the first time in his life. The little creature curled up against him trustingly.

It took Knud several minutes to tear his gaze back to the other eggs in the pile of leaves. Just like Vivilla had said, most of them were moving except for the golden-brown egg.

"Why isn't it moving?" Knud said. He reached over and picked the egg up gently. From inside the hard shell he felt something shudder. "It moved!" He smiled and Vivilla floated up and down excitedly, her hands over her mouth.

In his arms the hatched baby gryphon opened its eyes, but Knud's attention was fixed on the gold egg. "I need to keep it warm," he muttered, and tucked it into his shirt.

"Knud, its eyes. It opened its eyes!" Vivilla hovered next to him and reached out towards the baby gryphon. It glared at her suspiciously with its piercing blue eyes and snapped at her outstretched fingers with its transparent beak. She glared back at it, offended by its reaction. Knud just laughed.

"It likes you," he chuckled.

"Well I hate you," Vivilla snapped back at it, and Knud could have sworn it cocked its head at her, one ear raised.

"Look! Knud, look!" She held his arm and pointed at the other eggs. They were all moving now, some more violently than the others, and they could hear claws scratching against the inside of the shells. They both watched, fascinated, Knud with one hand around the black gryphon and the other over the egg tucked inside his tunic.

The first egg to hatch was a milky-blue one, and Knud's breath caught in his throat as the first tiny paw broke through, all four fingers a pale baby pink, its claws almost as transparent as its eggshell. Unlike the black gryphon, it did not wait until it had been picked up by Knud to open its golden brown eyes.

They both stared at it and the gryphon stared back at them, curious and cold. With a little screech it toppled to the side and kicked itself out of the shell, its legs too weak to stand.

"What are you going to call it?" Vivilla asked. "You get to name three, remember?"

Knud said the name almost before he had time to think. "Lína."

Vivilla cleared her throat, a smile on her face. "Knud, it's a boy!" she pointed out as the gryphon fell onto its side again. Knud picked it up in his arms.

"I'm calling it Lína!"

"Fine, but it's still a boy."

"It's a gryphon, I don't think it cares," Knud argued. He looked back at the un-hatched eggs and nodded at a cream egg with blue streaks. "You can name that one."

Vivilla clapped her hands excitedly and crouched down next to the egg as small cracks spread up its side. "It's going to be a boy, I think!"

With a loud screech, the entire top of the egg was kicked off before a scrawny little body broke its way through. Its little foot kicked at the straw and leaves frantically as it tried to break its way through the rest of the egg. Vivilla laughed and reached for it.

"Shouldn't you let it get out by itself?"

She paused for a second and then promptly ignored his suggestion. Before she could help though, a second leg kicked away the side of the egg and a very disgruntled baby gryphon scowled up at them, its black beak wide open as it squeaked, its dark blue eyes hidden under a thick tuft of brown downy feathers.

Knud tried to help her break the gryphon out of its shell but Vivilla slapped his hand away. "It's mine, I'll help it."

The gryphon seemed to have a different idea though, and tried to run towards Knud. Vivilla ignored its desperate bid for freedom and picked it up in her hands.

"I will call it Bird!" She laughed and kissed it on its fluffy face.

"Bird?"

"Yes, Bird." Vivilla defended her decision indignantly, even as Bird tried to leap from her hands, its skinny wings with barely a feather on them.

Near Bird's broken eggshell, a speckled grey egg rolled to its side before it managed to knock itself upright again. "This one is mine, too!" Vivilla said quickly. Knud did not argue with her, his thoughts on the egg held tightly against his chest.

The fourth egg took a few minutes to break, but when it did it split in half perfectly to reveal a fuzzy grey gryphon, its black beady eyes alert and awake.

"Cloud; I'm going to call her Cloud."

"How do you know it's a girl?"

Vivilla picked up Cloud in her hand and held her up for a moment. "It's a girl!" She laughed and pointed at the first gryphon curled up against Knud.

"What are you going to call him?" The little black gryphon looked up at Knud, both eyes wide open.

"Fljótr?"

"Fljótr?" Vivilla scoffed.

"At least I didn't call him Cloud," Knud retorted.

"I like the name Cloud," she said, pulling her two small gryphon back into her arms.

"They're cold, they should stay with me for a moment," Knud said.

"I'm not that cold," Vivilla replied, slightly hurt at their obvious preference for Knud, but eventually she gave in and helped them into Knud's arms where they bundled together with their siblings.

With a loud snap, the last egg in the nest cracked open and a small bat-like wing protruded from it, the skin pink except for the few pure white feathers that speckled it. Worried it would cut its fragile skin on the edge of the eggshell, Knud broke open the rest of it and placed it in his lap with the other hatchlings.

"Hvítna," Knud named her, as she curled up next to the other gryphon and closed her albino red eyes.

"The last egg!" Vivilla smiled.

Knud reached into his shirt. "This one still hasn't moved."

"Maybe you should open it?"

Knud pulled it out from inside his tunic and gently pressed the top of the egg, but the shell was surprisingly strong.

"Use a stone," Vivilla suggested, and Knud stared at her, horrified.

"I'm not using a stone!" he gasped. "What if I hurt it?"

"It's going to die if you leave it in there."

Knud looked around the hut and eventually settled on a large pebble. Carefully, he tapped at the top of the egg, gently at first, but with more and more force until a small crack began to show.

"Open it!" Vivilla urged him impatiently. Knud ignored her and kept on tapping slowly at the crack until it spread down the side of the egg. He prised his finger into it until the entire top of the egg had been opened up. With bated breaths they both looked inside.

The little creature was pitifully small, its limbs little more than a thin layer of transparent skin over bones, which were no thicker than twigs. There was barely a single feather over its whole body and it shivered violently as the cold air reached it. With both eyes closed, it opened its mouth and tried to make a sound, but couldn't.

"It's going to die," Vivilla whispered.

"Don't say that!" He quickly pulled it from the egg and tucked it inside his shirt, its head under his chin. Vivilla pulled a face at the bald little creature, disgusted by the slime that covered it, though Knud did not seem to notice.

"If I keep it warm maybe it'll live."

"What will live?" Loba's voice asked from the doorway.

Vivilla screamed with fright and turned even paler, as transparent as glass. Knud just stared up at Loba, the gryphon in his arms.

Loba looked down at them, one eyebrow raised. Even in the low light she could see how carefully Knud held the baby gryphon. She crouched down in front of him and looked at them curled up in his lap, all of them asleep and completely unafraid of the dwarf boy.

"So that's why you've been running off each day, is it?"

Knud nodded. He knew there was no point in lying. "Can I keep them?"

"Yes," Loba said.

"Really?"

"Do you want me to change my mind?" She raised an eyebrow at him.

"No!" Loba smiled and reached for the bald little gryphon against his chest. "Let's have a look at this one, shall we?" Carefully she took the baby from him and looked at it, a sad smile on her face. "I can try and help you save it, but it might die. It's very small, I can't promise anything."

Knud nodded. "I just want to give it a chance!"

Loba smiled, a large genuine smile which reached her eyes. "Alright, we will give it a chance."

LQGBERG

Astrid had barely spoken for the past few days, her face fixed in an almost permanent frown. Jarl had tried to speak to her, but no matter what he said she would let the conversation dwindle until there was only silence.

Since they had seen Ragana, Astrid had struggled to sleep. Her eyes were rimmed with dark circles and Jarl had more than one bruise on his side from where Astrid had inadvertently lashed out in her dreams. More than once he had heard her whisper in Axtī and had been forced to wake her in case one of the elves on the wall heard her, worried about the questions it would raise. Dwarves were not known for their love of languages, let alone Axtī.

Fortunately, none of the elves who watched them seemed particularly interested in them as they trailed behind the caravan. And with each day that passed, fewer elves lined the wall until eventually the walkway that ran alongside it was all but deserted. Ahead of them, Astrid could see the wide open gate that led out of the forest, only a handful of elves on the walkway above it.

"I can see it!" a voice called out from the front of the caravan. "Logberg!"

Jarl rode the pony a little faster and Astrid strained her neck to look over his shoulder, a large knot in her stomach at her eagerness to see the city. With her half elf eyes she was able to see a lot further than Jarl could, the mouth of the city a mere blur on the side of the mountain to him.

The entrance was enormous. In true dwarf form it had been built to be as imposing as possible. It was curved, as if a great giant had taken a bite out of the mountain side. The stone pillar that stood in front of it had the likeness of a dwarf king carved into the front, or at least that was what Astrid had thought until she saw the obvious breasts the figure had.

"That pillar is of Ása Amma, the Mountain Breaker," Jarl explained to her. "Legend says she lived for eight hundred years, the longest any dwarf has ever lived. Her body was buried in the pinnacle in front of the Great Gate. The dwarves of Lǫgberg think that so long as her body remains there the city can never be taken. Not that anyone has tried," Jarl laughed. "Even the elves would not try to attack the city. Lǫgberg has the strongest army in all of Ammasteinn."

"Maybe the strongest, but not the largest. King Titus has eighty thousand men just on his own. The others have twice that number," Astrid said quietly.

"That many?" Jarl asked, surprised, and Astrid nodded. "I thought Titus was the strongest of the human kings?"

"He used to be."

"Not anymore?"

"No. Not since Marcia married Attilio; her sister Maxima rules the desert cities."

"I don't know much about the human world," Jarl admitted. Astrid grinned to herself.

"That's alright. They don't know much about our world either." Jarl turned in the saddle to smile at her. "What?" she asked, confused by his expression.

"Nothing."

"What?" she insisted.

"You said *our* world."

"I meant my father's world," she replied quietly.

As they rode down the hill she could not help but imagine another dwarf walking beside them. A dwarf with grey eyes and copper hair. His face blurred in her memory but the warm aura around him was as strong as ever and she heard the ghostly echo of Arnbjörg's deep laughter in her ears. *I wonder if he would ever have brought me here if he had lived?* She quickly changed her train of thought and looked up at the city to distract herself.

She could not deny the city was magnificent, the mountain above it so high she could not see the peaks that were half hidden in the clouds. The gigantic gate, made of black granite, stretched from either side of the pinnacle to the sides of the mountain, the doorway in the shape of an upright hammer. With no hinges to hold the sides to the walls, it was held up by a series of pulleys that hung over the gate like a row of teeth, ready to plummet the moment the pulleys were loosened. It was a thick three metre wall of oak and steel.

"Breathe," Jarl whispered to her over his shoulder as her grip around his waist tightened. "It'll be alright."

Behind them, the gate that led out of the forest closed with a loud rumble. Astrid turned in the saddle to look and realised that the forest was lined entirely by tree walls - a wall of green that stopped abruptly at the edges of the yellow fields, which lay between them and Lǫgberg. She breathed slowly and leant her head against the back of Jarl's neck.

"Are you alright?" he asked, and drew the pony to a halt.

Astrid nodded. "I'm just being stupid."

Jarl jumped down from the pony and reached up for her, his hand around her waist as he lifted her off the saddle. "We can walk from here." He leant down to kiss her and laid his arm across her shoulders as they made their way down the beaten path, the caravan already half way down the slope to the city.

Astrid looked around at the fields as they passed them, some empty except for the animals which grazed on them, others with large groups of farmers with scythes in their hands. The corn they cut was picked up by the children who walked behind them.

Jarl looked down at Astrid who looked like she was about to run at any second. "Would it help if I told you I'm frightened too?" Jarl said, leaning down to kiss the side of her face.

Astrid smiled, her eyes closed, and leant her head against him.

"That song, the one you sang to Knud. Where did you learn it?" Jarl asked suddenly.

"My parents used to sing it to me, Faðir especially. Why?"

"I know that song, it's from Lǫgberg, but you sing it differently. More like an elf." He grinned at her.

"I always thought they made it up."

"The words are very different."

"How?" Astrid asked.

"The old song is different. It's about despair, not hope, like in your song."

"How does it go?" Astrid asked curiously.

Jarl turned a little red as he did his best to sing the tune, and if Astrid was honest it was not one of his talents.

Cry and despair, the moon is away.
No light in the darkness,
No hope now remains.
Only the howling,
The wolves and the night,
Your fears they have found you, you're too weak to fight.

Astrid shuddered as he sang it, the tone of the song so much darker than the hopeful song she knew. The image it conjured in her mind was of tombstones and misery.

The sun is a liar,
No hope in the light.

The darkness around me,
No end in sight.
No light in the darkness.
Only your fears.
No matter what comes,
You'll never be free.
No matter your love,
There is only my tears.

"I hate it," Astrid whispered. "It's horrible."

"They sing it at funerals."

Astrid was surprised at his reply. *Funerals? Why would her parents change a funeral song? Out of all the songs they could have picked, they changed one about death*, she thought to herself.

She stopped for a moment and reached up for her bag, her hammer ax partly visible from where it was tucked into the top.

"What are you doing?" Jarl asked, as she pulled out a spare tunic and wrapped the hammer ax in it.

"I don't want anyone to see this. It could cause problems."

They moved on in silence for the next hour, the distance between the forest edge and the city deceptively far. As they walked down the road, Astrid noticed a huge stone mound in the middle of the fields that shot up from the earth, its surface bare.

"What is that?" she asked.

"I think that's the Kāsni Kroukā." Astrid was surprised to hear him say the distinctly elven words.

"Why has it got an Axtī name?"

"I'm not sure." Jarl shrugged his shoulders. "I could be wrong about it, I just know that it used to be a middle ground between Lǫgberg and Kentutrebā for settling disputes. I don't think it has been used since the Rojóða."

Astrid glanced back and noticed it had the destroyed remains of several buildings scattered around it. Marks in the mound implied they had once been on top of it but had long since been knocked down. "I wish Dag would have told me more about Ammasteinn before the Rojóða," she murmured.

"There are books in Bjargtre you could read."

"I can't read Mál."

"Dag didn't teach you?" Jarl asked, surprised.

"He taught me to speak many different languages, but I was never very good at reading. I didn't think it was important. I preferred to learn to fight with Ragi," Astrid said regretfully.

Directly in front of the gates a market sprawled for the larger part of half a mile, with a few crudely constructed wooden inns dotted in-between the tents.

Humans, dwarves and even a few elves bartered their goods. The noise was incredible, and Astrid was able to pick out snippets of Axtī from the elves they passed. More than one trader tried to stop them and sell them their goods and Astrid smiled as she recognised some of the colourful silks from Bayswater and the beautifully carved palm wood boxes, the smells of the wood and silks making her feel acutely homesick.

Now that they were out of the forest Astrid took a little more time to look at the elves they passed and, without realising it, she began to look for her own features in them.

You're not like them, Astrid, stop looking! the harsh voice whispered. *Don't forget what they did to your ear! They don't want you, you're just a Mewa to them.*

Astrid shook her head and ignored the voice, her grip on Jarl's hand tighter. Nervous, she made sure her veil was held in place and looked over at her bag to check her hammer ax was still covered by her tunic.

She kept her head slightly bowed and huddled close to Jarl as they approached the wall gate, sure that they'd be stopped. But the guards did not even look in their direction, too interested in the heated conversation two dwarves were having with a human trader who insisted on being allowed to enter the city.

As soon as they had passed, Astrid looked up at the mountain and the city entrance, her jaw dropping in amazement at the incredible architecture. The statues of the kings and queens of Lǫgberg were carved into the mountain by the Great Gate, all of them enormous and with weapons in their hands: spears, axes and several large swords.

Astrid shivered, her heart in her chest, as the mountain blocked out the sunlight, but the moment they passed the Great Gate a warm breeze drifted towards them from the inside of the mountain, the smell of copper and stone in the air. Her mouth dropped open as she saw the city before her: a huge cavern in the mountain that had been hollowed out to house it. Some of the houses had been built inside the gigantic stalactites that hung down from the ceiling, and thousands of little yellow lights twinkled in the darkness.

The far end of the city was far from dark, illuminated by a bright beam of light that shone down from the mountain top onto the exterior of the palace. The palace walls were covered in white marble and gold, and it gleamed as bright as snow. Two enormous statues were erected outside it, which looked so life-like that Astrid wondered for a moment if there were indeed two giants sat there.

"That light...what is it?" Astrid asked.

"That's the Ríkr Gluggr."

"Is there a hole in the mountain?"

Jarl shook his head. "They have hundreds of small tunnels, and mirrors on the mountain top reflect the light down into the city."

"It's beautiful!"

As they crossed the drawbridge that led from the Great Gate, Astrid peered down over the edge at the city below, the buildings so far down they looked like houses children would make in the mud.

He lived here, the soft voice whispered in her head. *He gave this up for the Aldwood. He must have loved us so much.*

Instantly, Astrid felt ashamed that she even needed to consider the idea that Arnbjörg had not loved them, and the feeling was quickly replaced by an enormous sense of pride in her father.

He was so brave, to give this all up.

"Are you going to the palace now?" Astrid asked Jarl as they walked down the long steps from the drawbridge and into the city. Jarl took a deep breath and nodded.

"The faster it's over…I just want it to be over."

"I want to come with you."

"No!" Jarl replied quickly. "No, you have got to stay away."

"Why?" Astrid snapped. "I want to be with you!"

"And if Vígdís recognises you?"

"Why would she?" Astrid said, pretending not to know what he meant.

"Your father was nobility. We both know where the order probably came from."

Astrid's face dropped. "What if she kills you? I know you said the queen can't kill a dwarf, but she managed it before!" Her hands gripped his as though she would never let go.

"Your father was in the Aldwood; she probably thought nobody would find out what happened. She can't do that to me, not here, and not as long as she doesn't know about you. She wouldn't have any reason to try to hurt me."

Astrid dragged her hands down her face and groaned frustratedly. She knew he was right but she was afraid, especially now he had said out loud that he suspected Vígdís was involved in her parents' murder. It was a nagging thought that had always been at the back of her mind but one she had deliberately avoided and never spoken about.

"Astrid, if you love me I need you to stay away."

She glared at him. "That's not fair!"

"I know," he said, smiling.

She looked down at the ground for a few moments before looking back up at him, a scowl on her face. "Promise me they can't hurt you?"

"I promise."

Walking through the city, Astrid was overwhelmed by the busy sounds, sights and smells. The houses were all made of stone, hardly a wooden beam in sight, the stone a peppered mixture of black granite and limestone.

As they neared the palace, Astrid noticed Jarl was walking a little slower and eventually he stopped completely, his heart in his chest. He turned to Astrid and leant her head against hers. "Just wait here."

"For how long?"

"I don't know. Just promise you won't try and follow me into the palace."

"I'll wait three hours, then I'm going to come and find you."

Jarl nodded and held her in his arms, his heart beating so quickly that Astrid could feel it against her hands like a drum. She reached up and brushed his hair from his face, his blue eyes more than a little afraid. Astrid clenched her fists. She had never seen him scared like this and more than anything she wanted to protect him as she had for the past few months.

"If you're not back in three hours I will find you," she warned him. "I'll take the wolf skin if I have to, but I will—"

Jarl suddenly leaned down and kissed her passionately, one hand on the side of her neck and the other against the back of her head, his fingers knotted into her hair. Astrid's stomach fluttered and she kissed him back, her hands against his chest. Finally Jarl pulled away and took a deep breath.

"Three hours," Astrid repeated, and let go of his hands.

THE WOLF IS COMING

The crowd surged forward as they saw two figures walk out onto the balcony, Haddr too small to be seen by them, but they were held back by the thick row of soldiers in front of the palace. The plaza was heaving with all kinds of dwarves: women, men and even young children. The protective veils most people had adopted to protect them from the plague hung loosely around their necks, their anger too immense to compete with any sense of caution.

Haddr tried to look over the edge of the balcony but he could not, just tall enough to rest his chin on the edge. Hálfr was the only one who was tall enough to be seen from the balcony; Halvard stood a little further behind them, only just obscured from view.

Mistaking Hálfr for his brother, the crowd began to scream at him.

"You! You brought this on the city!"

"Your reign is cursed!"

Hálfr looked down at his brother, unsure what to do, the crowd's anger palpable. Haddr look terrified.

"What do I do?"

"I don't know."

"You need to speak to them," Halvard suggested.

"I'm not tall enough."

"I can hold you up." Halvard offered, and Haddr nodded.

Despite their anger, even the crowd were shocked into silence as the King of Bjargtre was held up on the shoulders of a soldier. Even from so far down they could see just how small the boy was and how deformed his feet were, his limbs like little twigs, both feet too large and curled inwards.

For such a small boy, Halvard had expected Haddr to be quite easy to hoist onto his shoulders, but the boy was so light and frail he was worried he might be blown away if someone so much as coughed.

"Tell me what you want to say, My King."

"I don't know," Haddr replied, his voice so quiet even Halvard struggled to hear it. "I...I just want to tell them I didn't mean for this to happen."

Halvard cleared his throat. Yes, you're most definitely going to be made a soldier by morning, he thought to himself again.

"King Haddr the Third regrets the toll the Hætta has taken on the city." As the words left his mouth, Halvard couldn't help but wish he was a little more eloquent. *I sound like a fool,* he thought. Nevertheless, he kept going.

"What else do you want me to say?"

"I...I don't know," Haddr whispered. "Tell them I'm sorry." Haddr tried to speak up so that his voice could be heard. "I'm sorry!" he said, but nobody could hear him. Hálfr suddenly climbed up onto the balcony and stood proudly next to his brother so both their heads were at the same height.

"My brother, the king, is young, the youngest king to ever sit on the throne!" Hálfr's voice was strong and clear, not as loud as Halvard's but loud enough to be heard by the majority of the crowd. "Our council advised that the Hætta would send a clear message that Bjargtre is just as great as it was in reign of Queen Ása Amma."

"No, no don't do that!" Halvard whispered quietly. "Don't blame the council, they will find a way to make you pay for it if you blame them!"

"But I'm the king? Don't they have to do what I say?" Haddr asked, confused.

"You might be king, but they can make life very difficult for you."

Halvard was impressed at how quickly Hálfr adapted his speech.

"They advised that we let the general..." Hálfr realised to his horror that he did not know the general's name and paused for a moment as he tried to remember. "The general..." he started again, "would lead the Hætta against the goblins. I advised against it, not my brother, the king."

Before the roar from the crowd could pick up again, Hálfr shouted out over them. "We have sent crows to Queen Vígdís to ask her to send her armies! Her armies are still the greatest in Ammasteinn. The goblins cannot break past the Mad Gate! Against Vígdís they will lose!"

Halvard could not believe his ears as the crowd began to quieten, impressed by the young boy's boldness.

"How did you do that?" Haddr looked at his brother in awe.

"I don't know."

"We should go." Halvard helped Haddr down from his shoulders.

"Wait, what's that?" Haddr pointed over the edge of the plaza to a large mural painted on the wall with chalk paint, the words underneath it painted in red.

"It's nothing," Halvard lied. "You should go."

Haddr nodded and walked away with his brother, both of them relieved to be out of view of the crowd. Halvard did not move from the balcony for several minutes, his eyes on the wolf's head painted in white on the wall of the plaza, 'the wolf is coming' written underneath it. The shape of the wolf was almost an exact copy of those on the goblin cuffs, which many people had taken as trophies after the Hætta. It had the same open jaw and harsh angles, except its eyes had been painted red with an excessive dash of paint. Four long drips spread down from the red eyes and across its cheeks like scars down its face.

* * *

Halvard dropped onto his bed like a stone, so exhausted he couldn't even bring himself to untie his boots. He knew Holmvé would have his head on a stick for getting mud all over his bed but he decided it was worth the risk even if it meant she would make him wash his bedding himself. Just as his eyes were about to close, the door to his room opened and Holmvé walked in. Halvard groaned loudly into his pillow, sure she was about to scream at him at any moment.

"Holmvé, what do you want?" He looked up at her, his eyes so tired they were almost completely bloodshot. For a few seconds she just stared at him, her face completely blank, her mouth slightly open and both eyes as large as saucers.

"Holmvé?"

"Halvard, the city is under attack. There are goblins at the gate."

"What?"

"Goblins, at the gates!"

Halvard sprung out of the bed and quickly caught her as her knees gave way. "Goblins! Hundreds of them outside! They've closed the gates!" she muttered in a panic.

Halvard made a move to leave, aware that if what Holmvé had said was true he would be needed, but she clung onto him like a frightened child.

"No! No, don't go!" she pleaded.

Eilíf, Gísla and Hlín hurried into his room and huddled together at the doorway.

"We're going to die!" Eilíf muttered.

"No!" Halvard yelled, making them all jump. "The king sent birds to Lǫgberg and Jarl will be there already. We only have to hold out a bit longer."

"What if we can't?" Hlín mumbled. "We can't keep the city closed with the plague in the city. We have to bury the bodies."

Suddenly, a terrible thought occurred to Halvard. "He planned this!"

"Who?"

"Ulf! He knew we were coming and made sure he could trap us in the city with the plague." He stood up and passed Holmvé to the others. "Stay here! I'll be back soon!" he promised.

This time, as he left the house, he did not even reach for his cloak but ran down the city streets as fast as he could, the sound of a bell he had never heard before ringing out through the night.

As he reached the gates he was just in time to see them close with a loud thud. The massive locks were pushed into place behind it and several steel beams slid down from the battlement above, slotting into several holes in the ground. Soldiers ran in from every direction.

"Halvard!"

Halvard turned to see the general standing behind him. "What are you doing here? I won't have a man at the gate who can barely stand. Go back home and get some sleep!"

Halvard waited patiently as the general barked several orders at his men before he asked if what Holmvé had said was true. "I heard there are goblins outside."

"Just a few!" The general replied sarcastically. "They've set the entire bloody mountain on fire!"

It was only then that Halvard noticed just how much smoke was in the air, and for once it was not the stifling smell of incense. The smell was of burnt wood and grass and the air was hot and heavy as great plumes of smoke billowed over the battlements.

"I should stay here," Halvard insisted. "With my men."

"Do you want to be demoted?" the general barked at him, and Halvard quickly shook his head. "Good! Then go back home and don't come back here until you've had at least six hours sleep!" He stopped Halvard as he was about to go. "I heard that the king had your family name re-instated," he said, a smile on his face. Halvard nodded, a little unsure why the general was so pleased. "Well, what is it?"

"What is what?"

"Your name, Halvard! Your family name!"

"Oh, it's Löfgren, sir."

"Löfgren, that's a good name!" The general smiled and patted him firmly on the back. "Now go back home and sleep."

"Sir?" The general growled as Halvard dared to ask one more question. "Who is attacking?"

"I haven't asked them but if I had to make a guess I would say it's Ulf."

"They said the wolf was coming!" A soldier nearby mumbled, visibly shaking with fear. "The seer warned us!"

"The seer was just a drunk man dying!" the general shouted at him. "I make similar horse shit predictions when I'm drunk! Now get up there and man the battlements!"

THREE HOURS

You should follow him! the quiet voice whispered. *What if something goes wrong?*

Astrid shook her head and made her way through the city, the pony behind her, its reins in her hand.

Follow him!

"Shut up!" Astrid hissed under her breath. "I won't! I made a promise!"

Keen to distract herself, she ambled into a market where hundreds of stalls had been set up for the day's trading. There wasn't a single elf or human in sight but goods she recognised as being theirs were for sale. She tightened her grip on the pony's reins as she walked through the busy crowd, everyone in such a rush to get where they needed to go that they rudely pushed past her, almost pulling the reins from her hands more than once.

She couldn't believe how big the city was and how many people there were, and wondered if Bjargtre was the same, but then realised this was the capital and Bjargtre must be smaller. She made a mental note to ask Jarl what his home looked like when he returned, her train of thought taken instantly back to where he might be.

He's trying to save his city and they'll take everything away from him! How can dwarves be so cruel? Why would you punish someone and humiliate them just for trying to help? Go and find him! You can stop this! the quiet voice begged.

Astrid stopped for a moment in the middle of the street and rubbed her face, scowling at a dwarf as she rudely jostled past her, in too much of a hurry to care.

Everything was different. The sights, the smells, the look of the clothes. It was all completely alien to her. The air smelt of cold stone, copper, and dust and the ground along the tunnels was covered in a coppery mud that glinted in the sunlight. There were ponies everywhere with large baskets on their backs, lumps of unrefined gold and copper inside them. The animals were unlike any she had see before: strong and muscular with distinctive red coats and white snouts, their hair long and twisted into thick locks.

She stopped for a moment on an empty corner next to one of the stalls as a large entourage of nobles pushed their way through the crowd, all of them held up in wooden litters. She turned to the stall and saw several small glass bottles laid out on the counter, the distinct smell of jasmine in the air.

Noticing her eyes on the bottles, the stall owner approached her and asked if she liked the smell of Jasmine. Astrid nodded and picked up one of the bottles in her hand.

"One Fé and it's yours."

Astrid put the bottle down and moved away, the scent bringing back memories she did not want to remember. She glanced at the rest of the stall and saw several knives in beautiful ornate sheaths made of leather.

"How much for that one?" Astrid asked, and pointed at a small dagger with a red handle.

"That one?" The stall owner paused for a moment as he quickly tried to assess how much he could ask for. "Five Fé."

She picked up the dagger, impressed by the craftsmanship. The handle was made of some kind of red metal she did not recognise and the blade was sharp enough to ring as she ran her thumbnail across it.

"I only have Feoh."

The innkeeper pulled a face. "I would have to ask for more then."

"How much more?" Astrid asked unfazed.

"Six Feoh."

She raised an eyebrow, fully aware that the dwarf took her for a fool, nevertheless she reached into her pocket and pulled out the Feoh that remained from Shaala's price of passage through the Kato Pass.

Surprised that she had agreed to the price, the stall owner happily took the coins she passed him. "Is the dagger for you?" he asked, as he bit the Feoh Astrid had given him to check that they had not been tampered with, a smile on his face as he saw that his teeth had left marks in the silver coins.

"No," Astrid replied, and tucked the dagger into her bag.

As she turned to go, the stall owner asked if she wanted the jasmine oil and held one of the bottles out towards her, sure that he could pressure her to part with a few more coins.

For a few moments Astrid looked at the bottle in his hand before she finally shook her head and walked away, a deep feeling of calm over her as she did so, as if a small ghost had been pushed from her soul.

I don't need it anymore. I have a new family, she thought.

She smiled and rubbed the pony's snout as it propped its head on her shoulder. "You're not afraid of me anymore, are you?" she said, and the pony snorted loudly in reply. "I think Knud will like the dagger, but maybe I'll ask Jarl to give it to him. Maybe he won't be as angry with me then."

Astrid made her way out of the market and towards the bright light of the Ríkr Gluggr, the streets a little less crowded the closer she got. As she reached the enormous plaza in front of the palace the light from the Ríkr Gluggr hit her and she looked up, her eyes blinded for a moment before they adjusted. She was surprised to see that it was not so much a window but an enormous dome in the mountain with hundreds of small tunnels at the top that looked just like worm holes. Polished pieces of silver and copper were attached to the surface of the rock to reflect the light into the tunnels.

Astrid looked down at the rest of the plaza and her eyes settled on a large platform that had been raised directly in front of the palace, a pillory at its centre. She stared, horrified at the figures, their expressions enough to make her heart want to cry. Broken and ashamed, their eyes were far away, as if they had forced themselves to shift their consciousness to the back of their minds, a defensive mechanism to numb the humiliation. Two of them had their heads and faces shaved, only one still had their hair. Several people near the platform stopped to laugh and throw rotten fruit at them.

Suddenly, a woman stepped onto the platform and wiped away the muck that covered the face of one of the dwarves to a chorus of jeering from the crowd. Astrid watched her curiously before noticing a red thistle embroidered into the hem of her tunic.

As the woman stepped down from the platform, Astrid felt her heart stop in her chest, the woman's features as familiar as a ghost.

The pony whinnied in protest as Astrid darted into the crowd, almost dragging the animal behind her in her hurry to catch up with the woman. For a brief moment she thought she had lost her in the crowd before she spotted her turning into one of the tunnels nearby.

Behind her there was a large commotion on the platform but she did not turn to look, all her attention focused on the woman.

Careful to keep her distance, she followed her down numerous streets until, finally, the woman walked up the steps to a large house. Astrid stopped not far the steps and watched silently.

With a jolt, her heart went from pounding like a drum to freezing mid-beat as she saw four children in the courtyard, their eyes a stone grey. The woman smiled as one of the children tried to jump into her arms and she crouched down to greet him.

A small dog, sensing Astrid's gaze, turned and yelped in her direction, and she stood as still as a statue by the courtyard gate. She could not help the loud whimper that escaped her throat as she saw the woman's face, and felt a pain in her chest like a thin shard of glass had been pushed simultaneously into her heart and through the front of her head. She knew that face. That nose, the way her eyebrows moved when she smiled. They were the same as Arnbjörg's.

For the first time in years the foggy image in her head began to clear and piece by piece the image reassembled itself until Arnbjörg smiled back at her.

"Who are you?" the woman shouted from the courtyard. "Auðr! Arnbjörg! Birna! Faði! Go back inside!" she ordered the children behind her. Astrid gasped at the name of the second child.

She looked at the little boy she thought the name belonged to, her eyes stinging with tears. The boy had the same eyes, the same stone grey, his hair a curly copper blond.

The woman stormed over to her, a small knife in her hand. "Did Eklund send you?" she asked, stopping a few feet away from Astrid but close enough to lash out with her knife if she felt threatened.

Astrid tried to open her mouth to speak but the words seized at the back of her throat in a painful knot.

"Who are you?" the woman screamed at her.

"Arnbjörg!" Astrid blurted out. "Arnbjörg Hvass!"

"What do you want with my son?" The woman stepped closer and Astrid was able to see the deep worry lines on her forehead and how tired she looked, more than one grey hair on her head.

"His uncle," Astrid whispered through the lump at the back of her throat. "I knew his uncle."

The woman lowered the knife slightly but not completely. "You're lying," she scoffed. "He's been dead for years."

"Arnbjörg Hvass, he had grey eyes and gold hair." Astrid spoke quickly, every single detail she remembered escaping her mouth before she even had time to think about them. "When he smiled you could see the wrinkles around his eyes, he had a small scar under his left eye, he said it was from when he had fallen over and hit his head on the side of a table when he was small." The woman's face turned ashen and the knife clattered onto the floor. Astrid carried on. "He liked to sing, he was always singing, his favourite song was—"

The woman suddenly lunged forward and pulled away the veil that covered half of Astrid's face, her other hand raised as if she were about to hit her. She screamed as she saw the deep scars down Astrid's cheek and down the centre of her lips, but when she noticed Astrid's different coloured left eye, every last bit of colour drained from her face.

Astrid stared at her, unsure of what to do with her veil completely removed. Slowly she reached up and untucked her left ear from under the veil, exposing the tip of it.

Why, why did you do that? the harsh voice hissed. *Stop it before people see!*

"She's the only one here," Astrid replied to herself out loud. "She is family; maybe if she knows me—"

"Go away!" the woman screamed, picking up her dagger from the ground and holding it up defensively. "We don't want you here!"

The reaction should not have surprised her, but still Astrid felt as though she had been disemboweled.

As quickly as she could, the woman raced into the house and slammed the heavy oak door behind her. Astrid heard the click of several bolts behind it.

She did not move, her arms limp by her side. She looked up at the building and noticed that for all its grandeur it had fallen into disrepair. Several of the windows had been boarded up and the two statues that guarded the outside of the courtyard were chipped and broken, one with an arm missing and one with its head completely gone. An ugly steel gate was built into the doorway that led to the courtyard, several of the bars bent from where they had been struck with large tools.

Behind her, the pony nudged Astrid's back and she quickly covered her face. From one of the only windows that had not been boarded up, the woman looked down at her niece, the look of fear and disgust on her face. For a moment their eyes met before the woman darted away from the window.

"Go away!" she screamed again. "We don't want you here!"

As she turned, Astrid saw that one of the statues was carrying a hammer ax. She let go of the pony's reins and walked up to it. The pattern on the handle was the same as the one hidden in her bag. She smiled sadly for a moment and ran her fingers over the stone. There were scrawls scratched into the stone that she could not read, though she doubted that they were nice words. Astrid rubbed her tears away and looked up at the building one last time, trying to imagine how it would have looked before it was vandalised.

The pony butted its head against her shoulder and snorted loudly as they walked away.

"What do you say to waiting for Jarl and then going home?" she said.

JUDGEMENT

If the Royal Palace in Bjargtre made Jarl feel nervous, the palace in Lǫgberg made him feel utterly insignificant. Each pillar was covered in murals and vivid blues, reds and greens in thousands of tiny mosaics adorned the walls. The floor was a black polished granite with silver veins running through it, the domed ceiling covered in gold. Jarl did his best not to look up and stare in wonder, aware that every eye in the hall was on him.

With his family plaque in his hands it had not taken long for him to convince the guards to allow him to wait outside the throne room. He did his best to not show how nervous and impatient he felt, but could not shake the worry that at any moment he would see a wolf with grey and green eyes approach him followed closely by the palace guards.

Finally, the doors to the throne room were opened and he was ushered in.

It was painfully silent and the clunk of his boots echoed on the cold stone floor. Jarl could feel his hands shake a little, his palms covered in a cold sweat. As shaken as he was, Jarl did not show it, he held his head high and fixed his eyes on Vígdís on the other side of the throne room. He ignored the dwarves in the court as they tittered amongst themselves at his worn clothes and the tattered cloak he wore, the ends still ripped from when he had bound Knud's leg with strips of it.

Vígdís stood in front of the throne. Her hair, tied in a thick and complicated braid, was impossibly long for a dwarf of her relatively young age; the ends of it were almost down to her feet. Pearls and diamonds were sewn into the bright blue ribbon that was woven into it and tied in a thick sash at the bottom. Her dress was the same colour, a bright royal blue, and the very top of her ivory shoulders were exposed. A white cloak was draped around her, held up by two large brooches on either side, each with her family crest, a purple thistle, embossed into it. Her lower arms were draped in a thin, almost transparent, white material with a netting of pearls over it. She wore several heavy gold rings on her fingers, a different seal on each of them.

But the most striking thing about her was her face. Sharp grey eyes lined with a dark blue pigment only served to make her eyes appear paler. And her nose, without a dip between her brows, was sharp and straight. Her strong jaw line looked as if it had never lowered itself in its entire life. She looked proud and beautiful.

Jarl wondered if she had known Arnbjörg and if it had been her to give the order. She would have been young, he thought to himself. Why couldn't she just have left them alone? They were in the Aldwood, they were never going to come back. Why did she have to destroy Astrid's life?

As they came to a halt in front of the throne, Jarl did his best not to let his thoughts show on his face, angry that in all likelihood he was asking for the help of a woman who had tried to murder Astrid and had succeeded in murdering her parents.

The guard walked away from Jarl as they reached the bottom of the steps and took his place by the throne. There were two raised platforms between him and the queen and he glanced at the throne, covered with heavy gold plates to conceal its unusually plain structure.

"Your name?"

Her tone was low and strong; years of public speaking had left her with a voice that could carry a great distance without the need to shout.

"Jarl Vǫrn," he replied, his voice just as audible as hers, though considerably deeper.

"Vǫrn? Your family is from Bjargtre?"

Jarl nodded. "I am."

"Well then, I hope that whatever you have to say was important enough to cross all of Ammasteinn." She smiled and reclined on the throne.

"My Queen..." Jarl paused for a moment to take a deep breath. "Bjargtre has not had the Hætta for many years now since the city was infected with a goblin plague, and because of this the goblins have become powerful and are a threat to the city."

Around him, the other dwarves in the court murmured between themselves. The queen looked deeply unimpressed.

"Why didn't you resume the Hætta after the city had recovered?"

"A third of the city died, My Queen," Jarl replied. "We were afraid to bring the Red Plague into the city again."

The entire court was in silence as they waited for Vígdís to reply. Jarl was sure he could have heard a fly rub its wings together; the silence was deafening.

Vígdís pressed her fingers together. "How strong are the goblin numbers?"

"I'm not sure. But enough to destroy the route to Einn."

Jarl saw her eyes dim and she looked away. A few members of the court went so far as to laugh out loud.

She was bored. In her mind the threat he described was barely worth mentioning, trouble his city had brought upon themselves by abandoning the spring tradition of the Hætta.

"And they have Agrokū," Jarl said quickly.

"An Agrokū?" Vígdís's eyes lit up and she sat up, alert. "How do you know?"

"He was seen in the mountains by Knute Villieldr."

"And why is this Knute Villieldr not here to tell me this?"

"Because he died from his wounds after he fought with the Agrokū," Jarl replied somberly.

"Why did the king only send you?" Vígdís asked suspiciously, her eyes narrowed. Inside his chest, Jarl's heart stopped for a second before it pounded faster than before. *This is it.*

"Because King Hábrók did not believe that the Agrokū was a threat. I came to Lǫgberg on my own to ask that you send help to my city."

There was a loud gasp from the court and an excited murmur. They knew what Jarl's admission meant. Vígdís had quite a different reaction. She stood up and walked slowly down the steps towards him until she was only a few feet away. Her stone grey fixed eyes on his blue ones.

"You know the law?"

Jarl nodded. "Yes."

"And you came regardless?"

Again Jarl nodded. "I would not have travelled so far if I was not sure. I know the law, but I won't stand by and watch my city burn for the sake of my name."

Vígdís looked curiously at the dwarf in front of her. As queen, she knew every noble family name, and she knew the Vǫrn's were a noble family famous for their service to the royalty of Bjargtre. To disobey King Hábrók would not have been a decision to take lightly. She was sure of only two things: the dwarf before her was either desperate or reckless, and he did not strike her as the reckless type. He was too calm and composed, his did not turn away from her as she looked at his face, instead he held her gaze, completely resolute.

"I will send birds to Bjargtre."

Jarl visibly breathed a sigh of relief.

"And I'm sure you know what the law requires for disobeying the orders of you king?" Vígdís added quietly.

Jarl closed his eyes and clenched his jaw. This was it. He nodded, resigned to what was about to happen.

Vígdís turned and walked back up to the throne, the small beads and pearls sewn into her robe clinking together as she did so.

All this way and now it's over in a couple of minutes, Jarl thought to himself.

From the throne, Vígdís nodded at the two guards who stood by the steps. Jarl knelt on the floor, his hands by his sides and clenched into tight fists.

The guards didn't bother to hold his arms behind him. It was clear Jarl was not about to struggle. The first guard grabbed the side of his head and dragged a sharp knife through the long hair. The court fell silent, all eyes on him as the abrasive sound of the knife's edge cutting through it drifted through the room.

Behind him, the second guard took a large handful of his hair and ran the blade up against the back of Jarl's neck. He winced as he felt it nip the skin but he did not say a word.

While the first guard hacked away at his hair the second drew his dagger and began to cut away at Jarl's beard, the edge sharp enough to cut away most of it, though it still left uneven patches, the skin partly exposed for the first time in over ninety-five years.

Images flashed through his mind: The first day his father, Jókell, had noticed that Jarl had stubble on his face and how proud he had felt that his father had noticed. How his brothers Jóð and Jón had argued with him about who had grown their beard the earliest. Jarl smiled a little as he remembered his mother, Elin, had been the one to confirm that Jarl was indeed the youngest of his siblings to start growing a beard. Jóð and Jón were furious at her verdict.

Jarl opened his eyes as he heard the blade slice through the last few strands. The hair was crudely cut and dishevelled, some strands as long as his smallest finger and others so short he could feel the air brush against the bare skin of his head.

Suddenly, the guard behind him grabbed his arms and held them tightly behind his back as the second guard strode up to the steps and lifted one of the burning torches. As he realised what was about to happen, Jarl closed his eyes and bit down on the insides of his cheeks with all his might. He inhaled sharply in pain as the torch was held so close to his face that what remained of his beard was set alight. It was over in seconds, the hair along his jaw and chin mostly cut away, the flames little more than a brief flash of heat, followed by a smarting pain.

As the guard behind him let go of his arms, Jarl took a deep breath and stood up, the hair that had collected falling in a large clump to the floor. Even Vígdís seemed impressed with how calm he was. He stood tall, his head held high, and refused to let his humiliation show on his face.

Vígdís studied him silently for a moment before she spoke again, impressed by his calm acceptance of her verdict. It was not unusual for dwarves to scream, plead or even threaten when faced with the loss of their family name and the public humiliation of an Ósómi. But he had not made a sound, he had barely flinched. Even now as he stood before her, his face bare and burnt, the skin red, and his once long thick hair gone, he stood tall and to attention. Every bit a soldier and a noble as he had been before.

"Your family plaque, you have it with you?"

Jarl nodded and reached into his tunic. Before he passed it to the guards he looked down at it one last time with a numbness in his chest as he gave it up.

"Four hours in the pillory, and you will wait in the city until the crows return from Bjargtre. If you are right, you will keep your title."

Jarl could not hide the shock on his face as he heard her sentence. Four hours! At least an hour had passed since he had told Astrid to wait for him. Astrid...if Astrid found him... Jarl felt his blood run cold at the thought.

Both the guards took hold of his arms and firmly waltzed him back through the throne room. Not a single person in the line waiting to see the queen avoided looking at him as he passed. Some appeared amused, others horrified, but most curious about what had earned him such a punishment.

Jarl wracked his brains to think of a way out of the situation, even though he knew there was none. If he tried to run the punishment would be more severe. His only option was to pray that Astrid would not find him.

It took several minutes for them to walk out of the palace and back into the plaza. They marched him up onto the platform, this time holding his arms roughly behind him, unwilling to take the risk that he might try to run. Jarl could feel everyone's eyes on him as a loud murmur built up in the crowd.

He looked ahead and felt his heart jump into his throat, sure for a moment that he had seen the back of Astrid's head. In front of him the guards marched up to the centre pillory and unlocked it. The dwarf who had been held there quickly scrambled away, his legs stiff, and in his desperation to leave as quickly as possible he fell down the stairs.

Jarl stepped forward and did his best to ignore the crowd but several loud bursts of laughter rang in his ears. It had been a while since there had been a noble in the stocks.

The guard grabbed him by the little hair that remained and roughly pushed his head down into the open neck brace. The pillory brace snapped down around his neck and Jarl winced as the edge nipped his skin. His hands were locked into cuffs that hung just beneath the neck brace. The two guards behind him laughed as they kicked his feet out from under him and locked them into the foot stocks a little behind the pillory so that he could not stand properly. Jarl gasped, his neck pressed down in the brace, unable to breathe for a moment. The pillory had been deliberately built so that he had to stoop a little; only his arms and back were able to stop his own weight from pressing down on his throat.

He tried to look up but found he could not, the brace too thick for his head to lean back. *Nothing has burst into flames yet...she can't be here,* he thought, relieved.

A loud shout rose from the crowd amid the laughter and jeers. Jarl closed his eyes again and braced himself.

FAMILY

Ótama could feel the heat from Systa's forehead through the wet cloth she pressed on it. Her eyes were closed, her mouth half open and her lips dry. Ótama leant her head down over her sister's mouth for the hundredth time in the last few hours, relieved as she heard her quiet but determined breathing.

"I'm still alive!" Systa rasped. She opened her eyes and managed an exhausted twitch of a smile.

"Good!" Ótama grunted. "Because I'll kill you myself before a silly injury like this does."

Systa tried to laugh but instantly whimpered in pain, her hands clasped over the bandages on her lower abdomen. "At least you would kill me quickly," she groaned.

Ótama moved the wet rag from Systa's head and dipped it back into the bowl of water next to her to cool it. Systa's talk of death made her nervous. "If I didn't kill you for that I'd kill you for leaving without me," she snapped, and Systa opened her eyes again to look at her. Ótama's eyes filled with angry tears. "Did Ulf ask you to go?" she demanded.

"No!" Systa replied quickly. "I only told Garðarr and Skógi."

"You took Skógi instead of me?" She placed the wet rag back on Systa's forehead. "I'm your sister! You should have told me!"

"Ulf would never have let me go if I'd told him, and he couldn't afford to lose two of his generals," Systa said. "I did like Skógi, but I would rather he died a hundred times rather than you." She reached for Ótama's hand and held it tightly. "It took me seven years to escape and get back to you; I knew I could do it again!"

"You should have told me!" Ótama shouted at her, fresh tears down her face. "I want you to promise you'll never leave me like that again!"

Systa nodded. "I promise, never again."

Ótama leant down over her sister so that their foreheads touched. "Good."

Systa's face suddenly scrunched up in agony and she pressed her hands over her stomach, trying but failing not to whimper in pain. Ótama looked down helplessly at her.

Garðarr appeared in the tent doorway, his face wracked with guilt. "Ótama? Is there anything I can—"

"Get out! Get out!" Ótama shouted and tossed her dagger towards him, Garðarr only just dodging it in time. His face was still several shades of purple from Ótama's previous beating.

"It's not his fault!" Systa gasped through the pain. "I made him promise!"

"Well next time I promise I'll kill him!" Ótama threatened. She hurried over to the door and firmly tied the bison hides that hung across the frame so that nobody could enter, then sat back down heavily next to her sister and held her hands.

"You know the worst part of it?" Systa groaned. "Part of me missed that smell, the smell of dwarves." She shuddered as the pain ebbed away a little. "But I still felt trapped. I know Ulf wants us to live in the mountains but I don't know if I can ever live under a stone roof again. It feels too much like a cage."

"Do you want more honey root?" Ótama asked, the sight of her little sister in pain enough to make her want to beat Garðarr into a pulp all over again.

Systa nodded and Ótama took some of the roots that Gríð had collected earlier. Using the small knife that she always had tucked into the side of her boot, Ótama cut the root in her hand into small pieces and tipped it into Systa's open mouth.

Systa ground the root between her teeth, each bite a little less vigorous until, finally, her grip across her abdomen loosened and she breathed a sigh of relief. "Thank you."

Ótama shook her head and curled up on the ground next to her, her head against her shoulder. "Don't ever do that to me again."

"If Ulf takes the city, neither of us will ever have to run from the dwarves again." Systa smiled, unrestrained hope in her voice. She closed her eyes, too tired to keep them open.

"You always did trust him far too much," Ótama grumbled.

"You swore yourself to him like I did. Don't you trust him?"

"Not as much as you do. He is my Agrokū, not my family."

Systa turned and leant her head against her sister's.

"Skógi? Did he die well?" Ótama asked, keen to keep Systa awake.

Again Systa opened her eyes but she would not look at her. "No," she mumbled. "He died in a sewer buried in dwarf shit. He died exactly how the dwarves want us all to die!" She looked up, her green and yellow eyes alight with an angry passion. "Ulf will stop that for all of us! Skógi died, but because of him we have a chance."

"No." Ótama shook her head and kissed her sister's forehead before she wrapped her arms around her protectively. "If Ulf takes the city it will be because of you."

Systa closed her eyes as Ótama stroked her head to calm her, tears running down her face even as she began to drift into a restless sleep, and Ótama could not tell if they were from the pain or if she was crying for Skógi.

* * *

The entire mountainside was set alight like an enormous stone pyre. The pines cracked and creaked as the flames ran up from the dry grass and consumed them. The sound was deafening and there were loud hisses as thousands of tiny bugs under the tree bark and in the grass burst with the heat of the flames.

Barely a single goblin had stayed behind in the camp as Ulf had announced the long awaited attack on Bjargtre. Even Ótama had left her sister's side, though it had been at Systa's insistence, determined for her not to miss the event they had all anticipated for the past three years.

"It's beautiful!" Ótama smiled, the red glow of the fire on her face.

They looked down over the ridge as the flames rippled towards the mountain, a thick black cloud of smoke darkening the dawn sky. In the distance they heard the dwarf horns sound, and then a low rumble amid the screams as dwarves ran for the Mad Gate as it closed.

Ulf turned to look at Ótama and Garðarr who stood beside him. "When those gates open again the city will be ours!" He smiled, his blue eyes fearsome in the red glow from the fire below them.

Bál snorted loudly and clawed at the burnt ground, the thick smell of smoke irritating his nostrils.

"The wolf will lead us," Ótama said, and Garðarr nodded in agreement.

If had not taken long for Gríð's prediction to spread through the camp and, before they had left, every single goblin had heard it, or at least some variation of it. There had been many re-tellings, vastly exaggerated.

A slow, confident smile spread across Ulf's face and he looked back down at the city, the gates now closed. Soldiers were visible in the battlement at least two hundred feet above the gate, which had been carved into the shape of a pair of eyes. Two enormous torches had been lit, making the eyes glow orange.

"Look!" Garðarr tried to smile, his swollen face a patchwork of blue, red and black from Ótama's beating. His left eye was completely covered by his bloated upper lid and his smile was more of a forced twitch at the side of his mouth. "Now the Mad Gate looks like it's screaming." Ótama tightened her grip on the reins and smiled with him. "Just imagine how it will look when it's burning *inside* the city." She laughed. "Hide little dwarves, the wolf is here!"

LET'S GO HOME

The light from the Ríkr Gluggr had changed from a warm yellow to a cold blue tinged with white as the many tunnels above him reflected first the sunset and, eventually, the moonlight outside. It would be another hour at least before he would be released from the pillory, an hour too late. Time was crawling by at an agonisingly slow pace.

She would be looking for him already. He wasn't sure what would be worse: for her to see him like this, or what she might do when she did.

His neck felt like it had been grated repeatedly with sand, the pillory around his neck too tight, the edges rough and rusted. His wrists felt the same, a red mark around them. His clothes were covered in mud and what he hoped was just rotten fruit. But most of all he felt cold. His beard was gone and only a thick, scraggy layer of hair was left on his head.

A large group of dwarves had waited until most of the crowds had dispersed before mixing stones with the rotten fruit and tossing it as hard as they could at Jarl from the edge of the platform. The guards did nothing to stop them until they saw a trickle of blood run down his bruised face and a deep gash above his eye.

Once they had been chased away by the guards, the silence set in. Jarl prayed under his breath as the minutes crawled by. Each second that passed seemed longer than the one before as every small sound magnified in his ears.

From across the Great Hall he heard a large object clatter to the ground. He tried to look up but the pillory did not allow him to. His heart was in his mouth. *Astrid…please, please don't do anything stupid!*

The guards laughed. "Got it! That's ten Fé for me!"

Jarl breathed a sigh of relief. It had been them, not Astrid.

The guards suddenly stood to attention and Jarl heard footsteps approach, light footsteps with the unmistakable swish of heavy, embroidered robes. Vígdís's long braided hair came into view, blue silk cords wound into it. She stood a few feet away from him.

"I received a swallow from Bjargtre. Several in fact, from the new young King Haddr. He writes to say that Bjargtre is in danger." Jarl's heart jumped into his mouth, afraid she would say that the city was already under attack. "The city is sick with the Red Plague and there is a large threat on the plains, over one hundred thousand goblins led by one named Ulf. He asks that we come to his aid as quickly as possible."

There was silence for a moment. Vígdís didn't move, only her eyes made the slightest motion. She looked at him with an expression that could almost have been confused for respect. Jarl tried to look up again and noticed that the family plaque she had taken from him earlier was in her hands. She crouched down and set it down on the floor in front of him before she turned to the guards. "Hold him for another hour and then let him go."

He breathed a loud sigh of relief. The army would leave and soon Bjargtre would have the dwarves they needed to fight the goblins. His city would be saved.

Vígdís's footsteps had barely faded away when he heard someone else approaching, their footsteps slow and heavy. He could hear someone speak with the guards followed by the loud clink of coins but he was sure it wasn't Astrid. She would not have talked to the guards.

Jarl swore under his breath as the unmistakable gilded hem of Áfastr Gull came into sight.

Without a word, Gull slammed his knee into Jarl's stomach as hard as he could. Jarl gasped in pain, unable to breathe and desperate for air. Another blow. He couldn't gasp this time, only inhale in a frenzy, deep breaths that were cut short each time.

Something wet and slimy hit his face and Áfastr Gull spat at him several more times before he stopped. Jarl was unable to wipe it away.

"You should have stayed in the city!" Gull hissed at him. "This was my moment! And you took it from me! Months on the road sleeping on the ground and all the queen could say when I arrived is how she is going to reward you!"

Unable to defend himself in any other way, Jarl suddenly spat back at him and Gull stumbled back, revolted. "You're cheap, Gull! I only had to pay the innkeeper a few Fé and managed to get you to tell him everything! Half the inn heard the news before Vígdís did, and you're stupid enough to expect to be rewar—"

Gull's foot slammed into his abdomen with a fury and Jarl's neck pressed down on the pillory so hard that he nearly choked.

"Stop!" one of the guards warned Gull. Jarl's whole body heaved for breath and his hands clenched together as he tried desperately to resist the urge to curl up to protect himself from further blows. His throat was on fire; the pillory had grated across it so much he could feel small shreds of skin and blood on it. He wasn't sure if he could take another blow. The pressure on his neck was almost unbearable.

Gull's hands clamped around his neck and he began to squeeze down with all his might. Quickly, the guards pulled him away. Gull kicked and screamed at them to let go but they did not. Instead, they dragged him off the platform and tossed him down the stairs. Jarl could taste blood in his mouth as the side of Gull's boot clipped him on the jaw as they dragged him away.

Gull tried to push past the guards and climb back onto the platform but they pushed him back. He swore loudly and offered them more money to be allowed back onto the platform but they refused. He re-adjusted his cloak and brushed off the dirt that had stuck to it. "It was my moment! The queen was meant to notice me!"

"Get lost!" the guards yelled. "You had your fun, now leave!"

Few a few seconds, Gull considered trying to force his way back onto the platform, but one look at the physique of the guards had him changing his mind. As he walked away towards one of the nearby streets, he smiled as he heard Jarl still gasping for air.

No sooner had he turned the corner out of the plaza, a hand snapped like a viper around his neck and pulled him further down the street. The torches that lined the walls flickered and faded in a puff of pale blue smoke.

"They said...stop!" a voice hissed. Two eyes, one green and one grey, glared at him out of the darkness.

Gull yelped and tried to claw at Astrid's grip around his neck, but he found he could not move. His arms dropped down by his sides like limp, wet rope as the hand that suspended him in the air began to glow blue. A terrible pain spread from his neck as if it was pressed against a hot poker. He tried to scream, but he could only rasp a horrible constricted whimper.

Astrid's face was as hard as stone, the edge of her mouth curled into a revolted sneer. The wolf skin was so low over her head that both of her eyes seemed to glow in the shadow it cast on her face. Gull's skin turned a sickly shade of grey and began to shrivel. Every fibre of his body - muscles, flesh, even his bones - felt dry. Within seconds his beard had turned grey and then bone white. His face, his arms and his hands shuddered as the skin twitched and convulsed before it began to sag like drips down the side of a candle.

Without warning, Astrid let go of him and he fell to the ground, a crumpled heap in the dirt. His clothes, which had fitted him perfectly before, were suddenly loose and ill-fitting, underneath them his body thin and scrawny.

"Who are you?" he wheezed. He clutched at this throat, horrified as he heard the sound of his own voice.

Astrid stooped down towards him, her face inches from his, a crazed look in her eyes. "I'm Ylva!"

Gull, terrified, tried to crawl away from her but she stood on the edge of his gilded robe and held him back. Gull was too weak to pull it out from under her and he spluttered, staring down at his hands as he tried to pull his robe from under her foot. His eyes widened as he saw how wrinkled they had become. The hair on the back of his arms and knuckles was pure white. He tried to scream but found he could not, his lungs too shrivelled to make the sound.

"Can't scream?" Astrid mocked, and leant down so that her head was at his height. "Here, let me do it for you!"

From the Great Hall the guards heard a blood curdling shriek, the sound so loud it cut at their ears like shards of glass. Everyone froze, their blood running cold. Jarl's especially.

"Astrid?"

The guards raced out of the plaza and towards the noise, leaving Jarl alone on the platform.

"Help him! I saw...there was a wolf! I think he's bleeding! Please! Please help him!" Astrid shrieked, huddled on the ground not far from Gull, her veil wrapped to cover half her face. The wolf skin lay crumpled on the ground, the head hidden underneath the rest of the fur. Gull was unable to make a sound, he gasped like a fish out of water on the dirty ground, his now claw-like hands flexed like dying spiders, shuddering and twitching.

"We'll take care of him," one of the guards reassured her, his hand on her shoulder. Astrid winced at his touch and pulled away from him instantly. "Which way did the wolf go?"

"Um...I...I think that way!" Astrid trembled and pointed down the tunnel. "Please be careful!" she whispered, her hand over her face. "The wolf, it was huge!"

"Don't worry! We'll find the wolf."

The guards picked Gull up from the ground as another rushed down the tunnel, weapons drawn. They carried him away, all the while asking if he had been bitten, surprised by the lack of blood.

Astrid got to her feet, Gull's eyes fixed on her as they carted him off, and laughed dryly under her breath, waving slowly at Gull as he disappeared around the corner, her expression cold, angry and vengeful.

In the plaza, Jarl had managed to stop his lungs from fighting against him as he tried to breathe, though now his heart had decided to perform acrobatics as he waited to see who the high pitched scream had belonged to. He was terrified that at any moment he would see Astrid's body tossed onto the platform in front of him.

He heard someone running towards him through the deserted plaza, Astrid's quick, light steps instantly recognisable to him. His heart jumped into his throat; he was painfully aware of how he looked. Leaving his injuries aside, his hair was so short he thought even Knud would have laughed at him. *What if she laughs at me?*

Her hands slammed against the pillory on either side of his face as she threw herself towards him. There was a flash of blinding blue light and a burst of heat surrounded him before he fell towards the floor in a sheet of black smoke. The entire pillory and most of the platform around them disappeared in a burst of blue fire-like ripples and there were hundreds of sparks of blue magic in the air.

Astrid caught him before he hit the floor. Even with her arms around him he could not bear to look at her, afraid that he would see her look back at him with disgust or even revulsion in her eyes.

Her hand moved to his chin and she lifted it so she could look at his face. "I waited three hours," she whispered, her forehead against his, unfazed that he was covered in spit, muck and a little blood.

Jarl's gaze met hers and Astrid smiled, her hands warm against the side of his face. Jarl ignored how uncomfortable it felt, the skin where his beard used to be was burnt sore and red.

"You know that I love you, don't you?" she said.

He did not try to hide the tears that rolled down his cheeks as she kissed him, unable to put into words how he felt as she'd finally said it. His hands cradled the sides of her neck as pain, relief and joy washed over him, all rolled into one. Astrid gently wiped his tears away before she kissed him again, a slow lingering kiss, and for the first time she moved her arms around him, and held him as tightly as she could, as if she were afraid that at any moment someone stronger than her would force her to let go.

"Let's go home."

THE END

BOOK DEDICATION

To Ronald Warwick. You're not here any more, but thank you for being the best English teacher I could ever have asked for. Without your encouragement I would have quit years ago.

WEB LINKS

Website:
www.klairedelys.com

Elaine Denning (Editor):
www.facebook.com/ElaineDenning

Harrison Davies (Formatter):
www.harrisondavies.com

11784487R00328

Printed in Great Britain
by Amazon.co.uk, Ltd.,
Marston Gate.